The Mage's Daughter

The Mage's Daughter

Leslie Kennedy

Copyright © 2012 by Leslie Kennedy.

Library of Congress Control Number: 2012923638
ISBN: Hardcover   978-1-4797-6795-3
               Softcover   978-1-4797-6794-6
               Ebook   978-1-4797-6796-0

All rights reserved. No part of this book may be reproduced or transmitted in any form or by any means, electronic or mechanical, including photocopying, recording, or by any information storage and retrieval system, without permission in writing from the copyright owner.

This is a work of fiction. Names, characters, places and incidents either are the product of the author's imagination or are used fictitiously, and any resemblance to any actual persons, living or dead, events, or locales is entirely coincidental.

This book was printed in the United States of America.

To order additional copies of this book, contact:
Xlibris Corporation
1-888-795-4274
www.Xlibris.com
Orders@Xlibris.com
125659

Contents

1. DESTRUCTION OF THE EVIL MAGE 9
2. AID FOR THE CHILD 18
3. NEW ALLIES, NEW ENEMIES 29
4. MAVS AND THE MAN 39
5. THE CHILD AND PRASS TO THE RESCUE 43
6. WHERE TO GO 54
7. ARRIVING AT THE REFUGE 62
8. MESSENGERS OUT TO THE RESCUE! 74
9. TO THE RESCUE 86
10. HOW CAN YOU HOPE? 95
11. FINALLY TO BATTLE 100
12. HEARTEN'S CHILDREN – OLD CHILD'S NEW NAME 112
13. UNITING IN WORK AND WAR 127
14. RESCUING THE HUNTED 139
15. THE FAMILY ENTERS THE FRAY 153
16. CLEARING OUT THE ENEMY 166
17. STRATEGIES OF THE RESCUER 184
18. THE MAGICAL STAIRWELL 203
19. THE RESCUE BEGINS 214
20. CLEARING THE OUTPOSTS BY THE SEA 218
21. GETTING A FEEL FOR THE ENEMY 225
22. INLAND OUTPOSTS AND TRADERS 233

Acknowledgment/Dedication

Thank you to my family: Nate (my husband) and Paul and Justin (my two boys). Also to Caroline who has been there throughout the long writing and editing process.

CHAPTER I

Destruction of the Evil Mage

IN A THRONE room so sinister that the heart raced and fear tried to steal one's breath sat atop the throne a Mage of such darkness that light seemed to be consumed.

He sat, a dead white hand with blackened nails supporting a face paler than death and just as still. The only parts that seemed alive were his black eyes that seemed to flicker with flames from hell.

"Well, daughter," he said to a disheveled lump of filth before him, "you will tell me whom you love, for if you cannot worship me, then I will destroy the being that holds your regard."

A weary but determined voice rose from the lump of filth and said, "I will not tell."

"Oh, you will," said the Mage with an evil laugh.

"No, I won't," came the determined reply.

"Yes, you will," said the Mage as he casually lifted a finger, sending shocks of agony through her body.

In a voice quivering from pain, she said, "I will not."

The Mage laughed darkly and commanded, "Stand." With a wave of his hand, his daughter stood, body quivering in agony, appearing ready to collapse.

"You will tell me whom you love," commanded her father in a voice of icy rage.

"I cannot, for I know not his name," replied the child.

"Oh, that will not stop me from finding him, and when I do, I will destroy him utterly. There will not be a memory of him in the entire world," said the Mage with relish.

"Even you, Father," said the child through teeth gritted in pain, "cannot destroy my memories of him nor his soul."

"Oh, yes, I can," said the Mage emphatically; and with the wave of his hand, he threw his child against the wall, shattering her bones and saying in a voice filled with disgust, "Throw her in the darkest cell. I will call for her when I want her."

◊ ◊ ◊

Two weeks later, walking into the throne room with such evil glee in his step that he practically flew, the Mage took his seat. "Fetch my child," he commanded, and his minions hastened to do his bidding.

They pulled before the Mage a bundle even filthier than before, smelling of dankness and mold.

"Stand up, my little moron," said the Mage snidely, and The Child slowly, with great effort, arose and stood before her father with her head hanging, appearing too weak to even hold it up.

"Tell me whom you love," commanded the Mage.

"No," was the quiet reply.

"You will not defy me," said her father with a steely cold rage in his voice. "Tell me whom you love!"

"No," she replied with quiet determination.

The Mage, out of habit, sent shafts of pain through her and then stopped. He looked upon her with eyes of such cold loathing that she shivered, but still, she would not say whom she loved.

The Mage smiled with delight, a sight so frightening that there are no words to describe it. "Oh, you will," he replied in a gleeful hissing voice. Standing, he cast his spell upon The Child. After casting it, he explained its workings, relishing the furthering of her fear, "This spell has been created so that no matter what safeguards your love has, he will be destroyed utterly. You will have no memories of him, and his soul will perish."

"I will not tell you," The Child said determinedly.

"Oh, you will have no need to speak. The moment you point, the spell will be released." And saying a magic word so dark that the mind refuses it, the Mage engaged his spell.

The Child tried to hold completely still, but her body moved against her will. She put in greater effort, sweat rolling from her face. Her father, surprised by her strength, added more of his will into the spell. Slowly, her arm rose; and she pointed, sorrow in her eyes.

The only sound the Mage had time for was a shriek of horror as the spell he had crafted did his bidding and destroyed whom his daughter loved . . . him.

His eyes rolled back into his head, his hair turned white, his face and hands seemed to age so quickly that in less than a minute, he was nothing but a disintegrated pile of dust on the floor.

His daughter stood still for a moment and then healed herself completely in almost the time it takes for one breath. She glowed with power as she gathered energy from around her and shouted in a voice that could be heard throughout the Mage's keep and land, "Flee, all is being destroyed." Running from the keep into the kennel area, she set the people imprisoned there free. Then she hustled into saddlebags and swiftly started depositing their children into the attached bags. She did this with her own hands and simultaneously with magic. This done, she bounded up five flights of stairs to the aviary and proceeded to deposit the children into special bags that had straps the avians could hang on to when flying.

When all was done, she joined the rest of the Mage's slaves as they headed for the only way out of the Mage's lands, the Western Pass. They ran for several miles across a flat plain of packed earth to reach the pass. When they were halfway to their goal, the ground began to vibrate, and soon a low rumbling was heard.

"Faster, you must go faster," called The Child, magnifying her voice with magic, even as she used the magic she was gathering to add speed to everyone's flight.

Just before the pass, she paused and waited, gathering even more power. When the roaring destruction of the Mage's keep reached a pitch, she threw up a shield protecting the other slaves to the best of her ability just as, with a mighty roar, the magic the Evil Mage had stored broke its bindings and exploded. The waves of power from the blast tossed the slaves like leaves in an autumn breeze.

When the explosions ceased, the other slaves got to their feet; and taking stock of their surroundings, their families, and their friends, they supported the injured between those who were sound and continued to make their way as quickly as possible from the Evil Mage's land. Once they reached water, they stopped. Everyone was exhausted and excited. Finally, at last, freedom!

A feline person looking about urgently asked, "Where is she? Has anyone seen The Child?"

"Which child?" asked a canine person.

"The Mage's child," said the feline with growing concern.

"The Mage's child?" said still another incredulously. "Who cares about her? We are free at last, and you are worrying about the child of that foul creature?"

"I was there in the throne room when the Evil Mage died," said the feline.

"Elder," said a tawny-coated feline of delicate feature coming upon him, "thank goodness that you are safe!"

"Tawny, my beloved," said Elder, "the Evil Mage is dead for all time. There will never be a rebirth, if such a thing is possible, of another like him!"

"I gathered that from the fact that we are free, and his land and keep have been leveled by mighty explosions," said Tawny dryly.

"But you don't understand. He was defeated by his daughter! She tricked him into the destruction of himself!" exclaimed Elder. "And now she is not with us. She set us free and used magic to get our children in the bags and the bags upon us so that we could flee."

"Elder," an old canine, graying at the muzzle, interrupted, "I was one of the last into the pass and only because The Child tossed me in. She stayed behind, seeming to wait, gathering power to herself, until she was hardly visible; then she threw up a shield across the face of the pass."

Elder groaned and sat down. "We must go back for her. We must find her."

"Go back for her? Find her?" snarled several voices. "Why should we help the daughter of that foul creature?" called another.

"Because she saved our lives, the lives of our children, and set us free," replied Elder, determined to be heard and heeded.

"Only to further purposes of her own I am sure," said a snide voice from an avian.

This received much grumbling of agreement; and Traw, always an angry one, said, "So she set us free probably just to become free herself. Still, she is the get of that evil one and cannot be trusted. Remember all the cruel and hard tasks she put us through."

The snarling, growling, and hissing had barely started up again when Tawny gave such a loud rude snort of derision that, coming from a creature of such delicate beauty, it shocked everyone. "Stop and think you. We are no longer beasts, and if we act like beasts now, we will give the victory to the Evil Mage that we have been denying him for all our generations. He has always wished to lower us to the level of beast. Wasn't that what he always called us? We are intelligent creatures. We are people, and we will not lower our standards of behavior to that of the foul one.

"Have you reflected on our escape? Everything she forced us to learn, especially the carrying of very fragile loads quickly, aided us in saving not only ourselves but also our children. Think who opened the door to our cages? Who loaded us with the carriers? Who climbed at a run five flights of stairs and helped the avians load their children into sacks? Who stayed in the rear of our flight and threw up a shield to protect us from the worst of the Mage's blast? Well, who?

"We don't owe her anything. She's the Mage's daughter. Like father, like daughter," Tawny said with a derisive sneer in her voice. "Bah! How has anything she has ever done caused anything but small amounts of hurt and that mostly to pride? Well, I am listening!" That last was said with such passion that her gray/blue eyes shone like silver lightning, and most were so ashamed they could not look her in the eye. Silence reigned, and sheepishness replaced the anger.

"Do you not know the curse that she is under?" asked Kriss, an elegant canine male.

"What curse?" asked a younger feline.

"She cannot die," said Kriss. "She is cursed to always appear a child."

"True," said Elder, "but what really concerns me is that she cannot die, and with the Mage's power unleashed, will it pervert her to his evilness?"

"Oh!" came from the group with some alarm.

"I am too weary to fly now, Elder," said a male avian. "But in the morning, when I have good sight and am rested, I will go in search of her. The Mage, as usual, did his most evil spell casting at night, so light should be upon us in an hour or two."

"Thank you, Alaw," said Elder. "Let us all rest, for life, though free, is going to become more challenging."

As the sun rose, Alaw readied himself for flight, careful to ease muscles that had been strained and bruised from the magic blasts. In a few minutes, he was airborne and headed back to the Mage's land. From up high, he spied The Child's unconscious form just on the other side of the pass from the Mage's land. A strange force seemed to be trying to reach her, so he landed in the pass behind her and, grabbing her tunic, pulled her to the other side. Alaw heaved a sigh of relief when he noticed that the force couldn't seem to enter the pass.

"Elder," he mind called, *"I have pulled her to our side of the pass, but she is too heavy for me to carry."*

"Thank goodness you got her. Was any of the Mage's power trying to reach her?" asked Elder.

"Yes, and in such force that I could distinguish it, but it seemed unable to reach her, as though there was a barrier preventing it from coming near her," answered Alaw. *"It can't seem to cross into the pass either, thank goodness!"*

"Kriss, Tawny, Yass, and I are on our way, and your mate, Aloo, brings a bag for us to use," Elder mind spoke to Alaw.

"I will stand guard here, and when you gather her, I will fly guard for you," responded Alaw. "Ah, here is my lovely mate now!"

"Aloo, my beloved," Alaw mind called to his mate, "I am happy to see you, and I have just thought of something. We will all be able to go back to our natural color!"

Aloo landed beside her mate and said, "I find that a very happy thought, dear one, but do you know I have no idea what color we actually are?"

"Hmm, true, even as nestlings, we were required to be dyed black," answered Alaw. "It is going to be fun to see what our true colors are, and to never have to be dyed again will be a delight!"

"How true that is," said Aloo happily.

Nodding in happy agreement, Alaw said, "I hope the others will be here soon, but you need to be back with our people. We and the ones coming are the war elders, and though we are not at war, this is a situation that could erupt into violence."

"Yes, I wonder if the other ex-slaves realize what a perilous situation we are in," agreed Aloo who walked some distance away and took wing.

"Mention it to them, sweet Aloo, and start them thinking of us united," mind spoke Alaw.

"I will, my love, for one thing all our training in warfare taught me is that our diversity is strength!" replied Aloo.

"Well put, beloved," agreed Alaw.

"Alaw," Elder mind spoke the great avian, "we will be with you in half an hour. The dark was deceptive, and we are not as far from the pass as I thought we were."

"Good," replied Alaw, "there does not seem to be any life other than myself and The Child in this area. At least I didn't spot any as I flew in search of her, but then it might have been too early for them to be stirring."

"Or the sight of such a huge predator has them hunkered down in fear," said Yass who had been listening to their conversation.

"Ha!" said Alaw with a chuckle in his voice. "You are probably right, and with Aloo's flight, they will stay hunkered down until thirst or hunger drives them to move."

Agreed amusement was felt on the mind-speech net from all the leaders, and a comfortable silence reigned.

"Has there been any change in her since you found her, Alaw?" asked Yass with concern as she peered at The Child.

"No, she seems to be just barely breathing. Her injuries have healed much more quickly before, so they must be severe," said Alaw.

"Maybe getting some water into her will help," said Kriss. "Let us be gentle as we put her onto the bag."

"Yes, very gently," agreed Tawny. "I have a plan for getting her on the bag with the least amount of jostling. Let us four-foots hold down the corners of the bag and you, Alaw, grab her by the tunic and tug her onto it."

"Excellent plan," said Alaw, and the other elders nodded in agreement.

With great care, the enormous avian pulled The Child onto the bag, centering her on it to the best of his ability.

"Excellent," said Tawny with satisfaction, "now let us get back to the others. Being this close to the Mage's land makes my fur stand on end!"

"I must confess to having a similar sensation," said Alaw with a shiver as he moved away from them before launching.

The four four-foots lifted the bag and, careful of their footing, went as fast as they could back to the rest of the freed slaves.

"Elder, Tawny, Kriss, and Yass," called Alaw with mind-speech, *"Aloo went back with the intention of getting our people thinking about the future, a future where we stay together so that we can be stronger than if we split into species groups. Our training certainly showed us that together we are stronger."*

"That is a good thought," said Kriss.

"True," agreed Tawny, *"and we owe that knowledge to The Child."*

"I wonder if she has a name," said Elder. *"The Mage never called her anything but child, daughter, and anything uncomplimentary he could think of."*

"She had to have one," said Yass. *"How else could he have controlled her?"*

"Yes, that is how he controlled all of us," agreed Alaw.

"I wonder if she even knows it," said Tawny. *"He must have taken it when she was a very small child."*

"When she comes to, maybe we will get some answers, but for now, I think that we had best be thinking of how to survive, where to go, and what we want to become as a people," said Elder.

"What we want to become as a people?" asked Kriss, a bit stunned by the notion.

"Yes," said Elder, *"having the misfortune to spend more than my share of time with the foul one, I know that one of his greatest fears was that his power should weaken and we would discover that we can be whatever kind of people we choose to be."*

"Well, that certainly gives us plenty to think of now and for days to come," said Alaw, who felt the agreement of the others.

"Aloo," called Alaw, *"we are drawing near."*

"Alaw, my love, I am glad to hear that," said Aloo. *"I have planted the seeds of what we are to become. But the suppressed rage within our people, especially our youth and those more sorely hurt by the Mage, is darkening the thinking here, and I believe that the sight of The Child will not be well received."*

"Thank you for the warning," said Elder. *"We will be on guard."*

Aloo's warning was in good time, so the elders were not surprised by the hate, rage, and anger the sight of The Child generated.

"Listen, people, Avian, Canine, and Feline," said Elder loudly with speech and mind-voice as he and the rest of the elders circled The Child and stared down those in a rage. We told you last night of her efforts to free us, starting with the death of the Evil Mage."

"So she killed her father. Doesn't that just make her like him?" asked Traw, whose scarred face was frozen into a perpetual scowl.

"Traw," said Kriss, *"the only reason she doesn't have worse scars than you is because she is bespelled to always heal. She was the Mage's favorite victim, and he often took out his rage at us on her."*

Traw froze in shock. *"But she is his child,"* he said incredulously.

"One time, when he was ranting at her, it came out that he only had her so he could have a servant trained by himself, loyal only to himself, one who because of blood ties he could control, if not her mind, at least her body. Many times, he had her do cruel things against her will, and if she cried, he enjoyed it more so that he would lengthen the time she was forced to watch her body hurt someone, thus torturing both his victims for a longer time. She learned long ago not to display her feelings," said Kriss.

"How did she kill him if she was so under his power?" asked another from the crowed.

"She became happy," said Elder.

"Happy?" asked Alaw.

"Yes, as you know, the Mage could not bear happiness. He would seek it out and do whatever it took to destroy it. He felt if anyone was happy, he did not have full control over him or her," said Elder. *"Can you imagine the fear and rage he felt when he realized that the happiness was coming from his child?"*

Total silence greeted this thought.

"He would want to destroy utterly, through her, whatever made her happy," said Yass with understanding.

"Let us unite in a mind net and I will show you what happened," said Elder.

All agreed, and except for the children and youth who it was deemed too dark a thing to see, all linked into the net, and Elder remembered what he had seen in the throne room. When he was done, everyone gasped, and many fears were eased.

"That is the only way he could have been defeated," said Yass. *"I wonder how long she had been planning this."*

"For decades," said Elder flatly.

"Decades!" exclaimed several in the crowd.

"Of course," said Tawny. *"She had to train us to survive before we could be free of the Mage. All those awful lessons even reading and writing. She taught us to hunt and*

to give aid to each other when we are hurt. She taught us everything to the best of her knowledge so that we can survive what lies beyond the borders of her father's land."

"But she hated teaching us anything," said a young voice from the crowd.

"True, and her father assumed it was because she was jealous of our good treatment from him," said Tawny.

"Good treatment?" exclaimed several.

"Compared to how he treated her, we were honored guests," said Kriss dryly.

Many in the crowed looked shocked. "Those of you who have never had throne room duty do not know the truth about her life. Imagine being the favorite victim of such a creature and not able to age or die," said Elder.

"But with the death of the Mage and the loosening of his magic, shouldn't she have perished also?" asked an older voice from the crowd.

"I believe that this was her hope," said Elder. "I think when she becomes conscious and realizes that she has failed to die yet again, she will be disappointed."

"Then she never planned this escape for her freedom, only for ours," said a youth in very sober tones.

"We have been in her care for many years, now she is in ours. Surely, we can do our best for her. She certainly did her best for us," said Aloo with sorrow in her voice as she realized the full extent of the horror of The Child's life and her amazing efforts to their good.

The feelings of the crowd had sobered and shifted. Those gathered started to walk away to think. "Wait, our people," said the elders in unison. "We must choose a direction to go and figure out how to move such a large crowd without destroying the environment we are in, especially if we have a need to come back in this direction."

"I think," said Alaw, "that for now, we need to move to where there is food and water. We avians will be able to arrive at the group's destination in enough time to set up guards for our children and to hunt for the group, but not for a long period of time. We need to have another solution."

"True," said Elder, "but for now, your solution is the most practical and will give us time to think."

"There is one thing though that we need to decide," said Alaw. "I do not want to call us the ex-slaves of the Evil Mage. We are people and of fairly good number. This makes us a nation, and we should have a name."

"You are right," said Yass, "a name that will break us free from the way we have been taught to think of ourselves when we were the Mage's slaves."

"How about The Family?" asked Tawny.

"That is excellent," said Alaw. "It doesn't give more importance to one species over the other and defines the best relationship for us to have with one another."

"All those who agree with this answer yes," said Elder. And thousands of voices and minds answered with a resounding "YES!"

CHAPTER 2

Aid for the Child

"*E*LDER, *ALAW, TAWNY, Aloo, and Kriss,*" Yass mind called.

"*Yes,*" answered the five.

"*It has been three days now, and all The Child takes is water. Also, she seems to be losing weight. We must get her to a healer,*" said a concerned Yass.

"*Let us call a meeting at our next stop,*" said Elder.

"*There are enough avian scouts to search for a healer among the humans that dwell at the edge of this land,*" said Aloo. "*So I have sent some of the more mature scouts to find one. I have also cautioned them to seek wisdom and kindness within the healer. We do not want to be subject to an evil human again!*"

"*That was an excellent thought,*" said Elder. "*When we stop for the night we can let our people know what is going on.*"

That evening, Elder said to the gathering, "*Good people, The Child is losing weight and has not regained consciousness yet. Also, she only takes water. The avians are scouting for a healer for her with these cautions: that the person be wise, kind, and open minded.*"

"*Good,*" said one of the youth, "*now we won't have the burden of The Child anymore.*"

"*You need to rethink that,*" said Aloo. "*The Child is one of us, us being the ex-slaves of the Evil Mage. She is less likely to know how to behave within a group of her own* kind than we are, and have you thought who will heal us of our more serious hurts if she dies or lives with others? She has always been our healer. And have you ever noticed that when she would heal us, she never touched our minds?"

"Oh," came from several in the crowd. "I guess we were not important enough to elicit healing from the Mage."

"Thank goodness!" said Elder. "When he tortured her past the point that the magic power she had could heal her, he would, and I think it was almost more painful than the torture that injured her in the first place!"

This statement was met with silence, creating sympathy in the minds of these refugees from bondage for the Mage's Daughter.

"I propose that we send a guard to keep watch of her well-being," said Kriss.

"I agree," answered Elder. "But who should we send?"

"Aloo," said Alaw with regret, "for she has the most sensitive mind touch and is well versed in concealed observation."

"Will you do this, Aloo?" asked Yass. "I know that you have young children just getting ready to have their flight feathers."

"It is not a welcome idea," said Aloo. "But I am the logical choice. I want in my team another avian, two canines, and two felines."

"How about Brak?" asked Alaw.

"Yes, he is an excellent choice," said Aloo. "How about it, Brak, will you be on my team?"

"It will be an honor, elder," said Brak, proud to be chosen.

"Who will you choose?" asked Aloo of the four-footed elders.

"We will choose Prass, but I don't know who else to choose," said Elder.

"What about me?" came a voice from the crowd, and a young feline pushed his way to the front.

"Mavs, even with the knowledge we have given you, you still hold on to your hatred for The Child. We cannot risk her safety to your prejudices," said Tawny.

Mavs said in reply to this, "I am not a beast to act on my feelings, but an intelligent being of honor who will guard The Child with my life to ensure no dishonor to myself or my family."

Seeing the doubt in their eyes, he said, "Use deep mind-speech with me then and know that I don't lie."

So they did, learning Mavs heart, and he became the second feline of the guard.

"The avian and feline parts of the guard have been taken care of, so next are the canine parts. Who will you choose Kriss and Yass?" asked Elder.

"I will choose Kerr if she is willing," said Yass.

"I am willing, elder," said a nondescript canine of mottled browns.

"I will choose Aris," said Kriss, smiling at a young silver-tinted canine male. Sensing the attitude of the crowd, he went on to say, "I am not showing *favoritism. Aris has been in training for two years in the art of stealth, observation, and assassination. I do not send him because he is my son. In fact, in this new and strange time we are in, I would rather keep my family near me."*

The tension in the crowd eased, and most of the people were pleased with the choices.

"Elder Aloo," came a mind call.

"Yes, Scout Zeth," answered Aloo.

"We have found three healers, but only one meets your specifications," said Zeth.

"How far away from us is this healer?" asked Aloo.

"She is about a half day to the south of us, four-foot time," replied Zeth.

"Thank you for the report. I will tell the others," answered Aloo.

"Our scouts have found a healer that meets all of our requirements. She is about half a day from us, four-foot time," Aloo announced to the gathering.

"If we get her close enough, we can fly her to The Healer and leave without being seen," said Alaw.

Upon hearing this, Mavs, with his black nose wrinkled in a snarl on his mottled brown and black face, whined, *"If you, avians, can fly her, why then did we have to drag her all this way? And why do we have to drag her closer?"*

This seemed a good question, even though it was asked with whining, and everyone waited with interest for the answer.

Alaw answered by calling his son. *"Af, get a sack like what The Child lies on and bring it here."*

Af quickly did as his father told him. *"Now,"* said Alaw, *"settle on it. Good. Now, Mavs, you and another one grab the straps and very gently pull the sack."*

They did as Alaw instructed and stopped in just a short distance. Mavs said with surprise in his voice, *"He is larger, but he weighs much less than The Child!"*

"Yes," replied Alaw, *"that is why we can fly our young, but not The Child, at least not for any great distance. It will take four of us and two bags to do this successfully. We will only be able to use our best fliers for this kind of synchronized flying. It is something The Child taught us to do to help rescue people from the battlefield, but not something that we have actually ever done. It is fortunate that she was concerned about the wounded and designed these bags so that, with a little manipulation on our part, they can be put together in a way that will carry a weight considerably greater than hers."*

After Alaw said this, his brow furrowed with worry, and he said, *"I wonder whom she and the Mage thought we were going to have to fight. We must be very, very cautious on our travels, and though we need to travel far enough apart so that there can be hunting for everyone, we had best stay close enough together to give mutual aid in case of an attack."* Everyone agreed with this wisdom, and their seriousness grew to almost gloom. But still, free for the first time in generations, their spirits couldn't stay dampened for very long.

They dragged The Child closer. And when their canine and feline spies said the time was right, the avians, with great care, strain, and an awesome display of coordinated flying, flew her to the healer. The healer, in her dwelling, did not see them land.

As soon as they landed, they gently pulled The Child from the bags. Then bundling up the bags, they, along with everyone else, hid. When Prass was sure that none would be seen, she let out a realistic groan to get the woman's attention.

The healer came from her cottage and, seeing The Child, quickly went to her. She paused about three feet away, sniffing The Child, and then cautiously circled her. She moved closer and scrutinized her carefully. Then suddenly making up her mind, she lifted The Child and carried her into her house.

The first thing The Healer did was to get The Child out of her filthy clothes. Once these were off of her, they were pitched outside. The Healer, smelling the stench of evil magic, put on a large cauldron of water to boil, went back to The Child, and bathed her in warm soapy water to get the initial grime off of her.

Once the water reached boiling point, she put in herbs and some odd crystals. Then going over to her work table, she made a tincture that she had The Child drink. She very slowly gave this to The Child, and once it was finished, she lay The Child down and went back to the cauldron, checking the solution in it.

Pulling out a tub, The Healer started putting the steaming concoction from the cauldron into the tub with equal parts of cold water from a well inside her house. When the tub reached a level that satisfied her, she carefully lifted The Child and gently set her into the tub. She used straps attached to the tub to hold The Child upright while she washed her hair. Once the water had cooled and might chill The Child, she took her out of it, wrapped her in a blanket, emptied the tub onto the heap of filthy clothes she took off The Child, and repeated the process again. She did this three times, stopping when there was no more solution in the cauldron. Then putting a large diaper on The Child, she tucked her into a cot next to her bed.

After three days of similar treatment, The Child opened her eyes and was aware but seemed to have no more knowledge than a newborn babe. The Healer patiently taught her how to take care of her bodily functions, how to walk, how to do small tasks around the cottage, and how to speak and understand simple instructions. Once she was sure The Child would not tumble, she allowed her to go outside and taught her tasks in the garden, such as milking, picking berries, and doing the laundry.

◊ ◊ ◊

Once the first two weeks were over, The Child began to heal at an amazing rate and learned The Healer's language swiftly. She was also remembering some of the language that was common to her, and sometimes, her sentences would get mixed up. This frustrated her considerably, but The Healer gently taught her to be patient with herself.

The guards watching could have told The Healer, if they dared to be discovered, that the reason The Child was so hard on herself when she made an error was due to the terror she experienced at the hands of her father for even an imagined slip up.

◊ ◊ ◊

This quiet, peaceful time in The Child's life came to an abrupt end one day when The Healer and The Child spied some soldiers riding to The Healer's house.

The Child was frightened by them, so The Healer said, "Stay and pick berries until they leave. I imagine they just want some directions. No one who does not live in this area comes out here, and they are obviously strangers."

The Healer went through her back door and, worried for some reason, closed and barred the door. She also hid the evidence that there were two people living in her cottage.

The men who came to seek The Healer seemed to be from two different lands. The man in command of the group, having similar coloring to The Healer, appeared to be from her land.

"Good Healer," said the man, leaning toward the woman from his horse, "the Regent is looking for healers versed in the old methods of healing when it was done with magic and stones. Do you know how to heal in this manner?"

He had just finished this sentence and was about to sit back upright when the darker soldiers drew their swords, others putting arrows to their bows, and slew the fairer soldiers.

They tried to take the leader captive, but he lost his seat on his horse as he tried to protect the woman, making him less of a target to those with the bows. Both he and The Healer ran into the cottage.

When the dark ones realized that the fair leader's skill and ferocity in battle were too much to allow capture, they launched a flurry of arrows through the door of the cottage. But even though wounded, the leader and The Healer managed to get the door shut and barred.

The dark ones, realizing that they could not get to their prey, set the roof of the cottage on fire, leaving the wounded warrior and Healer trapped in the burning building. The evil ones surrounded the cottage until the roof was an inferno. Then they gathered the riderless horses, their leader sending two after the warrior's horse which had run away, and went their way.

"*My scouts,*" called a shocked Aloo with mind-speech, "*two of you go after the ones following the horse. Two of you guard the road in case of the return of these evil ones. I will go to The Child. Brak, you need to see if this is an isolated incident.*"

The Child saw the attack from where she hid on the hill, and as Aloo was about to go to her, she came down to the cottage. Upon seeing Aloo, she smiled in recognition.

"You are Aloo, one of the avian elders," she said in way of greeting. "The Healer and the man are still alive inside. Are there any more here with you?"

"Yes," replied Aloo, relieved at being recognized, "I, another avian, two canines, and two felines. We are your guards."

"Good. I have a guard? That will have to wait. I need help to rescue The Healer and the soldier," said The Child. When she saw Aloo's reluctance, she added, "This is a strange land, not only for me, but also for you. These two will have information we need to survive in this land, and the aid we give here could be the seed of goodwill directed at us later."

Seeing the sense of her argument, Aloo nodded in agreement and called in the two guarding the road to The Healer's cottage and also mind called to Brak. "*The Child remembers me and has requested that we help her rescue the man and the woman in the cottage. She has pointed out that they know this land, and if we help them, we will be planting a seed of goodwill toward ourselves for the future. I agree with her and will need you to take over guarding the road from Prass and Aris who are needed to help her get them out of the cottage.*"

Prass and Aris, obedient to Aloo's command, returned. They and The Child entered a concealed way under The Healer's cottage. Once there, she gathered some blankets from a shelf and, getting water from the inside well, soaked them down. Then she secured them to the four-foots. Covering herself with another one, she said, "Come, these stairs lead into the cottage. We will have to crawl across the floor under the smoke while avoiding hot spots until we reach them. Then we will drag them out the closest door."

The cottage, so full of smoke and flame, made it hard to find The Healer and The Warrior. "I smell them toward the front of the cottage," said Aris to The Child and Prass. On hands and knees, The Child and the four-foots, crouching as low as they could, made their way to The Healer and The Warrior. Once they reached them, they grabbed them by their clothing and dragged them to the front door, staying as near the floor as possible. Reaching the front door, it took The Child and Prass to move the bar from across the door, as it was quite substantial. They went out, dragging the wounded two-foots as carefully as they could.

Aloo got a bucket from the woman's outside well and started dumping as much water as she could on the smoking fur, hair, and clothing of rescuers and injured alike. The Child seeing what she was doing helped her with that task.

When The Child was sure that everyone was free of sparks, smoke, and smoldering fur or cloth, she straightened up and said gratefully, "Oh, thank you so much for your help! I must go back in and get the supplies I will need to attend to their wounds, but first, let us put them on the bedding we covered ourselves with and take them up to the berry patch where they can be hidden. I will join you there. You might want to drag The Warrior first and The Healer second,".

"Why?" asked Aris.

"Good question, Aris," said The Child, startling him with the knowledge of his name. "The Warrior is the heavier of the two, especially in armor. So when you return and pull the woman up the hill, she will seem much lighter."

"Oh," said Prass and Aris at the same time and proceeded to do as she requested.

Taking a bucket, she refilled it from the outside well and started dousing the flames at the front door, working her way in. It was so smoky that she ripped off some of her garment and used it as a mask. The Child seemed to have a goal in mind, and once she reached it, she gathered some things and put them in a sack. Crawling on hands and knees under the smoke, she exited from the cottage, but only to get more water to aid her in having a safe path to the things she needed. This time, she came out with bedding and things to cook with. Then she went up the hill to attend the wounded.

The Child got a pot of water boiling and put some herbs in it. While this was cooking, she checked her patients and began removing the armor from The Warrior.

Taking the boiling pot off the fire and adding another with different herbs in it, she added cold water to the first pot she had set to boil and started to work on the woman. Once she was done removing arrows and stitching closed the wounds of The Healer, she seemed exhausted but continued on to The Warrior whose armor had kept him from being as severely wounded.

Aloo, watching this with great interest, asked, "Why don't you use your power to heal them?"

The Child looking up at her said, "My power seems very low, and even though I am sure that The Healer can use power to heal, she is afraid to do so. She does not seem like a person who is intimidated easily, so there must be a good reason behind her reluctance."

"Oh, that is not good news," answered Aloo.

"The fire seems to be most of the way out. I am going to get The Healer's mule and gather more supplies from the cottage," The Child informed the avian.

The first things she retrieved were more medicines and more of the special thread and needles that she had used to close the wounds of the grown two-foots. The Child kept all the supplies she gathered in separate groups, depending on use and immediate need.

"You do realize, Child, that we will need to leave this place in case the evil ones return, don't you?" asked Aloo, who was becoming alarmed at the large pile of stuff.

Just as The Child was about to answer, Brak flew in. Landing a short distance away from the berry thicket, he walked over to join them. "Aloo, the dark ones have attacked the next farm down the track, killing men, boys, old women, babies, young children, and doing such harm to those that remained that, between the shock and the pain, they seem to passively accept the evil done to their loved ones!" he reported in horror.

Alarm went through both the avian and The Child as they looked at each other and then at their patients.

"Do you suppose, Aloo," asked The Child, "that they will come back searching for The Warrior? He seemed important to them."

"I don't know," answered Aloo. Then turning to Brak, she asked, "Have you spotted any of the burden beasts we have observed?"

"Yes, they are scattered in every direction," he said.

"Go and spot them for Prass and Aris so that they can start them our way. Begin with those closest as we may only get one or two of the animals before full dark arrives."

"That was what I was going to do," said a slightly smug Brak, who had looked with concern on the piles of supplies The Child had gathered.

"Aloo," said The Child in wonder, "I do not remember anyone having such an attitude as Brak just displayed before."

"You are right. He is quite smug, but he is young. Maybe the young will recover from the effects of being under the Evil Mage's rule faster than we elders," replied Aloo.

"The Evil Mage?" asked The Child.

"Yes, don't you remember him?" asked Aloo.

"I remember you and the other people, and you are people, even though you are not like me and these other two. But I seem to have huge gaps in my memory, and it makes things seem very disjointed," answered The Child.

"Elder showed us the end of the Mage. Part of the spell that he cast upon you, to his own downfall, was to eliminate any memory of whom you loved from your mind," Aloo told her kindly.

"Why would he want to do that?" asked The Child. "And why would he eliminate himself?"

"It is a long tale, Child, but the short of it is that you were his daughter, his favorite slave, and victim. You are bespelled to heal quickly and not to age. I do not know how old you are, but you came to hate your father for the way he treated you and to hate us because we were treated with more value than yourself. After a while, however, you became happy. The Mage hated happiness, and when he discovered your happiness, he was sure that you loved someone other than himself. You would not tell him who you loved no matter how he tortured you. He went to his spell room and worked up a spell of great magnitude. He wanted it to destroy the one you loved utterly so that you would not even have a memory of him. He intended to even destroy the soul of the one you loved. It turned out that he who you loved was the Mage, so he destroyed himself utterly as he promised he would do."

"Oh," said The Child, eyes wide with shock. "But with him dead, wouldn't the spell wear off and wouldn't I start remembering him?" asked The Child.

"I do not know much about magic, but this I do know," responded Aloo kindly, "what magic has destroyed doesn't come back into being when the wielder of it is gone. If it were a spell to mask something or make a change in something, then it might reverse itself, but I am not sure. But nothing that is destroyed completely can be revived, even with magic, and the Mage was destroyed very completely."

"He was truly evil?" asked The Child.

"There was not one faintly glowing ember of good in him, and I think this was so from before we were enslaved," answered Aloo, who, hearing the approach of horses, turned her head to see Kerr and Mavs returning with not only The Warrior's horse but also the horses of the two dark ones.

"How do you keep them calm and doing what you want, being as it would be quite reasonable for them to assume you are predators and so a most feared enemy?" Aloo queried in greeting.

"Ah, fortunate for us, Aloo, they respond to mind-speech and can be calmed by us in this manner," replied Mavs.

"How are The Child, The Healer, and The Warrior, Aloo?" asked Kerr.

"The Child is well and has started their hurts to healing. She ran up and down the hill bringing supplies to the hiding place until she either had everything she wanted or was exhausted. I have sent Brak, Prass, and Aris to gather beasts of burden from the farm the evil ones have taken over. Just a moment, I want to call to them and let them know that they can use mind-speech on the beasts."

"Brak, Aris, and Prass," called Aloo, *"the burden beasts can be led and calmed with mind-speech."*

"Thank you, Aloo," was the response from all three, *"that will make staying hidden much easier."*

When her attention was back with them, Mavs queried, "Taken over?"

"Yes, they murdered the men, old women, children (boys mostly), and infants, enslaving the rest," she answered.

"We must help them," responded Mavs and Aris together.

"Would that, we could, but Brak has spotted many more doing much the same as these did," Aloo told them. "I am pretty sure we can get away with the elimination of the two you relieved the world of, but to do more might cause them to find The Family," Aloo sadly responded.

With downtrodden looks, the two brought the horses to The Child. She took them and went back to the cottage to gather more supplies.

"Darkness is approaching, Child," Aloo said as she arrived with yet another load of supplies. "We need for you to stay here in the berry patch so that we can eliminate any traces of your presence or the survival of The Warrior and The Healer."

"Will this be all that I will be able to get before we leave?" asked The Child.

"Yes, but maybe we can find more along the way. Why are you gathering so much stuff?" asked Aloo.

"I don't know how we will get more, and once we find a good hiding spot, it will be better if we do not move around much. If we don't move, we leave no tracks. And if we have enough supplies, we can be still for a long time," answered The Child.

"Oh, good plan," said Aloo with approval and was startled at the shy blush that appeared on The Child's cheeks.

"You have done an excellent job today," Aloo added, and The Child turned red clear to her hair. Aloo's heart ached for The Child's past as she realized that even in captivity, she and the rest of The Family had been able to appreciate one another and say so.

The Child tended her patients diligently but kept nodding off as she herself was not completely healed. Aloo, seeing this, said to her, "Child, rest. We will guard and watch. If there is any need, we will wake you."

"Thank you, Aloo, I am very tired. Wake me every two hours so I can attend to them sooner if they need me," said The Child, yawning and startling the great avian again with not only her knowledge of her name but also the realization that The Child had thanked her many times, and that was something she was forbidden from doing in the past. The Child was asleep the moment she lay down, and Aloo gently covered her sleeping form.

Prass grinned at Aloo and said, "I was startled when she knew me also."

"It was not only that she knew me, but do you remember how she was never allowed to say a kind or encouraging thing to any of us without being punished?" asked Aloo. "But now that I think about it, I realized that she thanked all of us several times for our help."

"True," said Prass, "and you are right, that is quite startling." Then with a yawn, she put her head on her front feet and went to sleep.

CHAPTER 3

New Allies, New Enemies

JUST BEFORE DAWN broke, Mavs awakened Aloo. "It is time to rise, Aloo," he said quietly, and she opened her eyes.

"Thank you, Mavs," said Aloo. "Your watch was uneventful then?"

"Yes, I woke The Child to attend to the other two-foots. I am still surprised that she knows who I am. I thought that the Mage's spell would have eliminated her memory."

"Only of him, and from the conversation that we had yesterday, she truly does not remember him, and I doubt that she ever will," answered Aloo, stretching.

"Why do you think that?" asked Mavs.

"Because he set out to destroy the memory of the one she loved, not change or conceal it," the great avian replied.

"Oh," said Mavs quietly as he thought about this.

"She also said that The Healer was afraid to use magic," said Mavs.

"Yes, she told me that too," responded Aloo. "When I asked why she wasn't using her power to heal the two, she said that her power is weak and that she was sure that The Healer could use magic to heal but was frightened to. Then she said that something that would intimidate The Healer was something to worry about, for the woman is not the type to intimidate easily."

"We are in more trouble than I thought then," said a worried Mavs, consternation in his voice.

"We are indeed, and we can't go anywhere until The Healer or The Warrior awakens. They know this land and will have a better idea of what is going on," said Aloo. "I am going to take an early morning flight to see if I can spot the enemy getting ready for the day. Maybe it will give me an idea about their plans."

Aloo spotted more farm animals and the evil ones preparing for the day. After they had eaten, they tied the women and children neck to neck, with their hands behind their backs. They left the farm with their line of prisoners in the middle where they could be watched and guarded.

As they left, some of them fired the house and the barn, seeming to delight in the sorrow this caused the people who had lived there. The delight of those who did this deed didn't live very long, for the officer in charge had two of them killed and had three more tied up with the prisoners. They left the bodies of their soldiers and the loved ones of the prisoners out in the open to feed the carrion eaters. Distressed by such cruelty and a lack of respect even for their own, Aloo flew back to camp and awoke her team.

"Awaken, the enemy is about, and the leader of the foul ones from yesterday is sending two soldiers back. So be very still," Aloo called with mind-speech.

From the berry patch, they watched the soldiers arrive. They tried to open the door, but the four-foots had relocked it as they were hiding all trace of The Child's activities. It was also helpful that two of the beams fell down, further blocking the door. The beams and some unburned thatch hid where The Warrior's and Healer's bodies would have been.

The soldiers, not being able to enter through the door, tried standing on their horses, but the horses would have none of it and both ended up falling. Then one tried standing on the other's shoulders, pulling himself up to the top of the wall. He looked in but didn't seem to see anything that aroused his suspicions. They left satisfied that they had looked at all that was necessary.

Once it was safe enough for her to land without being noticed, Aloo did so, and Brak took her place in the air. When she came into camp, the patients were awake.

"Greetings and well met," she said.

The look of shock on their faces at being talked to by an avian would have been funny if the situation weren't so desperate. The Child introduced the others and Aloo to them, explaining that the avians and four-foots had been changed into people eons ago; and though they get their food from hunting, they are people, not simple predators anymore.

"Greetings and well met," said The Warrior. "I assume that it is through your efforts that The Healer and I live."

"Ours and The Child's. She also is a healer and has tended to your wounds and nursed you through the night with our help," Aloo answered him. Then she looked at the man with sorrow in her eyes and said, "I know that you are wounded and sorely hurt, but we are in a dangerous situation and must have information in order to go undetected by those who attacked you. Am I correct in assuming that they are from a different land than yours?"

"Yes," said the man, "they are here at the bidding of the regent of this land. What can you tell me of their activities?"

"I noticed as I flew that people from the farms were being led away in identical fashions. They are marched single file with their hands tied behind them, and they are tied together neck to neck. They killed all of the infants, small children, boys, men, and elderly at each place. But with the exception of The Healer's house and the farm down the road, no other place has been set on fire," Aloo reported grimly, becoming concerned at the increased paleness this news brought to the wounded warrior.

"It is hard news to hear when you are so hurt," said The Child quietly. "But if we are going to survive, you must know the situation or you cannot advise us properly."

The man closed his eyes and said, "You are correct of course, but it would seem that my land is invaded." Then looking to Aloo with hope in his eyes, he asked, "Is there any way you can tell how far through the land this invasion goes?"

"I am sorry to say that within a fifty-mile radius, the story is the same," answered Aloo, and then added before the man could say more, "The Child's protection is my and my team's priority, and we will not risk further flight out."

"It would seem," said the man, "that going to the least settled areas would increase our chance of safe travel, and if we head northeast, there is a place in which we can hide." Then looking around at all the stuff, he asked, "How are you going to move us and this stuff at the same time?"

The Child answered him, "It will take me a little time, but I will have slings for you and The Healer to ride in in between horses, and I will have packs on all of the other animals." Then hearing the distressed sounds of mooing from the barn near The Healer's house, she looked to Aloo and said, "The cows are in distress for they are bred to be milked. When their udders are too full, it hurts them, and we are behind schedule with the outside chores."

The man said, "Now that they have checked for me, is there any way that you can see what the response from their commander is?"

"Yes," Aloo answered, "why?"

"Because if they assume that I and The Healer are dead, they will not come back, and we can free the animals and give them some relief," said the man.

"Brak," Aloo mind called.

"Yes, Aloo," answered Brak.

"Can you tell if the soldiers who came here have reported to their officer? And if so, what was his reaction to their report?" asked Aloo.

"They reported to him. He seemed satisfied with what they told him and had them get into formation," answered Brak.

"Thank you," said Aloo. Turning to The Warrior, she was shocked to see how pale he and The Healer were.

"Were you using mind-speech?" asked The Healer worriedly.

"Yes," Aloo answered.

"Oh dear," said The Healer, "something is attacking those with magic in them, and we are not sure that mind-speech is not magic. You may be attracting whatever it is to us!"

"That is grim news," said Prass, "for we used mind-speech a great deal yesterday."

"Then we had better see how quickly we can leave this area," said Kerr.

"It will be afternoon before we can go," said The Child. "These two need more rest before they can be moved, especially The Healer." And she turned to her charges that had fallen asleep from their efforts to be helpful.

"I will let them rest and go milk the cows," said The Child with a sigh.

"Why the sigh?" asked Aris.

"I don't really like to milk the cows, and they very much prefer for The Healer to milk them," she answered as she trudged to the barn.

"We had best stay away from the barn or the animals will give her an even harder time," said Kerr. Then she asked, "Aloo, is it all right for us to go hunting?"

"Yes," answered their leader, "but be careful and do not come back smelling like blood. The animals we have gathered would get too excited, and we would never get out of here." The scouts went in pairs to hunt and were back in a short time.

"This close to the wilderness, Aloo, the hunting is very good," said Aris, coming back with a well-satisfied stomach. "We brought down two extra deer, one for you and one for Brak. They are well away from here, and Kerr and Prass are guarding them for you."

"Thank you," said Aloo who walked some distance away and took flight. She met with Brak in the air and signaled him to follow her. They spotted the two four-foots waiting for them and landed.

"Before we start eating, Brak, you need to know that magic is under attack in this land. It is feared that mind-speech is a form of magic and will draw an attack," Aloo told him.

"We had better get away from this area then," said Brak.

"That is our goal. The Child knows that most of the task for successfully leaving falls to her, and with two patients on her hands, she says that we will not be able to leave until afternoon. After you eat head northwest and find an isolated place for us to be this night. Also, Kerr, Prass, you two will need to let Aris and Mavs know that we will be using the sign language that The Child taught us during combat training."

"Yes, ma'am," they said and started back to the berry patch.

When they arrived at the berry patch, it was to see that much of the supplies had already been bundled for travel, and The Child was creating carriers for her patients. Spying the buckets of milk, Prass asked as she came near to take a whiff, "What is that?"

"It is milk and comes from cows," said The Child. "There is more there than I can consume, so if you want any, do have some."

Prass gave it a taste and said, "Hey, this stuff is good!"

"Really?" asked Kerr coming up to try some. "You are right. Have you two tried this yet?"

"No," said Aris, "not after the face The Child was making when she drank it."

"I can't imagine not liking this stuff," said Prass.

"Let me give it a taste," said Mavs walking over to the buckets and putting his nose in.

"You are right. This is delicious! Child, how can you not like this stuff?" he asked.

"It is easy," she assured him. "But I am glad that you four enjoy it."

"If you don't like it, why do you drink it?" asked Kerr.

"Because it is good for me," said The Child with such a sour face that the four-foots burst out laughing.

Aloo returned from her repast and was quite surprised at how much The Child had gotten done during her absence. "You have been very busy!" she exclaimed in pleased praise, causing The Child to color up again.

"Thank you. Once I have the mechanisms figured out so that we can lift and lower the cots for the wounded, we will be able to leave," answered The Child, quickly getting her composure back.

"What is that enticing smell?" asked Aloo.

"A healing broth for my patients," answered The Child. "I have made a good supply of it so that if we cannot build a fire, it is still available to them."

"Good plan. You know that is the oddest contraption I have ever seen," said Aloo, peering at the mechanism that The Child was working on, "and in the Mage's land, there were plenty of odd mechanisms."

"It isn't pretty, but it is effective, and it will not profile should the horses be seen. It will appear as though they are companions who like to be together. I don't want to arouse any curiosity," answered The Child.

"Ah, so it will look like they used to be a plow team and they still have some of the harness on them," said Aloo, then questioned, "But what if one of the enemy decides to remove the harness?"

"I think from the way they treat each other, other people, and the way their horses act around them, they most likely won't bother," answered The Child.

"True," said Aris, "I noticed that the horses we brought back are happier with us predators than they were with the riders, and they think The Child is the most wonderful of all."

"One of them keeps trying to nibble her hair and lick her." Mavs laughed.

"Yuck, horse slobber," was Prass' reply to this.

"Ah, that's got it," said The Child with satisfaction, seeming to have ignored the four-foots' conversation. She tested the mechanisms several times then attached them to the pallets she had found in the cellar, then tested them some more.

"I believe that once my patients have awoken and we have taken care of their bodily requirements, we will be ready to go," said The Child. She went over and gently awakened the soldier first, asking the four-foots to help support him to the necessary. They did this very carefully. Then she woke up The Healer, and the process was repeated. When they got back, she had a place where they could recline and drink their broth more easily.

As she gently started to feed them, The Warrior tried to take the bowl from her, but she would have none of it. "Your hurts are deeper than you know, and you will not do anything that makes me have to stitch them closed again. You will keep your arms to your sides and try not to move too much," she said sternly.

Much to the surprise of The Family's guard, he behaved and did just what she told him to do. After she was done feeding him and had gotten him on the pallet that would carry him, she went to attend to The Healer.

The Healer looked like she was going to be stubborn also, but The Child looked her in the eye and said, "You know better!" And trying to scowl, The Healer did as she was told.

Aloo peeked over the horse to see how The Warrior was and said, "I am surprised at your quick obedience to The Child."

"In this land, we are taught to honor and obey our healers. You would not believe how unpleasant they can make getting well be if you don't!" he answered, grinning weakly, and then was asleep.

"Have you noticed that the animals we brought in yesterday do not seem to fear us?" asked Prass.

"Yes, but I don't think the other animals The Child will gather as we go will be so accepting of you," said The Warrior, awakening from his drowse. They had stopped for a break allowing the horses and cattle to graze.

"We need more horses or anything else that can carry supplies, and we need more supplies," said The Warrior.

"Why?" asked Prass, her emerald eyes wide remembering the large pile of stuff that The Child had salvaged from The Healer's home.

"We might not have the chance to get them later, and we may find some of my people fleeing also," he replied.

"But how will The Child manage so many animals?" asked Aris.

"She can string them together with lines long enough for them to graze, but not get tangled in. Horses and cattle are herd animals, and once they get used to being with us as we travel, they will follow us whether they are tied together or not," he answered.

"Oh," they said together. So out they went, the four-foots accompanying The Child, while Brak kept watch overhead. Without mind-speech, the scouts could not calm the animals, so The Child, on a horse, had to herd them.

They came back with ten more animals, and The Child asked, "Where will we find supplies for so many animals to carry?"

The Healer, awake and looking a little better, said, "The reputation of the Regent of this land before he ever became Regent was awful. When he came into power, the farm folk, especially those farther from the capital or any town for that matter, had hidden fields, granaries, and cellars."

"What are cellars?" asked Aloo.

"They are the rooms beneath a dwelling place, like the one under my cottage," answered The Healer. "I know where all the hidden storage places are in my area."

Seeing The Warrior's puzzled look, she smiled and said, "We all know where each other's secret stores are hidden, and while we have been waiting for the Regent's rule to end, we have been stockpiling goods in hopes that the lines of trade that have been closed to us, due to his greed and arrogance, would be opened again. By knowing each other's secrets, we felt that these secrets would be better kept, and none of us could be threatened with disclosure, for all were guilty."

The Warrior, with a rueful look, said, "That was very sensible of everyone, but didn't the Regent get suspicious?"

"Oh, not very, and if he sent someone who was overly curious, he ended up discredited, distracted, or worse case, injured and unable to do his job due to an accident," she replied, wincing as she raised a hand to move her reddish brown hair from her face, her brown eyes darkening in pain.

Aloo and her team, along with The Child, The Warrior, and The Healer, wandered slowly from storage place to storage place, gathering supplies and more animals. When they reached twenty-six animals, The Child said, "I cannot manage any more animals, especially with all those dairy animals following us. Thank goodness we found those calves. They are happy to get a meal anywhere they can."

"It is unusual for a cow to allow a calf not her own to feed from her," said The Healer.

"I think they are just happy to be relieved of the pain," said The Child. Then she smiled and said, "I am also rubbing them with a strong herb and petting the cows with the same herb so they smell alike."

"That was very smart of you," said The Healer.

"I was desperate!" said The Child.

"I think the animals that have been on the lines will follow us. So if you take the lines off of them and attach those lines to new animals, plus have lines of your own, I think we can have more animals," said The Warrior.

"I can give it a try, but it is more the attention that they want than anything else," said The Child.

"They don't need as much attention as they let on," said The Healer. "They are taking advantage of you."

"Oh, they are, are they?" said The Child.

"Oh yes," said The Warrior with a chuckle.

"Well, that will have to stop. I am exhausted by them!" exclaimed The Child.

"A few pats as you go by and a nibble of something every now and then will be enough," said The Healer with a smile.

"You will have to teach me this for I do not have any memory of dealing with animals," said The Child.

"I wish we had found some refugees," The Child said later that evening when her patients slept. "It is unbelievable that the takeover of this land could be so complete. It makes me nervous, like there is something that I should remember but can't."

"If you are that concerned, we need to take extra precautions," said Aloo.

The next day, Aloo told her team, "We will have to take greater precautions. The Child feels very nervous, like there is something about this situation that should bring up a memory, but she cannot grasp it." Seeing the startled looks on The Warrior's and The Healer's faces, she explained, "The Child had the training of us for the past decade and more, and though she has lost much of her memory, if her mind is trying to piece something together causing unease, we will heed it."

"She had the training of you for the past decade?" queried The Healer. "She only looks to be nine."

"The Child is bespelled to always heal and never age, and the death of the Evil Mage did not remove this burden from her," said Aloo sadly. "We do not know how old she is."

"But her behavior is much like that of a child's," said The Warrior.

"True," said The Healer, "but when she came to me, she was so magic-blasted it was as though she were an infant. That was only four or so weeks ago. Generally, when someone has taken such an injury, they never fully recover from it, let alone to the extent that she has done in four short weeks. Also, the healing that she has done for us was not anything that I taught her, and she did everything perfectly."

"Oh," said The Warrior quietly.

"I believe we should be moving on, Aloo," said The Child, uncomfortable at being the topic of conversation.

"You are right. I will signal Brak that we begin and join him in the sky," answered Aloo.

"Lady Aloo, could you and Brak watch for anyone who could give us some information?" asked The Warrior.

"All the villages and farms seem deserted," said Aloo. "Where should we look?"

"When you and Brak are on patrol and spot a road, could you see if there is anyone there?" asked The Warrior. "If they are trying to make a quick escape that is the route they will use."

"Warrior, this is a good thought, and being able to plan is better than guessing," said Aloo, startled at the title he had given her. Then with curiosity, she asked, "Warrior, what is your call name? If we get more than one two-footed warrior in our group, what should we call you and what is your rank?"

With a sparkle in his eye, he said, "Aaron is my name, and as of now, I don't have a rank."

Soaring high to remain out of sight of the two-foots (*really they have such puny distance vision, thought Aloo*), Aloo saw a man on a horse, about ten miles from her group, being chased. The horse appeared to be staggering as though it had run a long race, and the man scanned the country ahead intently. Seeing what he was looking for, he broke to the right and plunged off the road. Hiding in a thicket at the edge of the road, he watched his pursuers pass him by. When their sounds had faded, he fled deep into the forest.

At first, Aloo lost him, and then she saw him going swiftly across a meadow and then plunging back into the brush.

On the road, his pursuers, more of the dark ones, rode on for several more miles until they realized that they had lost him. Realizing this, they yanked their horses around and went back, but at a slower pace, searching for where he had left the road. This gave the man more time to distance himself from them.

Using the time his ruse had bought him, the man slowed and cooled his horse. Coming upon a stream, he removed the bridle, saddle, and bags, and then set the beast free. Hiding his gear, with the exception of the bags, he took off up a path that only the deer could possibly have used.

Aloo flew back and, landing in a meadow that would intercept the four- and two-foot's route, waited.

Prass, who was in charge on the land, called the rest when she saw Aloo.

Bobbing her head in acknowledgment, Aloo went to Aaron at a pace that would not upset the horses. "Aaron, I have seen a man being pursued on horseback. He has escaped his pursuers for now, but they follow him still. I have signaled Brak to continue to watch the man and the pursuers and to land if there is something new to report."

"Describe the man to me if you can," said Aaron.

"He was mounted and then moving, so I cannot tell of his height. But his hair is pale, almost white, except the hair on his face that has a reddish cast to it. He has broad shoulders and seems to ride with great ease. Also, after his horse was done drinking, it went searching for its rider."

On hearing how the horse was following the rider, Aaron's eyes sparkled, and he said, "I think I know this man. If we can get him free of his trackers, he is the perfect person for the information we need!"

"If an opportunity of acceptable risk comes, we will do our best to free him," said Aloo.

"Thank you, my lady," said Aaron as he closed his eyes and promptly fell asleep.

"I wish you could use your healing power on these two," said Aloo. "It would make things much simpler."

"Wishing for what cannot be, at least for the present, only leads to frustration, and that is a waste of energy and time," replied The Child in very adult tones as she looked about the clearing. "Would this be a good place to camp, Aloo?" she asked.

"Yes, and it is getting toward evening time. We are far enough from those pursuing the man to be able to have a fire," said Aloo.

CHAPTER 4

Mavs and the Man

Brak landed shortly after they had set up camp and reported, "The man, horse still following him, is heading even higher into the mountains and across areas that look treacherous."

"The evil ones have found where he left the road, but they are setting up camp for the night. Also, it looks like one is a mage, for he worked a sending. A short while after the sending, he received a reply, and he seemed quite pleased when he reported back to his leader."

"How far away is the man?" asked Aaron, who had awoken upon hearing Brak's voice.

"Hmm, maybe four hours on foot," answered Brak.

"We must warn him," urged Aaron with a worried face.

"I will go," said Mavs. "My night vision is very good."

"Go then, Mavs," Aloo said. "But please use every bit of caution and stealth you can."

"Yes, Aloo, I shall be very careful. I do not want to be mistaken for a predator," answered Mavs.

Aloo looked about camp to see if anything needed doing, but The Child had everything in hand and was checking her patient's wounds while she waited for the water for their medicines to boil. When it had, she set it aside to steep.

This task done, she turned to the second pot of boiling water and added meats and vegetables to it, moving it slightly so it would cook a little slower.

When the medicines had steeped enough, she handed Aaron, who was finally well enough to take his medicine himself, his medicine and the delicious broth. Then she went to The Healer helping her to take her medicines and fed her the delicious broth to get the medicine taste out of her mouth.

The Healer watched Aaron, feeding himself, with envy, and The Child seeing this said, "Your wounds are worse than Aaron's. He had on armor, and you didn't."

"I can still wish I was mending faster," grumbled The Healer.

"It has only been a few days since you were hurt, and you are already impatient to be well!" exclaimed The Child, shaking her head.

◊ ◊ ◊

Mavs, entering the cool dusk of the forest, used the moss growing on the ground and the deadfalls to cover his tracks and muffle all sound. The gloom of the forest succeeded in making him less than a shadow as he flitted through the trees.

He went to the place Brak had seen the man last, and because he came from another direction, he avoided the unstable mountainside. Once he picked up the man's scent, he followed swiftly, but not so fast that he would leave a trace of himself.

The man was not within view, but Mavs could tell from the scent that he was very near. Unwilling to be taken as a predator looking for a meal, he slowed even more until he got the man located. Coming upon him, he said, "Greetings from a warrior named Aaron."

"Aaron is dead," the man said in a flat voice, startled at being spoken to by what he thought would be a predator, at least from the way his horse was acting.

"Not so," said Mavs from a different location in order to not be a target. "He was wounded and left for dead, but my people have aided him. He said to warn you that one of those who hunt you is a mage. He did a sending and seemed well pleased at his answer."

"Ah, this is dire news indeed," said the man, voice grim, but resolute. "They have sent for the kill hounds. I am sure of this, for I know the mage they sent to hunt me, and I have delighted in spoiling his plans many times," he added with a grim chuckle. The moon revealed a glint in his eyes. Then he continued, "Tell the warrior Aaron that I shall lead them to the giant's shower in hopes of killing them before I die. Take my steed. He will serve you well."

"Not so," said Mavs, having shifted yet again. "A steed cannot travel the road I take, and I would not want to lead the foul ones to my people."

"You are right to display such caution," said the man in a sad voice. "The horse will have to fend for itself. But now that I know their plans, I can make some of my own."

"Fare-thee-well," said Mavs as he silently crept away.

"Fare-thee-well," said the man to the air.

Several hours later, Mavs reported in. "Entrance I seek," he said formally to Brak, who was on-guard duty.

"Enter and welcome, Mavs," said Brak, who then woke Aloo.

"Mavs has returned, Aloo," he said quietly, and they both saw Aaron stir and realized that to hear Mavs's report, Aaron had forced himself to remain awake. The glow of the fire showed that he was looking very tired and very much in pain.

"He thanks us for the warning," said Mavs, not only to Aloo, Brak, and Aaron, but also to The Child who had risen to hear his report.

"He said that he will lead them to the giant's shower and try to kill the hounds before he dies," added Mavs.

"I know the falls he speaks of. It is two hundred feet tall with sharp pointed boulders at its base. But here is a thought, we are closer to it than he is and behind the falls is a cave. If we can figure a way for him to swing into it, he will be protected from the hounds. Help me mount my horse, and we can arrive there with time to set up some surprises of our own."

Aloo said, regret in her voice, "No, I am sorry, Aaron, to be wet feathers on your plan, but we cannot endanger all for one. We did not even do that for The Child."

Before Aloo could continue, The Child spoke, "In what direction does the falls lay, Warrior?"

"About two miles to the west and south," said The Warrior.

"I will go, and you will stay. I have done much work to save your life and ensure that you will heal, and undo it, you will not!" she stated quite emphatically. "I will leave in the early light of day, I and one other if anyone is willing to volunteer to assure we arrived there before him."

"I will go with you, Child," said Prass. "We felines are better climbers than canines, and Mavs has had his share of adventure. I claim this next turn."

The warrior protested, but it did no good.

Aloo protested, and The Child looked at her and sweetly said, "This feels right to do, and we have much rope. I will take the war steed and the plow horse. I have a plan, but it may have to change if the terrain isn't what I hope it will be. Now as the healer here, I insist that all not on guard duty get some sleep." And after making sure that Aaron took his medicine, she watched him drink it down, looking like a cranky old woman. He grinned and drank it down, looking quite unrepentant.

"What is going on between you and Aaron, Child?" asked Aloo.

She answered, "He dumped his medicine so he would not sleep. He was so anxious to hear Mavs's report."

CHAPTER 5

The Child and Prass to the Rescue

BEFORE TRUE LIGHT, The Child was up stirring the fire, mixing medicines, and setting out food and water where Aaron could easily reach them, for he would have to aid The Healer while she was gone. She helped them to stand and do what was necessary, and then she gathered up what she thought she would need and left.

"How can you let a child go on a mission of such great danger?" asked Aaron, his voice filled with frustration, anger, and worry.

"She has always had the responsibility of many things, as she was her father's assistant, and I know that she is capable of much. In all the time I have known her, I have seen her receive injuries that should have killed her, and they didn't. She simply looked at her hurt and watched herself heal, or if she was unconscious, she healed without truly awakening until the healing reached the stage where she became conscious. Then she would wait patiently for the healing to be complete and continue about her business.

"When we escaped the Evil Mage, she threw up a shield to protect us, but we were still hit with part of the blast of his stored power, and we tumbled about on the ground and through the air like leaves in the wind. The blast should have killed her, as she received the brunt of it. I imagine that The Healer can vouch for the unnatural way in which she heals," Aloo explained.

"Yes, I can vouch for her remarkable healing, but I didn't realize she had taken a blast of such intensity. Remember also, Aaron, that she is older than she appears. And I know this, not just from the words Lady Aloo has spoken, but also from the healings she has done on us. I did not teach them to her, and I don't know how she knows them, but she has done everything quite correctly. I couldn't have done any better, and this reinforces what we have been told about her age. Where do you come from? I know it is from the same land as The Child, for you speak the same language," asked The Healer.

"We come from a land to the west of here. It was controlled by the Evil Mage. When he died, suddenly, the spells that held everything together came undone, and the magic he had stored exploded. If it weren't for The Child, we would not be alive, and I am thinking that neither the Mage nor we of The Family ever truly knew the power she had."

"Ah, the only mage I know of who came from that direction was from times long gone. If you are talking of the Evil Mage of old, that must have been some shield. The Mage of old had legendary power, and even if it had dwindled, he would still have been a force to be reckoned with. His power was such that it took several mages to contain him. They never could kill him. It was a happy time for us when he seemed to lose interest in his neighbors after his defeat," said The Healer.

"We hired some mages and warriors of our own to free us of his evil powers," Aaron informed them, "and when the war was over the mages put up a ward against him, but that was centuries ago. It is shocking to realize that such an evil creature lived to such a great age, and it is good that he is gone, for the mages we hired are long dead." With that last statement, he yawned and went to sleep. When Aloo looked, The Healer also slept.

◊   ◊   ◊

"Prass, I will need your help in springing the trap and letting loose the guy rope I will use to carry myself and the man into the cave behind the waterfall," said The Child as she and the great feline padded quietly through the forest, leading the animals. "I hope my idea works and that the trees and terrain will provide the best situation for both the rescue plan and the trap. Otherwise, you and I could be fighting for our lives.

"The trap I will be making is going to be a water trap hidden above the heads of the evil ones so as not to give our positions away," continued The Child.

"You have chosen the animals for this adventure well, Child," said Prass, changing the subject, as she thought about what The Child had said.

"Thank you," said The Child, "I chose these two for they are calm and seem intelligent for their species, and as you of The Family have protected them on occasion from wolves, they seem to view you in the same light in which they view human beings. Also, I think that you have the smell of humans they know upon you," The Child replied.

"Why do we need a water trap?" asked a curious Prass.

"Somewhere, I read about certain kinds of mages who lose power or have it blocked if they become wet. They have certain runes written either on them or on their garments. These mages usually come from desert lands and tend to be dark of skin as do the enemies of The Healer and The Warrior. When we get to the falls, I will show you the runes. If nothing else, the trap will be a distraction and buy us time. But there is a danger to you, and I am not happy at the risk you will be taking," said a concerned Child.

"It is my risk, not yours, as it is my choice, not yours. You have told me true of the danger, and I knew that there would be danger when I volunteered to come with you," said a determinedly independent feline as she strode beside The Child, her black fur revealing glints of gold as she moved. "I do not feel that I need to follow your dictates anymore for you are a child, and though you controlled us through the will of the Evil Mage, your father is no longer alive to give you power."

"Good," said The Child, "for I have no memory of the one you call the Evil Mage, although I do have memory of training you and the other people who were enslaved by him. As my memory comes to me in bits and pieces, it is much more comfortable to do something dangerous with someone who is willing to share the danger than it is to send someone into danger."

"I can see how that would be so, and if I were in your place, I would be much more comfortable with such a companion myself," answered Prass.

Prass and The Child continued on in silence. The Child kept a fast pace, and if she seemed to lag or get tired, she would mount one of the horses.

Breaking the companionable silence, a very curious Prass asked, "Child, how at the top of a waterfall are you going to get a mage wet?"

"With tall trees, a waterproof tarp, and rope I hope," answered The Child. "Aaron says that the waterfall is about two thousand feet up in elevation, although it is only two hundred feet in height. At this elevation grow a variety of trees, and he told me that I would find oak, maple, and some pine trees at the rim of the canyon above the waterfall."

They arrived at the falls about twenty minutes after Prass' curiosity had been satisfied. "The air is filled with the smells of the forest. It is a delight to the nose, for it smells of freedom," said Prass.

"Yes, it is a delicious scent," said The Child, "and the scent of autumn is new and fresh upon the air."

"We are two to three hours ahead of the man, the mage, and the kill hounds," said The Child, sounding much relieved as they spied around a rock to get a view of the hunted and the hunters. Looking the terrain over, she found the best place to swing into the cave behind the waterfall. She set to work guessing the amount of rope she would need, anchored it to a tree, tied herself to it, and then dived at an angle toward the cave entrance.

Prass, who had no warning that The Child was about to dive, felt her heart jump into her throat and all of her muscles tensed as she watched The Child climb back up the rope. Aloo, watching from above, had much the same reaction that Prass did and found herself holding her breath. Both members of The Family watched, Prass with a posture of concern and Aloo with bated breath, as The Child did this three times before she successfully entered the cave.

Prass' heart continued to race as she watched the rope that The Child was attached to become taut, slacken, and then remain taut. In a short while, The Child was climbing like an inchworm along the length of the rope and back up to the top. Both Prass and Aloo felt they could breathe now that she was back on land.

"How have you managed to keep from drowning?" asked Prass. "And how did you manage not to be torn from the rope?"

The Child smiled and took off a harness of rope that was padded with cloth, the color of the clothes she wore, and showed Prass how it could slide forward and upward with her along the rope.

"It seems to catch a bit," said Prass with concern.

"It is why I chose this type of rope. It helps me to climb. Otherwise, I would keep slipping back into the cave," answered The Child as they both stood comfortable on the large tree limb overhanging the falls. Then she went to the spot in the tree where she had anchored the rope, untied it, and retied it with a special knot that would allow Prass to untie it quickly when they were in the cave.

Next, with the waterproof tarp, more rope, and the help of Prass, she set her mage trap using the same knot as before. Running thinner lines from the ropes in such a manner that they were only visible if you knew where to look, she went up into the pine next to the oak where Prass would hide, as it gave more cover and she could easily see what the evil ones were doing. She tied the same knot yet again. Prass would use her judgment on which line to pull first.

"I assume that you expect me to pull the ropes and disappear while my victims are in a state of confusion," said Prass, enjoying the idea of the confusion she would cause.

"Yes," said The Child. "Now let us scout our escape routes and move the horses. I suspect the sound of the kill hounds will panic them."

"It is good we are so far ahead of the man and the evil ones then," said Prass.

They could faintly hear the baying of the kill hounds, and the animals they brought were very jumpy, so they moved them about half a mile away and hid them from sight. The Child tied them very securely, muffling them so they would not give themselves or the rescuers away.

"Muffling the animals seems extreme to me," said Prass.

"The baying of the hounds seems to induce fear," said The Child. "I do not think that anything will move until well after they are silent, so the animals should be safe enough."

"I thought that I was the only one feeling fear," said Prass. "You say that their baying seems to generate it?"

"Yes, I suspect that it would normally cause a person to freeze from fright or faint," answered The Child grimly.

"The man we have come to aid must have a very stout heart to continue the race then," said Prass admiringly.

"You are right. Now let us hope to be as brave," said The Child.

"Then it is time for us to get to our intercept point," said Prass.

"And now silence must reign," agreed The Child, worry in her eyes.

They reached the lookout point and realized that the baying of hounds had fooled them, and the man was not near enough. "Good," said The Child, "I had one more task I wanted to do."

They returned to the falls, and The Child went back into the cave, then climbed down the cliff and secured still another rope to a stout piece of wood under the water. She climbed back up the side of the waterfall and joined Prass. Taking off the harness that she had made, she quickly sized it for someone larger than herself. "Do you think it is about time now?" asked The Child in quiet fear.

"I think we can rest a moment. While you were working at the falls, I signaled Aloo, and she will signal when we need to move into place," answered Prass.

Aloo, signaling them from above, watched as The Child and Prass went to intercept the man.

They saw him, but he was too far away to get his attention without warning the evil ones. So they waited, Prass out of sight on a rock shelf above The Child and The Child just after the turn in the trail.

Aloo, watching the chase between the man and the evil ones, noted that he chose his route well. It was very treacherous, and often, he showed so little caution that it looked as though he would cause his own folly as the mountainside slid and shifted. But he made his way up the side of the mountain and along the narrow ridge that led to the waterfall safely.

As fast as the kill hounds were coming, it was a good thing that he had the lead on them by several miles. They were unbelievably fast and were steadily closing the distance. The route the man took made it obvious that he knew of the hounds' speed and had chosen a path that worked against them. Even high in the air, Aloo could hear their whines of frustration with the slide area.

The evil ones fared poorly on the mountainside and lost at least four of the eight who followed the mage's leading. Unfortunately, none of the hounds shared their fate. Of the troopers who came to hazard on this treacherous area, only one was killed.

To The Child and Prass, waiting with mounting fear, each minute seemed like an hour. The baying of the hounds constantly frayed at their nerves. It came as a relief when the man finally came abreast of them. The Child, hearing the sound of the man very near, showed herself, grabbed his hand, and said, "Come quickly." She swiftly led him to the edge of the waterfall as Prass went to her station unseen by the man. Then with sure, swift movements, The Child helped the man into the harness.

By this time, the kill hounds were close, and their baying ran a chill down the spine, even from where Aloo watched in the sky. The Child was determined that the kill hounds would be destroyed, and after attaching herself to the same harness that the man was in, she told the man, "Project your fear. I will project mine. It will be like drink to them." So they waited, with The Child holding tightly to the man.

As the hounds drew closer, their baying became more frenzied as they sensed the fear of their prey seemingly at bay. The joy of the kill excited the hounds past thought, and they increased their speed, bounding toward their prey with lathering jaws. When they were but a bound or two away, the man and child launched off the cliff, taking the hounds with them.

Aloo and Prass, watching this, felt as though their hearts had stopped with fright for the two. Prass waited a slow count to ten and released the rope to the cave, going swiftly to where she could see if it was being pulled in and sighed with relief when she saw it was. Quietly, she returned to her hiding spot.

The mage and the rest of the hunting party, missing the noise of the hounds, hurried to the edge of the falls. But there was nothing to see, except the mists at the base of the falls.

The mage, believing that the man had, even at his death, created a victory against him, started to shake, his skin darkening even further. Aloo could see his mouth move as he began to speak. The words he spoke were dark and wrathful, and the rest of the hunting party gazed at him in fear. Fearing that he would take his wrath out on them, those in front of the mage dropped to the ground. The one to the side and a bit out of the mage's sight swung a limb he had found at the mage, distracting him. Quickly, while he was distracted, the others got limbs of their own and pushed him off the cliff. The soldier to the side of the mage got in a lucky last blow as the mage was falling from the cliff and knocked him out.

Aloo, with her keen sight, shifted her angle of flight and watched the water at the foot of the falls. The mage came bobbing up his face contorted in agony as his flesh melted away from his bones. In a short time, only his bones remained in his robe which was snagged on a submerged tree limb.

Prass, in her hiding place, waited for the hunters to leave. Then she triggered the unused trap and went to wait for The Child and the man at the place they had chosen earlier.

◊ ◊ ◊

The Child and the man, arriving in the cave, dropped to the floor. A few moments later, the rope fell loose, and The Child began dragging it in. The man was quick to help her.

"Will there be more kill hounds?" asked The Child, shouting in the man's ear to be heard above the roar of the falls.

"No, they are very expensive, and the accursed ones have few with them," the man shouted his reply back to her.

"Let us rest," shouted The Child. The man, unable to hear her, put his ear to her mouth, and she shouted again, "In a little while, we will go down the rope and meet my friend." So they sat or moved around, depending on how cold they were, careful to stay away from the mouth of the cave where the light shone through.

After about a half hour of this, The Child decided it was time to climb down from the cave. The man went first, fearing for The Child and wanting to be able to help her. She nodded her understanding when he shouted this in her ear and let him go first. Their cold muscles made the climb down difficult, and it seemed to The Child that it took longer than when she had done it earlier.

The man, waiting at the foot of the falls, steadied The Child on the last bit. She looked at him in surprise and went to where she had anchored another rope underwater. The man, realizing that she planned to use the current to move them to the near shore, positioned himself so that if The Child had trouble, he could help her. They launched into the water, the current carrying them to the shore. Once there, they scanned for the enemy and, not seeing any, climbed out of the gorge.

Once they reached the top, The Child led the man to where Prass waited. When Prass stepped out of hiding to greet them, the man, in fright, jumped back, pulling The Child behind him and drawing his knife, determined to protect her from the huge cat.

Prass, laughing, said, "Relax, man, I am with The Child and will guide you to the horses and from there to the warrior Aaron."

The shocked look on the man's face to have a large cat talking to him caused Prass a great deal of amusement which she stifled, saving it to share with her friends later as she led them to the horses.

The man, however, was so stunned at being talked to by a cat that he just stood in the pathway, and The Child with a look of inquiry took his hand, saying, "Come. The climb up the cliff helped to warm us, and now the movement will help us to stay warm. Also, I have some food in the saddle bags, and I am hungry!" So a bemused man followed a child and cat to the horses.

"Aaron's horse!" he exclaimed in joy. "Now I have more belief in the voice in the dark!"

"Before we head for our camp, we need to go back to the trap and remove it," said Prass. "We removed any traces we made, setting it before you arrived, so if we are careful where we walk, we will have little to do."

The man and child both nodded, too busy eating to answer.

As they got closer, the horses began to get skittish. "The scent of the kill hounds must still be in the air," said the man.

"Then you stay with them while The Child and I take down the trap," said Prass.

"As good a plan as any," agreed the man between mouthfuls of food.

Returning twenty minutes later, The Child and Prass carried the tarp and ropes over to the plow horse and started to load him. The man hurried to help, and in five minutes, they were on their way back to camp, the man riding Aaron's horse and The Child perched on the plow horse, except for when she felt the need for movement to warm up.

When they arrived in camp, the man, seeing Aaron, leapt from Aaron's horse and ran to him. Kerr blocked his path so quickly that when he stopped short, he practically fell on his face.

"It is all right, Kerr," said Aaron with a smile. "This is Hearten, the Arms Master for the elite soldiers of this land."

Before Kerr moved, she spoke to the man, "Arms master, Aaron is sorely wounded, and you must be gentle around him and The Healer."

"Yes, I see that now, and I will be very careful of my friend," said the man, who approached Aaron at a more sedate pace.

The Child brought out some cheese and fruit and gave some to the man while having some herself. She ate ravenously. The food she had brought for their return trip hadn't done much to appease the hunger of either her or the man. As she ate, she and the others listened while Aaron and the man talked.

"What can you tell me, my friend?" asked Aaron.

"No good news, but one do I have for you, my lord, my friend," said the man, kneeling beside Aaron, gently touching his hand. "The Regent, your uncle, has lost control of the whole situation, and we are truly invaded, with most of our people being carried off on slave ships or murdered. Some few have escaped, but the planning of our downfall was very complete.

"They enslaved large parts of the army with drugs in their food, then killed the men and bound the women in chains. The outlanders that the Regent brought in for his protection really worked the divide and conquer well; eliminating anyone who would be able to stop their plans and making sure those who came into power were the ones who fawned over the Regent. If they couldn't eliminate them, they managed, through the Regent, to keep vital people and groups away from the capital. I am afraid, my prince, that we are a country no more."

"But what is the one piece of good news you said you have for me?" queried a grim and sorrowful prince.

"Your uncle's head now rests on a pike at the main gate of our capital," responded the man, grim satisfaction in his voice.

"Aaron, Arms Master," Aloo said to get their attention, "we need to be able to find a place where you and The Healer can mend, and we cannot be found."

"I am sorry to hear about what has happened to your people, more sorry than you can know, but we cannot do anything to counter the evil that has been done, Aaron, unless you and The Healer are mended. I take it that you are the crown prince of this land, and your uncle has been trying to kill you?" asked Aloo.

"More so since my prince comes closer to legal age for ruler in this land," answered the Arms Master.

Aloo nodded acknowledgment of what the Arms Master said and continued speaking with the prince. "The Regent's attitude toward you must have been obvious to your people, who seem to have understood his nature very well. And if we should meet any of them as we flee, this will give you favor with them. This is important, for those of your people who have escaped death and enslavement will need someone to rally around and lead them."

"Your understanding of the situation here in my land is quite good, and I am very surprised at it," said Prince Aaron with inquiry in his eyes.

"We have been forced for years to study governments and the politics within them. Your uncle, as an evil Regent, seems to follow the path of all those who wish for power but do not have the right to it. The Child had us learn all that we could about governing and the pitfalls that people encounter. How she got the Evil Mage to allow such learning is beyond me, but we do have this knowledge."

The Child looked at Aloo and the others and, shrugging, said, "I have no idea either. I remember you and the rest of The Family, but not the Evil Mage, and some things even of you are not clear yet. I wonder if my memory will return fully. Also, Aloo, am I considered part of The Family?"

"I cannot tell whether your memory will return or not, and quite frankly, your life was so horrible I hope it doesn't," said Aloo. "Yes, you are part of The

Family. All of us who were the victims of the Evil Mage are of The Family. It is our strongest connection with each other, and you, Child, were his favorite victim. Also, you are our only healer."

"Well, that my life was that bad is uncomfortable news, but I am happy to know that I am not outcast by the other survivors," said The Child, sounding relieved. "But life is so challenging right now, and my memory so spotty, that I think I will just concentrate on surviving. I do, however, seem to remember a feline named Elder. Is he not one of our leaders, and did he survive the magic blast?"

"Yes, he is and did, why?" asked Prass.

"For some reason, it is in my mind that it is he whom I should ask most of my questions," answered The Child who, upon seeing the relief on Aloo's face at not being the one she intended to ask most of her questions, said with gentle amusement, "I still have quite a few questions about the here and now." She looked at all the members of The Family, eyes twinkling at the groans she received.

"Who are you of The Family?" asked Prince Aaron who had been watching the play.

"The Family consists of the species you see in camp with you and The Child. We are new to your land, and it is obvious that your people have never encountered the likes of us before," answered Aloo.

"How very true, but if you had not come to our aid, The Healer, Hearten, and I would be dead," answered the Prince.

"We are willing to give aid to you and your people. Are you willing to give aid to us?" Aloo asked.

"By 'us' do you mean your nation called The Family?" asked Hearten.

"Yes, we have always considered ourselves people, but not a nation until very recently," answered Prass.

"Most nations do live in single locations, but there are some that seem to have a lust to wander or have had such a terrible thing happen to their country that they find themselves homeless. Still they are nations for they have laws and government among themselves that are separate from that of whatever lands they wander in," explained Prince Aaron.

"Then I believe that we are truly a nation, for we have developed over the last few years a loose form of government among ourselves," Aloo answered.

"I accept your proposal that we become allies giving mutual aid one to another," replied Prince Aaron. "It is a relief to me that we have allies in our time of need, but I understand that this is a mutual pact and that your people are in need also."

"Yes, we are. We had been enslaved, much as your people are now, for generations. And now that we are free, we are learning that as much as The

Child tried to teach us, we still do not know how to truly survive in a land that is not magic controlled.

"Besides understanding the evil that has struck your nation, we have in common the fact that The Child played a major role in our freedom and rescue as she did in yours," answered Aloo. "But brilliant as The Child is, this burden is too great for her to deal with. She received great hurt from taking the brunt of the magic blast when she threw up the shield to protect us. In our hurry to escape the evil ones who have invaded your land, we have forgotten that she too is healing. Look, she sleeps, but not before making the medicines that you and The Healer require. Also, Aaron, could you give formal introduction of us to your Arms Master?"

Aaron looked startled and said, "Yes, this is Hearten. Hearten, the Lady Aloo, who leads our band of rescuers."

Hearten leapt to his feet from beside Prince Aaron and bowed to Lady Aloo. Then with great concern on his face, he said, "Forgive me, Lady Aloo, but if you are enchanted creatures, you must go from this land before the magic suckers find and kill you."

"Worry not, Arms Master Hearten," said Aloo, "although magic was used to alter us, we are not enchanted, merely people, instead of predators."

"But you are right, Lady Aloo," said Aaron. "We need a safe haven, and I apologized for not realizing the danger you and your people could be in with the magic of this land under attack."

"No apology is necessary, Prince Aaron. There has been no time for any thought other than escape, and you were asleep much of the time as your body needs all its energy to heal. Speaking of healing, I do not want to answer to The Child why you haven't taken your medicine, so do so," said Lady Aloo kindly, but firmly.

The Healer finally coming into the conversation said, "Yes, Prince Aaron, do not fuss. We need to take our medicine. The Child is weary and still healing, so let us not give her any trouble. Also, Hearten can use a nap."

Prince Aaron, looking at them with exasperation, said, "Very well, I can see that I will get no peace until I do so, but I feel a great urgency to be doing and resent the time healing takes."

"Rest is what we need to give our bodies the energy to heal. If we stay still, we will leave no tracks. As a healer, I suggest we stay here for at least a day. It will help in our recovery, and as The Child's healer, I believe she has had enough activity for the day. This place has plenty of grass in the meadow for the animals. Let us leave in the morning and today rest and plan," The Healer answered, giving Prince Aaron a kind and understanding smile. "Now, Hearten, if you will be so kind as to give Aaron and me our medicine, we will rest."

Hearten did as he was asked, and after eating a little more, he too slept.

CHAPTER 6

Where to Go

PRASS, LYING COMFORTABLY on the ground, grinned up at Aloo and said, "You should have seen the look on Hearten's face when he heard me talk. I kept grinning the whole way back!"

They all laughed at that.

"My scouts," said Aloo, sharing her worry, "this is the end of harvest time, and The Healer tells of extreme cold, snow, and rains that are frozen. We have never experienced a time when acts of nature kept us from food, and in the last years, there was never a time we could not hunt. Yet Prince Aaron says that many of the creatures that dwell in these northern parts sleep through the worst cold and can't be got at. I worry about our people. We need to find winter shelters.

"Brak, I am sending you to report to the elders and the rest of The Family telling them not only what has taken place but also warning them about the season The Healer calls winter. It may be that as this land has lost its people, this will be a good place for us, at least for the winter. But instead of thinking of hunting only, we must gather what stray animals we can find and food for them, becoming herders of beasts, so that our own people will not starve when winter's harshness arrives."

"When should I leave?" asked Brak.

"Not yet," answered Aloo, "we need to have an idea of where we are going before I send you on your way."

"I will fly patrol while they sleep," said Brak, impatient to be doing and not liking the waiting or the planning.

Aloo looked after him with envy and then at Prass, the oldest of the four-foot guard, and said, "Ahh, to be so young again and not loaded with responsibilities. Hmm, come to think of it, growing up under the control of the Evil Mage, I never had a time when I wasn't loaded with responsibilities. I wonder if Brak even realizes his freedom. Impatience was always severely punished when the Evil Mage was alive."

"No, he doesn't, and watching him shed some of the discipline we grew up with would be good under any other situation. But during this time of crisis, it is not good," said Prass "And, Aloo, I wouldn't worry about the place to take refuge, for the prince indicated that the direction we are heading will lead to such."

"I had forgotten," said Aloo. "Thank you for reminding me, and if it is not large enough, the hidden barns of the people of this land would make for dry, warm, and cozy hiding places."

"True, and they all seem to have fodder stored there. So instead of having to gather food for the animals, we can move the animals to the food," agreed Prass who, with a yawn, was asleep.

The two-foots slept for a long time, and the wounded reaped the benefits of their first good rest since they had been injured by the evil ones.

Hearten woke first, and Aloo happy to have one of the men awake to answer some of her questions asked, "Hearten, can you think of a place where we can shelter for the winter? A place that is large enough for many refugees and has lots of supplies as well as animals and their food?"

"That is a good question, and it would be better if it were not on any maps," answered the arms trainer.

"What are maps, Hearten?" she asked.

"Hmm, they are a drawing on a surface such as leather that is a kind of picture showing where things are," he answered.

"Can you show me what you mean?" Aloo asked.

"Yes, I can," Hearten answered. Then picking up a stick, he started to draw in the dirt as he explained. "This dot," he said, referring to a round mark, "represents where we are, and this dot, the falls, this line represents the road, and this small house, a village. Maps are always oriented with the top being north, the bottom south, the right is east, and the left is west."

"Ah, that would give people a fair idea of where places are and where to look for certain people," she responded.

"Yes, my lady," he answered. "And at the palace, the maps are even more detailed."

"But not quite complete," said Aaron from his bed, startling both Aloo and Hearten, as they had not heard him stir. "My uncle, while acting as Regent, sent me too many places. And at eighteen, I was sent to the northern border with the hope that while chasing brigands, they would kill me. He sent me with a too small patrol, and I barely escaped with my life.

"The local lord, disgusted with the Regent and loyal only to himself and his people, was desperate to get rid of these criminals. So when I came up with an idea to entrap them, he was very helpful in spite of his doubts about my age and experience. and though I wished to capture and question them he villagers who suffered the most were showing no mercy and there were no prisoners."

"Later, finding time to backtrack them, I found their hideout. I have never seen such an immense group of caves in my life, and when I was back at the palace for a short time, I checked the maps, and they weren't on them much to my delight."

"I can imagine," said Hearten dryly. "With your uncle trying constantly to kill you and make it look like an accident or ill fate, it is only logical that you were in want of a place where you could hide when it got closer to the time of your coronation."

"You are right, and I wanted it to be in a place where I could shelter those who are loyal to me and in danger from my uncle, such as yourself, Arms Master Hearten."

"About how many people do you think could dwell in them?" Aloo asked the prince.

"I did not see all of them," he replied. "But of what I did see, there was room for at least a hundred people."

"How far would we have to go?" asked The Healer.

"About a four-day journey to the northeast," Aaron replied. "But the way we travel with us being injured, plus avoiding the evil ones, it will take us eight days to two weeks to get there."

"Don't forget to add in the amount of time it will take us to cover our trail, and the amount of beasts we have with us already makes that task difficult," reminded Kerr.

"I didn't," said the Prince. "But since the beasts traveling with us, even in their wild state, are mostly herd beasts, it will not create curiosity in anyone to see their tracks in groups. And at the pace we will be going, they will have plenty of time to graze. This will help to create the illusion that they are beasts just wandering for food. So the only tracks we need to eliminate are those of two-footed people, enormous avians, and very large four-footed people. We have these species, but in smaller animal form, and we do not want anyone to become curious."

"Good," said Aloo with relief. "The winter approaches, and we need a safe haven. Let us make this our goal. Now that we have Hearten with us, maybe it won't take us so long to get there. With him with us, we have more flexibility."

"Thank you for your confidence, my lady," Hearten said, bowing to Aloo. "I will go through what we have and arrange the packs. Come, Child, you can help."

The Child went with the arms trainer, and they rearranged very little.

"For a youngster, you did a very good job," Hearten said approvingly to The Child.

"Thank you, Arms Master Hearten," she responded, approval in his voice, making her shy and putting color in her cheeks as she blushed with pleasure.

"I learned mostly by doing," she said in a shy, quiet voice. "When you have to keep searching for the things you need, you learn to put them where you can find them."

"Ha! How true that is," agreed Hearten with warm friendliness.

Having the packs ready for the morrow, they started on food, medicine, and the general well-being of the hurt.

Hearten, helping The Child to bathe their wounds, lifted his eyebrows in astonishment as he realized that all of the stitching and care given to the two had to have been done by her. Listening to her as she spoke to her patients only added to his amazement. When The Child had accompanied The Healer to take care of necessary body functions, he looked at the prince and then at Aloo and asked, "How old is she? I have never seen wounds so well-tended."

"We don't know," answered Aloo. "But she also has suffered injury and is still healing. The magic blast that she protected us from knocked her unconscious, and when she came to The Healer's cottage, she seemed to have the mind of an infant. That was a little over twenty days ago."

"She heals remarkably fast then," said Hearten.

"Yes, she is cursed to always heal and never age. I think she believed that, with the end of the mage, her life would also be ended, but the spells to heal her and keep her from aging seem to be holding," answered Aloo sadly.

"What saddens you that she is alive?" asked Aris, coming in from a scout.

"Can you imagine living on and on with all those you love dying around you?" asked Aloo.

No one spoke as they thought about this.

When The Child returned, they all looked at her with great concern.

"What?" she asked, somewhat alarmed.

"We are concerned that the spells to keep you young and healing haven't worn off, not that we aren't happy that you are alive. But I would have thought that with the death of the Mage, you also would perish," explained Aloo.

"Oh, I had not thought about that, and I don't think that I will with so much of my memory missing. I don't have the information to even make a guess. Besides, we need to stay focused on the tasks at hand," answered The Child, shrugging off their concern.

"Besides surviving, what other tasks do we have?" asked Mavs.

"We need to survive, but to do that well, we need to learn what we can about the enemy. We need to learn more about this land, how it is set up, and the customs of the people of this land. We need to be sure that we understand their language correctly and discover the purpose of the enemy and how the magic is being stolen from this land. And I am sure there are some things I haven't thought about," answered The Child calmly.

"Oh," said everyone in camp. Quiet reigned as they tried to take this in.

"Excuse me, Arms Master," said The Child, "but I believe that we should get an early night's sleep and an early start tomorrow. With you here, it will take far less time to get going in the morning, and I hope that will enable us to get to the shelter Prince Aaron has mentioned before two weeks are out."

Prince Aaron looked about to object to the command for an early night, but The Child said, "Neither you nor The Healer are as pale and drawn looking, but you will be even better and heal faster for the extra sleep."

Sighing with acceptance, the prince ate his food and took his medicine, falling asleep shortly afterward. The Healer, having more mending to do, was asleep before him.

Once she was sure that all was prepared for the next day, The Child also went to sleep, and Hearten, not really sleepy, sat by the fire and thought.

"Prass," he said, "has she always been that bossy?"

"She had to be, and she has always been our healer. And from the way her two-foot patients are behaving, it would seem that healers in this land are bossy also," answered Prass with a feline grin.

"True, true, and we are taught from our infancy to obey them," answered Hearten. "Still, she had many good points giving us all much to think about."

"A caution, Arms Master," said Prass. "When she is acting as healer, she is bossy. But unless there is an emergency, you will not find her so at any other time. I think that having so much of her memory missing has undermined her confidence."

"It is well that we take on the task of seeing that we survive successfully," said Aloo. "It is part of what we were trained for. Also, the Prince is already getting anxious to be out and about, and I imagine that The Healer will not be any less so when she feels better. The Child has her hands full for a good while yet."

"You have the right of it, my lady," said Hearten. "Healers are notorious for being bad patients." Then rising and stretching, he went to his bed.

At first light, Mavs and Aris went out for short-range scouts.

"Brak," said Lady Aloo, catching him before he launched for his morning scout, "I will have you stay with us maybe a day or two more and then go to

The Family. We avians can go over a hundred miles in a day, unlike the rest of our people, so you will easily catch up with them."

"Yes, Aloo," said Brak, and he left to launch into the early dawn. Brak flew above them for a long view of the area around them and would give warning with certain calls they had devised, along with natural-seeming body language that could be read from the ground.

While out scouting, Mavs and Aris came upon Hearten's horse and brought it back with them. Aloo, seeing the horse following them, was surprised that it did not seem to fear them.

"You didn't use mind-speech, did you?" Aloo sharply questioned them.

"No," replied Mavs, "but we were all in camp with Arms Master Hearten last night, so maybe it smells him on us."

"I am amazed," said Hearten. "Where did you find him?"

"I think that he followed you to the falls and from there to where we found him," said Aris.

"I agree," said Mavs. "We backtracked him, and his trail led from that direction."

Prince Aaron chuckled. "Hearten raised him from a colt, and he was forever trying to follow him into places that don't welcome horses."

"He has the nose of a hound, I swear," said Hearten. "But being a war horse, he is breed for intelligence and can puzzle out things. Also, I noticed that you of The Family do not smell quite the same as regular predators do. So when he realized that I was coming with you willingly and there was no scent of my fear, he would not have feared you, I guess."

"Sounds like a new chapter in the continuing history of our war horses," said Prince Aaron. "I guess you will have to write it down."

"May the One God grant that we find a scribe," said Hearten in mock fear. "I have never enjoyed writing any more than I had to, but scribes seem to delight in it."

"Do you have further to report?" Aloo asked the two scouts.

"We have not seen a trace of the hunters, with the exception of their dead comrades," said Mavs, his brow furled. "It was obvious that they killed their own people and left them to the carrion eaters. What type of people care not for their injured, but instead kill them and leave them where they fall, showing them no honor?"

"If they do not care for their own, it will be bad for the people of this land," said Kerr quietly so that Aaron would not hear.

"You are right," said The Child. "But please wait until the Prince and Healer are healthier before you bring this subject up. Fortunately, the morning's efforts have both of them sleeping, so they did not hear. Hearten, however, did, and I will speak with him."

She went over to Hearten to caution him about what to say to the Prince. Aloo, watching from a distance, saw the Arms Master nod in understanding to what The Child said. Then he walked over to Aloo and the scouts.

"Not respecting life at all," said a worried Hearten in a low voice once he was near. "I could understand that attitude toward our people, but toward their own, this I don't understand."

"We do," growled Kerr. "We have the example of the Evil Mage to look back on. I hope that we can find enough of your people to free this land of these evil ones."

"Let us continue on while my patients sleep," said The Child quietly and went to gather the beasts of burden to her. She didn't have far to go as they would seek her out, preferring to remain close to her.

Prass, curious about this, asked, "Child, why do they follow you so willingly?"

"Ah, The Healer told me that you could win them through their stomachs and with kindness, so I have been giving them little treats and lots of pets. They really like being brushed and groomed. Also, if there was a need for them to scatter, I wanted them to want to come back to me," answered The Child.

"Good plan, and now we need to be on our way," said Prass. "Brak has already found the next campsite, and says that it is well away from the enemy."

◊ ◊ ◊

When they reached the next meadow, both the Prince and The Healer were looking much better. Once The Healer had her needs taken care of, The Child propped her up with some of their baggage.

Aloo told The Healer, "The enemy is still far enough away for us to have a fire."

And The Healer answered, "That is good news. It is still early, and The Child and Hearten can make enough food to last for several days. Oh, by the way, Lady Aloo, and the rest of you who do not know me, my name is Mavis."

Aloo was so embarrassed to have forgotten to get her name and to realize that she had not been treating The Healer with proper respect that the skin around her beak turned red. "I apologize, Healer Mavis," she said contritely. And The Healer, more amused than offended, graciously accepted not only Lady Aloo's apologies but those from the rest of the group.

Then Mavis looked at The Child and the Arms Master, and seeing that she had their attention, she gave clear and easy instructions to them. Before long, they had a good meal prepared and food for several days cooking.

"Why don't you and the others of The Family try this stew?" Healer Mavis invited Aloo and the rest of the guard. "It is fairly tasty for a meal with little herbs in it."

"Thank you. We will," said Aloo, and The Child brought her some in a large bowl, which she shared with the others.

"I find it strange, but good," said Prass and then added with a feline grin, "and I don't know what herbs are."

"They are plants that enhance the flavor of food and can be used for medicinal purposes," answered The Healer.

After the meals had been cooked, Hearten borrowed the prince's tack and set out to retrieve his riding gear along with the tools he had stashed. Aris had assured him that the stuff was still where he left it and had no scent of the enemy on it. "The evil ones paused to look at it, but they were so confident in their hounds they wasted no time making them a trap," he told Hearten.

Their confidence caused Aloo to ask, "Hearten, has anyone ever escaped the kill hounds?"

"The kill hounds are highly effective and have never failed before to my knowledge," he answered and turning to Prince Aaron added, "I wish, my prince, that I could have gotten to you before this mayhem struck our people. You would have believed the warnings I gave, unlike the majority of our leaders. There was no point in warning your uncle, since the closer the time came for the invasion, the less accessible he was."

"That might have stopped some of the mayhem, but this plan seems to have been laid very, very thoroughly," answered the prince, lying back on his mat, exhausted from personal chores, feeding himself, and sitting upright. "And I am not sure how effective we could have been even if I had received your warning in time. In fact, the reason I didn't expect treachery from the foreigners was that I was expecting it from those my uncle had assigned to me from our own people." With that, he closed his eyes.

Kerr approached the Arms Master and Lady Aloo. "It has been slow going, Arms Master, Lady Aloo," said Kerr. "May I accompany Arms Master Hearten on his task?"

"That is a good idea," said Lady Aloo. "We do not need any more surprises or anyone else hurt."

Hearten, startled at this request, was ready to object when Prince Aaron roused and said, "My beloved friend, you we cannot spare, and I will rest easier for knowing one of The Family travels with you."

"Yes, my prince," answered the man. Then grinning at Kerr, he said, "I know what you mean. I don't think I have ever traveled so slowly or with such caution before in my life. Some brisk movement will ease the stress!"

Kerr grinned back and nodded in agreement.

"Be on your way then," said Lady Aloo.

CHAPTER 7

Arriving at the Refuge

BRAK AND ALOO launched into the air using dawn as concealment, Aloo doing aerial reconnaissance and Brak heading for The Family.

The canine and feline scouts ran through the understory of the forest, where Aloo could not see, for at least a mile from their camp, searching for any sign of the enemy. By the time they returned, Aloo remaining in the sky, everything was packed and ready to go.

In order to prevent drag marks, Hearten continued to use the method The Child had devised, with the stretchers slung between horses. The rest of the horses were connected together with the rope long enough to let them graze, but short enough for them not to get tangled in, with the exception, of course, of the Prince's war mount who kept an eye on the horses carrying his rider.

When Hearten took up the leads of the horses carrying The Healer and the Prince, Kerr asked, "Child, why does the Arms Master have controls of the patient's horses and you the herd beast? You are, after all, their healer."

"I do not have much experience with animals," explained The Child. "And before Hearten arrived, Prince Aaron's mount was better able to guide Mavis's and Aaron's horses than I was. It is a relief to me that Hearten can handle the job."

"Sensible as usual," commented Prass. "But then you have always been sensible. Even when we didn't understand what it was, I can now see that the things we learned were important to our freedom." Then she went over to Hearten. "Hearten," said Prass, "we will need to exercise silence for we go toward the enemy, and from Aloo's signals, the enemy is also coming toward us. Are you able to pick up nonverbal signals quickly?"

"Yes, we have hand signals and body signals of our own in the military," answered Hearten. "I will try to quickly learn yours." Then he mounted his horse, and taking up the reins of the patients' horses, he followed Prass into the forest.

Prince Aaron's horse followed his master, keeping an eye on the horses carrying his stretcher, giving proof to The Child's claim about him.

They left the meadow about two hours into light. The forest was full of shadow and gloom, causing shapes to lose their definition and helping to mask their movements, while the noises and soft debris muffled their sounds. The four-foots went through the forest moving in a rhythm that caused their steps, when they could be heard, to sound more like the rustle of wind through the autumn leaves than footfalls.

The scouts guarded those in their care in a compass point pattern with one north, one south, one east, and one west. Those they guarded had to travel in a stop-and-go pattern, not only to imitate the movement of a herd, but also to allow the four-foots time to scout ahead before they moved forward again; and as they needed to use body signals, they had to remain in line of sight or move to it to communicate to each other.

Hearten was quick to pick up the signals which helped a great deal.

It would have been unnatural for herd beasts to stay in the forest and avoid meadows, so they traveled from meadow to meadow through the forest. Hearten kept his animals at the edge of the forest, and The Child accompanied hers into the meadow.

At a lunch stop one day, The Child took the leads off of the heard beasts and stored them away.

"Are you sure that is wise?" asked Kerr. She and Prass were coleaders on the ground.

"If we come upon any soldiers, it will look as though these animals are pack animals whose owners did not escape their sweep," said The Child. "And going by how they seem to crowd around the camp at night, I believe that they will not leave us unless panicked, and then they will try to find us again."

That day, they did not come near any of the evil ones; but on the next day, they needed to cross a road that was heavily patrolled. The closer they got to the road, the thicker the enemy patrols became.

About midmorning, with the enemy all around, The Child sat down in a meadow with the herd grazing to be out of sight. It was a good thing that she did, for three of the enemy patrols converged upon them.

The enemy paid no attention to the halters on the animals, if they even noticed them. They were focused on glowing orbs that seemed to be guiding them through the intensity of the light they emitted. Aloo, seeing this from up high and knowing that The Child could not see the soldiers, gave a call, mocking the sound of a local falcon to get The Child's attention. The Child heeding her warning and seeing the enemy before they saw her quietly left the meadow. As she was leaving, the globes became dark.

This caused a frenzy of activities from the patrols, scattering the animals into the forest until they had the meadow to themselves. After not finding anyone, the leaders of the patrols took to shaking and banging their orbs. Having grown up around magic objects all her life, Aloo gave a call and flew a warning pattern, and then she darted away as fast as she could go.

It was fortunate that the animals had left the meadow, for minutes into her flight, there was an explosion that lit the sky, flattening many of the trees surrounding the meadow and killing all of the enemy there as she discovered when she flew back over.

◊ ◊ ◊

The refugees had vanished into the forest, and as Aloo could not see within it, she remained soaring until they became visible again.

Hearten, having seen the patrols coming into the meadow, had eased himself and the wounded farther into the forest and was moving silently and cautiously when he heard Aloo's second warning cry. Then he started to hasten them.

Aris coming upon him cried, "Run for your life!" And following his own advice fled through the forest.

Hearten had ridden his horse but a short distance when he heard the blast and moments later felt it. Then his escape became more treacherous as he dodged falling treetops and flying debris. Because he was already on the move, he managed to get out of the affected area quickly, breathing a sigh of relief when he came to a small narrow gorge with a steam running through it. He followed the stream to a hollow that was surrounded by briers offering a good hiding place.

Taking his time to find the best way into this hiding place, he left the horses in the stream bed where the swift moving current would wash away the tracks they made. Following a moss-covered bank, he discovered an opening into the thicket on the other side of the stream. Leading the horses into this area, he set about camouflaging the opening.

◊ ◊ ◊

Once the enemy was distracted with the darkening of their globes, The Child went in the direction Hearten would have taken. She arrived just in time to see the tail end of one of the horses he was in charge of disappearing and followed as best she could. The Child came upon the stream very shortly after he did, and seeing from the fading impressions in the stream bed the direction that they had gone, she ran along the bank keeping to the moss and leaving as little trail as possible. When she caught up with Hearten, she immediately started to help.

Shortly after they finished camouflaging their hiding place and getting their patients comfortable, the four-foots joined them, and all settled in to wait.

Breaking the silence, Prass said in a whisper that could barely be heard, "I am sure that blast will draw other soldiers." The others nodded, and silence resumed.

In tense silence, they waited, listening intently. The four-foots heard them first, the two-foots a minute later; and all tried to be quieter still, even though the soldiers were very noisy as they trampled through the brush.

"It will be better, Hearten, if you and The Child remain here until we four-foots have a chance to patrol. When we deem it is clear, we will come and signal you," said Kerr when it seemed the enemy was far enough away.

As she turned to leave, Hearten said, "Hold a moment. It is important that we leave before full dark is in the understory hindering our travel. The habits of our enemy have proven to be consistent. They always set up camp before dusk. With all the tracks that they have made and those of the herd, we will not need to be so cautious of our tracks here in the woods or as we cross the road. It is important that we be in the woods on the other side to set up camp."

"A good plan," said Kerr. "We will scout not only for the enemy but also for a quick way to the road." With that, she and the other four-foots slipped quietly from the shelter, not even snagging fur on the brambles.

◊ ◊ ◊

The enemy took a long time to satisfy their curiosity over the blast, so it was almost evening before they could leave.

"We have found a route, and the road is not that far from here. If they see your tracks, I doubt that they will be able to tell them from their own," said Kerr, agreeing with Hearten's earlier observation.

Hearten and The Child swiftly loaded the wounded, and they hastened on their way with Aris leading them.

It was almost dark when they reached the road and, after a quick scout for the enemy, crossed. After traveling for another half hour, they were forced to make camp due to darkness.

The next morning, The Child had them check on the closeness of the enemy before she built the fire she needed to brew medicine for the wounded. As Kerr crept through the forest, she was shocked to see that they were within fifty feet of an enemy encampment. She scouted and watched for a while, then silently went back to her camp, indicating that none should speak.

As quietly as possible, The Child and Hearten readied the horses the scouts had found and loaded them. Prass came in from her scouting and signaled that the enemy was near on that side also. Mavs, who had gone back toward the road, reported that troops were stirring along this route. Aris, who had scouted the direction they were headed, signaled that he had found a narrow way between the troops in the direction they needed to go.

With the enemy so near, The Child could not brew the medicines that cut down on the pain the Prince and Healer were in. She gave them leather straps to bite on when the pain got too great.

◊ ◊ ◊

It took three hours of silent going, with many near mishaps, before she could have a fire to brew the medicines. When she took the leather straps from their mouths, they had been nearly bitten through. Even though the pain was so great that they didn't feel like eating, The Child forced them to do so. She fed them a broth made from dried meat and some leftover pan bread. As soon as she was sure that their sleep was deep, she and Hearten, with help from The Family, got their stretchers back between the horses, and they journeyed on.

◊ ◊ ◊

The patrols were so thick that it was two days before they dared speak to one another. They had small intense fires made with a practically smokeless wood so that The Child could make the medicines, and once she was done, they were promptly extinguished.

The evening of the second day, Aloo was able to rejoin them, and she recounted to them what she had seen in the meadow. "Do you know what was going on, Child?" she asked.

"Yes, Aloo," she answered grimly, "I not only possess the ability to do magic, but magic is also part of my physical being, as it is with all who can work magic. Those globes were designed to seek out magic. When I realized what was going on, I tamped down my magical energy and shifted it so that they could not detect it. The globes were crudely made and could not detect the shift."

"Oh," said Hearten and Prince Aaron at the same time.

"It would seem," said Prince Aaron, "that The Family are not the ones endangered by the magic sucker, but you are."

"Yes, and Healer Mavis is also threatened by whatever it is. Magic attracts magic, and Healer Mavis, like me, carries magic within her," The Child told him.

"How can I be rid of the magic, and if what you say is true, why once you had disguised your power, didn't they discover me?" asked The Healer.

"Your injuries have depleted your magic store for now, but once you get well, it will blossom again. You do not realize how sorely you have been wounded. All of your body's energy is going into healing you," The Child explained.

"Oh," said Mavis. Then suddenly weary, she drifted off to sleep.

"I didn't realize that her injuries were so severe," said Prince Aaron, concern and fatigue coloring his voice.

"I know. She is a very strong-willed person who resents being helpless, so she does her best to mask her discomfort," said The Child, adding, "which is why I lace her medicines with a strong sleeping potion."

"Stronger than mine?" asked the Prince, making a face over the thought.

"Yes, quite a bit stronger," she answered with an amused smile.

"Yuck!" exclaimed Aaron quietly. "That stuff tastes terrible! What a staunch person she is. I think even most healers would groan over having to take that potion!" he added, his voice full of disgust. This statement brought smiles to all as they settled down for the night's sleep.

◊ ◊ ◊

The next day saw fewer and fewer patrols, and they made better time. On the day after, Prince Aaron was riding his mount for short periods of time, much to his delight.

That night as they sat around their small campfire, Aris said to Hearten, "You seem to be at ease in the forest, and the war horses move as silently as the wind through it, how can this be?"

"I grew up in a forest, hunting for my food and fur for clothing and trade. Prince Aaron is also an expert woodsman, as he had to learn forest stealth in order to survive his uncle. War mounts are trained to silence as well as to combat," Hearten answered.

His reply gave those of The Family plenty to think about. What kind of land – what kind of world are they part of now that they are free?

◊ ◊ ◊

Though the pace had been nerve-rackingly slow, it seemed to have been beneficial to the wounded; and on the tenth day, as they drew near their hiding place, Prince Aaron insisted on riding until they had arrived. The Child, The Healer, nor Arms Master Hearten were very pleased with the idea.

"I know that you three do not approve of this," said the Prince in a cranky autocratic voice. "But I am the only one who knows where this place is, and I will not be able to find it lying in a stretcher between two horses!"

"You are right of course, my Prince," said an unhappy Hearten in a very formal voice, causing the Prince to look a bit ashamed of himself over his attitude.

"I am sorry," said the Prince. "None of you deserves that attitude, but it still doesn't change the necessity of my riding this day."

"You are correct, Prince Aaron," said The Child in such a formal voice that it had the Prince wincing. "But once we are there, you will follow my instructions completely if you wish to be of any use to your people."

"Yes, ma'am," said the Prince. Then giving her a sheepish grin, he led the way.

The more confident Prince Aaron became of his landmarks, the more excited he became and the straighter he sat in his saddle. His excitement was contagious but did not break their disciplined silence.

Coming to a wall of brush, the Prince indicated with sign language that the four-foots should try to locate a stream. His use of their code after such a short time in the saddle had them quite surprised. They located the stream by smell, and following the scent, they came to the wall of a bluff. Here the Prince had them stop.

"Child," he said, "in some spots, the way is too narrow for two horses abreast. Healer Mavis will need to ride upright, or you and Hearten will have to carry her on her cot."

"If she rides before Hearten, she should be safe enough," answered The Child. "We have come this far without leaving any two-foot trace, and I do not want us to do so now, not so close to our hiding place."

Then she went over to Healer Mavis. "Mavis," she said, gently touching the woman's hand, "the way through the gully is too narrow for horses side by side. I am reluctant to leave any human tracks. If Hearten were to hold you before him, could you ride on his horse? It has a very smooth gait."

The Healer looked at The Child and answered, "You are right to be so cautious, and I will be fine riding before Hearten. In fact, it will be nice to see something besides a horse for a change."

The Arms Master had The Child mount his horse, sitting behind the saddle to steady The Healer as he gently lifted her onto his mount. Once The Healer was steady, The Child dismounted, and Hearten took his seat behind her, holding on to her firmly but gently to keep her safe.

Then being careful not to disturb the brush at the entry of the gully, they entered the stream. The four-foots held the brush apart, and the animals went through, following The Child (perched on a plow horse), as she had hoped they would.

The sides of the gully became higher the farther up the stream they went, and in some places, the walls became so narrow that there was barely enough room for the horses with riders to go through.

Kerr went before the Prince with Prass, while Aloo kept watch from up high. Aris and Mavs brought up the rear and later reported that it was a good thing there was a hole farther downstream for the water the animals had muddied to fall through.

Aaron led them out of the water about two hundred feet up the gully, and after wending their way through a maze of boulders, they came upon the concealed entrance of the caverns.

Hearten and The Child were only minutes behind Kerr, Prass, and the Prince. And when The Child took one look at the Prince, she said in a voice that brooked no argument, "Stay mounted. Hearten will help you dismount after we have assisted The Healer."

The Prince grimaced but did as she said, an indicator of how badly he hurt.

"My Prince," said Hearten, looking about with satisfaction, "this is an excellent hideout. No wonder no one could find the brigands."

"Yes, it is even more amazing once you get inside," said the Prince, his face pale and his smile weary.

The Child said to Hearten, "Arms Master Hearten, once we have Healer Mavis settled, I want you to help the Prince off his horse."

Hearten took one look at Aaron and said, "An excellent idea. I know the wounds you have, my Prince. And if you try to dismount, as tired as you are, you will destroy the good healing that The Child and your body have done."

Prince Aaron, making a face, replied, "I have no desire to have one healer mad at me, let alone two. Can you imagine what they could come up with? I will do as The Child has already instructed!"

Hearten chuckled at this, and it even got a weary smile from Healer Mavis.

As Aloo flew overhead, she noticed how narrow the gully was and couldn't help being glad she didn't have to walk. Avians do not like spaces that confine their wings. The other thing she noticed was a ledge on the other side of the bluff. She landed there without being seen and made her way to the others.

"Lady Aloo," said Hearten as she came around the side of the bluff, "would you be as kind as to come and stand beside my horse so that you can steady Healer Mavis while I dismount?"

"Yes, certainly," Aloo replied, wondering how his mount would react to her close presence. She had no need to worry for a better trained animal than a war stead would be hard to find.

Taking her place as Hearten instructed, she partly unfurled a wing to steady Mavis as he dismounted. Once dismounted, he very gently lifted The Healer down and carried her to the pallet The Child had ready for her. Then he went to Aaron and helped him dismount. Aaron was so weakened that Hearten all but carried him to his pallet.

The Child gave the wounded their medicine and a drink, saying, "I suggest that you sleep while Arms Master Hearten and I clean up in the caves. Prass and Kerr have given the all clear, so it is safe to go in."

While Kerr, Prass, and Aloo stood guard, The Child and Hearten entered the cave with Mavs and Aris. They were gone for about twenty minutes, and when they came out, The Child reported to Aloo. "This is a huge complex of caves, Aloo. The main cavern is too large for our small group. We did find one cave that will do and some that will be handy for the animals that are close to the front." Then she went back inside to help clean the smaller cave.

The cleaning done, they carried Healer Mavis in on her stretcher. Mavis, looking around in the lantern light, said with approval, "You two have done a nice job of setting up a house. We should be quite comfortable." The Prince was next; and Hearten assisted him, while The Child brought in the pack animals, unloading them, and led them to their caves.

Once the Prince was settled, Hearten, Mavs, and Kerr left to eliminate their tracks leading into the gully and to scout around and learn the lay of the land.

"I think, Child," said the Arms Master upon returning, "that we can have a fire. The smoke holes are covered by brush and trees, and they will dissipate the smoke."

"What about the scent of it?" The Child asked.

"The outlaws who used this cavern system left a large supply of wood that is generally smokeless and odorless, even if our enemies can smell it. With the brush and the trees dissipating it, they will find it almost impossible to locate," he answered.

"The brigands seemed to have had several fires," commented Aris looking about. "Which place will you choose?"

"Hmm, I think this one that is farthest back. It will make the flame hard to see should any happen on the cavern entrance," said Hearten.

"Good," said The Child, "I will need you, Arms Master Hearten, to take the second largest pot and fill it with water to heat. I want to wash Prince Aaron and Healer Mavis's wounds and make sure that they are not becoming infected." So saying, she went to the packs and started taking things out and organizing them into piles.

Her assumption that Hearten would obey her and his amazement at being ordered by a child, even though the instructions were practical and necessary, had him looking at her warily; and as he came by Aloo, he asked in an undertone, "Just how old is she?"

Stopping to think back, Aloo answered, "I cannot say, I remember her always being in my life."

"Well, I am happy to hear that," he said in a quiet voice. "I am afraid I take exception to having my dignity battered by having to take orders from a child!"

"But she is a healer, and according to Healer Mavis, she knows more than expected. In some instances when The Healer has questioned her, it turned out that the ways she knew to do some things were more advanced than Healer Mavis's knowledge," Aloo pointed out.

"True, she is a healer and just as bossy where her patients are concerned, as all that lot are," answered Arms Master Hearten. "But in our culture, we do not accept being ordered around by children. And when they try it, they are chastised."

"Oh dear," Aloo responded. "She has always had the directing of us and does not know how to communicate, except when she is requesting information, quizzing us on knowledge, problem solving, reporting to her father, giving instruction, or issuing orders."

"And I need to remember that she is not of this land or our culture," agreed Hearten. "And way older than she seems. I think you and the rest of The Family will have an easier time adjusting to the ways of my people and being accepted by my people than she will."

Aloo looked at him with concern and asked, "Why do you say this?"

"I have watched you and the other members of The Family interact with one another, and your behaviors are more like those I am used to. The Child, on the other hand, withdraws unless she has something to say or sees a need that needs attending to. She does not sit and have conversation. In fact, she seems to avoid casual conversation completely and often acts worried when she is not exhausted and there is nothing for her to do. This is not normal behavior. What kind of life did she lead?"

"One horrible beyond imagining. We do not believe that she was ever allowed to be a child, and her slightest infraction was met with horrendous punishments," answered Aloo grimly.

"Still she acts like a child with the same indecisiveness that a child her age would have," he replied.

"Yes, but she received the brunt of the magic blast. That is why we came to your land. She would not awaken, and we could see that she needed a healer," Aloo responded.

"Well, I will try not to take it personally when she orders me about," Hearten replied with a smile.

"Hearten," Aloo said before he could go further, "remember, she doesn't remember the Evil Mage or the tortures he put her through."

"Oh, the blow she took was more serious than I thought then, for she remembers you and the others," he said.

"The magic blast did not cause this. The memory loss is part of the spell he put on her. It was a spell to kill utterly, including the memory of whom she loved the moment she pointed at him," Aloo said.

"With such ill treatment, how could she have loved him?" asked Hearten.

"We do not know, and as she doesn't remember him, she will not remember why she loved him either," said Aloo.

"Thank you for telling me this, but I had better get this water to the fire. Healers are so cranky when they are not obeyed swiftly," said Hearten with a smile as he strode over to the fire.

"Thank you, Arms Master Hearten," said The Child when he arrived with the water. "Do you think it would be best to keep the grooming tools closer to the animals? And where should we store the tack?"

"You are welcome," he replied. "Yes, having the tools and tack near the animals will make life convenient. Maybe you can find a small cave near them."

"Good," she answered and went to do as he had instructed.

"It would seem that she not only can give instructions," said Prass with a feline grin, "but she can take them as well."

"You are right, of course," said Hearten, grinning ruefully, "and I should take a lesson from her. She doesn't seem to take anything personally."

"I think that if she had done that, she would have lost her mind," said Prass. "Her father treated her only with hatred. If she had taken it personally, with her inability to die, she would not be the sane person we know, who taught us so much that is coming into use now that we are free."

"She taught you the skills that you need to be free?" asked Hearten, his eyebrows rose.

"Yes," said Prass who rose, stretched, and left Hearten with much to think about.

Hearten busied himself around the fire, preparing a meal and checking the way that The Child had organized things. He did very little rearranging, as she had picked up his patterns for doing things and had organized them accordingly.

While Hearten was busy with the meal, he said to The Child, "Don't you think that you should take care of the milking?"

"Yes," she answered with a quiet sigh and went to do so.

Prass and Aris, not on guard duty, accompanied her as she went to do this chore. And they secretly wanted her to hurry, so fond had they become of milk. Waiting for her to finish drinking what she could of the milk, they didn't show their impatience for their share.

"If we get more refugees, we will need more cows," said Aris, licking milk off his muzzle. "Otherwise, you and I won't get such a large share of this delicious stuff."

"You are right. Maybe more will come and join the herd!" said Prass with bright hopefulness.

"Oh great!" The Child said in disgust. "More cows to milk, how nice."

Her four-foot companions laughed, and Prass said, "Maybe some of the new refugees will be able to milk the cows, and you will be free of that chore."

"Now that is a cheerful thought," said The Child brightening up.

When they returned from the milking, Prass and Aris were still grinning at The Child's reaction to milking more cows, and Aloo asked, "What is so funny?"

"Aris was saying how he hoped that if we get more refugees, we would also get more milk cows, and you should have heard the disgust in The Child's voice at the thought of milking more cows," replied Prass, chuckling.

"Oh," said Aloo with a smile in her voice. Then she added, "I must confess to being amazed at the many uses two-foots put their animals to and how, even though they are not of the same species, if they are familiar with each other, they will stay together."

They quickly settled into a routine with only The Family going out for long-range scouting or with the herd animals to pasture to protect them from predators. At night, they brought them back to the caverns to keep them safe.

CHAPTER 8

Messengers Out to the Rescue!

T HEY WERE IN their hiding place for two days when Aloo, spotting a winged one, flew to greet and guide the messenger to their camp via the hidden ledge she used when she entered the caverns. The view from the ledge side of the mountain was all wilderness with very few of the enemy in the area. She always launched from there, as its height allowed her to get airborne without the sound of her giant wings giving her away.

Brak, as Aloo had surmised, was the return messenger, and she was surprised to notice that the self-importance he had displayed when he left them was missing. She was greeted by a much more likable person.

"Aloo, The Family should be here in five days," said Brak, somewhat breathlessly as he came to a landing behind her.

"What wonderful news!" she exclaimed as she led him along the hidden path to the caverns.

"They are taking care not to leave a trace or they would be here sooner. The elders have decided to send Anvar to you. They feel that her ability to see and sense magic will help to make the people of this land, and our refuge, safer," he told her after he had eased his thirst.

"Good! And well done, Brak," Aloo said with approval.

The skin before Brak's beak glowed red with pleasure at her approval.

Prince Aaron and Arms Master Hearten greeted Brak as they entered the cavern, "Welcome Brak. It is good to see you again. What news do you have of The Family's arrival?" asked Prince Aaron.

"They should be here within five days," answered Brak. "They are taking care to leave no trace. The young, who are not being carried, can only go so far and so fast in a day."

"That is good to hear," said Prince Aaron and, turning to Aloo, said, "Lady Aloo, we have decided that our guards of The Family should come in so that you can have news not only of all your people but also of your individual families. We will keep watch."

Aloo looking startled and pleased said, "This is a courtesy I didn't expect, and I thank you, but I don't think that I can call them all in. The beasts need to be guarded as well as our shelter."

"Go ahead and do so," said The Child, who had quietly joined the men. "Healer Mavis is well enough to tend the fire. I can take the up high lookout point. Prince Aaron can take the lower level, and Arms Master Hearten can tend the animals."

Both men looked startled at her coming forward, as she rarely said more than three words at a time. Also, they continued to fall into the trap of treating her as though she really was nine, and she rarely corrected them.

"An excellent duty roster," said Prince Aaron with a grin at Hearten. "I don't think you could have put together anything better, do you, Arms Master?"

"No, I couldn't have," said Hearten, somewhat sheepishly, for the Prince had saved him from taking umbrage at what he thought of as The Child's high-handed manner and so embarrassing himself.

"I apologize, Child," said Hearten with a sigh. "I forget that you are not from our land with our traditions. Your solution is excellent and will allow our friends to get the news I am sure they have been longing for."

"It is all right, Arms Master," she responded. "Sometimes, I feel as I look like a child, but other times rather like a very old woman. It is nice to know that I am learning your ways well enough that you forget that I am not of your people." With that, she left to take Aloo's place as the overlook guard; and the men, grinning, went to their posts.

Mavs and Kerr came in carrying two good-sized rabbits. "Welcome, Brak," said Kerr. "Come, eat, refresh yourself, and give us news of The Family." Waiting for Brak to finish eating so they could find out how the rest of The Family fared required great patience. Aloo, greatly missing Alaw and their children, could barely keep from fidgeting.

When Brak was done, two of the four-foots took the remains from the cavern and buried them. He waited until they returned to give his report. "The Family is doing very well. They are a little leaner for all of the traveling they have done on light rations, but the children are growing. And your children, Aloo, are taking their first practice flights. Alaw and your children send their love, as do the rest of your families," he finished, looking around at the other members of The Child's guard.

Aloo sighed, and you could hear the sorrow of missing her children's first flight efforts in her voice. Brak continued, amusement in his eyes, "Your young ones are so excited to be getting back with you that Alaw had to gather them under his wings and hold them so that they didn't damage themselves or anyone else. And, Aris, your mother is expecting to deliver your new brothers and sisters within the month. From listening to their heartbeats, your father can tell that there are three of them and reports, after one kicked him when he was listening for their heartbeats, that they seem very strong. Your mother said, 'I could have told you that.'

"Prass and Kerr, the elders of your family are very proud of you, and your siblings and cousins are quite jealous!"

"Well, that can be considered bad news or good news," said Prass. "Some of my siblings and cousins, even when we were under the control of the Mage, would act out when they were jealous."

"Mine also," said Kerr.

"The elders are aware of this and have set about giving them tasks so that they will not feel they are less than you and therefore need to be in competition with you. I think the trick is going to be keeping them from thinking that they are superior," said Brak ruefully. "But they got my arrogance in check quite quickly, so I imagine that they will manage."

"We noticed the change for the good," said Aloo kindly. "I am amazed at how differently we all respond to being free."

"It is a heady realization," agreed Brak.

Aris was delighted to learn that he would soon be a big brother and had many questions. "Brak, are they making sure my mother gets enough food?"

"Yes, all of the pregnant females get first choice," answered Brak.

"What about carrying loads?" asked a concerned Aris.

"She is not allowed to do that," said Brak, and then added, forestalling the next question, "and at the stage she is in, she is not allowed to hunt either."

"Do my other siblings then have to travel the whole way by foot?" asked Aris.

"No, there are more than enough volunteers to carry them and the other children also. Being able to share the burden has increased our travel considerably," answered Brak.

"Thank you for this news," said Aris.

"Yes. Thank you," said the others.

"You are welcome," said Brak, nodding acknowledgment of their thanks. He continued his report. "The area they have been traveling through is very much wilderness, although you can see where people used to live. We have gathered what two-foots we can find, and they too slow us down."

Just as they were about to ask more questions, they looked at Brak and curbed their curiosity. Their valiant messenger was sound asleep. Quietly, they left Brak and went back to their posts not completely satisfied, but they were heartened at the news they had received.

The excitement of knowing The Family was so close, and that she would be seeing them in a matter of days made it hard for Aloo to sleep that night, so she moved away from the others to pace and ponder how best to organize everyone into a harmonious mix of people. As she paced, she muttered to herself, "If we changed from hunters to keepers of domestic animals and find ways to combine the talents of The Family with the talents of those in this land, we would not have to live in the small groups that made us easy prey for the Evil Mage. This I will discuss with the elders of The Family."

"One thing is certain," she continued muttering to herself, "the training given to us by The Child and our experiences since then have shown that all four species, acting together as a people, make us very strong indeed! I will talk to Aaron, Mavis, and Hearten about how to work together so that we can stay as a strong and free people.

"Hopefully, they and The Family will see that by creating a foundation of goodwill and trust, neither the people of this country nor we of The Family will be devastated again." Then stifling a yawn, she said, "Ah these speculations will be better in the morning. A rested mind eliminates muddled thinking." And she went to her perch and slept.

◊ ◊ ◊

"Aaron, Mavis, Hearten," said Aloo after all had eaten, "before we go to our tasks, may I speak with you?"

"Certainly," said Prince Aaron, and the other two nodded, looking at her with interest.

"Last night, the excitement of seeing my family in a few days made me restless, so I spent the time thinking. It seems to me that if The Family and you and your people join forces, we will be stronger and more able to prevent the chaos that is happening to you, and that happened to us, from happening again."

"I have been having such thoughts myself," said Healer Mavis. And upon seeing the startled looks on everyone's faces, she grimaced and said, "Healing can give you time to think or to fret. And as a healer, I know that fretting gets in the way of a speedy recovery. So having plenty of time to think, I have pondered these things."

"I myself think it is a good idea for both nations to combine," said Hearten thoughtfully.

Prince Aaron looked startled. "How can you say so? I am sorry, Lady Aloo and the rest of you, but you are strange to me. And as we have been overrun with aliens, I do not feel comfortable in trusting The Family completely just yet. You I know, but the rest of your people and your customs, these I don't know."

"That is a wise thought, especially considering your recent past," said Aloo, not taking offense.

"But it is not the time to be cautious on this subject now," said Hearten.

"Why do you say so?" asked the Prince.

Hearten looked to The Child and said, "I am sorry, but he has to know."

She nodded, giving him her consent to tell the Prince and The Healer what they had kept from them.

"My Prince, Healer Mavis," Hearten said to them in the voice of one who hates to give grievous news, "our avian scouts have noticed, as we have moved, that the lands they fly over are deserted. The elderly, infants, young children, and men all slaughtered and left for the carrion eaters." Seeing the look of horror on their faces, he grimly continued on. "When I was escaping, some of the enemy soldiers were hurt in the rock slides. The next day when our scouts went out, they found that the enemy had simply slain them and left them to be eaten."

"Their behavior causes my stomach to tie into knots. How safe can our people be with such creatures, and how cruelly are they being treated?" asked Prince Aaron in great distress.

The Healer laid a comforting hand on the Prince, saying, "It would seem that they only hold on to those who are useful to them. Let us pray that the ones they have enslaved are useful."

"My Prince," said Hearten, bringing the topic back to The Family, "an alliance with The Family will give us the people we need to rescue ours and free our land from these people. Also, if you will recall, the behavior of our enemy was always stand-offish, and never very friendly. We have clearly seen the character of The Child's guard displayed to us every day, and it is so much more like us and so much friendlier."

"You are right," said Prince Aaron, closing his eyes wearily. "But The Family also has to agree with this alliance. Thank you, Aloo, for speaking with us first about this."

"Will you take this idea back to your people for thought?" Prince Aaron asked Brak.

"Yes, Prince Aaron, I will. Does this mean that you are in favor of the alliance?" asked Brak.

"I am still uncertain," said Prince Aaron. "But not as unsure as I was before."

"This too I will report to our elders," said Brak, and turning, he left the cavern heading for the ledge. But before he left, he reminded them, "Watch for Anvar. She should be arriving today."

"I will," Aloo replied. "Good flight." And Brak was gone from the cavern.

"Let us look to the here and now, doing what needs done today," said Healer Mavis. "We will be having a large group of diverse people here, and we need to think how best to set things up for their physical needs."

"There are many caverns, some not as large as others, but all of about the same height, except for the large central caves," said Prass.

"That is odd," said Prince Aaron. "But now that you mention it, I noticed it the first time I explored here."

"The different sizes of caves are mixed together, and some of the larger ones have smaller ones off from them," added Kerr.

"That is good to hear," said Healer Mavis. "That way, if we get large groups of people who belong in one family, or in a guild, we will be able to accommodate them better. The smaller caves can be for different numbers of people which should nicely mix up all our peoples so they can start learning to live together."

"I had not thought of that," said Aloo, respect in her voice at The Healer's planning.

"Remember," said Healer Mavis kindly, "I have had plenty of time to think."

"So have I," said Prince Aaron ruefully. "But I didn't do the thinking that you have done."

"You are trained for governing, war, and, with the way your uncle was always trying to kill you, survival in the most trying of conditions," said Mavis kindly. "You were focused on our need to reach this point and what went on about us. I, however, am a healer and am very focused on the practical needs of people. This reminds me. We need to see if there are any more of those handy pit areas for people to relieve themselves in."

"We will also need food available not only for ourselves and The Family but also for any other refugees that we can lead safely here," said Hearten. At the startled looks at such practical thinking, he grinned and said, "Soldiers always think about food, and as we usually travel in large groups, we think of the need of the whole group."

"True," said Healer Mavis. "You know, Lady Aloo, you avians will be the hardest people to mingle, cave wise. You require room for your wings, and closed tight places make you uncomfortable."

"Hmm," said Aloo, "you are correct, with the exception of when we are nesting. During nesting time and during our children's downy time, we like to keep them in secure tight areas, and they prefer it themselves. It makes them feel safe."

"Our children also like warm small spaces," said The Healer.

"Coordinating our people to help us learn to accept each other is all good, as is the practical aspect of getting prepared for large numbers," said Prince Aaron. "But our first thoughts need to be of defense and provisions."

"Arg, I agree with the Prince," said Mavs.

"Arg, we agree with Mavs and the Prince," said the rest of the scouts.

"I agree with all of you," spoke The Child. They were all startled to hear her speak, especially voicing her opinion.

Mavs, who disliked The Child, sneered, "And what would a child know of these things?"

"Ah, Mavs, you let your dislike of me deceive you into believing that I am as I appear. But while we have journeyed, along with the quiet time of healing I had before the evil ones attacked, my mind has unfuddled. I remember you coming to the keep, well, not you exactly for you were born there. But I remember your people, many parents ago. And even though there are blanks in my memory, I can think back to before your people arrived. I remember many changes of the keep. I assume the changes were the Evil Mage configuring it to his needs and many, many lessons.

"Healer Mavis says I have the appearance of a nine-year-old, yet I have greater knowledge than she in many things, knowledge she feels it would have taken me decades to acquire. So it is most likely that in actual years lived, I am at least fifty or sixty. And most likely, I am well older than that. This being the case, kindly leave off thinking you are an elder to me and so should warrant special respect from me. Indeed," – The Child smiled gently – "it is quite the other way around."

Mavs and all but Healer Mavis stood with their mouths open.

"I apologize, Child," said Aloo, feeling the skin around her beak turn red at the consternation that she felt. "We avians were slaves to the Evil Mage for at least a decade longer, if not more, than the four-foots, and I remember you from my fledgling days. I know for a fact that you looked to be a child of about the same age then as now."

"Awk!" said Aloo, turning redder still. "I called you 'child' again!"

The Child burst out laughing for the first time in her life, a delightful sound, joyful and full of life. Everyone stood looking at her, puzzled at what she could find so funny.

Finally getting her mirth under control, she said kindly, "Don't you think I should have a name? I can't remember having one, but I don't want just any name. Getting people to take me seriously is difficult enough as it is, looking as I do."

"You are right," said Prass. "It must be a name unusual and associated with authority."

This comment of Prass had them looking at her with curiosity. She gave a feline shrug and said, "Well, she is a healer, equal to Healer Mavis, I believe. And Healer Mavis is a master healer. If we don't find a name that gives her authority, how will she be able to help the injured and sick? They need to be able to take her seriously."

"Thank you, Prass," said The Child, "and while we are thinking on this, we need to first and foremost think on defense, supplies, and cohabitation of our people. I believe that the need for defense, especially of the children, will cause all the rest to fall into place.

"The example that will be followed by most, if my studies are correct, will be the one we set. If we continue to treat each other as valued people when other people of the Prince's land come to be with us and when our people join us, then the example we set of valuing one another will be followed by the new arrivals. The tricky part is to combat the fear of difference and firmly plant into the minds of all people that because of our differences, we are a very strong people indeed.

"The need to protect our children, those we love the most, will be common ground that all people, no matter what species, will understand. We will need to locate our children in an easily defensible area where they will be taught and supervised, and because they will be together, it will help us understand and appreciate each other's differences. It will eliminate the strangeness factor.

"Also, when teams go out foraging, it should always be a mixed group with people from each species if possible. Those who can't blend will need to be assisted to go elsewhere."

Even Healer Mavis, knowing that The Child was old, was still startled at the wisdom that flowed from her, and they all felt a sense of her great age.

"Excellent thinking, Old Child," said Hearten, recovering first from this tremendously, at least for her, long speech. "This is what we do in training soldiers so they can be a team. But I must add that we will need to train them to work together, to know what they can expect from one another, to eliminate any false notions of what each species or individual is capable of, and to fight together."

"Excellent, and again, the need to survive will be the impetus that causes this to happen," Aloo exclaimed. "Let us give this more thought."

At about noon, Aloo saw Anvar from her guard perch on the launching ledge. Making a careful check, she flew to meet her, signaling her to follow, and led her to the ledge.

"Sister's daughter, what a delight to see you," said Aloo, giving an avian equivalent of a hug by caressing her niece's neck with her neck.

"Greetings, mother's sister," said Anvar, returning the embrace. "As I winged my way here, I saw many interesting things. But I think the priority of my telling should be of small groups of refugees fleeing in this direction. Some are pursued and others are not."

"You are correct in your priorities," said Aloo as she led her to the caverns.

"Prince Aaron, Arms Master Hearten, Healer Mavis, and, Old Child," Aloo called as they entered the main cavern. Those she called looked up from their tasks and came over to her. "Allow me to introduce Anvar. She is my sister's daughter and has a report I believe you should hear right away."

"Greetings, Anvar," welcomed Prince Aaron, "I am Prince Aaron. This is Arms Master Hearten, Master Healer Mavis, and of course you know Old Child who is also a master healer."

"Thank you for your welcome," replied Anvar. "Old Child?" she asked curiously.

"It is the best they could think up at the moment," said Old Child with a twinkle in her eyes, "and at least it is better than 'The Child.' I explained that I was most likely the oldest person here and suggested that I should have a name."

"You have ever been The Child to us, but I know that my parents remember you from their fledgling years," replied Anvar. "It is only now that I realized you have never had a name that any of us knew. Even your father never used a name when calling you. Still, 'Old Child' seems like a peculiar name to me."

"We wanted a name that would help people be mindful that she is old," said Arms Master Hearten.

"Yes," Aloo agreed with him, consternation in her voice, "it is embarrassing to be forgetting constantly that I am talking to an elder."

"Ah, that makes sense then," replied Anvar.

"What is this that you need to report?" asked Prince Aaron.

"On my flight here, I saw several small groups of people trying to escape your enemies. Some were being pursued, and others were not yet located by the enemy, although there are plenty of soldiers out looking for them," answered Anvar.

"Good news is what you bring. We have been hoping to come to the aid of those who have managed to escape the carnage that has beset this land," said Prince Aaron excitedly.

"We need to choose whom to rescue first," said the Arms Master.

"Sadly," said Aloo, regret coloring her voice, "I recommend that you seek first those who are not pursued, even though their need is not as great as those who are pursued. Keeping our existence secret is our best and only defense."

Prince Aaron and Arms Master Hearten looked at her, shocked and angry; but before they could say anything, Old Child spoke up, "You are correct of course, Aloo." And turning to look at the two men, she continued on. "We do not have the ability to defend ourselves nor time for argument. When those who are not pursued are rescued, if they are not in good shape, they can stand guard duty. If they are in good-enough shape, it might be that they will be able to help us rescue those being hunted. But even if they are not able to go out to battle, they will be able to protect our haven while we are out, and that will be a relief."

Swallowing hard, both men turned to Aloo and said at the same time, "Lady Aloo, we apologize for our attitude. You and Old Child are correct."

"Another thing, my Prince," said Healer Mavis, "your wounds would only cause you to be a liability, so Old Child and Hearten will be the two-feet going out on this mission."

The Prince was about to object when the Arms Master said, kind understanding in his voice, "My Prince, my dear friend, Healer Mavis is right, and this land will completely perish if anything should happen to you now. That you live will give hope and heart to our people. We must keep you safe."

"But what will my people think of a prince who will not fight for his people?" asked the Prince.

"Your exploits are well known throughout the land," said Hearten with a smile. "The people of our land already know that you will face great peril for their sake. The bards made sure of that, even when the Regent forbade their ballads of you."

"I think, Prince Aaron," said Healer Mavis, "that easing our people from their shock and fright will be your most important task. Unless they get over the shock and are in control of their fear, we, as a people, are doomed. Your job is to be the heart of our people: strong, brave, determined, caring, and loving. You will need to counter their fear and direct their anger. Not a simple job."

Prince Aaron looked taken aback at what The Healer said and looked questioningly to the Arms Master for confirmation.

"Master Healer Mavis is correct," replied the Arms Master. "You have been the heart of this land and its courage in defying the Evil Regent for all of his reign. You must continue on, and you must become well and strong. The time for you to go into battle, my Prince, will surely come."

Prince Aaron sighed but accepted the judgment of his arms master and the master healer with a glum look on his face.

"Anvar," said Aloo, "you will need to stay and brief the Prince and Healer Mavis on the needs of the family. I will fly guard and scout for the rescue team. Once you learn our modified silent signals, you may scout for the rescue teams also."

"Yes, Aloo," said Anvar, not looking very happy at being left out of the rescue. "But I do know the signals if they are the ones that Brak showed us."

"You do?" asked Prass.

"Yes, he taught them to us," she replied.

"Good!" said Prass. "That means we will be able to have two teams out tomorrow. Let us get under way!"

"Yes, let's!" said an excited Aris.

The Prince grinned ruefully at Aris and said, "I understand your excitement, but do not let it rob you of good judgment. You are not expendable either."

Grinning at the Prince, the young canine replied, "I will be cautious. Oh Prince, I don't want to hear from the old lady, I mean Old Child, if I'm not!"

Those of The Family laughed. During her training of them, Old Child had worked on discipline, discipline, and more discipline to ensure that they would not be ruled by their emotions in times of danger. She had a way of getting you to recognize your folly that was embarrassing to say the least, making it highly effective as a training tool. She just smiled at him and said, "I will need to exercise caution over my feelings also. I don't want to have a talk from me either!"

"It has only been truly safe to fly and land at dawn and dusk while our enemies are still within their camps," said Aloo. "I only say this to remind you of the danger we could be in, for we avians are not small people. Fortunately, the ledge we have been using is pretty much hidden from sight."

"I believe we all agree that this is an acceptable risk," said Prince Aaron. "Being too cautious can be as disastrous as not being cautious enough."

"Good, that was my own opinion, but I am not the only elder in this group and wanted a consensus," said Aloo, who then left to launch off the ledge while the rest gathered supplies and horses.

"I surely hope that the first ones they rescue will be fit for guard duty tomorrow," said Mavs to Kerr as they went to stand guard.

"Me too," Kerr replied with a sigh. "I would love to take part in the rescue, but we drew the lots, fair and square as Hearten would say, so there is no use complaining."

Having anticipated and hoped such rescue efforts would be needed, Hearten and Old Child had already gathered the supplies they thought would be useful, including a medicine kit for emergencies. The land team members were ready to go in about ten minutes and out of the gully in two more minutes.

Hearten and Old Child went out with his horse, a sturdy pack horse, and three of the other horses they had gathered. They were shod with a kind of boot to hide their tracks and dampen the sound of their hooves. The two – and four-foot people had already decided on the best pathways out of the gully to avoid leaving any evidence of their whereabouts.

With Hearten in disguise, they started down the chosen path, Prass on guard in the front, Old Child and Hearten handling the horses, and Aris bringing up the rear. Both he and Prass were equipped with a strange broom made of soft bows so when hiding traces, nothing that was not of the forest would be visible. They were also easy to take off and left their teeth free in case a fight ensued. Also, when held a certain way, it further helped to disguise their appearance.

About two hours after leaving their refuge, they met with the first group of refugees: an old man; a younger, sickly looking man; and ten children.

Hearten met them causing a bit of fright at first. Then Old Child stepped out, motioning for silence with a finger to her lips. Still maintaining silence, Hearten and Old Child led the horses to them and helped the children and sickly young man to mount. The old man and one of the older children walked. Old Child led the animals off, guided by Aris, on a route that made sure there was little noise and left as few tracks as possible.

Meanwhile, Hearten and Prass backtracked the way they had come for about a mile, hiding all traces of them.

This careful travel was slow going and silent. Aloo kept watch, guarding them from up high. While so occupied, she spotted five other groups who were not pursued within reachable distance from their refuge.

CHAPTER 9

To the Rescue

"WELCOME TO OUR refuge," said Old Child to her group. "We can talk now, though it is bests we do so quietly. Come to the fire and food."

As she extended the invitation, there was somewhat of a rush to the stew pot. Healer Mavis, stepping into their path with arms crossed and a stern look brought them to a swift halt.

"I know that you are well-nigh starved," she said with firm kindness in her voice. "But first you will wash your hands. While you are doing this, I will instruct you how to eat so that you do not throw up what I have spent much time preparing."

"Yes, ma'am," was the reply as they followed her to the washing area.

"You will take a bite, chew it slowly, swallow it, count to three slowly, and then you may take another bite. If you do not do as I say, you will be quite ill. And I, your healer, will be displeased!" she told them with another stern look.

After washing her hands, Old Child helped the Prince and Healer Mavis serve the new refugees.

After they had eaten a little, Mavis, Old Child, and Aaron proceeded to clean them up, wrapping them in warmed blankets while their garments were set to soaking to be cleaned the next day when the new refugees had the energy for it. The Prince and The Healer didn't dare to do this task, for their healer had forbidden it and was keeping a watchful eye on them. After hearing Aris' comment about not wanting her to have a talk with him, and the look of agreement between the rest of the guard, including Aloo, they decided that they did not want a talk from Old Child either.

Once everyone was clean and comfortable, Mavis and Aaron proceeded to serve them more stew. The young man looking up to thank Aaron as he was serving him gasped with shock, "My lord!" he exclaimed, trying to jump up but getting tangled in his blanket and falling over instead.

Aaron managed to catch his bowl of stew before he spilled too much of it and at the same time kept the young man from falling into the fire.

"You're alive!" shouted the young man in his excitement. "But we were told you were dead, that rebellious farmers had attacked and killed you!"

"Nay, not farmers, good scribe, but our allies from the lands to the south and over the sea. They left me and Healer Mavis for dead, but some very unusual people came to our rescue," said Prince Aaron who was being scrutinized by Old Child, who having witnessed his rescue of the young man came straight over to the Prince and inspected his wounds.

"How you managed to do that without reinjuring yourself I don't know," she said in a somewhat cross voice.

The prince grinned at her and said, "Let me introduce you, Old Child." And turning to the young man said, "This seeming child, who led you here, is Old Child." Upon seeing the look on the men's faces, he explained, "As far as we know, she does not have a name, and she received an injury that blocked her memory for a time. She was brought to Healer Mavis by her guards when she would not awaken. Let me introduce her guards that are here to you, and please do not be alarmed by these people. They are a type of people that you have never seen before.

"Anvar, if you will step into the light, thank you, let me introduce you to the good priest Father Flin and to Scribe Uther. They have aided me in surviving my uncle's regency."

"Well met, priest and scribe," said Anvar. "I am of the people species avian."

Aaron, Mavis, and Old Child grinned at each other and at Anvar as they saw the looks of astonishment on the faces of the men and the children.

"May I assume from the looks on your faces, Father Flin, and, Scribe Uther, that you have never spoken with people that is not of your species?" asked Anvar with kind amusement in her voice and a kind look at the children that went long ways toward reassuring them.

"Excuse our astonishment," pleaded the priest in his gentle voice, "but I knew not that such as you even existed."

Hearten, Prass, and Aloo entered the main cavern right then, and the look of astonishment Prass and then Aris caused was tinged with fear.

"Fear not," said Aris, "I guided Old Child back so you would arrive safely, and Prass helped Hearten to cover your tracks so you and us will not be found."

"Oh, thank you," said the priest fervently.

Then the priest jumped up and said, "Hearten? Hearten! You also are alive, but how? The kill hounds never fail."

"They did this time, priest. They failed the only way they can, by dying," answered Hearten in a grim voice, the fear from the hunt fresh in his mind.

"Praise the One God and His Son," said the priest.

"Amen," said Hearten with a wry grin on his face.

"Amen?" queried Aaron. "Amen from you, Hearten? I thought you believed in no God."

"With age come wisdom," responded Hearten, "and I aged decades on that chase, let me tell you!"

At this point, knowing they were safe for the time being and still very hungry, there was only the sound of eating from the rescued. Healer Mavis had been right. They had gone for days with little or nothing to eat.

Aloo, noticing how very carefully they ate, gave Healer Mavis a look of inquiry.

She smiled at them reassuringly and came over to her. "They have not had much, if anything, for days. And if they do not eat slowly, they will throw up what they need to regain their strength."

Aris, sitting next to Aloo, grinned and said, "As hungry as they were when they arrived here, they still had enough discipline to wait until they were invited to eat before they approached the food. Once invited, however, it was a mad dash that came to a quick halt when Healer Mavis blocked their way. I have concluded that the healers of this land are held in fearful respect."

"We are not feared, young canine," said Healer Mavis in a somewhat haughty voice. "We are, however, highly respected." Then she moved to see to the newest members of their group.

Hearten brought his own and another bowl and sat down next to Aris. "They are highly respected indeed, young Aris," he said quietly, "highly respected and feared."

Those who heard his comment grinned, but there wasn't any laughing. Healers **are** highly respected and feared.

After eating, the youngest of the children fell asleep where they sat, and Hearten carefully put them to bed a safe distance from the fire. Mavis and the Prince settled the other children with them. The priest and scribe, also weary, took places by the children so when they awoke in this strange place, people they knew would be at hand to calm their fears.

"It is good they rest, for tomorrow will be a busy day," Aloo told the others. "I spotted five more groups of refugees close to us. They are small, like this group, and not being hunted. But a sixth group is, and it is a running battle. In the morning, I will make a reconnaissance flight so we can better plan, but we should have the supplies we will need ready this evening."

"Good planning as always, Lady Aloo," spoke Prince Aaron. "Old Child, you and Hearten get some rest too. You will be doing all the legwork tomorrow. Healer Mavis and I will get your packs ready, and yes, Hearten, I know how you want them to be arranged after all you taught me."

"Yes, I did, and you always tried to get more in the space I allowed than was reasonably possible," answered the Arms Master.

"I was successful too," replied Aaron with a twinkle in his eyes.

Shaking his head, Hearten went to his pallet to sleep.

◊ ◊ ◊

Early that morning, Aloo made her flight and located the groups. This time Hearten went with one set of horses and Old Child with another, relying on Aaron, Mavis, Father Flin, Uther, and the children, who were able, to keep guard and get everything ready for the next groups of refugees.

"Aloo, Hearten, Old Child, and the rest of you," said Prince Aaron as the teams were about to leave, "it would probably be best if the avians remain secret until the people get here. They are refugees like ourselves, but we do not know them or what drives them."

"Oh," said Hearten, "and that would give us backup in case we met with any trouble from the other refugees." Nodded understanding was given to the Prince's choice, and the teams left. Old Child's went left, and Hearten's went right.

Aloo flew long-range scout for Old Child and Anvar for Hearten. Kerr and Prass accompanied Old Child, while Mavs and Aris accompanied Hearten.

Hearten met up with his group first: a woman, man, three young adults, and five children. In a quiet voice, he said, "My name is Hearten, and I come from a refuge. These are my companions Mavs and Aris." As he mentioned their names, each bowed and greeted their group with a "well met."

The refugees looked shocked to be spoken to by what appeared to be enormous predators but were too tired to be more than surprised.

"We have come to lead you safely to our refuge," said Hearten.

The people looking warily at Mavs and Aris, seemed undecided about what to do.

Mavs said, "Come, Prince Aaron waits." A glimmer of hope sprang in their eyes, and they looked questioningly at Hearten.

"Yes, he is alive," said Hearten, seeing the hope warring with doubt in their eyes. "You need to make your choice quickly, for there are hunters out. And if you wish to join us in safety, we need to be moving. Do you wish to accompany us or not?"

"Forgive our hesitation, sir," replied the woman, weariness lacing her voice. "We have met with such treachery that we do not know whom to trust."

"Mistress, fear not," said one of the youths to the woman, seeing through Hearten's disguise, as it was created more to fool someone from a distance rather than close up, "I know this man, and he was reported dead by the foul ones. This is Hearten, as he said, Hearten the Arms Master of the elite soldiers of our land."

"Thank the One God the reports were not true! Yes, we will follow you," said the woman in a relieved voice.

"Let us put the least able on mounts. Then follow Aris, while Mavs and I backtrack to eliminate your trail," said Hearten.

"Quietly now, and try to travel in the driest or the most leaf-strewn places. The rain we had last night has worked a boon, giving silence to our steps, but the mud makes covering and eliminating tracks very difficult," said Aris. They were slightly startled again at being spoken to by Aris, but they could see the sense of what he ordered and did as he commanded.

With the children and the older man mounted, they began their journey toward the refuge. It was a long, roundabout trip full of silence as they strove to go unseen.

Anvar and Aloo from up high could see the diligent searching the enemy was doing and felt chills go down their spines at the single-mindedness of it.

Old Child came upon her group about two hours from the refuge. She watched for Aloo's signal to make sure the way was clear, then stepping from the brush, waited for them to come upon her.

Shocked concern was on the faces of the adults, but before they could say anything, she put a finger to her lips, signaling for silence as she came toward them. When she was in whispering distance, she said, "My team and I come to ask if you wish to accompany us to refuge."

"Refuge?" questioned the man in a whisper, hardly daring to hope. "You have a place to hide from the devils who have murdered our people?"

"Yes," answered Old Child. "But you will have to live in the company of refugees very different from people you have ever met before."

"A place of safety is all we ask," said the man.

"I don't know if we can promise safety. Safer, but maybe not complete safety," said Kerr as she stepped from cover.

"A different people indeed," said the large woman traveling with the man.

"Yes," said Prass coming from cover behind them. "Do you still seek refuge with us?"

The man and woman looked at each other and the rest of their group, two couples with six children between them and two large youth. Then the man said to Kerr, "Yes, for what seemed normal and good to us turned out to be evil, so maybe it is that what seems strange indeed will be for good."

"Good, follow me while Prass and Old Child remove the traces of your passing. Speak not and be as quiet as possible with your movement. Try to step where there is no mud, and those of you leading the horses try to keep to the wet leaves for they will buffer sound and it is easier to hide a track among them." Once everyone who needed to ride was mounted, Kerr said, "It took us a long time to reach you, and it will take an equal or longer time to get back."

It was midafternoon by the time Kerr brought her group to refuge. Old Child and Prass followed her about an hour later, their journey having been longer, as they had backtracked the group to eliminate as much of their trail as possible.

Fortunately, the refugees kept getting closer and closer to refuge; so both Hearten and Old Child, with their teams, had time for one more rescue. This time Hearten went left, and Old Child went right. In a very short time, they both reached their groups.

Hearten recognized his group as border guards and, as he had long been in the service of Asalawn, knew the appropriate hand signals that would indicate that he was a friend, not foe. He stepped out into their pathway when he was ten feet from then and signaled. The leader of the group said in a low cautious tone, "Identify yourself."

Hearten replied, "Arms Master Hearten."

The one in the lead came up to him, sword drawn. Stopping out of arms reach, she eyed him warily. Then a smile of relief broke out on her face, and when her companions saw her body relax, they came forward.

Hearten, seeing that some were hurt so badly that they might not make back to refuge without immediate care, got the medicine kit out and started to work on the wounds of the soldiers. After all who needed aid had received it, they mounted them on horses, with the more able behind the less able to support them.

There were five men and three women in Hearten's group. The women weren't as injured as the men and had been doing most of the tasks needed for the group to survive.

The aid and mounting of the injured onto horses was done in silence. The discipline of the border guards was great, as they often need to go unnoticed. So the guards were startled when Hearten broke the silence with a quiet whisper. "I must introduce you to the other members of my team. One will guide you to refuge, and the other will help me to eliminate your trail. Mavs, Aris, will you step forward please."

When they stepped out, there was a gasp from the soldiers at the size of Mavs and Aris. The size of the canine and feline people is considerably greater than anything the guards were familiar with.

"Greetings, soldiers, I am Mavs of the feline people," said Mavs with a bow.

"Greetings and well met, I am Aris of the canine people," said Aris.

The guards didn't seem able to find any words to say, and Hearten, giving them an encouraging smile, said, "You will follow Mavs back to our refuge. Leave as little trail as possible and keep to your silence. Aris and I will go back the way you have come and eliminate any sign of your passage."

Due to the injuries of the guards, Old Child and her group arrived back at the refuge before the border guards, even though they were farther away. This group was from Potsfield. They had been on a trip to get some special clay for the porcelain vases and dishes they made. The area the clay was located in was difficult to get to, so they used pack mules. The mules freed them from road travel, and they shortened the travel time by going cross-country. This is why the enemy had not found them.

As they got closer to home, they became alarmed at the unnatural silence; and when they got into the town, they were met with the horrifying sight of all the elderly, men, boys, young children, and babes slaughtered and all the women and girls missing.

The animals had been left penned up to starve, so they freed them. Their leaders, though shocked, had the presence of mind to get more supplies, and then they slipped away.

This group consisted of four adults and ten youths, six boys and four girls. They had been trying to hide their trail, and though exhausted from grief and the need to be constantly alert, they were in better shape than the other groups.

When Old Child stepped out in front of them, there were no sounds, but a look of concerned startlement crossed their faces. She got close to them and whispered, "I am from a place of refuge, and your Prince Aaron awaits there, also others who have been fortunate enough to get away. If you choose to come with us, you will be taking refuge with not just human people but people of other species also. If you choose not to seek refuge with us, the friendliest border to this kingdom lies to the northeast."

Looking somewhat alarmed, one of the adults asked, "What kind of people do you speak of?"

With that question, Kerr and Prass stepped out of the brush on either side of Old Child and said, "Us."

Seeing that Old Child had no fear of these creatures, even though they were so much larger than she, they decided to come with her.

"Follow Prass, the feline, she will guide you to refuge," Old Child told them.

"Continue as you have been doing and leave as little trace of your passage as possible," instructed Prass. "Kerr and Old Child will follow along behind and cover any trail you may have made. Use the mounts we have brought to rest your horses."

"But what about the child?" asked the woman of Prass and, looking to where Old Child had been, was startled when no one was there.

Prass, seeing the startlement and concern on the woman's face, said kindly, "Old Child will be explained to you at our refuge, but rest assured we would never put a child in danger."

"Come," said Prass, "the sooner you are hidden from the evil ones, the better."

"Our animals seem to balk at the sight of you," said the man, somewhat embarrassed, for the horses that Old Child's team had brought were calm.

"Yes, I see that. These animals also were frightened by us, but they have grown accustomed to us and feel safe around us. Arms Master Hearten said that if we were to have this trouble, the animals should be blindfolded and led, also that I should try to be as far in front as possible, and if not in front, at least downwind."

"Arms Master Hearten? He has survived this invasion? Surely then the regent knows that we are invaded and will be sending troops from the city," said the woman.

"Oh, he knows all right," said Prass dryly. "The invasion started at the capital, but we do not have time for explanations, and we do have a need for silence. Blindfold the horses and let us be on our way."

Upon entering the cavern system, the refugees who followed Prass were surprised to find that they were so close to shelter.

"Thank you, Prass, for guiding us here," said the woman. "We would never have found this place, even though it was quite close to us."

"You are welcome," said Prass. "Let me introduce you to Healer Mavis, and I suspect you know Prince Aaron."

"Prince Aaron!" exclaimed both the man and the woman. "You have survived this invasion!"

"Yes," said Prince Aaron, responding to the happiness in their voices. "Thanks to Old Child, whom you have met, and her people of whom Prass and Kerr are but two. The invaders, posing as friends to the Regent, overthrew him and tried to kill me. When they couldn't, they left myself and Healer Mavis for dead in her cottage after they set it on fire."

"We were trying to reach the capital to warn them of the invasion," said the man.

"It is good that Old Child, Prass, and Kerr intercepted you when they did, or you would have walked right into a trap with the men and boys killed and the women and girls enslaved," said Prince Aaron.

The potters stood numb with shock, and when they realized what this meant to them in the loss of personal family members and friends, they stood shaking and weeping.

"Come," said Healer Mavis, putting a comforting arm around one of the young people, and the older potters and the Prince followed suit, "let us go to the fire, I know that you were cold and tired before you arrived, and this shock will not help. I have a broth I want you to drink. It will help to warm you."

They followed her to the main cook fire and numbly sat where she told them to and drank without even noticing the taste of the broth, so shocked were they to learn the completeness of the disaster.

CHAPTER 10

How Can You Hope?

"AH, FATHER FLIN," said Healer Mavis, walking over to him after she got the refugees settled, "we have refugees from Potsfield to add to our number. They have just found out how complete the invasion of our land has been," she added with concern.

"Oh dear, and having lived so far from the capital, they were insulated against the atrocities of the Regent, his advisors, and wizards. The shock must be tremendous. I will tend to them the best I can," said the good priest and hurried over to them.

"Welcome," said Father Flin with kind concern as he looked on faces pale from shock. "I am glad you have arrived here safely and am sorry for the ill news that you have received. It is our hope that more people will be found, even though our allies have let us know how complete the invasion is. It is they whom you owe your rescue to. They spotted you and guided the land teams to you."

"So some of them fly?" asked a youth.

"Yes, some of the people who helped to rescue us are avian people, and they are able to fly great distances. They have brought us reports of empty towns, cities, and farms throughout our land. I wish that the news was of a more hopeful nature."

"We thank you for the news," said the man from this group weakly. "But I feel as though my heart has been ripped out. It was terrible going through our town and seeing all the slain, but to learn that none were safe, that this horror has happened throughout our land is more grief than I can handle."

"I understand," said Father Flin gravely with sorrow, but still willing to hope. "But the only way to honor our dead is to survive and to find a way to free our land and those they have taken prisoner."

"How can you have faith now?" asked the woman, the peace of the priest grating on her nerves. "Your peace is beyond my understanding. How can you be calm, and these others, when all we have known and loved is destroyed?"

"My faith is battered and bruised," confessed Father Flin. "But if I didn't have it, I wouldn't have anything left, and I do not want to be without hope. Before Hearten, Old Child, Aris, and Prass came to our rescue, I was almost totally bereft of it. But just when I thought that we would all die of starvation or capture, when I had given up hope, it came to me in the form of a man, a child, a canine, an avian, and a feline, totally unlooked for and unexpected.

"Then today while helping with guard duty and the other refugees, I learned of the amazing events that led to my group's rescue, starting with the rescue of our prince by these different people, who call themselves The Family. They also rescued Arms Master Hearten from kill hounds, made it to refuge, and then before three days had passed were out rescuing us. They are always in the right place at the right time to our benefit, and though almost all of the men and boys are dead, still there are women and children who are being held captive. So we have hope for our land in the fact that though we may seem to be the only survivors, we are not. I thank the One God and His Son constantly for the hope they are giving me."

The potters heard the priest but had nothing further to say as they sat in sorrow and thought.

"Hearten, I am glad you are back," said Prince Aaron. "It is getting late, and I do not want anyone out after dark."

"True, it is hard to know if you have left a trace in the dark," agreed Hearten. "How are the guards?"

"Fortunately, Old Child beat you back for her services, and those of Healer Mavis were immediately needed. They say, however, that you did such a good job that it was easy to get to the wounds and attend them as they needed to be attended to," said Prince Aaron as he and Arms Master went to see the guards.

They came upon them lying on pallets on the floor in an orderly row. The most hurt were sleeping. The less wounded were leaning against the cavern wall, fatigue drawing lines on their faces as they sipped on The Healer's broth.

The guard who had investigated Hearten tried to rise when she saw him coming in and gave even more effort when she recognized Prince Aaron.

"No! No!" said Prince Aaron, gesturing urgently with his hands for her and the others to stay seated. "Are you trying to get me into trouble with our healers?"

"No, sir," said the guard, "I don't have anything against you!"

"Healers?" questioned another. "Do you mean we actually have two healers and an assistant here?"

"No, we have two healers here," said Prince Aaron, and upon seeing the puzzled looks, he added, "the seeming child working with Healer Mavis we call Old Child. No one, not even she, knows her name, but she is older than the oldest of our allies, the ones who went with Hearten to your rescue. She is a master healer. In fact, she is mine and Healer Mavis's healer, for we were both wounded."

"Oh," said several of the guards.

"I will save the rest of the story when you are more rested," said Prince Aaron with a smile.

"Come, Hearten, now that you have seen that our soldiers are well taken care of, we need to plan for tomorrow," said the Prince, taking a reluctant Hearten by the arm and pulling him to a small fire with no one around it.

They had just seated themselves when Anvar rushed into the main cavern practically breathless. "Prince Aaron, Arms Master Hearten, Aloo!" she called, in her rush, scattering people and creating minor chaos.

"What?" questioned all three as she came to a fast halt near the Prince, filling the air with dust and feathers causing people to cough and sneeze.

"Is the enemy about to come upon us?" asked Aloo, crest feathers bristling upright.

"No, but they are very close, engaged in combat with the group we have seen them fighting with. I do not believe that they are even twenty minutes from us, and none of their brethren are near. Please, elders, can we go to the rescue of these valiant ones?" Anvar pleaded, concern deepening the gold of her eyes.

"I vote we go!" said Hearten, practically shouting, so excited to engage in combat and rescue more soldiers.

"But what about keeping secret and safe," asked Father Flin.

"If we eliminate them all and hide their bodies and the evidence of the battle, we will not bring suspicion on us," pleaded Anvar.

"My Prince," said one of the border guards who had come to see what the commotion was, "we have so few soldiers, and there has been so much death, as the other refugees have witnessed. Please, please, can we go to their aid?"

"I believe, Prince Aaron," Aloo said, cutting into this conversation, "that this would be a good thing to do. We of The Family have only fought in mock battles and none with humans, but I believe that we are perfectly able to meet this challenge. Arms Master Hearten is a seasoned warrior and will be in charge of all who go to the aid of your soldiers."

"Very well," said the Prince and turning to Hearten added, "Hearten, it will be up to you to plan and choose those on the assault team. And yes, I know that I will not be included," said the Prince with bitterness at being left out of the battle. He gave a sour smile when he heard all of the sighs of relief coming from his people.

"Thank you, my Prince," said Hearten. "I have already given this much thought, and the only people in good-enough shape to arrive timely and fight well are those of The Family." Hearing the shocked gasps from everyone around him, he raised his hands and said, "You have gone through too much hardship and, with the exception of the guards who are too hurt to fight, do not have the training to fight. I have fought with our enemy, and they are very hard to kill. I believe that they wear a second armor under their first set. Those of The Family have been training for a very long time for combat, and I suspect against these very beings."

"We do not have the time to waste in discussion," said Anvar with a frantic sound in her voice. "The soldiers are about to be pinned against the face of a cliff with no escape available."

Upon hearing her words, Hearten said, "Come, members of The Family, we go to battle!" And sprinting to his battle steed, he was gone in a matter of minutes along with all The Family, all but Aloo that is.

Aloo had started to leave when Hearten did, but Old Child, the Prince, and Healer Mavis blocked her way. "I am sorry, Lady Aloo," said Prince Aaron, "but you, like myself, are too important to the well-being and future, not only of your people, but of mine, to risk."

"Also," said Old Child, "I will need you to be guard for myself and the others who venture out to bring the wounded soldiers back."

"If I could have some volunteers to create the stretchers that we might need and to carry them," said Old Child, turning to look at the people of Asalawn, "and those with some medical training and those good with horses, we will be able to give aid so that the loss of life to these valiant soldiers is kept to a minimum."

"It might come as a surprise to you, Aloo," said Old Child. "But I have no idea how to defend myself, so the rest of the medical team and I will be hanging back. And if you or Anvar will give me a signal when to come to the aid of the wounded, I will come with my staff."

This last comment along with the requests for volunteers had the refugees looking at each other with puzzled faces. Healer Mavis seeing these looks said in a voice brooking no nonsense, "Old Child is older than I am and a Master Healer. You will follow her instructions and not argue with her."

"Yes, Healer Mavis," was the reply, and those who were going sorted themselves out.

While Old Child watched the refugees sort themselves out, she said to Aloo, "Once we head back to refuge, Anvar can guard us and you can return here."

"Why Anvar and not myself?" Aloo questioned.

"You, Elder Aloo, as our leader representative for The Family, along with Prince Aaron, who is the leader of the refugees of this land, must get the fifty or so new refugees settled. Then you need to put your heads together and figure out what rules should guide us as a community. We are getting more and more people, and if order and rule are established early, it will eliminate a lot of problems. Also, Healer Mavis is a wonderfully practical woman, and I suggest you seek her advice. Some of the rules need to be sanitation ones to ensure the health of the people here," Old Child replied.

"Oh great," Prince Aaron and Aloo groaned at the same time. They had been too busy to think about this aspect of combining their people.

CHAPTER 11

Finally to Battle

THE MEDICAL TEAM left shortly after the fighters. The ten volunteers, led by Old Child, rode horses and led the others loaded with medical supplies, blankets, and water.

Those who were to carry the wounded on stretchers headed out once Aloo found a place for them to cut poles for the stretchers. They used extreme care trying to make it look like a natural or old thinning project even while making haste. Once done, they gathered up the wood chips or rubbed them into the dirt and hurried carefully to join the rest of the medical team.

◊ ◊ ◊

While in the air scouting and guarding her two groups, Aloo got an avian's eye view of the warriors as they moved swiftly through the forest led by Hearten. The rain they had the night before deadened their steps with soggy leaves. Upon Anvar's signal that they were getting close to the battle they slowed down for stealth.

At that signal, Old Child stopped and waited with her volunteers. By this time, the stretcher carriers were on their way, keeping an eye to the sky to get direction from Aloo.

The warriors of Asalawn had their backs to a cliff face and were outnumbered, eight to twenty. With grim determination, they used the cliff face to cover their backs and worked together as a team; giving no safe entrance into their ranks and for the time they were holding the soldiers at bay. They were sustained by cold anger and hate. Just when it seemed like this was not enough and they would be overrun, the scream of a demon was heard, and the soldiers took heart for only one person had such a battle scream, Hearten!

Suddenly, the enemy was fighting the battle on two fronts. When from the air came the battle-raged scream of a bird of prey, and an immense bird came diving down at unbelievable speed. The warrior in command, recognized by his greater size, had his head ripped off with such force he was thrown onto the blades of his own soldiers.

The war scream of Hearten, the battle cry of Anvar, and the death of their enemies' captain revived the soldiers of Asalawn, and they put forth even greater effort. The enemy, confused at the loss of their captain and not knowing how to effectively battle the warriors of The Family, were unable to withstand the onslaught from both sides and above.

When the last enemy soldier lay dead, Anvar flew a swoop and signaled that she would take over, guarding Old Child and her staff.

Realizing that there was no one left to fight, Hearten looked around losing his battle rage, but still very alert. He strode over to the commander of this group of soldiers. She looked at him, giving him a wolfish grin which he returned.

"Capt. Alessia!" he said in greeting, the rush of battle shining from his eyes. "Well done!"

"Arms Master Hearten!" greeted the captain, fierce joy in her voice and relief in her eyes, "I am surprised, sir, to find you still alive!"

"Ah, that is a tale for another time," said Hearten. "In the meantime, there is medical help coming. I need to advise you that the healer looks to be a child of nine, but is older than I am. You might want to pass the word, for though she is from a different land, she acts just like our healers do!"

"I will pass the word, but who or what are the creatures that joined in battle with us?" asked Alessia as she held a compress on a soldier's wound.

"They are members of a nation called The Family," answered Hearten, "and they are people not animals, so you might want to pass that along also."

"Oh," said the captain.

"Hearten," came a call from Prass, "will you please let these soldiers know that we are allies of theirs?"

"Yes," said Kerr, coming to stand beside him. "I think you can use your loud voice, as the only enemy to hear you are dead."

"I get the point," said Hearten. And standing with his hands above his head, he said to the soldiers, "Listen up! The giant canines, felines, and avian are people, not predators. They have allied themselves with us. In fact, I, Prince Aaron, Healer Mavis, along with the many rescued at our refuge, owe them our lives."

The soldiers visibly relaxed at this information and allowed the soldiers of The Family to give them what aid they could and in Mavs instance receive aid in turn.

Old Child arrived at the site of the battle and handed Hearten a shovel, then grinned and said, "We can't leave a trace of them, Hearten. I need my volunteers to help work with the wounded, and that makes you the only able one with hands to do the chore."

"You are not an old child," said Hearten as he faced the task of burying the forty enemy warriors and erasing all trace of the battle. "You are a mean old woman. I think that chore will have to wait as I help attend to the soldiers."

"Oh, I have plenty of hands for the job, but I can see that having their Arms Master alive and coming to their aid has put heart into them," she told him with a twinkle in her eye, recognizing procrastination when she saw it.

"That and the news that Prince Aaron lives has lifted our spirits more than you can know," said Captain Alessia.

"Old Child, meet Captain Alessia," said Hearten.

"Captain Alessia, meet Old Child, a most excellent healer!" said Hearten.

"It is nice to meet you, Captain. Can you take me to your worst hurt first?" asked Old Child in greeting.

"This way, ma'am," said the captain, and she lead Old Child to where the soldiers waited. They were lined up on the ground in the order of need.

"Thank you," said Old Child. And bending over a soldier, she smiled gently and said, "You have won the battle. Now don't lose the war. I am an excellent healer, and in fact, your prince is one of my patients."

She quickly evaluated and tended to the wounds of the soldier, moving with more speed than one would believe, her focus completely on her task.

"Angelica," said Old Child to the head of the stretcher bearers, continuing to work on the worst hurt first, "the severely wounded do not have the time the stealth we use takes when approaching our refuge takes. For this one time, take the quickest route back to our refuge."

"Won't there be a lot of consequences if we do that?" asked Angelica.

"I will answer for this decision," answered Old Child with asperity in her voice. "Now go as smoothly and swiftly as you can. I will follow not far behind you."

"Who will cover the trail?" asked Prass.

"Those not on stretcher duty can come along behind and cover the traces until it gets too dark. When dark falls come straight home and we will finish hiding traces of our presence in the morning," answered Old Child.

"That is an excellent plan," said Hearten, supporting her. "There is no time for delay, and I will be happier if after you have treated those who need you the most, you also leave. Surely, others can finish up here."

"I have only the stitching of Mavs's leg left, and then I will be on my way," answered Old Child. Mavs was the only one of The Family to need her aid, and though the wound was slight, it needed stitches.

While Mavs waited his turn, one of the wounded soldiers with a broken arm held a pressure pad on his wound to staunch the flow of blood with her good hand. Her fatigue was so great she was only slightly startled when he thanked her.

Upon completion of her last stitch on Mavs, Old Child packed her instruments and headed back to refuge, Prass running along with her. She arrived there in less than ten minutes and headed straight for the hospital area.

When the rescuers and soldiers arrived back at their sanctuary, everyone was startled at the quickness of their return.

"How is it that you have returned so swiftly?" asked Master Carter Hays.

"Old Child ordered us to be swift and direct. These soldiers are direly wounded," said Master Angelica, panting as she led the others to the healing cave.

The carter went to follow to ask questions as did others, but Prince Aaron blocked their way. "You heard what she said," he proclaimed. "Stay out of the way and do not delay the treatment that these soldiers need."

"But we are jeopardized!" shouted Master Hays, and his worry was supported by a rumble from the rest of the people.

"Old Child is extremely cautious," declared Elder Aloo, her voice sounding easily above the roar of worry coming from the crowd. "If she believes that this is an acceptable risk, then you must have confidence in her judgment."

At that moment, Old Child entered the caverns and headed straight for the healing cave, only to be intercepted by a frightened and ugly crowd.

"Are you insane!" shouted one of the refugees. "Your immature choice will be the death of us all! Why on earth did you allow a child to do an adult's job, Prince Aaron?"

"Contrary to her appearance, Old Child is the oldest person here at our refuge. She is a master healer as testified to by our own master healer, Healer Mavis. If she deemed the hurts so bad that the risk of discovery was the lesser of evils, then I will respect that," answered the Prince sternly, but with a worried look on his face.

"Think, you," said Master Potter Angelica of the stretcher bearers. "Everyone here owes his life and the lives of those with him to her and these new people who travel with her."

"I was rescued by Arms Master Hearten," shouted another.

"You were rescued by Arms Master Hearten, Mavs, Aris, and Anvar to be exact," said Prince Aaron, getting angry. "And if Old Child and Prass had not rescued Arms Master Hearten from the jaws of kill hounds, he would be dead. If they had not rescue myself and Master Healer Mavis from a burning building and tended our wounds, we would be dead, and there would have been no one who knew where this place is, and there certainly wouldn't have been anyone available to come to your aid. Enough of this nonsense! Master Healer Old Child has always shown excellent judgment and has saved my life and everyone else's too."

Old Child, looking at the worry and fear on people's faces, said in a stern voice that only master healers seem to have mastered, "It is unlikely that the enemy would be close to our refuge. We have been very vigilant about keeping eyes, nose, and an ear on the land close to us so that we would not have any surprises. I have confidence in the abilities and trustworthiness of our guards, especially those of The Family, for they have a keener sense of smell and hearing than humans, and in some cases, superior night vision. The avians of course have vision beyond any of us two – and four-foots put together. Also, it is the pattern of our enemy to always set up camp with the coming of dusk." With that stern admonishment, she hurried off to the hospital to attend the more severely wounded.

"She is telling you the truth," Aloo said to those standing about with gaping mouths. "She can't remember much of her life, but what she can remember was full of discipline and fear. Although she has little regard for her own personal safety, she values our lives, not just The Family's, but also yours, more than you can imagine."

"Why doesn't she value her life?" asked one of the border guards.

"Because she is unable to die, just as she is unable to age. The Evil Mage cast such spells on her in these two areas that even with his death, they have not come undone," Aloo replied.

Prince Aaron looked at Aloo, and then said, "That explains her attitude. I never could quite figure out why facing a challenge that would have a grown soldier trembling in fear didn't seem to be any big deal to her. It amazed me that Hearten, who is one of the bravest people I know, is still shook up by his memories of the hounds, and she just shrugs them off."

"You are sure that the Evil Mage is dead?" asked another refugee.

"Yes, elder, one of the feline elders saw his destruction and reported on the completeness of it. He said that if there is such a thing as rebirth of a person, we would not have to worry about the return of the Evil Mage," Aloo replied.

"The Evil Mage is dead, and Old Child contrived this," she continued, "and even though she is his child, none of us received the abuse that was her life.

He often punished her as an example to us. And we, avian, canine, and feline people, cannot forget her suffering or the fact that we owe her our freedom, as do you.

"She led us out of captivity, and the price was almost her life. As we were escaping through the only route possible, she hung back and threw up a shield to protect us, taking the brunt of the magic blast that was created when the Evil Mage died.

"Indeed, we are in your land at this time because we needed help in caring for her, so we were present when Healer Mavis and Prince Aaron were attacked, and we were able to help her to rescue them."

"Well, that certainly explains why she acts like an old master with every right to decide and direct without consulting anyone," said Master Potter Angelica.

"She has never had anyone she could talk to, let alone have aid or support in any of the decisions that she made," Aloo responded.

"But you are her friends, and you go out of your way to see that she is constantly guarded," commented a large man, a carter named Johnathan.

"We have only just begun to be her friends. She had the ruling of us under the watchful eye of her evil father, and she made sure that we did not like her if we even thought about her at all." Aloo paused after this statement and then said, "I have just realized this last, for trying to survive has not been conducive to thinking beyond what is necessary. I believe and have the example of her father's death to back this idea up, that if she had ever shown a preference for anything, it would have been destroyed before her utterly.

"Her father did not love her, but he was very jealous of anyone or anything that she gave her regard to. I remember one time she had a special case she used to carry things, but he decided it was a favorite thing to her and destroyed it on a whim."

"You say that she doesn't remember her father? How can that be?" asked one of the refugees.

"She became happy," said Aloo and smiled with her eyes at the confused look on the faces around her.

"Happiness was like a thorn in the Evil Mage's side," Aloo told her very interested audience. "He tried to weed it out wherever he found it. It took him a long time to find the source of the happiness within his keep, but he searched diligently and finally created a complicated spell to seek it out. He was shocked to learn that the happiness he felt came from his own child. He was sure that she had found someone to love, especially as years before she had professed her hatred for him. He was certain that it was someone other than himself. He tortured her greatly to find out who it was but couldn't get her to tell. So he spent two weeks working on a spell that would destroy whomever she loved utterly the moment that she pointed at him, and when he placed it on her and activated it, she pointed at him."

"Oh," said the refugees.

"He destroyed whom she loved so utterly that she has no memory of him," added Prince Aaron.

"So she wouldn't remember being the cause of his downfall?" asked Father Flin.

"Not even a glimmer," answered Aloo.

"Wow, what made her decide on this course?" asked Angelica.

"We most likely will never know for that would be associated with memory of him," said Aloo.

"The Evil Mage's downfall has been our boon," said Prince Aaron, "for it has led to our rescue."

"There is this also," said Aloo, "we are beginning to believe that the enemy we were being trained to battle with is your enemy."

"When the rest of your people get here, maybe you can compare notes and see if they get that same notion," said Prince Aaron to Aloo.

"There are more of her people coming here?" asked Smith Adela.

"Yes," answered Prince Aaron, grim hope in his voice. "My hope is that there are enough of them to give us a chance of not only surviving, but of rescuing those held captive and freeing our land from these evil ones."

"Please excuse me," said Prince Aaron to the crowd, "but I am terribly worried of our soldiers and wish to discover their condition." And he hurried off to the infirmary.

◊ ◊ ◊

Hours later, Aris, Kerr, Anvar, and Hearten returned to the refuge; and upon their arrival, people gathered around, with Smith Adela bringing drink and food to these brave ones.

After Kerr had satisfied her thirst and hunger a little, she said, "My compliments to the stretcher bearers. You did an excellent job of watching where you stepped. We barely saw a sign of your travels on our way here. We managed to hide most of the evidence of the battle, but it grew dark before we could completely hide all trace. It will be necessary for some to go out in the light of day and hide what we were not able to see."

The two-foot refugees nodded and looking grim talked among themselves to decide who would go and do this. It was decided that those fleet of foot and able bodied would go. No one under the age of sixteen would be allowed to go.

Aris listening more to their tone of voice and hearing their fear said to Aloo, "Elder Aloo, I volunteer to be one of the four-foots who go out on this expedition."

"I also would like to go," said Prass. "We will be able to guard the understory of the forest with our keener sense of smell and hearing."

"I also want to be in this group," said Kerr, "and we should leave at the start of day before we go to find more refugees."

"And I would like to fly guard for the ground crew," piped in Anvar.

"All of you?" Aloo asked.

"Well, except for me," said Mavs. "Old Child told me that I would be staying close to home until further notice. Are you sure we shouldn't have named her bossy woman?"

The rest of the refugees laughed at this, and one said, "Well, she is a healer, and that seems to be standard to their nature."

Knowing that they had such excellent guards eased many fears, and in a very short time, the two-foots had a roster of ten people who would go.

"I think that ten is too many," said Arms Master Hearten who had come back from checking on the soldiers. "I and four others will be enough. The rain and the season have helped us remain undetected, but too many people could cause us to be revealed. We only had so many because Healer Old Child deemed it an acceptable risk."

"So, Arms Master Hearten," said Prince Aaron, coming upon the crowd so quietly that he startled many there, "please report on how you, Aris, and Kerr disposed of the bodies."

"Oh, we dug a trench against the cliff wall and then loosed some rock in a slide area above it to cover them," Hearten answered in an off-handed manner.

Aris and Kerr who had stayed to guard Hearten looked at him with surprise. "Well, I guess that is the basics of what we did," said Kerr, "and though Aris and I helped dig the trench and carry the bodies to it, it was Arms Master Hearten who faced the danger of causing the slide area to fall."

"Oh," said Prince Aaron, "Maybe you two could give me a more detailed report."

"Once we got the trench dug and the bodies in it," said Aris, "Arms Master Hearten had us move to one side. Then pulling some string from his pocket and picking up a short stick, he climbed up to the slide area, tiptoed gingerly across the face of the slide area . . ."

"I didn't realize how ready the rock was to slide until he was almost halfway to his goal and his foot slipped, loosening some small rocks that threatened to have the whole slide falling down, him with it!" Kerr inserted.

"Yes, my heart was in my throat after that until he made it back to the two of you," said Anvar.

"Once Arms Master Hearten found the boulder he was looking for, he braced it with the stick. And slowly, carefully, one small rock at a time began to clear the debris that was holding it in place," continued Aris, "once he had that done, he ever so carefully came back, watching his step and unwinding the string attached to the stick at the same time.

"He rejoined us, and then with a sharp yank on the string, he pulled the support away from the boulder and gathered in the string as fast as he could. At first, the boulder did nothing. And then slowly, it began to tilt, then more quickly than I can tell it, it began to move, and the rest of the cliff's face joined it! First, it went slowly then faster and faster, covering the corpses and our trench completely!"

"It also helped to cover some of the traces of the battle that had been waged there," added Kerr.

"I hope, Hearten," said Kerr, "that I never have to see a friend in such peril again!"

"Me neither," seconded Aris and Anvar simultaneously.

Prince Aaron looked at Aris and Kerr, his face somewhat white from the thought of his friend's danger, and said, "Maybe I will not ask for such a detailed report next time. I do not know, Arms Master Hearten, whether to congratulate you or yell at you!"

Before Hearten could reply, Healers Mavis and Old Child came upon them with faces that bore ill news. "Old Child and I have done all that we know to do. I am sorry to say that three of the soldiers will not survive," said Healer Mavis.

Old Child, her face very serious but more like she was pondering, looked at Anvar and asked, "Anvar, are there any of the enemy near us?"

"No, Old Child, not within a fifteen-mile radius," was her reply.

"I have an idea, but I will only do it if I receive agreement on it." Then she explained, "If I am very close to the soldiers so not much energy is expended, I believe I could treat their worst hurts without signaling the magic sucker. This land is in dire trouble, and we are going to need all the warriors we can get."

"I could keep watch and let you know how far her magic reaches and if she does signal anything or anyone," said Anvar in a pleading voice.

Prince Aaron, Healer Mavis, Arms Master Hearten, and Aloo looked at each other and then at the refugees around them. No one could bear the idea of those valiant soldiers dying, and without a word, they looked at Old Child and grimly nodded their consent.

It was dark out, so Anvar launched from the wide area of the gully rather than the ledge. She hovered above their refuge for about an hour and a half, coming in when Prince Aaron signaled her with a torch.

"What happened, Prince Aaron?" said Anvar upon landing. "Was Old Child unable to use her magic?"

"She used her magic, and the soldiers are resting comfortably," Prince Aaron told her, gladness in his voice as they walked into the main cavern together. "They will be slow to heal as she only healed the life-threatening wounds, but they will heal!"

"Her control is amazing," said Anvar. "I couldn't see her magic at work, and I watched the cavern entrance very closely. It didn't alert the seeker/sucker either," she added.

"What!" squawked Mavis and Aloo at the same time, "You can sense the seeking?"

"Yes," she said, "It is a use of magic, so it is visible, just barely, as it is very secretive working hard at not being noticed."

"Come, let all those who are able eat," said Father Flin before any more discussion could be made, "Talk of magic and other things will be more beneficial when we have eaten and rested. I know that Old Child must be tired. Magic working can be draining, so ask her your thousand questions tomorrow!"

"Ah, Father Flin," said Scribe Uther, "Practical as always and right as usual."

"But how do you know the effect of magic on a person, Father Flin?" asked Prass.

"It is in the histories of this land, and in fact, it was by tiring the Evil Mage that the other mages were able to contain him," he replied.

"How many mages were battling him?" asked a curious Mavs.

"Twelve I believe," said the priest.

"Wow! And they could only contain him?" asked Aris. "They must not have been very powerful."

"Yes, they could only contain him. And next to him, they were the twelve most powerful mages alive at that time," answered Father Flin.

"It is a relief that we do not have him to be concerned with also," said Master Potter Ansar. Those hearing his statement nodded or murmured in agreement.

With the soldiers out of danger and the relief that Old Child's magic had not been detected, everyone went to their meals with less worry on their faces and better appetites.

Aloo had gone hunting for The Family's repast as the winged and four-footed people do not cook their food. They ate separately from the two-foots and came back when they were done and groomed, not wishing to offend or frighten their new allies.

Once everyone had eaten and the chores were done, the new rules that Prince Aaron and Aloo had worked on were read. Healer Mavis had given them good advice as Old Child had said she would.

"Keep it simple," she told them. "And remember the sacred rule, to treat people the way you want to be treated. Also, there is sanitation regulations that we will need to have put in place. While you two figure the conduct rules, I will have Scribe Uther write these up."

The rules were very basic: respect one another, no stealing, no fighting, and for the safety of everyone, no leaving the refuge without consent, for it is important to know where everyone is. After this, the chore roster was read, and there was very little grumbling about the next day's chores.

Prass said, "Now that we have taken care of the immediate business, I have a concern from the battle we fought."

"What is that?" asked Hearten.

"Although each of you humans has a different smell, it is part of a basic smell that says to me human. Those we fought looked to be human, but they smelled very different. Their fragrance didn't say human to me, at least not very strongly. There seemed to be a vast difference between your aromas," she replied.

"You are right," said Hearten. "They did not seem to be put together quite the same as we humans either. I didn't examine them as we needed to get them buried as quickly as possible and dark was coming. Does anyone here know anything about them?"

"I always thought they were human, somewhat different coming from a land far away, but still human. If they are not human what kind of creatures are we dealing with?" asked Father Flin worriedly.

"That concern is going to have to wait until later. We are all tired and need to look to our survival. Surviving is going to be quite enough for any of us to think about for the next few days or even weeks. To survive, we will need more supplies. But with the enemy around, getting to them and not being seen will be a dangerous task," said Prince Aaron, looking weary and worried.

Old Child came up to him then and said, "You and Mavis are not completely well, and it is time to rest. Here is your medicine. There is your bed, and I am going to watch to make sure you take it all."

With a sigh, the Prince took the medicine cup from her. She narrowed her eyes, standing with her hands on hips, eyes glaring, and looking very much like a grumpy old woman. He said, "I am taking it. I am taking it."

Watching Prince Aaron and Healer Mavis submit to Old Child helped many people believe in the age that the Prince claimed for her. They were also grinning at the awful face the Prince was making.

Healer Mavis rolled her eyes at the Prince and said, "I don't know what you are fussing about. I know that mine tastes worse than yours, and you don't see me acting that way."

The prince just sighed again and rolled his eyes, and then handing the medicine glass back to Old Child, he went to his bed.

"Off to bed the rest of you," said Old Child in a firm, but kind voice. And all but those on guard duty went to their pallets.

Those who didn't go on the rescue missions took the night watches to allow those who would be out again tomorrow a good night's sleep. Angelica took the first watch and was followed by Scribe Uther, Father Flin, and Journeyman Carter Johnathan.

Old Child had her hands full with the wounded soldiers, and whoever was on night duty was to awaken her every two hours to check on them, or sooner if their seemed to be a need. Fortunately, the healing that she and Mavis had done on them was sufficient so that they could rest comfortably; eliminating the need for her to lose any more sleep than necessary.

CHAPTER 12

Hearten's Children – Old Child's New Name

WITH THE EXCEPTION of those who were going out with Arms Master Hearten to hide any trace of the day before's activities, the weary refugees slept late into the morning. The four most recently rescued groups slept until midmorning, and the battle weary soldiers slept until noon. This extra sleep was good, not only for them, but also for the Prince and Mavis who rose before them, feeling better than they had in days and eager to be doing whatever they could to help their people.

"Child," called Aloo softly, "The Healer and Prince are awake. Do you think she will be fit enough to take over the care of the injured and sick?"

"Let me check on her and on the Prince," said Old Child who looked up from where she was stirring porridge and saw them coming toward her. "Good morning," she greeted them cheerfully.

"You are looking much better today," Old Child said, having given them a thorough scrutiny.

"I am feeling much better," said Healer Mavis.

"As am I," said Prince Aaron. "Being able to stay in one place seems to have helped both of us a great deal."

"Yes, it has," said Old Child, smiling as she handed them bowls of her porridge.

"This is quite tasty," said Healer Mavis. "I detect things in it that I have never tasted in porridge before."

"Yes," agreed Old Child, "it is made especially to strengthen one and to counter shock."

"There doesn't seem to be enough to go around," said the Healer.

"I have portioned out the oats and the herbs so that they can be made as people arise," said Old Child, indicating bags that were tied together a little ways away from her fire. "It is always best fresh. Also, this is our most common-sized pot, so I calculated the amount of ingredients needed for a batch of porridge this size."

The Healer went over to look at what Old Child had done and noticed that each bag had a flat piece of bark by it and each piece of bark contained the same instructions. She read these and said, "This seems simple enough. I believe that the Prince and I can handle it on our own, and I am sure that your people would rather go out with you than with some of the people here who they don't know."

"True," said Aloo, who had been listening to their conversation. "Also, none of these people know the signals that we use to communicate."

"True," said Prince Aaron. "And though I know that they have been hunted, as was I, the unwillingness to trust until I am fully confident in their character leads me to suggest that we do not teach them these signals until we know them better."

"It would seem, Prince Aaron, that you were as robbed of your childhood as Old Child was," said Aloo.

"I had a childhood until I was nine, with parents that loved me and taught me right from wrong. In that, I have a great advantage over Old Child. Although having to grow up so quickly certainly lends itself to understanding you a little better, I hope," said Aaron, smiling at her kindly.

"I am in the odd position, Prince Aaron, Aloo, and, Mavis, of being both very old and very young at the same time. For all of this life is new to me, and my father, who shaped my understanding of life, is gone from me so completely that there isn't even any memory of him. So I feel as though I am having a fresh start."

"Hmm," said Healer Mavis, "when you don't understand the reason someone is doing something, you had better come to Prince Aaron, I, or Aloo or the Elders of The Family. It is going to be hard for the people of our land to understand why you don't know the simplest of things."

Nodding, Old Child turned from their conversation and went on to the tasks at hand. "I have charted the conditions of our patients on some bark, as you and I agreed on, Healer Mavis. If you would look at those once you have finished eating, I would appreciate it. And, Prince Aaron, now that you are finished eating, will you and Aloo please assist me in making sure the packs are ready for Hearten and I to go out?"

"Certainly," they both said. And while Mavis finished her breakfast, the others went to the packs.

"You know, Prince Aaron, as Mavs is refuge bound, he can teach the soldiers and border guards our signals. And when they are well, they will be prepared to be out with us," said Old Child, as they approached the packs.

"That is a good plan, and I can help. Those are people I can trust," said Prince Aaron, smiling. "Healer Old Child, why don't you go join Healer Mavis. Lady Aloo and I can handle the packs."

Healer Mavis was startled when Old Child joined her after such a short time.

"Prince Aaron and Elder Aloo feel that they can handle the packs, and that it is more important to make sure you and I are communicating clearly about our patients," said Old Child, smiling at The Healer.

"Everything looks well-organized, and our patients are resting comfortably, Healer Old Child," was her reply. "I am surprised at how quickly you have been able to fully do the charting that we talked of."

"I seem able to remember everything from the time I became clearly conscious at your cottage, including every word spoken," said Old Child.

"Well, that should make for quickness in learning," said Mavis.

"Before I came over, I mixed your medicine, and I expect you to take it. You will find it less bitter, for except at night, there are herbs that I will not be putting into it," ordered Old Child with a twinkle in her eye as she watched the soldiers watching Mavis.

"I suppose I must follow The Healer's orders, just because I need to set a good example," said Healer Mavis with a sigh, much to the amusement of the patients.

"Exactly," replied Old Child, trying to look stern and not grin.

"Wow," said one of the soldiers, "she didn't even flinch or make a face!"

The Healer just rolled her eyes and said, "Of course! If I can take my medicine without fuss, I expect brave soldiers to do the same."

"Yes, ma'am," they said with a sigh.

"When Hearten comes back, will you be going out right away to seek more refugees?" asked Healer Mavis.

"Yes, the more people of Asalawn we can gather in, the better," said Old Child, the desire to be out and doing just that sounding in her voice.

"I am starting to think you enjoy the danger you put yourself in," said Healer Mavis.

"Hmm, I have never thought about it," answered Old Child as she looked about the cavern. "More people are stirring. I will get more porridge cooking for them." And she left the healing cave.

Arms Master Hearten and his volunteers returned shortly after the first of the refugees were rising. "We saw none of the enemy, but then only Anvar was in a position to see them. She will be along shortly to give us a report. I think she wanted to check where the next refugee groups are located," he said as he walked over to one of the kitchen areas to get a bite to eat.

In about twenty minutes, Anvar walked in. "Elder Aloo, Prince Aaron, Arms Master Hearten, and, Old Child," she called, "I come with a good report. There is a group of children to the west and two groups to the south at a greater distance."

"You should go for the children, Old Child," said Prince Aaron. "You will not frighten them, and you, Hearten, should go for the two groups farther away."

Hearten and Old Child nodded, and once the rescue teams had finished eating, they were on their way.

The group Old Child's team met up with consisted of fifteen children led by two youths, a boy and a girl of about fifteen. They were a woebegone group with the horrors they had seen shadowing their eyes and the exhaustion from running and hiding for days with scant food causing them to droop.

Before Kerr got them to their refuge, she stopped and looked closely at Cem and Senay, the youths who led this group.

"You are using mind-speech, aren't you?" she asked.

"Yes," answered the boy, "is that bad?"

"I don't know for certain. Let me check something out," replied Kerr.

Using body language, she signaled her request to Aloo. "Mind-speech is being used by the youths who lead, has Anvar check for seeker/sucker activity?"

Aloo signaled understanding and, getting Anvar's attention, passed on Kerr's message. Anvar signaled understanding, and the two switched places. After a brief, but thorough look, Anvar mind spoke both Kerr and Aloo. *"Great news,"* she said. *"There is no seeker/sucker activities anywhere near the children. Even though there are enemies close by with the same orbs, they almost caught Old Child with."*

"Wonderful!" exclaimed Aloo and Kerr together in mind-speech.

"Now we can be even more effective," said Aloo. *"Let me pass this information on."*

"Mavs, Prass, Aris," Aloo called with mind-speech, *"we have learned that the seeker/suckers do not register mind-speech as magic!"*

"That is great news," said Mavs. *"I will notify Prince Aaron and Healer Mavis.*

"And I will notify Old Child," said Prass.

"And I Hearten," said Aris.

"That is good news," said Hearten when he received the word from Aris spoken in a very quiet voice. "But we will still need to use the signals because not all Asalawnians are capable of mind-speech, and some are suspicious of it."

Aris reported this back to the rest of his guard and Old Child's guards.

"Understood," was the reply, and he passed this on to Hearten.

Kerr looked to the youths and said to them with mind-speech, *"Good news, mind-speech does not register with the enemies devices as magic. How is that you two are able to do mind-speech better than most of your people?"*

"We are twins," said the boy, *"and need no words between us."*

"Why don't you speak, girl?" asked Kerr and was answered with pictures and sensations of horror, pain, and humiliation from the youth.

"My sister was raped repeatedly by the Evil Regent," the boy mind spoke to Kerr. *"His treatment of her even disgusted our enemies, so they cut his head off."* This last comment brought a fierce pleasure to the girl's eyes.

"Now that I know that you will not bring disaster with you to our refuge, we can continue on," said Kerr with mind-speech and led them without further incident to the caverns.

Cleaned, fed, and safe, this group was asleep within forty-five minutes of their arrival.

Hearten's came in close to evening. His group ended up being both groups that Anvar had spotted. One was a forester family consisting of both parents and three children, two boys and a girl. The other group consisted of a farmer and his wife, their five married children, their spouses, and their children.

◊ ◊ ◊

Old Child approached Hearten as he was sorting supplies. He could either be found getting ready for the next day's tasks or tending to the injured, so he was easy to locate.

"Hearten," said Old Child with inquiry in her tone.

"Yes, mean old woman," said Hearten, looking at her fondly.

"Did you by chance have any children? Say a boy and a girl, twins?" asked Old Child.

Hearten jumped up, hope ablaze in his face. "Yes!" he practically shouted. "Cem and Senay are their names."

"Come, but gently for the girl has been abused," said Old Child, and she led him to his children.

The look of surprise, joy, and then fear on the girl's face was heartening and heartbreaking.

"Oh, my beloved children, I thought you dead or worse enslaved," said Hearten, holding his children to him and unashamedly weeping for the joy of having them in his arms.

"We escaped with these other children," said Cem. "The soldiers who held us captive were sent to track and kill Captain Alessia and her patrol."

"Was it these soldiers who caused this hurt to your sister?" asked Hearten.

"No, Father," replied Cem. "It was the Regent who harmed her. The soldiers of our enemy do not act that way with women. In fact, that is why they put his head on a spike."

"Yes, I saw that when I went back to try and find you," replied Hearten.

Fierce joy shone in the eyes of Hearten's children, especially Senay's. Her father hadn't deserted her, and he wasn't dead as the evil ones had told her.

◊ ◊ ◊

"Aloo," said Prince Aaron, coming to speak with the giant avian, the gold highlights in his brown hair gleaming in the torchlight, "we truly have a village here, for all of the crafts are represented along with a farmer and forester! This gives me confidence that my land can become a nation again."

"That is good news," agreed Aloo.

"Besides this good news, Aloo, I have a concern. I have the hardest time remembering that Old Child is really old, and she seems to have a trick of silence that causes you to forget about her," said Prince Aaron, sounding somewhat exasperated.

"You will be relieved to hear then, Prince Aaron," Aloo replied, "that I have the same problem."

"Well, that is a relief," he answered. "I wonder how she does it."

"I think that it is a survival trick for her," Aloo replied. "Her life was truly something of the darkest of dreams."

"She seems happy now," said the Prince. "I have even heard her laugh several times."

"Yes, and I cannot tell you what a shock it was to us, of The Family, the first time we heard her laugh," the great avian responded. "It is a sound that we had never heard before, and I must admit to finding it delightful."

"If this is true, Lady Aloo," said Prince Aaron gravely, "I hope that she never remembers her father or what her life was like."

"I agree," said Aloo.

"Pardon again, Lady Aloo," said Farmer Seth who overheard their conversation as he helped Old Child with the wounded, "but does this child not have a name? Old Child is no name for a person."

"I have wondered about her name myself," said Captain Alessia.

Aloo may be an Avian but the consternation she felt at them talking about Old Child as though she wasn't even there showed on her face, and that she and Prince Aaron had done so made it even worse. And when Old Child looking upon her saw her discomfort she started laughing. She laughed so hard she had to sit down.

Farmer Seth and Captain Alessia looked at her quite startled, and this only caused her to laugh harder still.

Mavis came over to see what was going on and had to pound Old Child on the back so she could catch her breath. While Old Child was getting her mirth under control, Mavis said, "I could use a laugh myself. What is going on?"

This started Old Child off again, and Mavis looked at Aloo, her brow lifted in inquiry. Seeing Aloo's embarrassment and bafflement at Old Child's laughter, she started grinning.

So clearing her throat to get Seth's and Alessia's attention, Aloo said, "She doesn't have a name. We have always called her The Child, but when we got here, she pointed out that she was probably as old if not older than the eldest of the avian, canine, and feline people."

"So," said Seth, turning a bright red with embarrassment, "I have been treating like a nine-year-old a person as old if not older than myself?"

"Um," said Aloo, feeling even more uncomfortable, "yes."

Alessia looked at her, at Old Child, and then at Mavis to confirm the truth of what she had heard.

"Yes," said Mavis and Aloo together. And Mavis added, "She is a master healer also."

Old Child taking pity on them told Seth and Alessia, "I was bespelled by an evil mage. He is dead, but I still remain a child. Mavis says that I have knowledge that it would take person decades to learn, and Elder Aloo's people were captured by the Evil Mage several generations ago. I remember their coming and my sorrow at their captivity."

"Old Child threw up a shield to protect us as we were fleeing after the Evil Mage's death. His death triggered a mighty explosion, and even with her shield to protect us from the worst of the blast, we were tossed about like leaves. Old Child received the brunt of the blow, and although she would take water, we couldn't awaken her. So we took her to Mavis for healing," explained Aloo

"Yes," said Mavis, "she was shocked by the explosion so badly that at first she was like a newborn babe, but she grew in strength and in wisdom by leaps and bounds once she started to mend."

"Oh," said Alessia, "I thought that she was a very gifted child and you were calling her master healer to honor her healing skills so people would respect her judgment. I know Prince Aaron and the others have told me she is aged, but it is hard to believe. Still Farmer Seth is right. Old Child really is a poor choice of a name. In our society, 'Old Child' denotes a very aged person who has started to lose his mind, putting him back into childish ways."

"What!" Aloo squawked, so horrified that she all but feel off of her perch. That set Old Child off again with Mavis, Alessia, and Seth grinning.

"Hearten!" she called with great indignation. "Hearten!"

Hearing her calling, Hearten and his children came over. "Yes, Lady Aloo," queried a concerned Hearten.

"Hearten, how dare you give The Child the name Old Child when in this society, it denotes an aged person whose mind is failing?" Aloo demanded in an indignant voice.

Seth, Mavis, Alessia, and Old Child were looking at Hearten with amused inquiry on their faces.

Hearten turned redder, if possible, than Seth had done. He looked at Old Child with even greater consternation than Aloo upon his face.

"Father," said Cem, "you didn't, did you?"

"Well," said an embarrassed Hearten in a weak voice and looking even more uncomfortable by the minute, "it is descriptive. She is old and is still a child."

"That is not factual," said Mavis. "For any human who has lived for decades no matter what she looks like is an adult."

"I agree," said Seth and Alessia together.

"Well, Captain Alessia," said Old Child with a mischievous grin on her face and her eyes twinkling, "when he got assigned by me to burial detail, he said, 'you're not an Old Child. You're a mean old woman.'"

"You are not a mean old woman," said Mavis, Seth, and Alessia together, looking at Hearten with great indignity.

"You are kind and gentle," said Alessia. "My troops say wonderful things about you."

"And you have been very patient with all of us, even those who know your age but are still treating you like a child," said Seth, looking at Mavis, Hearten, Aaron, and Aloo.

Grinning, Old Child said, "Thank you both. With the crisis situation we have all been dealing with, I thought I would bide my time until people could catch their breath and evaluate where we are, what we need to do, and how to go about it. Then with my skills needed, I would insist on the respect due my ancient age."

"Ha! Wise as well," said Seth.

"And remember, it has only been about six weeks since Old Child first came to my doorstep," said Mavis. "When she woke, she was like a newborn babe, but as the stench of dark magic was on her, I knew what to do. Sadly, I have seen the magic blasted before, but never have I seen anyone recover so quickly and completely. Except she remembers not the Evil Mage. This seemed strange to me until Lady Aloo explained his end."

"Well," said Old Child, "this has been very informative, but it isn't getting any work done."

"Right," said Seth, "and I think I will call you Wisdom's Child for you have acted with much wisdom in these difficult times."

"How right you are, Seth," said Hearten, quickly adopting the new name. "I have always thought that Wisdom's Child was directed by whichever of the four-footed or winged people who were with her."

"No," said Aloo, "Wisdom's Child has always had the directing of us as she was the Evil Mage's daughter, slave, and favorite victim."

"But," said Mavs who had come to see what the conversation was about, "she has not once directed us since we fled the blast."

"True, except when she took charge of the rescues of Hearten, Prince Aaron, and Healer Mavis," Aloo said. "But for several years, she has been training us to be free people, united even though we are of mixed species. You are quite right, Seth. Wisdom's Child is an excellent name for her."

At that, everyone but Mavs left. And when he was sure his conversation with Aloo would not be overheard, he asked, "Elder Aloo, why do all of you elders say that she was his favorite victim. You have said so time and again."

"Mavs," she answered, "I think you are ready to know this, but I need to show this with mind-speech. Let us go somewhere private, say outside."

When they got to where they would not be disturbed, Aloo said to Mavs, "Remember a time when you rebelled against the Evil Mage and your leader was dragged in to face the Mage's wrath."

Mavs did as she asked, and then she showed him what happened to The Child when the Evil Mage wanted them to understand what he would do to their children if they didn't obey quickly and completely.

Mavs responded as Aloo thought he might and got sick to his stomach. After he was done retching, she told him, "This happened every time the Mage even thought we might be going to rebel."

When he had himself back under control, he said, "That explains much that I didn't understand. Wisdom's Child knew that I and the other young ones of The Family didn't know this, didn't' she?" he asked in a worried voice.

"Yes, Mavs, even though she doesn't remember the abuse, she is aware that something went on that I and the other elders know about. She figured this out from the way I behave around her. I will always grant her great respect, and I will always feel that I owe her a debt for all of the pain she was caused because of us, even though it was the Evil Mage's choice to harm her. Now that we have traveled together in these new circumstances and I have come to know her, I feel awash with guilt that we didn't care what happened to her, only what happened to our children. I believe this is why she has been so patient with you in particular, as well as the others," Aloo said. "She told me once when I got exasperated with you that you were acting quite sensibly, considering you had only a limited amount of pertinent knowledge."

"She did, did she?" asked Mavs, perking up, "In that case, I can face her and not feel like a complete idiot every time I'm around her. You know, Elder Aloo, the other young adults will not like feeling like idiots because you elders withheld information. They need to make proper choices," said a concerned Mavs. "I am glad she is wise enough to figure out that we didn't have the same information as you elders have, even though she doesn't know what the information is. Farmer Seth is right. She is very wise and very kind."

"You are right of course, not only about Wisdom's Child, but also about the other young adults. The question is when would be the best time to show them this part of our history?" Aloo responded.

"The elders with The Family should show the young adults before they get here so that their behavior will not alarm our human allies. That would be my suggestion," responded Mavs.

"You are right of course and are showing wisdom of your own. I will attend to this matter at once." And she flew off to contact Alaw and the leaders about her conversation with Mavs.

"Alaw," Aloo mind spoke her beloved.

"Yes, my love," he answered. *"I thought mind-speech was dangerous."*

"We have learned that the magic sniffer cannot sniff out mind-speech," she replied.

"Well, that will certainly make things easier, heart's wings," responded Alaw. *"Let me tell the others."*

"Alaw," she said again.

"Yes, Aloo, is there something the matter?" he asked.

"Not really the matter, but I have had to acknowledge Mavs's adulthood by showing him how the Mage treated The Child and his poor excuse of why," said Aloo, and she remembered the conversation to him with mind-speech, starting with Wisdom's Child's name and Mavs's question, her response, and her conversation with Mavs afterward.

"Mavs is quite correct. We had to let the young adults know early in our journey, as they were poisoning the children's minds against Wisdom's Child," answered Alaw, as he adopted Wisdom's Child's new name. *"We had all of the children present when we showed the young adults the truth they didn't know. Also, Aloo, you had best show the rest of the guard. Anvar and Brak already know."*

"Yes, I will do that when they come in," she answered, and in concerned afterthought, asked, *"but wasn't this harmful to the children?"*

"We did not let the children see what we showed the young adults, but the sense of remorse and horror that the young adults felt was transmitted, along with the shame and sorrow they felt for what they had been saying about Wisdom's Child. When the children witnessed the young people throwing up because the memory was so bad, it curbed their curiosity. Since they learned the truth, they have been working hard to eliminate the damage they have done. It is good she has a new name. It will disassociate her from the boogeyman the mage's daughter was beginning to become to the children."

"See you soon, my love," answered Alaw.

"One thing more you might tell your young adults, Alaw," said Aloo, "Mavs got some comfort when I told him what Wisdom's Child told me once when I was annoyed with his behavior."

"What was that, dear Aloo?" asked Alaw, his mind-voice full of love for her.

"That she thought he was behaving sensibly considering the limited amount of information he had to go on."

"Ouch! That was rather pointed of her, wasn't it?" he responded.

"Yes," she said with a smile in her mind-voice, "but I deserved it, and she said it in such a gentle voice it was like a knife to my heart."

"Also, Aloo," said Alaw, "there are starting to be more of the enemy, and they may delay our arrival. We will send Brak to let you know of our choice."

"That is not news I want, but it is as it is," said Aloo, with a sigh.

"Aloo," called Alaw with a question in his voice.

"Yes, my love," she answered.

"What does The Child think of her new name, Wisdom's Child?"

"I heard her muttering as she went to her work, 'Oh well, it is better and something to live up to,'" Aloo replied.

Alaw laughed. "I must attend here, my love."

That evening, as Aloo was checking on enemy encampments, she saw a dark speck flying toward her; and when it was within sight, it danced in the air an identifying pattern.

"Brak!" Aloo greeted gladly with mind-speech.

"I have news. The enemy is thick between here and The Family, so there will be a delay. The war elders request council with you, Wisdom's Child, Prince Aaron, and whoever he has on his war council," Brack told Aloo with mind-speech.

"I will speak with Prince Aaron privately about this and also Wisdom's Child," said Aloo.

"Come, rest. There are many new people for you to meet and our first battle with the enemy to hear of," said Aloo.

"Were any of The Family hurt?" asked Brak with concern as he landed on the ledge.

"Only Mavs, and his injury only needed but a few stitches," Aloo answered.

"With so many pregnant females with us, many of The Family are wishing that Wisdom's Child was traveling with us," said Brak.

"That is also something that we should discuss. I believe that Wisdom's Child is healed as much as she is going to, with the exception of the memory loss due to the Evil Mage's spell, and nothing can bring that back," said Aloo.

"That may be for the best," said Brak.

"I think so myself," said Aloo as they walked into the cavern. "There is Prince Aaron with Arms Master Hearten preparing for tomorrow's rescues. A good place to have a private word."

"Prince Aaron, Arms Master Hearten," said Aloo formally, "Brak brings news of The Family."

"Our war elders will be here tomorrow morning to hold council with you. The enemy soldiers are thick between us. They are choosing to delay the arrival of The Family until passage is safer. They will want to speak to you and whoever you pick as your war council, Prince Aaron, also Wisdom's Child and Aloo."

"Why Wisdom's Child?" asked Hearten.

"Wisdom's Child is a war elder," said Aloo, shocking both men with this information. "You must remember it was she who had the training of us for war. Whatever we know about war, she knows about war. Also, The Family wants their healer back as they are traveling with so many pregnant females and with so many children."

"And we don't feel as though we can do without her either, but I can see where a nation on the move would have a greater need," said Prince Aaron.

"It will surprise you again to know that the decision to come or go will be Wisdom's Child's. She is the senior elder, and in the matters we will be discussing, she will probably be in full memory and therefore confidence," said Aloo, watching the looks of surprise and consternation cross their faces.

"Her silence certainly hides who she is," said Aaron at last, having taken several moments to soak in what Aloo had said.

"Remember, Aaron," said Hearten, "she is of The Family, not Asalawn, and would be reticent with any information."

"And in spite of the fact that she goes out on rescues facing the same danger as you do, Hearten, I need to quit seeing her just as a healer and often as a child," said Prince Aaron with a sigh.

Brak looked questioningly at Aloo, and she giving him a look of humor explained, "We keep forgetting that she is an elder unless she is acting as the master healer, and even though we of The Family don't worry about her going out into danger, we still fall into the trap of her appearance."

"Do you think the rest of The Family will have this problem?" asked Brak.

"Probably," said Aloo, "she has a trick of silence that causes her to go unnoticed. And with so much of her memory gone, she is starting over, and some of her behavior is childlike especially in social areas, although I think they would have been anyways. She had no social interaction until now in her entire life."

"Oh, so she has to learn everything I did as a child while being an adult with a lot of her memory missing?" questioned Brak.

"Yes, plus being our healer and rescuing people," answered Prince Aaron.

"I think I would be silent and disappear also," said Brak in sympathy for Wisdom's Child.

"I will go and tell her of the meeting," said Aloo with an avian chuckle while she looked around for her. She saw Wisdom's Child sitting at the weaver's fire, listening to the stories the weaver was telling the children.

Aloo waited until the story was over, enjoying it herself, and then asked Wisdom's Child to speak with her in private. They went outside of the cavern, and Aloo began. "The war council will be here in the morning to take council with you, I, Prince Aaron, and his council. The enemy is too thick between them and us for safe passage. Also, The Family would like to have their healer back among them if she is well enough.

"This last I will think on first for my power is growing and I fear I will activate a seeker/sucker close to The Family," said Wisdom's Child. "But I do know that I have lined the avian carry bags with magic-resistant fabric, so if we can get some here, I could make a tent and do some healings and make clothing for myself that will mask my power. I will ask Alaw when he gets here how soon some of the avians can fly their children here.

"This will need to be discussed in council," said Aloo. "Also, medicines that you would need to bring, what about them? I know you always had extra herbs and things for the pregnant females to eat and other things to sooth wounds and fevers."

"I have been making them up while we have been here. I gather what herbs I can find in the forest, making it seem as though something was browsing. I do this by tearing the plant rather than using a knife," answered Wisdom's Child. "Let us go back in. Tomorrow is soon enough to ponder these things, and I want to get my patients settled."

When they arrived at the infirmary, Master Farmer Seth was helping Healer Mavis with a soldier's bandage as Captain Alessia looked on.

Healer Mavis seeing Wisdom's Child said, "Good you are back, Master Healer Wisdom's Child. Master Farmer Seth is an excellent help in the infirmary."

"I am happy to hear that," said Wisdom's Child, who had been inspecting the bandage job, "and to see that it is so also."

"Master Wisdom's Child, if you will man the infirmary and if you, Lady Aloo, will find and hail Prince Aaron for me, I would appreciate it. We need to get people located and settled down. The main cavern is getting out of hand with all the noise and movement."

"Prince Aaron," hailed Lady Aloo, her voice caroling out above the noise of the crowd, "Master Healer Mavis would like to speak with you."

Prince Aaron came over to Mavis. "It is time, Aaron, to put our plan into action and get the main cavern settled down. We need to assign the caves as we planned earlier and get some order in our daily lives," said Master Healer Mavis.

"I agree," said Prince Aaron. "Lady Aloo would you get everyone's attention please?"

"Certainly," said Aloo.

"All listen!" called the great avian, her voice filling the cavern.

A hush settled over the people, and Prince Aaron, standing on a stump to be seen, raised his hands and said, "Master Healer Mavis and I will be assigning caves and giving the new arrivals instruction on the rules.

"The children without craft or family will have the two caves to the back and right of this great cavern. The soldiers will be quartered at the caves nearest the entrance. The families and guilds will be assigned caves according to the number of people."

"But we with crafts need more room," whined a voice from the crowd.

The prince looked grimly in that direction. "Take a look around you. Do you see anyone save the potters who have the tools of their trade with them?" asked the Prince.

"When we can safely get supplies, rest assured that the tools you need for your professions will be high on the list of priorities. But at the moment, we are at bay with the hounds of the enemy sniffing around trying to find us.

"Master Mavis," said Prince Aaron, "if you will kindly step forward and explain the layout of the caves off from this cavern and give the assignments, I would appreciate it."

"Certainly, Your Majesty," said The Healer, and the Prince helped her to mount the stump.

"The caves have been numbered in a clockwise fashion. And with the help of Scribe Uther who managed to bring paper, quill, and ink, we will make a roster of everyone here: name, age, family, guild, or soldier. If you will form an orderly line, we will begin and get this done as quickly as possible.

"Once I know how many are in a group, I will assign you a cave. The Prince and I have already decided which caves can hold which number of people."

Farmer Seth, who came in the night before, and his family were given a large cave. Upon receiving their assignment, he asked, "Thank you, but can I ask why you have not put us all next to each other?"

"I didn't put you next to each other because we will be having new people coming in, and it will make the transition easier for them if they have neighbors who know what is going on," answered Master Mavis.

Hearten and his children were put in a small cave next to the children's caves so that when he was gone, Cem and Senay would be with the children they knew and vice versa. Senay was worried about sleeping away from the children but was reassured when she saw that Healers Mavis and Wisdom's Child along with Father Flin would be there with them. She was further comforted that night when she saw that her father was sleeping across the threshold into their cave to protect them.

"Master Healer Mavis," said Master Potter Angelica, "wouldn't it be better to put the children in with the families or guilds?"

"I thought of that but came to the conclusion that they should stay with those they know right now. One because they know each other and life has become strange enough, and two we do not know what personalities will mesh yet."

"Also, Master Angelica," said Healer Mavis, "will you spread the word that we will have a standard bedtime for everyone unless they are on guard duty?"

"Oh yes, I will!" said the woman happily. "That is a good thought. This is like living in a large house with no furniture. Every sound echoes."

CHAPTER 13

Uniting in Work and War

"HEALER MAVIS," SAID Prince Aaron with quiet concern as he and The Healer walked back to the hospital area, "our people are frightened and seem to be stunned. What do you think will happen once the shock wears off?"

"We will have very angry people who will want to blame someone for their misfortune," answered The Healer.

"I think anger is not a wrong response," said Prince Aaron. "But this is a confined space, and we need to be able to count on one another. How can we keep the people here from acting out their fear and rage on each other?"

"That is a good question," Mavis responded. "I myself am not sure what to do. I think that we should talk with Father Flin about it, and a few of the masters seem promising leaders."

"Yes, they are," agreed the Prince. "Let us go and speak with the good father."

"Father Flin," hailed Prince Aaron when they were within a few feet of him, "I was wondering if I and Healer Mavis could have a few words with you."

"Just a moment, my prince," replied the priest as he helped a child with her shoes, "let me just finish up here."

"There, Courtney, they shouldn't come untied now. I see that Journeyman Johnathan is preparing to tell stories. Why don't you go and join your sister in his circle." Courtney ran off joining her sister, and Father Flin turned to the Prince and The Healer. "What can I help with?" he asked.

"We have realized that when the shock wears off, our people will be hit with rage, and we do not want them taking it out on each other or the members of The Family who will be here," answered Prince Aaron.

"That is true," agreed the Father. "If they are kept busy and encouraged to work with one another, they will be too tired to dwell on much and become friends. They will have a sense of community. The question is what to keep them busy with?"

"I know just the thing" said Mavis. "Let us get our caverns ready to welcome Aloo's people."

"That is an excellent idea," said Prince Aaron, "for The Family represents hope to me, and I hope that our people will see them in that light also. Who will organize and get them busy though?"

"I will recruit Master Farmers Char and Seth, the master carter, and the master potters to head this task," answered Healer Mavis, who then paused. "Wait, on second thought, you my Prince, should make this request of them. There will be less balking."

Prince Aaron looked at The Healer in consternation and groaned when Father Flin said, "Yes, of course, you are correct, Healer Mavis. The Prince will get the best response."

"Good," said The Healer with a grin, "I will get back to my patients now." She left before the Prince could object.

Prince Aaron looked at the priest sourly. Father Flin just grinned and said, "I am needed by the children, and I am not autocratic enough to get the type of cooperation that will be needed." And he too hurried off.

"Rats!" said Prince Aaron under his breath, as he squared his shoulders and went to speak first with the master farmers, and then to gather the rest together to plan an orderly way to complete the tasks.

He had little problem until he came to the master carter. "Master Carter Hays," said Prince Aaron as he and the rest came near the man. They were a little bit behind him, and the poor man nearly jumped out of his skin. "What?" he said in a surly voice, quickly changing his tone when he saw that it was Prince Aaron who had called to him, "may I do for you, Your Majesty," he ended ingratiatingly.

Smiling congenially, the Prince said to him, "I have gathered you and these masters to head the committee that will make our current home welcoming for the people of The Family. I know that most people are tired after their terrible ordeal, but getting the caverns cleaned up and orderly are something that will help us keep track not only of people but also things, and it will keep Healer Mavis happy as well."

The carter started to have a sour look on his face, and the Prince asked him with a shudder, "Have you ever annoyed a healer?"

With a sour smile, Carter Hays said, "Aye, and I don't really want to do it again. Who knew that you could be healed so unpleasantly?"

"True," said one of the master potters with a shudder. "I couldn't learn from my brother's example and had to test one myself. I don't want to do that again!" The masters and the Prince laughed and settled down around the carter's fire to decide the best way to proceed.

"I think," said Master Farmer Char after they had decided the best ways to clean the caves, "that we should talk to Lady Aloo about how many people will be coming and what their needs will be."

"That's a good plan. I suspect that Healer Mavis will be there to listen and to make sure we know what the end results need to be," said her husband, standing up and offering her a hand up. The other masters rose as well, and they went over to Aloo.

"Lady Aloo," said Prince Aaron, "we wish to get the caves ready to welcome The Family but do not know their needs nor how many to expect."

"Well," Aloo answered thoughtfully, "there will be at least two hundred families."

"Two hundred families!" exclaimed the carter.

"Yes," Aloo answered the astounded masters. "Wisdom's Child did an amazing job rescuing us from the destruction of the Evil Mage's land. These of course will be the families with the youngest children. The families with youths, no children, or single adults will stay in the hidden barns."

"Oh, gracious," said Master Char, "no wonder Healer Mavis assigned so many caves to your people!"

"How will we get so many clean?" asked Carter Hays sourly.

"We will have to divide and conquer," said Master Potter Ansar.

"Also," Aloo said, "the families will realize that they need to share accommodations until further exploration of this cavern system is done, and in fact, the children are used to being in nurseries where they were kept safe."

"Whew!" exclaimed Master Seth, wiping his brow. "We will only need to clean eighty or so caves."

"We are located on the four different sides of the cavern, so let us go from left to right," continued the master potter, "with crews headed by some of the other adults and older children. I imagine that we will also be able to find things to do for the youngsters."

"I won't have any children on my crews," said the master carter emphatically. "I can't abide children."

"We will not assign any children to you," said Prince Aaron, displeasure coloring his voice. "But you will learn to get along with children and to be a mentor to them. We do not have enough people for such prejudices to prevail."

The carter flushed and said, "Yes, my prince," in an unhappy tone at being chastised.

"So," said Master Char, "we need to call together the other adults and older youth."

"A visit with Scribe Uther for a look at the roster would probably be the best place to start," said Master Angelica, her husband Ansar nodding.

"Scribe Uther," said Prince Aaron, "have you broken down the roster into masters, journeymen, and apprentices yet? Oh, and of course those too young to be apprentices, we need them to get teams organized for cleaning the caves."

"Uh, I was doing that, but I don't have it finished. I have all of the masters listed and the journeymen, but I am still working on the apprentices and children," answered the scribe.

"Well, that will certainly get us started," said Farmer Seth, giving the scribe an approving smile.

Lists in hand, they went back to the carter's fire and gathered masters and journeymen to them in small groups so that the children would not be left alone.

When they explained what needed done to the group, Master Forester Nate was in. He said, "I will head getting things set up for the avians. I ran an aviary for hunting hawks. I will need some very stout lads for my team. We will need to bring in driftwood and large rocks to anchor the wood."

"Done," said Prince Aaron with a smile. "You might want to ask Lady Aloo for her assistance and advice."

"Let me call my boys," said Farmer Seth. "The five of you will be able to set things up, and the less burly groups can get the avian area cleaned first."

"Also," said Master Forester Fern, "we will need to get some foliage to make the caves more comfortable for the four-footed people. They have been sleeping in the forest and it is a much more fragrant and soft place than these caves are."

"I am sorry, but until the enemy does not hold us so much at bay, we all must make due," said Prince Aaron. Seeing the look of rebellion of Fern's face and that of the others, he went on to add, "Brak flew in with news this evening that the war council of the elders will be slipping past the enemy for a conference with me and my war council tomorrow morning. The report is that the enemy is too thick between us and them for them to risk their children."

"That is grave news," said Master Fern. "I am sorry that I did not realize how serious the danger is to them. I thought that with them coming from another direction, they would probably miss the enemy soldiers."

"No," said Aloo, coming into the conversation, "they are very serious about not leaving anyone alive. I wonder what they fear to be so thorough."

"A good question for the council meeting tomorrow," said Prince Aaron, yawning. "This is all we can do for now, and I see that Master Wisdom's Child is getting ready to send everyone to bed, so let us adjourn and get busy in the morning."

"Who will be on your war council, Prince Aaron?" asked Master Char.

"I, Arms Master Hearten, Captain Alessia, plus the head of the border guards that Hearten brought in," answered the Prince.

"A good roster," said Master Nate, also yawning and stretching, smiling as Master Wisdom's Child came up to Prince Aaron with his medicine.

"Aloo," said Wisdom's Child, "will you please get everyone's attention?"

"Certainly," said Aloo. "Attention, attention, Master Wisdom's Child speaks."

The refuge quieted, and Wisdom's Child spoke. "It is time for bed everyone, as I am sure most of you can see my bringing Prince Aaron his medicine." This got laughs out of everyone. "Tomorrow is going to be a very busy day, so to bed everyone and may your dreams be blessed."

Prince Aaron took his medicine and went to his cave, to his bed, and everyone did the same.

◊ ◊ ◊

Aloo, watching the work going on as she waited for the rest of the war council to arrive, sighed. "Master Nate, I truly envy you humans for your hands."

"And I, dear lady, envy you for your wings," said the Master Forester with a smile.

"In that case," said Elder Aloo, "shall we use what we admire of each other to each other's advantage?"

"An excellent idea," said the Master Forester as he continued with his work.

"Aloo," mind called Alaw, *"the four-foots have entered your gully."*

"Good, Prince Aaron waits at the cavern mouth," responded Aloo as she hurried there herself.

"Welcome," said Prince Aaron to Elder, Yass, Tawny, Kriss, and Alaw. "I am happy that we can have this council and we have set aside a private cave where we will be able to speak without being overheard. But first, may we meet your thirst or hunger needs?"

"No, we are refreshed from the stream and fed before we came," replied Elder.

"Then let us take council," said Prince Aaron, who led the way to the cave. It was down a hallway which was guarded by two of The Family and two Asalawnian soldiers. When they entered, Arms Master Hearten, Captain Alessia, Sergeant Marista, and Wisdom's Child rose to greet them.

"Happy I am to see that you are looking so well!" exclaimed Wisdom's Child in delight. "I know that we trained and trained and trained some more, but still I worried."

"And happy are we to see you so well," responded Yass, coming up to Wisdom's Child and giving her a canine caress. "The training you made us do has saved us many times, but now we face an armed foe, not an animal, which would not be any match anyways unless in a pack, and we have faced that too. The pack who had some of our people backed against a wall were very surprised to find themselves surrounded with a larger pack and left quickly. The mind-speech net has saved many lives as we have journeyed."

"Good," said Wisdom's Child, "but now we must speak of war and I think with the beings that you were being trained to combat. Arms Master Hearten, Captain Alessia, and those of The Family, except me and Aloo, can tell you of fighting them."

"The enemy warriors are not human," said Master Hearten. "Prass brought that to our attention the night of the fight. When Anvar killed the lead soldier, known by his size, the rest seemed to be confused, and they did not know how to do combat with any of The Family. They are hard to kill," Hearten continued, "I thought it was because they wear double armor, but now I am wondering if it is something about the way they are formed."

"It is something about the way they are formed," said Captain Alessia. "We found that the best places to wound them were the joints and the eyes. They still continue fighting, even though they are bleeding to death. And in fact, death is the only thing that stops them from fighting. But I agree with Arms Master Hearten. Take out their leader and they are easily confused and defeated."

"At the palace, there were also lizard men who were wizards, along with human wizards," said Hearten. "They need to be taken into consideration, for it is likely that they could be sent out if magic was thought to be a threat or if they are running the kill hounds."

"The kill hounds are somewhat magic wrought, that is why their bays and howls have such chilling effects and they are so fast," said Wisdom's Child. "Aloo, would you please have Anvar see if she can locate one of the seeker/sucker devices. And when she does, have her transmit what it looks like to someone, and then have them draw it."

"Yes, ma'am," answered Aloo. *"Anvar, can you find one of the seeker devices and then transmit what it looks like to one of the war council."* And she looked about, and hearing Elder sigh, she said, *"Transmit it to Elder please, so he can draw it."*

"*Yes, ma'am,*" replied Anvar and went straight to the task.

"Do you have a plan, Wisdom's Child?" asked Prince Aaron.

"The beginnings of one," said Wisdom's Child. "It is an artifact, so it can be used against its owner. If these lizard men wizards should pose a threat to my people, I want to have solutions at hand. Also, once I study these things, I may be able to use them to slow down or even partially disassemble the kill hounds."

"The lizard men are put together more short and squat than the soldiers," said Hearten. "It would seem that this might make it harder for an avian to break their neck or rip their heads off."

"That is something that we worried about in our training, and Wisdom's Child had us train with all types of dummies of different weights and with long and short necks," said Alaw. "But I wonder, do these people have tails?"

"Yes," said Arms Master Hearten and Captain Alessia together.

"And I," said Arms Master Hearten, "have seen them in combat training, and their tails are deadly. But once they are bereft of their tails, they lose all sense of balance. I saw them punish one of their fellows that way once."

"Elder, Elder," Anvar mind called, *"I have the image of an artifact."*

"And I have paper and pen. Show me what it looks like." And she did. Elder drew the most elaborate picture, designating gems and crystals, also colors. And when he was done, he showed it to the war councils.

"That looks like the luck tokens we see everywhere," said Captain Alessia. "Gypsies came through about four years ago, and every place that welcomed them received one. They were very serious about them, the gypsies I mean, and they had to be pointing just the right direction so as to bring the best of luck."

"The magic users didn't start dying off until two years ago," said Prince Aaron.

"Magic traps, which is what these are, can be triggered whenever the wielder decides too," said Wisdom's Child. "They most likely didn't want any suspicion to fall on their gypsies."

"There are some at farms also, smaller but there," said Captain Alessia grimly.

"And we know that they know how to detect if a person has magic within," said Wisdom's Child.

"Alaw, do you think that the avians, or at least some of them, can fly their children here to Refuge within a day?" asked Elder Wisdom's Child.

"No," said Alaw reluctantly, "maybe a day and a half. Why?"

"Here then is the start of my idea. The lining of your carry bags is made of magic-resistant fabric, and if I had that, I could cloak myself and study some of these devices. Also, we could use a bag or two to store such devices in. The leader of our enemy must be very confident of his slaughter, but should we remove all of the tokens between where The Family has been and beyond Refuge so that we will not be located, the loss of power flow from this area will be noticed right away. He will be sure that magic is involved.

"The only way their leader can find out what is going on is to communicate to those out in this area threw their wizards and soldiers, which we will eliminate and take their magic. I am sure they have a way of gaining their wizards' magic when they are dying. Their magic traps can be used to this purpose, I am hoping, although the lizard men's magic may not respond to them and we will have to find another way to gain it. If we can gather their magic and learn it, we can turn it against them, even their kill hounds," said Wisdom's Child, sounding very much what she was, eldest of a war council, and grimly determined to protect her own.

"With the area cleared of the enemy, we can send out teams of people to get all of the crafts' supplies, food, and other necessities for running a community here and an extra when we find the rest of the living Asalawnians. They will have sky and ground guards while they are on this mission, and we will be able to airlift the supplies to Refuge with the soldiers removed from our proximity. Without the seeker/suckers around, if I have the proper crystals, I will be able to use my magic to make things light in weight. But first we need to remove the enemy that is near us, and then farther and farther out. We also need to be alert for any that will be coming this way."

Prince Aaron felt a shiver going down his spine as he heard the hard determination in her voice and was amazed that she was the same gentle, though bossy healer that he was accustomed to. "I agree with you on clearing the territory, but won't the seeker/suckers be too dangerous to have near us?"

"No, I will study them away from here. They are an artifact, and what can be turned on can be turned off," said Elder Wisdom's Child, smiling. "I can also change the owner's signature so that the mage who created it or who it was created for cannot use it or even locate it."

"Also, Aaron, and you are going to like this," said Wisdom's Child with a twinkle in her eyes, "once I have the bags, I can do healings on you, the soldiers, the border guards, and anyone else. I will take the precaution of working farther back into the mountain, but there will be no magic detected and it will be a relief to get to use some of mine. It is getting kind of itchy."

"Magic can get itchy?" asked Captain Alessia.

"Yes," said Elder. "Magic is an energy that must be used or it can actually harm its wielder."

"Oh," said all of the Asalawnians together.

Prince Aaron, smiling with pleasure at the thought of being healed, said, "We will have to plan strategies that will incorporate the strengths of all four of our people, but for now, I suspect it will be what opportunity affords. Be careful of one another. Also, have you found many refugees?"

"Not many," answered Kriss sadly, "about twenty, and they slow our progress as some of them are injured. Since you told us of the secret barns and what to look for, they have fared better than yours with enough food" – and then he paused furrowing his brow – "with the exception of the bards, and I am pretty sure they are holding themselves back."

This had all of the Asalawnians laughing. "We do not know why, but you cannot seem to fill a bard up. At least not for more than fifteen minutes," answered Prince Aaron to the curious looks of The Family. "They are perpetually hungry, so much so that it is legendary!"

"Once the avians and their families arrive here, I can go about masked," said Wisdom's Child, bringing the conversation back to the subject. "I will be better able to go to The Family and attend to their needs. Also, the towns will have maps of this land, won't they?"

"Yes," answered Prince Aaron.

"Good, that will make planning much easier," said Wisdom's Child.

"I believe you are correct, Wisdom's Child, peculiar name," said Tawny. "And I propose we do careful scouting until we can move against the enemy. We need to know more about them. I am not satisfied with the knowledge we have."

"Still, it is more than we had before," said Yass.

"Also, Yass, as your healer dear," said Wisdom's Child kindly, "you are staying at Refuge."

"What!" she protested. "But we have other children to think of who need their parents."

"I am sorry, dear, but you are too far along and should not even have made this journey," said Wisdom's Child kindly. "Kriss will be with them, and they have many aunties and uncles to care for them, but you are staying here and can in fact be a great help in getting everything ready for the four-foots of our people. Aloo has no idea, and I only have the kennels and Healer Mavis's house to go by. You have traveled this land and seen much, so you will know what this land offers that will best suit you and the rest of the four-foots."

"But," she went to further protest.

"Dearest love," said Kriss, nuzzling her, "it will be such a relief to know you are here in relative safety, not only with our healer, but with another, that you cannot imagine. Our children will be fine, anxious about their mother, but fine. In fact, Tefla is going to say good, and you know it."

Yass gave a small grin and sighed. "All right, and you are right Tefla will say good. How a child that age can fret that much is beyond me."

"We must go then," said Tawny. "It is a long journey, and as we wish to be undetected, it is a slow journey. There is another thing about the enemy soldiers.

When they are focused on looking for just one thing, they do not have any curiosity about anything else."

"That is very good information to have," said Wisdom's Child as she saw them away.

Coming in from seeing the war council of The Family away, Prince Aaron looked around with concern and went to talk to Master Mavis. "Healer Mavis," said Prince Aaron with concern, "the people are staying in their same groups and not mingling. It will be important for them to be able to work together at all sorts of tasks. How do you think we can best mingle them so that they can come to know and trust one another?"

"Hmm, that is a good question, my Prince," Healer Mavis replied with a thoughtful frown on her fact. "I think that it is really important that we learn that we can rely on one another, but it might be too soon for some to be able to do this. I think in this instance, Father Flin and Arms Master Hearten will be the people that you need to go to for advice. Let me know what they advise."

"Prince Aaron," Aloo said, having overheard their conversation.

"Yes, Lady Aloo," he said.

"I remember when the Evil Mage had us of The Family come together for the first time. It was quite difficult for us to understand and trust each other, but Wisdom's Child managed to get us to cooperate in a very short period of time. I suggest you have her be part of your conference," she said.

"Yes," agreed Yass, "I remember that it was not easy, but she did it."

"That is a good suggestion, Lady Aloo, and, Lady Yass. I will do that. Do you happen to know where she is?"

"Hmm, she seems to be over by the weaver's fire, attending to the small hurts of the children," Aloo replied.

"Thank you, I will round up Father Flin and Arms Master Hearten, and we will join her there," Prince Aaron said, turning and striding away, his body moving with greater ease now that his healing was almost complete.

"Hearten," said Prince Aaron to the arms master, "I need to have council with you, Father Flin, and Wisdom's Child."

"What about, my Prince?" asked Hearten curiously.

"How to mingle the refugees so that we can learn to work together as a whole, not just as individuals and guilds," answered Prince Aaron.

"That is an excellent idea," said Hearten, "and there is Father Flin by the cavern entrance."

"Hmm, let us gather up Wisdom's Child first then and join him there," said Prince Aaron.

They walked over to the weaver's fire and waited until Wisdom's Child seemed to be done with her task. "Wisdom's Child," said Prince Aaron, "will you please join me, Arms Master Hearten, and Father Flin for a conference?"

"Certainly, Prince Aaron, what do you wish to discuss?" she asked.

"How to get the people here to intermingle and become one unit cooperating with one another for the good of all," answered the Prince.

"Oh my," said Wisdom's Child ruefully, "I don't know if I will be much help, but I will do the best that I can."

They joined Father Flin at the cavern entrance. "Father Flin," said Prince Aaron, "I have come to ask you to be part of a conference on getting the people here to intermingle and become a unit."

"Hmm, it might be too early for some," said the priest.

"Yes, that is what Healer Mavis said," said Prince Aaron with worry on his face. "But we do not have time on our side if we want to gather the supplies we need. We will need to split people up into work teams, and with so much danger present, they need to be able to depend on one another."

"What you ask is not going to be easy, Aaron," said Father Flin.

"He is right Prince Aaron," said Wisdom's Child. "Sketchy as my memory is, I do remember that it took some time to integrate all three species of The Family. And I had the fear of the Mage to help generate cooperation."

"Hard, but not impossible," said Hearten. "I think that the first thing we need to do is to be upfront with everyone."

"That could cause tremendous amounts of fright, and that would be counterproductive," said Father Flin.

"They are pretty aware of the grim realities of life right now, Father," said the Arms Master.

"True," said Wisdom's Child, "and you do not have to dwell on it greatly. Just state what is and outline a plan that will give them direction. The rules to live by, including sanitation, have already been set, and I believe many will be relieved to have things to do. You, Hearten, will have quite a bit to do in this area, for the people here, including myself, need to learn to become warriors, or at least to defend themselves and our refuge."

"Yes!" said Prince Aaron excitedly. "That is the direction that we should go. Master Foresters Nate and Fern can teach about the edible and medicinal plant life. Also, you Master Wisdom's Child, and, Master Healer Mavis, can teach battlefield medical aid. This way, if we cannot get to supplies, we can live off the land. And if any are injured, the others can take care of them. I do not intend for anyone to go out alone."

"Prince Aaron, this is all we can plan for at this time," said Wisdom's Child. "And you, Healer Mavis, and many others here need to have extra rest to ensure speedy healing. I don't have the avian bags yet."

The Prince looked at her with exasperation, and Father Flin said, "Even if you can't sleep, people will know that your healer has insisted on rest for you and will leave you alone. This will give you uninterrupted time to think on these matter and decide how best to present your arguments to our people."

"Very well, I can see the wisdom of both of your arguments, and I certainly do not want to be on the bad side of my healer," said the Prince with a smile. "Why even Healer Mavis follows her orders!" This ended the meeting, and everyone went their separate way.

After everyone had risen from their naps, Wisdom's Child had insisted that everyone rest. Prince Aaron gathered his people around and told them, "My people, we are in a dire situation. If we are to survive, we will need to be able to work together and rely on one another. To this purpose, I will be having you work with people who are not from your group or family.

"Arms Master Hearten will be heading the training of us all as warriors or at least defenders, and this includes making this place as defensible as possible. Master Foresters Nate and Fern will be teaching about surviving in the forest. I am sure all of you wish you already had that training," he said with a grim smile and received equally grim nods.

"Healers Mavis and Wisdom's Child will be instructing us in battlefield first aid. There is a lot we need to be able to learn and a lot we need to do in order to come out of this terrible time triumphant! You are my people, and I owe my very survival to your resourcefulness during my uncle's rule. So I am confident in your ability to rise to this current challenge."

The people heard Prince Aaron out in silence and, nodding in agreement, started to become better acquainted with one another and see how they could be of help to each other.

Hearten and Wisdom's Child went out to rescue at least one group each for that day. "Some days just do not seem to have enough hours in them," said Wisdom's Child to herself. "But the meetings and planning done were important and could not be put off."

CHAPTER 14

Rescuing the Hunted

"I AM CONCERNED," SAID Anvar to Aloo. "There are less and less people who are not hunted. How are the land teams going to free the ones who are being hunted?"

"I don't know," said Aloo. "Let us go and talk to Prince Aaron. He, Arms Master Hearten, Captain Alessia, and Wisdom's Child are by his cave."

"Prince Aaron," said Aloo as they came upon the group, "there are fewer and fewer people who are not hunted. Soon we will be rescuing the hunted. How are they to be rescued without us giving ourselves away?"

"That is a good question," said Prince Aaron. "Are there any suggestions?"

"If we use the land itself as an excuse for their deaths as we did with those we battled, we will be able to get away with some deaths," said Hearten.

"There are also large predators such as bears and large cats who could account for a few more, and then the refugees themselves could also be held responsible for the deaths of their pursuers. If they cannot trace them, we should be able to get away with the deaths," said Captain Alessia.

"How would people, not soldiers, kill the enemy?" asked Wisdom's Child.

"They could trip them and then crush their skulls, stab them with a thick sharpened branch, or maybe shove them off cliffs," said the leader of the guards who had come to listen. "I am recovered almost completely and would like to go out with Wisdom's Child. I know that she can heal from almost anything, but

I am uncomfortable having her out there by herself, even though she rescued Arms Master Hearten from kill hounds and The Family is with her. I can't get my head to accept that she is not as my eyes see."

"I think that is a great idea," said Wisdom's Child to everyone's surprise. "How have you been doing with the body signals?"

"She does very well," said Mavs, coming over.

"Good," said Wisdom's Child.

"I also think," continued Wisdom's Child, "that Prince Aaron is well enough for at least one outing a day, but only if we have another person along with him."

"How about one of the master foresters?" asked Captain Alessia. "They are well versed in going silently through the forest."

"Or the farmers, any that is an adult," said Hearten. "They aren't as silent as the forester, but they are close."

"We will need to ask them," said Wisdom's Child. "It will be best if it is you, Prince Aaron, along with Arms Master Hearten, who do so. Be sure you tell about the methods that can be used to kill the enemy and ask for any other ideas. They may have killed some already."

"We will do so," said Prince Aaron, rising from the fire, eager to find people who would accompany him on rescues.

"Do you think sending the Prince out is a good idea?" asked Aloo.

"Yes," said Wisdom's Child, "he is well enough for it, and he is getting to frustrated being cooped up inside. He has spent most of his life outside avoiding his uncle's plans for him. Healer Mavis and I discussed this yesterday and agreed that this is for the best."

◊ ◊ ◊

"Sergeant Marista," said Wisdom's Child, "do you find mind-speech objectionable?"

"Umm, well, yes, ma'am, I am afraid I do," answered the good sergeant, turning red. "I am always afraid someone will take control of my mind."

"You are right to be concerned," said Prass. "But are you not taught to shield as a child?"

"Shield?" asked Marista. "I don't have any mind powers."

"Everyone has mind powers," said Kerr. "Even those who cannot do mind-speech can shield. We teach it to our children who do not develop mind-speech abilities until they come into their youth."

"So I can have a mind shield and not be worried about being around those who use mind-speech?" asked the sergeant.

"Yes," said Wisdom's Child. "A shield will also enable you to receive mind-speech, but only in the part of your mind where you communicate, not where you think or anywhere else."

"So then we would not have to talk, and it would be faster than signals when we are rescuing the other refugees," said Sergeant Marista in understanding. "I would like to learn this. I am a soldier, and a soldier wants whatever gives her the advantage for her job."

"I can teach you this evening," said Prass. "When we rescued Hearten, one of those pursuing him was a mage who did a sending. If they can do that, they can knock you out with a mind blast if you are not protected."

"That gives me the shivers," answered Marista. "Would it be all right for me to invite the other guards and soldiers?"

"I think that would be a great idea," said Prass. "Once you practice your shield, you can keep it up even in your sleep."

"Wouldn't having an opening so people can communicate with you leave you vulnerable?" asked Marista.

"No," said Kerr. "Prass will teach you how to shield behind that area, so all that will happen is that you are alerted to a threat and can strengthen your shield even more."

"Oh," said Marista.

"Aloo signals that the refugees have shifted to the west and that the enemy is getting closer to us than them. Let's lead them away from their prey and turn the tables, time for silence."

Prass told Aloo their intentions with mind-speech, and she veered her flight to the direction they needed to go to reach the terrain that would cause the enemy to spread out, making them easier to kill.

They ran silently away from the refugees and deeper into the forest. The thickness of the underbrush made the going a little difficult but did not slow them down greatly. Aloo signaled that the enemy was on the chase and starting to string out. Marista and Prass dropped into the brush and disappeared. Kerr and Wisdom's Child slowed enough to be visible and gave the leaders more zest for the hunt, and the enemy passed by the other two without realizing it.

Silently, Marista and Prass waited for the last enemy soldier. He reached them and had just gone past when Prass with a mighty leap landed on his back and, with a quick bite to his neck, broke it. Marista came forward and seeing that the enemy was dead signaled that they should continue the hunt. Prass agreed, signaling caution. When they came in sight of the next soldier, they moved farther to the left and went up ahead of him to see how close he was to the others. Aloo signaled Kerr and Wisdom's Child that their ambushers had caught up, and they put on more speed, taking a path full of twists and turns and more brambles.

The enemy soldiers' shadows went a little ahead of him, still to the side, keeping him in view; and when he was out of sight of the others, they had their second victim. This time Prass knocked the soldier down, but Marista did the killing, cutting his head off. There were two soldiers left, and they started missing the others and made sure they stayed together. Wisdom's Child signaled Kerr, and they looped around to join Marista and Prass, trusting Aloo to communicate what they were doing. There they set their third trap, ambushing the other two.

Getting their breath back, Wisdom's Child signaled Aloo, asking where the refugees were, and she indicated that they needed to go northwest about five miles to get to them. Also, they were not near any enemies.

Panting but satisfied with their efforts, the four headed toward the refugees and catching up with them asked the same questions. Did they want to come to refuge, and could they live with people unlike themselves?

To be safe, they believed they could live with anyone but were worried because they knew that they were being hunted.

"No longer," said Sergeant Marista, "my team and I have taken care of that situation."

"With a child!" exclaimed one of them in shocked horror.

"I am not what I seem," said Wisdom's Child with a kind smile. "I am a master healer and am the oldest person at our refuge. I am cursed to never die and always look this age. Quite annoying, I assure you. Now if you will be so kind as to let me see that arm, I will attend to it and the leg over there. We would normally have horses, and in fact, we need to figure out how to get them to people once we have gotten rid of the hunters." Then she went about her business, cleaning and stitching wounds and resetting the leg of a young man.

"You know," said Kerr, startling them and pointing to the one with the broken leg, "he isn't that big. I could carry him. We might need more rest stops, but I could manage."

"Thank you, Kerr," said Wisdom's Child with a smile. "Sergeant Marista will be able to steady him, and that will leave Prass and I free to eliminate their tracks." With the young man being carried by Kerr, the refugees got on their way, making much better time.

◊ ◊ ◊

Prince Aaron could not keep from smiling as they left Refuge, free from its confines at last and able to go to the aid of his people. Hearten grinned knowingly it is very hard for a warrior to be cooped up.

Master Forester Nate had agreed to accompany them and carried a large limb sharpened into a lance. He and his family had killed several of their pursuers, and he knew all kinds of ways to lay traps for the unwary, as did both Aaron and Hearten.

They were out so early you could just barely see in the understory of the forest. They wished to set up ambushes and to lead the refugees first in the direction of their traps, and then hiding all traces of them toward Refuge.

Prince Aaron intercepted the refugees, and putting his finger to his lips, he came close to them so they could identify him. They sighed with relief, and hope lit their faces when they recognized their prince.

"I am going to lead you to a safe place, but first we must rid you of the evil ones. You must follow me and my companions exactly so that you do not trigger what is meant for the enemy," Prince Aaron said as he waved Mavs and Aris forward.

"Well met, people of Asalawn," said Mavs, bowing.

"Keep up your courage," said Aris, also bowing.

"These are some of the people who rescued me from the enemy," said Prince Aaron as he handed them food bars that the cooks had created to give them energy, cautioning them to eat them slowly. They nodded and eating followed their Prince and his companions from their night's camp.

Aaron realizing how tired his people were led them carefully, watching Anvar for word on how close the enemy was to them. Pretty soon, she indicated that they needed to hurry for the enemy was drawing closer, and he rushed them past the traps that Hearten and Nate had set. At a stream, he veered off, going up a ways; and then reaching a mossy bank, he exited the stream. From there on, he led them where little tracks could be found, and they tried hard not to leave any.

Mavs stayed with Aaron and with body language told him that the enemy was fooled and no longer followed, although there were still plenty about. Aaron slowed his pace, letting his people catch their breath, and headed for Refuge.

The enemy was excited. They had sighted the escapees and would overtake them easily. They loped through the forest, not caring about the noise they made, sure to catch up in minutes, then death.

Death, yes, but theirs. They had hit the first of the traps, and two were lifted up and flung onto sharp stakes. They were not immediately dead, but their companions finished the job. The remaining two exercised more caution but now were in a frenzy. Their prey had escaped them, and they started to speed up.

Forester Nate showed himself to them, just a glimpse, and they were hounds on the hunt. He let them draw closer and veered from his path, dodging trees, then dived over a log.

They came on faster, sure that they had him, and were caught in a deadfall trap, crushed by a tree.

Hearten and Nate checked to make sure that they were dead. Assured, they dismantled the trap so it would look like an accident and went to dismantle the other and hide the bodies. Then they journeyed to join Aaron on the way to refuge.

"Arms Master Hearten," Anvar mind spoke, "I hope you do not mind mind-speech?"

"No," said Hearten. "What is it?"

"If you will veer to the left, about two miles from you are many refugees who have eluded their hunters. They pushed them off a cliff," she replied. "I am having Aris join you as Mavs and Aaron are making good time traveling to Refuge."

"I feel nervous with Aaron out with only one guard," said Hearten.

"The people with Aaron are a teacher and students from a military school that the elite send their children to," said Anvar.

"Who is the teacher?" asked Hearten.

"A fellow named Zephron," said Anvar.

"Zephron is a good fighter," said Hearten with a sigh. "He is an aristocrat and may not fit in well at Refuge, even worse than Master Hays. You might send warning to Master Mavis and the other masters. But I am content at the Prince's guards and am heading for the refugees you spoke of."

"Master Nate," said Hearten, "I have just had mind-speech with Anvar, and we need to veer left and gather in some resourceful refugees who just pushed their pursuers off a cliff. Prince Aaron's people are from a military school for the elite, an instructor and four students. I know the instructor and am content with the Prince's guard," Hearten added when he saw Nate about to object.

"That's all right then," said Forester Nate, and he and Hearten set off at a mile-eating pace to gather in the other refugees.

Aris caught up with them and then scouted ahead. Finding the people, he came back to Hearten and Nate and signaled for them to stop.

"Hearten, Nate, what kind of people go so silently? Even their children are silent, not like silent because they are afraid, but because that is how they are. They are mostly women and children, and the women are obviously warriors."

"If they have even invaded these mountains so deep as to haze the Hazbastas out of their homes, we are invaded worse than I thought," said Nate.

"The Hazbastas!" exclaimed Hearten. "This will call for some negotiations. They only treat with women. Is there a meadow that Anvar can land in?"

"No," said Aris.

"Maybe in this emergency, they will treat with you," said Nate Worriedly.

"Let us hope," said Hearten.

"Lead us to them, Aris," he commanded.

When the Hazbastas came near, Hearten, Nate, and Aris stepped from cover and waited, hands at their sides, weapons sheathed.

The Hazbastas stopped, and Hearten spoke. "Hail, I am Hearten, Arms Master to Prince Aaron. Our whole land has been invaded, and the evil Regent is dead, killed by his own guards from foreign lands. We have a place of refuge, but to dwell there, you will have to accept equality of men and women and will have to dwell with people of different species than just us humans."

"So," said the lead woman, "this foulness is throughout the land?"

"Yes," said Hearten with sad grimness. "They murdered the men, old people, boys, small children, and infants in every farm, town, and village across the land. Very few have escaped."

"This is grimmer news than I believed possible," said the woman with alarm. "Arms Master Hearten, you are the one who trains both women and men. Who would not follow the dictates of the Regent when he tried to eliminate women from being soldiers?"

"It is against the laws of the land to prohibit women from being soldiers," answered Hearten. "My wife was a soldier, and many of the queens of Asalawn have been soldiers."

"Our people became as we are due to abuse, abuse to such a degree that men could no longer be trusted. The idea of trusting and seeing men as equals is a hard thing. Let me talk to my people. I do not know if they can do this," said the leader.

"Well, she is honest," said Forester Nate.

"The Hazbastas are famed for their honesty," said Hearten dryly.

"My people want to know if there is someplace else that they may go," said the woman.

"I do not know," said Hearten. "We have only found the one place that is not being searched and where the magic sucker is not active."

"Magic sucker!" exclaimed the leader.

"Yes," said Hearten, "all of the people in our land who have magic have had their magic and their lives sucked out of them. We have just recently learned through the new people that are with us that there is a magic being worked that sucks magic and life out of people, and we are afraid even the land."

"We too have lost magic wielders. Some thought it is was because we decided to become a settled people, but you say it is because a magic is being used to suck the magic and life from them?" asked the leader.

"Yes," answered a grim Hearten, "it is what killed my wife."

"A warrior and a magic wielder, what a powerful woman you married," said the leader. "Were you frightened of her?"

"No," said Hearten, smiling at the memory of his wife, "there is no fear where there is love, and we loved one another greatly."

"I will go back and speak with my people some more," said the leader, pondering Hearten's last statement.

"My people," she said as she returned, "they know of nowhere else to go. And I believe that we have the truth for Arms Master Hearten is known for his trustworthiness. He has also given answer to the reason we have lost our magic wielders, and he is afraid that it will eventually suck the life completely out of the land. The place they are hiding has no such magic going on."

"This is grim news, Hildy," said an elderly woman. "How did they learn this?"

"From the new people who are not human that come to dwell with them, Eldest," answered Hildy respectfully.

"The reason we settled here in Asalawn was because women are treated with equality. It is our prejudices against men that has kept us from interacting with the rest of the land," said the Eldest. "Maybe now is the time to change our ways and become healed people returning the trust we have withheld for generations back to our men. They certainly have earned it. Don't say it. I know that some have not, but then again, some women have not either. I think trustworthiness is an individual thing, not an entire gender thing. It is a thing of character. Let us go with these people and learn to be part of our land."

"Yes, Eldest," said Hildy, bowing and looking at the rest of the people, seeing that they agreed with their Eldest.

"Arms Master Hearten, our Eldest has spoken, and we shall journey to your place of refuge and learn to be part of the land of Asalawn," spoke Hildy. "She says it is time."

"You will be joining us as we become a new land then," said Hearten, "and will have some say in how we grow."

"Prince Aaron will allow this?" asked Hildy in surprise.

"Prince Aaron insists on this," answered Hearten with a smile at the shocked look on her face.

"I must tell this to the Eldest, and then we will be ready to travel," answered Hildy.

Hearten led them, and Aris and Nate followed, eliminating any traces of which there were very few.

When they arrived at Refuge, Prince Aaron came forward to meet the Hazbastas, bowing to their eldest. "Greetings and welcome," he said to them.

"Thank you for accepting us into your shelter," replied the eldest.

"You are welcome here, Eldest. I see that you are hurt," said Prince Aaron. "May I offer you the services of our healers? Both are women."

"Thank you," said the Eldest, "I would appreciate that for myself and my people."

Prince Aaron led them to the healers' area where both Mavis and Wisdom's Child were checking on the progress of injured border guards and soldiers.

"Master Mavis, Master Wisdom's Child," said Prince Aaron, coming upon them, "I present to you some new refugees of the Hazbastas people. As you can see, they are in need of your attention."

"Welcome," said Master Mavis. "Let Master Wisdom's Child and I treat the worse hurt first, and then she must be back out to rescue more refugees." They treated Eldest first and made her as comfortable as possible as her injury was to the spine. They had to figure a way to brace her back so that she would not cause herself further hurt and so that people could help her without causing more damage either.

Once done with the worse injured, Wisdom's Child left with her team to rescue more of the hunted.

"How can you send a child on such a mission?" asked Eldest sternly of Prince Aaron when he came to see how she was doing.

"Master Wisdom's Child is the oldest person at Refuge as we call this place. She was bespelled by her father, an evil mage, to remain a child and never die," answered Prince Aaron. "She rescued myself and Healer Mavis with the help of her people: the Lady Aloo; Aris, who you have met; and two other of the four-foots, along with another winged person. And she was the one in charge of their training in the art of war and many other studies. They all remember her from their childhoods, and she looked the same then as now. In fact, she is so resourceful that she and Prass, a feline four-foot, rescued Hearten from kill hounds."

"Those devil beasts!" exclaimed Eldest. "They set them loose in our lands, so we fled. Once we passed a certain point, they seemed unable to go past it, and my people took great delight in killing them as they paced back and forth frustrated. We must have killed fifteen of those things, and I know there are still more."

"That is grave news," said Prince Aaron. "It is good to know that they can be killed, but that they have been set loose, we must have care and more care. If their mages move the parameters, we could be in serious trouble. Thank you for this information. I will speak with the elders and masters about this and have the people of The Family warned of this," said Prince Aaron who went striding away.

"Master Seth," Prince Aaron said as he approached the man, "I would like you to double the guards. I am going to see if any of the guards or soldiers is healthy enough to stand guard duty with you. One thing, I want you to have your nonpanicky people pay attention to this if they get a sense of fear greater than what they already have or should find normal for this situation. I have found out from the Eldest of the Hazbastas that the enemies have set the kill hounds loose in their lands, but they couldn't cross a certain boundary. She says her people must have killed fifteen there, and she knows that there are many more. If their mages change the parameters of the boundaries, we could be in serious trouble, and fear is their first weapon against their prey."

Master Seth's face paled and turned grim. "From what I have heard of Hearten's story, those things only live to kill. It will be as you wish, Prince Aaron."

"Captain Alessia," said Prince Aaron, coming upon the woman in the infirmary, "come with me while I talk with Master Mavis please." And he strode over to where Mavis was mixing up herbs.

"Master Mavis," said Prince Aaron, "I am sorry to interrupt you. I know that mixing herbs can be exacting, but Eldest of the Hazbastas has told me that the kill hounds were set loose upon her lands, and there was nothing to do but flee. She says once they reached a certain point, the hounds couldn't cross it, and they managed to kill fifteen of the creatures while they paced there in frustration. Are any of the soldiers or border guards in good-enough shape to just sit at the guard posts and monitor for fear? Fear seems to be the first thing they send out to confuse and panic their prey."

"Yes," said Master Mavis, "and you are forgiven for the interruption. You should also have some of the Hazbastas on guard duty. They know how to kill the things, and you should have them teaching the rest of us how to do so. Anything the memory of that leaves Hearten trembling in fear is nothing I want near us."

That evening at war council, Prince Aaron started it by introducing Hildy. "This is Hildy of the Hazbastas. They are a group of people who chose to settle here in Asalawn many decades ago. She has grim news to report to us."

"I speak in place of our Eldest who is hurt," said Hildy. "The enemy has set loose kill hounds as you call them, devil hounds as we do, upon our lands. They are restricted to a set area, and once we crossed that boundary, they could go no farther. We have been teaching your people how to kill them since we have come here. It was difficult for us to find a place to cross the border, for they have soldiers stationed at areas to keep us from doing so. It was only by going along a cliff face that we managed to escape the hounds and cause the soldiers hunting us to fall. Our Eldest, unfortunately, fell also. But we were tied together, and the fall was short, so not fatal."

"Hildy," said Master Mavis with kind sadness, "did gypsy people come through your land and leave luck tokens with your people?"

"Yes," said Hildy, "why?"

"Elder Wisdom's Child, who is also Master Healer Wisdom's Child, is a mage, and she has explained to us that these are magic traps and are what have been sucking the magic and life out of our magic wielders and will suck the life out of our land," said Master Mavis.

"But the wielders did not start becoming ill until two years after the gypsies visited us," objected Hildy.

"Magic traps can be set and left sitting for years, even centuries, before they are triggered," said Wisdom's Child kindly. Seeing the look on Hildy's face, Wisdom's Child continued, "Hildy, what Master Mavis has told you is true. I really am a mage, and my power is coming back. I have studied magic for decades, if not centuries, for I have no more idea of how old I am than of what my name is. All this was lost at the death of my father."

Hildy looked to Prince Aaron for confirmation.

"Yes," said Prince Aaron with a wry grin, "and because Wisdom's Child took such hurt when she threw up a shield to protect her people, who are the four-footed and winged people, she sometimes acts as unsure as a nine-year-old. And I forget that she is my elder, which I assure you is quite embarrassing."

"Oh," said Hildy.

"She rescued me from kill hounds, Hildy," said Arms Master Hearten. "And when I remember the incident, I am still shaken, yet she is not. This is because she is cursed to neither age nor die."

"That would not be good," said Hildy.

"Yet that is how it is for me," said Wisdom's Child. "Now let us get back to the enemy. If we can free up the borders set by the enemy of their guards, more Hazbastas can escape the hounds."

"We would need to find and eliminate their leaders," said Prince Aaron. "Actually, it would be good if we focused on eliminating all of their leadership. From what you have reported about your battle with them, Captain Alessia, they do not function well without it."

"You are right, my Prince," said Hearten, "that would be a more effective way to fight them."

"We avians can spot the leaders. In fact, Anvar and I noticed that some of the leaders are the lizard men that you told us about," said Aloo.

"Ah, the lizard men," said Hearten and Aaron at the same time. "They are very clever and have a strange kind of magic of their own."

"I wonder," said Wisdom's Child, "if avians couldn't find seeker/suckers, put a carry bag over it, and drop it in the proximity of the lizard men."

"See where their section of the border is and use the seeker/sucker on them?" asked Aloo.

"Yes," said Wisdom's Child, "I do not want my magic revealed, and I do not want anyone coming against a magic user without some protection, so why not use their magic against them? Also, I worry that the lizard men are the mages sent out because they are not affected by the seeker/sucker, or do they have some device that they wear that protects them? It is my hope that when they are weakened, the use of a strong arrow from a distance can kill them."

"They are able to make the arrows turn to ash," said Hildy.

"If they are weakened, they cannot make all of them turn to ash. And if traps are set up and they are harassed into them, they will die just like any other creature," answered Wisdom's Child with grim sternness.

"You are truly an eldest," said Hildy, shocked to be hearing such words from the mouth of a seeming nine-year-old.

"If we destroy all who are with it, it will need to flee," said Captain Alessia. "And if we have set its course, we can bring an end to it. Are some of The Family close enough to come and help with this Aloo?"

"Yes," said Aloo. "Tomorrow, we will need to scout, plan, and get people into position so that we can do what we can for Hildy's people."

"We also need to be rescuing those who are hunted in our area," reminded Prince Aaron. "We will need more volunteers to guide the people back and more to eliminate the hunters, but I think if we work on eliminating the leaders, we can cut down on the efficiency of the hunters. From what Aloo and Anvar have reported on their hunt patterns, they have a certain amount of territory that they search and they only do that area. If they are not told what to do the next day, I wonder what they will do."

"Now that is a very interesting question," said Arms Master Hearten with a grin.

"So then," said Wisdom's Child, "let us for tomorrow continue to rescue those hunted with the emphasis on hunters lead by leaders. While Aloo contacts The Family to do the scouting needed along the boundary that the enemy has set to keep the kill hounds and Hazbastas in. We will need packs of precooked food supplies, medical supplies, shovels, and weapons which I will leave to Hearten and Captain Alessia to gather."

"I can take care of the preparation here," said Master Mavis. "Captain Alessia is able to go out on the hunt. Also, a couple of Master Seth's sons would also like to go out."

"There are those of my people whose injuries are slight who would be willing to lead people back. We know that we are not able to fight yet," Hildy added hurriedly when she saw the looks that both Master Mavis and Master Wisdom's Child gave her. They both grinned and agreed to her suggestion.

"I believe that this is all the planning we can do for this evening, and we know what we are doing tomorrow, so let this meeting be adjourned," said Prince Aaron, rising from his seat, and the rest followed.

"I couldn't help but notice that you seem to have a very healthy respect for our healers," said Captain Alessia as she walked with Hildy toward the infirmary.

"We are taught young to respect and obey healers quickly and to not get them mad at you," said Hildy.

"You know that is funny," said Captain Alessia. "We are taught the same thing, and some have learned from experience why you don't want them mad at you. Also, the people of The Family have this same training."

Hildy grinned. "It would seem that, in this at least, we have something in common."

"Indeed we do," said Captain Alessia with a grin and went her separate way.

"Eldest," said Hildy coming to report, "They have a plan to free the boundary area of the enemy soldiers."

"That is good news," said the Eldest. "Did it take much persuasion on your part to show them the need for help?"

"I did not even have to mention it," said Hildy. "Once I gave my report, they instantly went to work, figuring ways to get rid of the soldiers and the lizard men wizards."

"I am ashamed of how I have always thought of these people," said the Eldest.

"I think that it is Prince Aaron who sets the tone for the attitude of the people. He and the mage Wisdom's Child, Master Mavis, Arms Master Hearten, and Lady Aloo," answered Hildy. "They continually remind people that it is their intention not to go back to the ways of the evil Regent's reign."

"So what Arms Master Hearten said about starting over and building a new country with safeguards against the errors of the past that has led to this downfall are true," said the Eldest. "Prince Aaron is hoping that I will become well enough to become part of the ruling council and help keep things running smoothly here at Refuge. The other councilors he has chosen have come to speak with me to learn our customs and to tell me what theirs have been."

"Do we have much in common?" asked Hildy, who then grinned.

"Why the grin?" asked Eldest.

"We at least have the way in which we respond to healers in common," she said with a laugh. "Captain Alessia had a word with me on that after we were leaving the meeting. I had volunteered our less injured to go out with the teams, and the looks I got from Masters Mavis and Wisdom's Child had me hastily adding that we would be leading people back to refuge, not fighting."

Eldest laughed at this and added, "Yes, we do have many things in common. With the exception of our attitudes toward our men and them never being allowed to learn how to fight, we are much the same. Well, except the men and women share being head of the household, and we do not. I must tell you, our men are quite uncomfortable with the expectations that the Asalawnians and the people of The Family have of them. They are not sure they want equality and are frightened about the change."

"Oh dear, that is not something that I would have expected," said Hildy. "I will go and be with them and the children and see if I can help them."

"Do that," said Eldest, "but first finish telling me what was planned at the council."

CHAPTER 15

The Family Enters the Fray

A LOO LAUNCHED INTO the sky with the predawn arrowing toward The Family. She was greeted, having gone but a short distance, by avians with their children riding safely in their carry bags. She turned and led them to the ledge where they landed in an orderly fashion, each couple hurrying to make room for the next.

"*Yass,*" Aloo mind called, "*you finally have company. Won't you introduce these members of our nation around?*"

"*Certainly,*" said Yass, hurrying to meet the arrivals. "How wonderful that you are here. I have been treated very well and included quite nicely, but when you are used to having your children lying beside you, it is hard."

"Yes, but if the war elders' plans go well, they will be here in a few days. It has been hardest on Aloo I am thinking," said Laftra, giving Yass a head caress in greeting.

"Indeed," said Yass, "and I was so concerned about me, I hadn't even thought about the sacrifice she has made. I am ashamed and appreciate her sacrifice even more now that I can feel the sting of it myself. Come, let me introduce you to our other healer, Master Healer Mavis. She is also in charge of lodging. They have found another cavern off from this one, not quite so large though, and have set it up in a manner that they hope is suitable for avians. Aloo supervised when she was in, so I imagine that they did a fine job with what they had to work with." She finished speaking as she led the way to The Healer.

◊ ◊ ◊

"Alaw, the avian families have arrived safely, and Yass is showing them around," mind spoke Aloo.

"Good, now we can have healed human soldiers to add to our ranks," answered Alaw on the war elder mind net, getting the rest of the elders' attention.

"Our scouts are showing that there are many Hazbastas cornered but are inaccessible to the kill hounds. If we can reach them with a message of hope, they will stay where they are, and we will be able to come to their aid," said Alaw.

"Maybe a note from the Hazbastas Eldest at Refuge could be flown to them," said Aloo. *"I have sent a scout to request such notes. He wants to know how many."*

"Five so far," said Alaw.

"I have told him, and he continues his flight," said Aloo.

"Alaw, rest of the council, have our people learned the modified body language for communicating with the humans?" asked Aloo.

"Yes," said Kriss, *"why?"*

"If we can send some further in to join with those who are freeing the hunted refugees, it will make it easier for them to seek out and kill the leaders of the troops. From the reports, the lizard men are solely occupied with the kill hounds and holding a border against them. I wonder if Wisdom's Child has thought of this, that they are holding the border not only against the people but against the hounds."

"It looked this morning like they did a ceremony to reinforce it and last evening also," said Elder. *"That was the report I was given by one of our scouts."*

"It may be that we need to do something about the kill hounds first," said Tawny.

"I wish Wisdom's Child was here. Her knowledge and magic is what will make the difference in this situation," said Elder

"Even with so much of her memory gone?" asked Kriss.

"She is older than you think, and much of her study was done with tutors brought in by her father. So what she learned is not associated with him," answered Elder. *"He rarely if ever taught her any magic. He did not want her to learn any magic above a certain level. But seeing how she gathered magic about herself, healed herself, and used it to free us, I think she long passed what he wanted her to know."*

"It is good he never realized this," said Tawny, shivering at the thought.

◊ ◊ ◊

"Sergeant Marista," said Wisdom's Child as they left the gully, "when the enemy gets far enough away, we will have to camp to be within striking distance. I look forward to when all of the soldiers and guards are healed and when Hearten has more of your people trained in combat practice."

"It is good that duty can be assigned to a wounded sergeant," said Marista with a grin. "But Sergeant Corey says everyone is taking it very seriously, and he sees them putting in extra practice time, even the parents."

"I think going past all those villages with dead children would have every parent practicing extra hard," said Wisdom's Child soberly.

"Aloo says that the avian families have arrived and will be landing in back. Yass is going to see to them," said Kerr. "I am glad that we have three elders here and that Yass is tied to Refuge. It will be better to have an elder supervising the new arrivals while they settle in."

"True, and having the extra avians means we will have extra teams going out tomorrow. But now for the hunt, Brak signals that we are within two miles of our prey," said Wisdom's Child with an odd excitement in her voice, causing all three of her companions to look at her strangely. No one said anything, but all were startled at the warrior like attitude that she displayed.

It took thirty minutes of careful going, but they caught up with the hunted and led them one way, while making a false trail that led the hunters another way. It looked like the hunters weren't going to take their bait when the leader pulled out his globe which was shining brightly in Wisdom's Child's direction. This decided them on their prey, and they went swiftly in the direction that the globe led.

Wisdom's Child seeing this tamped on her magic a little bit, and they hurried faster, thinking that they were falling behind. Then she too sped up, letting their globe lighten back up.

While the refugees followed Prass, Kerr and Marista ran with Wisdom's Child, and she took them into an opening in the forest of bare rock. With the enemy almost upon them, she dampened her magic completely out of their globe and signaled for the two to follow her swiftly, which they did.

The enemy went berserk. The leader held the globe and moved all over the rock clearing, and then he began to shake it. Brak knowing what had happened the last time did the warning cry and flew for his life while the land team put on more speed. In a few moments, they heard a tremendous explosion and ducked low while still running to avoid any flying debris.

Brak signaled the all clear from the air, and they rested. "I think you need to go back to Refuge and use some of your magic, Wisdom's Child," said Kerr quietly.

"How close to us are the next refugees?" was her reply. "I can let them see my magic or not with those globes. They were sniffing the scent where we tried to muddle the trail and looked to be ready to follow the refugees, so I thought what would distract them. Magic is what their masters hunger for, so let them hunt for magic. And of course we know how they reacted in the meadow that one time, so I was hoping they would do so again."

"Oh," said Kerr, while Sergeant Marista just looked puzzled and then said, "Explain it to me back at Refuge. I think it may take you a while."

Wisdom's Child smiled and said, "You are a woman of wisdom, and Brak says the next refugees are about to run right into our laps and the hunters are hot on their trail."

"All that in sign?" asked Kerr.

"No, mind-speech," said Wisdom's Child.

"From the picture he is giving me, let me run with them and head them up the stream farther back the way we came. There is a deep hole that seems to flow under an overhang, and maybe I can hide their scent and them there," said Wisdom's Child. "You two will need to ambush wherever possible, and I have given Brak permission to help with what combat you might get in."

"Yes, ma'am," they both said, and in a short time, they heard people running toward them.

Wisdom's Child jumped up and joined the runners, saying, "This way." She led them to the stream, in it, and up it. Then she started to swim. When some balked at it, she came back and said, "You must hide. They are almost on you, and this is the only place to hide I know of. If you don't know how to swim, lay on your back and I will tow you. People float, you know." It was a sign of their desperation that they did what she said, and those who could swim helped with the towing. Once they were under the under-cut, they found that it was long and fairly deep. They crowded back as far as they could and seemed to hold their breaths.

Marista and Kerr hurried out of sight and watched as the hunters passed by. They were evenly matched in pace and ran together well, but they gave no thought to the amount of sound they made which made following them easy.

Once the hunters reached the bank of the stream, they seemed to stop and smell about more than they used their eyes. They decided to split up, two going up stream and two going down, with one on each side of the stream.

Kerr and Marista decided to take out the ones going upstream first, and then go after the two going downstream. The forest cover made stalking the soldiers easy. Choosing the soldier on the side that the cut bank was on, they waited until the brush blocked him from the sight of his mate and took him out silently with Kerr knocking him down and Marista cutting his head off. Then they crossed the stream and did the same to the other one.

"We have killed the two near you. The others went downstream, and we seek them," said Kerr, standing above the cut bank. "Wait and stay hidden."

"Thank you," whispered one of the adults, shivering in the dark.

Wisdom's Child patted her hand comfortingly, and they waited for what seemed hours.

"We got one, but the other almost caught us!" said Marista on their return. "Fortunately, Brak saw him and dove down to our rescue, removing the threat."

"That is good," said Wisdom's Child. "Now we need to get these people safe and dry."

"Thank you," said a woman, looking weary and eating gratefully on the food bar that was provided.

"You are welcome," said Wisdom's Child and watched with a smile at the surprised look on the adults' faces as she took charge. "I am named Wisdom's Child because they couldn't think of anything else to help them to remember that I am old. I am older than any of the adults here or at our refuge. This is Kerr who is of the people species canine, and this is Sergeant Marista of the Border Guards."

"Who is Brak?" asked a youth.

"Brak is of the people species avian," said Kerr, "and he is flying guard over us and says we need to be moving while the way is clear."

"Oh, you really are people," said a man.

"I hope you can live with people whose species is different from you," said Wisdom's Child. "Otherwise, we will try and find you a safe route out of Asalawn and get you supplied, but you will not be allowed to remain at Refuge for it is an integrated community."

"She really is older than us," said Sergeant Marista. "She is a Master Healer and a War Elder of her own people."

"We will come with you," said a woman. "We will do the best we can to learn to live with people other than ourselves. But I agree with Brak. We should be moving on. Let us try this new life before we say we cannot live it."

"Agreed," said Wisdom's Child, who led the way to Refuge while Sergeant Marista and Kerr hid any trace.

When they arrived at Refuge, Wisdom's Child introduced them to Healer Mavis and left them in her care while she went to greet the new arrivals from The Family.

"Greetings," said Wisdom's Child as she came upon them. "Are your quarters satisfactory?"

"Yes," said an avian named Jaspaw, "they have been put together with great care and good thought. It is nice to have the small rooms off to the side for the nurseries."

"Excellent," said Wisdom's Child, smiling at everyone as she looked around, "you all seem to be in fine shape and even stronger than when we left the keep."

"We have kept in practice and have done most of the hunting for The Family. Getting the children moved safely is a big enough job without having to hunt also, and as we can arrive at our destinations earlier, we have taken on this task," answered Clarrifia.

"Excellent and well done!" said Wisdom's Child, giving heartfelt praise that shocked the avians and Yass. Seeing the looks on their faces, she burst out laughing, further astounding them.

"When the Evil Mage robbed me of all memory of himself, he actually set me free to be me, a person, who can laugh and cry, be happy, and even get angry," she told them kindly. "The person you knew me to be does not exist, and I don't believe ever really did."

"Well," said Yass, "we never really knew you, except as a teacher or commander who was strict and never satisfied."

"Ah, well," said Wisdom's Child, "it will be nice to get acquainted with you. I seem to have some vague notion that doing so was a bad idea during our time under the Evil Mage's rule."

"That would be putting it mildly," said Yass dryly. "And it is nice to meet you, Wisdom's Child."

"I don't mean to be in a rush to greet you and then run off, but I need the bags you brought your children here in. And then I will tell Master Mavis that I do not want to be disturbed for a while as I figure out a few things," said Wisdom's Child, gathering the bags from where the avians had stored them.

"You had better put some across my back. There are quite a few," said Yass as she watched Wisdom's Child turn one inside out. Suddenly, she stopped, ran her hands across the fabric again, and smiled with glee.

"My library!" said Wisdom's Child. "I hid it between double layers so the Evil Mage would not discover it. I hope what is here has the information that I need!"

"Quickly, everyone, help me to gather these and take them deeper into the mountain so that I can access it," she said excitedly. After they had gathered the bags, she said, "Wait, I will go and tell Mavis what I am doing."

Running, she found Mavis and drew her aside. "Master Mavis, the bags not only contain the fabric I need but also part of my library. My memory of it was triggered when I handled the fabric. I am going deep into the mountain to open it. I believe it will give me some of the information that I need. If it is not in these bags, I can take the bags back with me to The Family and switch until I find the right one. I know people want me to stay here, but I need to check on my people." And she grinned. "You should have seen the shocked looks on their faces when I praised them and the even more astounded looks when I burst out laughing."

"Yours and their life were very grim," said Mavis. "It is a shock for them to realize that they do not know you at all."

"Truly," said Wisdom's Child in agreement. "Now I must hurry so we can help the Hazbastas."

Wisdom's Child was gone for several hours, and when she returned, she was grim. "I need to speak with you and your war council, also as many of our war council as we have here," she told Prince Aaron.

"Certainly, I will call one now," he answered. "We can have it at the same place as before."

"Good," said Wisdom's Child, "I will get Yass and Aloo."

"Yass, Aloo, we will need to meet with Prince Aaron's war council within a few minutes. My library offered up the name of the soldiers we are fighting," Wisdom's Child told them.

"We are coming," said Aloo, getting down from her perch as Yass arose from a pallet laid there for her comfort.

Once they entered the conference room and everyone was seated, Wisdom's Child spoke. "The beings we are fighting, at least the soldiers, are called Wanz. They come from an insect origin and were developed during the same era as the winged and four-foots. They are not born as we are but are hatched and have four stages: egg, larva, chrysalis, and their developed form. They belong to a hive community and do not function well as individuals. They implant their eggs once fertilized into living beings, and once it reaches its larval stage, it eats its host. This is why I believe they chose women and girls for slaves." Everyone looked ill and frightened, not for themselves, but for the captives of the Wanz.

"It is more important than ever that we get them free from the enemy," said Prince Aaron, despair in his voice as he looked beseechingly at Aloo and Yass.

"Our plan to rid this area of their presence may cause them to delay shipping out," said Wisdom's Child. "Also, since they made their soldiers magically multiply from chrysalis to soldier, what are they going to do with all of them? Do they want the slaves more than they want the soldiers? Do they actually have enough room on board their ships for all of their people? Is there a hive established here? Will they take the magic they have sucked out of Asalawn so far and leave with things set up so that the continued leaching of magic and life goes on, and will they leave the lizard men as caretakers of the containers?"

"If they have established a hive here, then the women and children will not be taken aboard the ships. But if it is elsewhere, they will go," said Captain Alessia.

"When I was escaping, I did not notice that many ships in the harbor," said Hearten. "Could they be expecting ships to arrive, and those that are here are mere underlings to others?"

"These are questions that the whole war council of The Family needs to hear and ponder," said Wisdom's Child. "In the meantime, we need more scouting than ever done to find the answers to these questions. Now that we have carry bags available, we will be able to use darkness to penetrate enemy territory and find answers too many of these questions. Also, Prince Aaron, I would recommend that you have those on your council from other parts of your land who can speak for how those connected to your government behaved and to give information on how the land lies for best surveillance."

"I will consider who we have among the masters and other refugees that would be good upon the councils," said Prince Aaron.

"On a better note," said Wisdom's Child, "I can do a complete healing on everyone here, or at least those soldiers and guards who will be going out to battle along the border held against the Hazbastas, along with some of the worst hurt. Anvar said my use of magic did not alert the seeker/sucker, and I have set up a tent where healings can be wrought. Master Mavis, I will start with you first to settle any fears, and then the worst hurt, including the Eldest of the Hazbastas. When we get more of her people here, it will be best if she can smooth the way."

"I will fly to my meeting point with Alaw and let him know what has been discussed and that the plans we have made for infiltrating this area and removing the enemy are still viable, even though they need to be firmed up. With Aaron, the soldiers, and the guards, well, do you think we could meet at a point in between?" asked Aloo.

Prince Aaron looked startled at being overlooked as the war leader and saw that the rest of his team was also. He then sat back, realizing that Aloo was speaking to her war elder on what her war elder's assessment of his and the others' limitations as their healer.

"If I boost their energy magically, we should be able to do this. It will mean of course that our meeting will need to be held in a secret barn," said Wisdom's Child.

"Is it an acceptable idea to you?" Aloo asked Prince Aaron.

"Yes," said Prince Aaron, "and bringing the soldiers and people of Asalawn who will be participating in this event so that we can get right to work is a good idea."

"Is there anything further, a question or idea that has been thought of?" asked Wisdom's Child as she looked at the members of the councils. "None? Then I will go and have the wounded brought to me so that I may begin their healing."

"You will get no complaint from me," said Healer Mavis, ready to be back at full health. "If you are to magically boost those going with you, you will not be able to do a complete healing on everyone here."

"True, also I will need to do your healing very publicly with as many as can fit into the small area I have to work in. Master Char is bringing in a nourishing soup to help people regain energy. In a short period of time, after you're healed and rested for three or four days, you will be able to magically heal the least injured, and I will leave the tent up for that purpose."

"Excellent," said Master Mavis with a smile. "To be able to use my powers to heal again will be a treat!"

Gathering the patients together, Wisdom's Child signaled for silence. "I have created a tent of magic-resistant fabric and want to do a complete healing on those who have serious injuries or will be needed to confront the enemy. I am going to start with Master Healer Mavis so that you will see what happens. Will those of you gathered to carry cots bring them forward and those of you singled out follow. When Master Healer Mavis has rested three to four days, she will be able to start healing the rest of you, but she will have to be very careful on how much energy she expends. I will be having the very watchful eyes of Master Char and Elder Yass on her to make sure she does so."

Once they reached her tent, she went about the business of healing The Healer very publicly as they had discussed.

"It doesn't look like you did anything," commented one soldier, "but the look of relief on Master Mavis's face belies that. Can I be next?"

"Certainly," said Wisdom's Child as she helped Healer Mavis up. Triss seeing what she was doing came to her assistance.

"Healer Mavis, if you will please take a seat until you feel stronger, you will be able to help me keep things organized and running smoothly."

"Why is Master Mavis weak?" asked Triss. "I thought you healed her."

"A good question," said Healer Mavis, "and one that I happen to know the answer to. In order for her to heal all the people she wishes to, Healer Wisdom's Child must get some of the strength from those she heals."

Mavis had just finished speaking when Master Char arrived, with help, carrying a large pot of soup and dishes. "Prass came with your message, Wisdom's Child, and we have done as you requested."

"Thank you. If you will feed those who have been healed so that they may get their energy back more quickly, I will appreciate it," said Wisdom's Child.

Char, nodding, set about putting the pot of hot broth on a fire and, after she was done, brought a bowl full to Healer Mavis.

Turning to the pallet that she had Mavis lay on, Wisdom's Child was surprised to see the soldier who had volunteered already laying there grinning at her, ready to be healed. Smiling, she bent over him and said, "Corey, this is going to be uncomfortable and a bit painful, for I am accelerating your body's natural healing rhythm."

"Yes, ma'am," said Corey, "and thank you for the warning. You hear that, you mugs?" he asked his comrades.

"Yep, but what's a little discomfort or pain if we can finally get out of the infirmary, no offense," said another soldier, looking apologetically at both healers.

"None taken. You do know the amount of discomfort corresponds to the amount of healing your bodies have left to do?" Master Mavis reiterated.

"Yes, ma'am," everyone answered.

Smiling, Wisdom's Child went back to her work, pausing after every third patient to eat some of the soup.

"Eldest," said Wisdom's Child to the Hazbastas woman, "my healing will in no way touch your mind, only your body, and you will need several more days of rest than the soldiers and younger people will need."

"Thank you for explaining that to me. My people and I wish to be part of the goings on, and I think it will be easier for them if I can be with them," replied the Eldest.

When Wisdom's Child was finished with her work, she looked at those she had healed and said, "Remember that I used a lot of your energy to do this healing, and all of you, except those going out to free the Hazbastas, will need to rest for at least three days before you can take up more activity, and only then at a level that Master Healer Mavis or I will determine. When she was done talking to and accepting the thanks from her patients, Wisdom's Child looked up and saw Prince Aaron. "I wondered where you were. I know that you do not want to miss these encounters with the enemy," she said.

"It would seem that my people want to wrap me in wool and keep me safe, and only Hearten and Hildy coming to my aid convinced them at all that it was necessary for me to be part of this action," said the Prince wryly.

◊   ◊   ◊

"I have sent the scouts out," said Alaw to the councils. "They know to fly high."

"And I have gathered some of the seeker/suckers and studied them," said Wisdom's Child. "The magic seems rather simple, but highly effective. I have removed the owner signature from them and shut them down."

"How do the lizard men rest at night, Alaw?" she asked.

"They seem to like to sleep in a sandy bed. In fact, they make the soldiers lug a bed of sand from place to place and groom it for them every morning before they go to their work," answered the great avian.

"That is excellent," said Wisdom's Child, smiling. "I will construct a net and put it at the bottom of their box. It will draw power from them I hope. If it does not, that fact alone will give us the information we need and some suppositions to draw from."

"It would be nice to use the nets to weaken the hounds or kill them, but they would also weaken the people, wouldn't they?" asked Prince Aaron.

"Yes, they would weaken the people. The magic is too general, and I do not have what I need to make it more specific," answered Wisdom's Child. "But here is a thought. How well would the hounds do if they were tangled in nets?"

"Their speed would cause them to tangle tight before they knew what was happening to them," said Hearten excitedly.

"Then if they were put in other nets, they could be held until any use for them is passed, and they could be killed," said Elder Tawny.

"That is a good thought," said Hildy in admiration.

"I was thinking that if we put them in the pit with the lizard men, they would take care of the wizards nicely, especially if they are weakened," said Elder Tawny.

"A lot of that depends on how they are controlled," cautioned Wisdom's Child.

"What do you mean?" asked Prince Aaron.

"We have not seen a handler, yet when they were chasing Hearten, they stayed to a set task, and neither the mage nor the soldiers felt in any danger. This time, however, the mages and the soldiers feel as though they are in danger," said Wisdom's Child. "It might mean that they are controlled through a mind connection, and at this moment, there are too many hounds for the controller to handle, or the handler was so tight into the chase after Hearten that the death of the hounds was his death also."

"I had not thought of that," said Captain Alessia. "It is not something any of us from Asalawn would have thought of."

"Nor we of The Family," commented Aloo.

"You are not remembering the Hands," said Wisdom's Child.

"How do you remember them?" asked Kriss.

"Part of my library is a journal, and they are mentioned as being under complete mind control of the Evil Mage," answered Wisdom's Child.

"So the hounds could be like them in that aspect," said Elder thoughtfully. "How will we be able to tell without alerting whoever controls them?"

"I will look," said Wisdom's Child calmly. "It says in my journal that I would do a light look at the surface of my father's mind in order to anticipate his mood and demands and that he never detected such a touch."

"You were much braver than any of us knew," said Elder with a shudder. "To even have that much mind contact with such an evil creature would have been sickening, and the price you would have paid if he had ever caught you would have been to have your mind removed from your body!"

"It must have been necessary," said Wisdom's Child with a lack of concern that had everyone looking at her with worry. She smiled and said, "To me, reading that journal even though it was written by me is like reading something written by a complete stranger. Now back to planning. Once the kill hounds are out of commission, are there ways for the land teams and the Hazbastas to sneak out?"

"Yes," said Alaw, "we have marked them in our memories and will be sure that the four-foots will have this knowledge as well as the winged."

"Excellent," said Wisdom's Child. "Have the locations been chosen for the lizard men pits?"

"Yes, ma'am," said Tawny, "also the paths for their retreat, ones that hamper the use of their tails."

"Good planning, let's get the nets made and people into position so that we are able to move quickly when the time is right," said Wisdom's Child.

"Alaw, how large are their sand beds?" Wisdom's Child asked.

"About six feet by eight feet," he answered. "Also, they seem to give off heat, and we have noticed that the lizard men do not like the cold."

"That means if I do not want them to realize that they are losing power, they need to feel as though they are warm and comfortable until they arise," she said thoughtfully then she smiled and set about setting the stones from the old seeker/suckers onto her nets.

That afternoon, before the soldiers and wizards returned to their camp, the nets were in place, and you could not tell that the sand had been disturbed. Also, the net traps for the kill hounds were in place, and those whose job it would be to lure them went to the task.

◊   ◊   ◊

Quietly, Triss and her group came through the brush and once they spotted the hounds at a distance veered away, snapping a branch and giving a worried whisper. This was all that it took, and the hounds were after them. Triss, Kerr, Hildy, Prass, Corey, Andsel, and Marista ran like the wind, magically boosted to go faster than they had ever gone before; and still they felt the hounds gaining on them. They put on a burst of speed and wove through the trees, trying to slow the hounds down, but they kept gaining. *They have never been this fast before*, Hildy thought to herself and worried pressed harder, trying to go faster. And just when they were sure the hounds would have them, they passed the net casters, and the hounds were trapped. Tawny ran beside them and said, "You can slow and cool down now," which they did.

Getting her breath back, a very worried Hildy reported to Elder Tawny, "Elder Tawny, they have never been that fast before."

"Wisdom's Child," called Tawny on the War Elders' net. *"Hildy reports that the hounds have never been that fast before."*

"They were being ridden by more than one mage, and they sensed the magic enhancement of our runners. Their lust for the magic had them feeding some of their magic into the hounds," replied The Family's Mage. *"When I realized what was happening, I put more speed into our runners."*

"Our mage says the hounds were being ridden by other mages who sensed the magical enhancement of your speed, and their lust for magic of any kind had them lending power to the hounds. When she realized what was going on, she added more power to your speed," Tawny told her runners. "But with the hounds being ridden by the mages, we will need to kill them."

"Unless Wisdom's Child can get them free of the mages and cause them to become inaccessible to them," said Kerr.

"Wisdom's Child," said Tawny, *"Can you find a way to keep the mages out of the hounds?"*

"I am thinking on it," said Wisdom's Child. *"They would make such a neat end to the lizard men. I have masked the magic enhancement of the other runners. Also, the mages riding these hounds do not seem to be as interested in keeping control over them. Let me look at the minds of the hounds that we have captive."*

Wisdom's Child looked at their minds, blinding their sight, removing their sense of smell, and blocking their hearing, so they would not be able to be used to report anything. With these three senses blocked, the mages who were riding the hounds' minds seem to think them dead and left them. Wisdom's Child finding their path to where they controlled the hounds shut it down and created one that only she or those she told about it could access.

"Tawny, War Elders," mind called Wisdom's Child, *"I have managed to get the mages to believe in the deaths of the hounds. I will do so with the others. Also, I have managed to close their path to the area where they controlled the beasts and created one of my own which I will share with you elders. This way, what was their weapon becomes ours, and our avians can use them to drive the lizard men along the path we want them to go quite effectively."*

"That is a good plan," answered Tawny with a pleased purr in her voice. "Our people are gathering the Hazabastians and guiding them to the safe borders."

"The mages are putting up their safeguards against the hounds crossing the borders for the evenings," said Aloo.

"It would seem that there is not a lot of trust among our enemy," said Wisdom's Child thoughtfully.

"Yes," answered the elders on the elder net to her thought, *"something to think about."*

CHAPTER 16

Clearing Out the Enemy

BEFORE DAWN HAD settled in the sky, the soldiers of Asalawn, the Hazbastas, and The Family were in place. They waited silently while the Wanz soldiers took their places and the lizard men went into their trances. Once they were well into their trances, the allies struck. In teams of two-foots and four-foots, they attacked the soldiers, while the kill hounds, controlled by the avians, charged the lizard men, unnerving them. In a panic, they fled only to find their paths blocked by soldiers of The Family, who they took to be enormous predators trained to kill. Not being able to find time to regroup, they were driven relentlessly to the pits where they fell to their doom, with the kill hounds following after to assure their deaths.

Meanwhile, the soldiers of the Wanz were attacked in a fashion that showed that they had been studied – all of the leaders were eliminated from the groups first. Still they fought valiantly with never a thought of surrender, though they were outnumbered by The Family and two-foots. It did them little good as none survived the attack.

◊ ◊ ◊

Those who were assigned to rescue the hunted Asalawnians found them before they broke camp, if they were close enough, and introduced themselves, asking them the question: can they live with other people not of their species?

"You are being hunted," said Master Forester Fern. "We will lead you on a path that will cause the death of your hunters. We must be careful because there are many hunters out, but we also have many teams out to attack them. Thanks to the members of The Family, the four-footed and winged people, that we have the people and the ability to rid ourselves of these hunters. Have you finished eating?" At their nods, she said, "Good, let us be off." And she led them in the direction that Questa, a young feline, indicated they needed to go. Forester Fern proved to be a good leader and husbanded her group's strength for when they would need to run.

At Brak's signal to Questa, she indicated that they needed to start going faster for the hunters had found their trail, and she put on more speed. Finally, after running for half an hour, Brak signaled that the hunters were taken care of and they could slow down and that they were not near any hunters at the moment.

Fern slowed the pace and let the group cool down properly. Then she asked Questa, "Questa, can you find a stream for us? I am quite thirsty, and the travel food while nourishing is rather dry."

"Yes, ma'am," said Questa and found a quiet stream where they took a rest and ate some more travel cakes.

While Questa was lying at rest, but alert, one of the children, a child of about three, came over and crawled between her front paws under her chin, snuggled in, and went to sleep. Questa was so surprised she just looked at his parents. They were sitting with their mouths open as surprised as she was.

"Well," commented Forester Fern, "he certainly knows where to feel safe now, doesn't him?"

"It would seem so," said the boy's father. "I have never seen him take to anyone like that before."

Questa sighed. "I have this effect on our four-footed and winged children also. Anywhere I sit or lie down, it isn't long before I am surrounded by children."

"Only exceptional people have that effect on children," said the boy's mother. "I have only met one other person, and he was a priest."

"You are right. Only exceptional people do have that effect on children," agreed Master Fern. "What was the priest's name?"

"Why, Father Flin," said the woman.

"You will be happy to know that he survived and is at Refuge," said Fern, and the woman's face lit up.

"It is time for us to move on," said Questa, "Brak has mind spoken that from here to Refuge, there is very little enemy activity and that the attacks at the border the enemy had set up to keep the Hazbastas from escaping the kill hounds were a complete success."

"That is good," said Master Fern. "But he is right. We must get back, and silence must reign," she added kindly when she saw the looks of curiosity on their faces. "We will explain everything once we get to Refuge."

◊ ◊ ◊

Wisdom's Child spoke on the War Elder net out loud so Prince Aaron and those with him could hear. "Alaw, Aloo, I would like you to have the avians direct the kill hounds that remain at the remaining Wanz hunt groups, especially the leaders. If any of the troops try to break away to give warning, be sure they are hunted down. Let the rescuers know what hunt parties you are aiming for and guide them to the hunters' prey. Then have their avian guide lead them away.

"I would like those of The Family and those soldiers who are assigned outlying duty to gather their packs and head to the refugees at the farthest point reachable in two days of two-foot time for now. We need to get the people gathered in.

"I will be gathering in seeker/suckers from beyond where The Family is now and on forward. This will make the towns and farms safe, and we can send people with guards to gather supplies to bring to Refuge. We need to be able to withstand a siege of long standing, say years. I don't propose letting them lock us up in our Refuge. I don't propose letting them even find it or get their balance for one moment. But if I end up fighting the master mage over the container that the magic is currently flowing in, there could be a magic explosion that would cause us not to be able to plant or grow any food in the land for a substantial time. We need to have breathing room to find a solution to such a problem," she finished.

Prince Aaron stood there in silence, shocked, and then said, "It shall be as you command, Eldest" – and bowed – "you have heard elder Wisdom's Child of the War Council. Follow her orders and do so quickly. We need to get every bit of our land back as quickly as we can so that our enemy cannot have its victory." Those who were assigned to go the far distances ran to their packs and joined The Family team they were assigned to and headed back into Asalawn to reclaim what was theirs.

"*Elder Tawny,*" said Wisdom's Child on the War Elder's mind net, "*we need to set spies about. First avian, then four-footed, and even two-footed. I need you to make sure that the two-foots are capable of the tasks we will ask. If I can find the right crystals, I can make whatever is in the bags seem light, and the avians can fly them in the night to wherever we want to place them.*"

"It will be as you desire, Eldest," said Tawny, taking up Prince Aaron's title for her.

"Eldest," Wisdom's Child sighed. *"Well, that will certainly get the point across."* The mind net hummed with humor over this statement.

◊   ◊   ◊

Deep within the Asalawn forest, a family is at bay where the soldiers of the Wanz have them cornered. The parents and larger children are doing their best to defend themselves and the smaller ones with pitchforks and sharpened poles. Then in quiet deadliness, out from the forest comes salvation as the kill hounds leap on their attackers, rendering them to nothing and feeding, ignoring The Family completely and fortunately the rescuer, an avian, who landed with some difficulties through the trees and walked to them.

"Hello," said Scaaz, bowing, "I am of the people species avian and come to lead you to the refuge, which Prince Aaron has found for his people and for ours. That is if you don't mind living with people different from yourselves."

"Can we talk elsewhere?" asked the woman.

"I was hoping you would want to," said Scaaz. "Those things are scary."

The Family carefully made their way around the hounds and their meal and joined Scaaz as he led them deeper into the forest.

"I can't hear them now, and we have a nice stream with a clearing. This seems like a good place," said Scaaz.

"Yes, it is," said the woman. "I am WyAla, and I am a healer and an herb woman. This is my husband Masson, and he is a fashioner of wood."

"I am glad to meet you. The other species people you would be living with at Refuge are feline and canine. Ages ago, we were changed by magic into people with thought, song, and law," answered Scaaz. "Normally, you would have been met by at least one human and a canine and feline group to guide you safely back, but you were in such peril that it was deemed that this was the best plan. Also, you were heading toward more hunters."

"Oh my," said Masson, "we were trying to get to the capital and warn the Regent."

"From what I have been told, this invasion started at the capital with the Regent as one of the victims. Those he brought from foreign lands to protect him from those who had cause to hate him slew him," Scaaz told the shocked couple.

"The enemy tried to kill Prince Aaron and almost succeeded but were thwarted by an amazing twist of fate which caused some of our people. We are of the nation called The Family to be in place to rescue him," Scaaz further reported.

"Our head war elder and her guard rescued your prince, and they also rescued a master healer named Mavis, who is helping to attend to our people."

"Master Mavis survived!" exclaimed WyAla with delight. "Then someone of healing power in this land has survived!"

"Yes, one of our avian people who can see magic discovered what was stealing the magic and life from people and all life from this land," Scaaz informed them. "They call it a seeker/sucker, and it was put in place two years before any of your magic wielders started to become ill by gypsies. It is a magic trap according to our war eldest and can be triggered at any time."

"If that is so, the downfall of our land has been planned for a long time," said Masson.

"But where did all the warriors come from?" asked WyAla.

"They are a people who were developed when we winged and four-footed were and have a chrysalis stage that a mage can hold them in. A mage can hold them in stasis until they are desired, and then have them come out fully, ready to fight," answered Scaaz.

"Are your children able to journey on? My avian guide says that there is a good way clear. If we leave now, we will make it so that we will more quickly meet up with the land team that will be taking you the rest of the way to Refuge. I will be your guide from up high then, and you will be better protected, for the people coming will have soldiers among them," said Scaaz.

"Yes, we can go some more now that the rest and water have refreshed us, along with the journey food you brought," said WyAla with a smile. "Going through this forest with all this brush is not going to be easy for such a large avian."

"It is the tail feathers that can cause the most trouble and I have to walk leaning forward all the time," said Scaaz, as he led the way.

They went until dusk at a gentle pace, coming to a snug little clearing where a fire wouldn't be noticed. They stopped there for the night.

"You do not seem worried about our enemy at night," said one of the boys with concern.

"They always make camp at dusk, and they do not leave their camps until morning is well established. Master Healer Mavis and Master Farmer Seth both believe that they do not have the best eyesight," answered Scaaz.

"Oh," said Masson, "that would explain why we did so well eluding them. We go longer and start earlier."

"My guide says that there are none within two miles from us," said Scaaz, "and there are no lizard men wizards or any other kind of being besides the Wanz soldiers that belong to our enemy for very long ways toward the capital."

"You use mind-speech then?" asked WyAla.

"Yes, can you imagine trying to communicate while flying without it?" answered Scaaz. "We only use mind-speech with those of The Family or if we have been given permission by others. And we only call them if it is an emergency. Speed or silence is vital. We were shocked that you do not use it," went on Scaaz.

"We are afraid of being mind controlled," said Masson.

"A rightful fear," agreed Scaaz. "But are you not taught as children how to shield your mind?"

"How can you do that if you do not have mind powers?" asked Masson.

"Everyone's mind has power. Some do not mind speak, and others do. But everyone's mind has power, and all can shield and should. It is reported that the mage who was hunting Arms Master Hearten used a mind sending. If he could do that, then the mage who answered him could do a mind blast on you and your family, and you would be witless and in their power. So do you want to learn how to shield your and your children's minds also?" asked Scaaz.

"Yes," said WyAla, "I would love to know this. It will make living with people of different species not such a fearful thing, and yes, I would like my children to know how to do this."

"Once you get good at it, you can put it in place. And unless you remove it, it stays in place. Also, there is a way to put the shield behind the communication center of your mind and a light one in front of it. That way, people can communicate with you in an emergency. That is the kind of shield I use. They kind of put a little pressure on the light mind shield to get my attention by thinking my name at me, and then they wait for me to lower it and answer. This is the shield I will teach you if that is all right." WyAla nodded.

"All right," said Scaaz, "let us begin."

After his students went to sleep tired but happy with the idea that they could protect their minds, Scaaz sent out word on the mind net to Alaw, "*Elder Alaw, my people did not know they could shield their minds from others, and this caused them great fear about living with us. Could you have the other people of this land receive this training right away? It made my people quite a bit happier. The husband Masson is a powerful sender and needs some guidance in this area.*"

"*I will report this to Prince Aaron. It will certainly make his people much more comfortable with ours,*" answered Alaw. "*Thank you for your excellent problem solving and suggestion, Scazz, good job.*"

"*You are welcome,*" came a pleased but shy reply over the net.

◊ ◊ ◊

"*Alaw, Elders,*" Wisdom's Child called as she woke Prince Aaron, Arms Master Hearten, and Captain Alessia.

Wisdom's Child speaking aloud and in mind-speech said, "I have put further guards on the kill hounds so that they cannot be wrested from our control. Today should see the rest of the refugees rescued and tomorrow the last of the enemy in the territory we have designated. To ensure that we retain our hold on these lands, I propose that we use the kill hounds as border guards and use them to harass the enemy whenever they are close to the lands we have reclaimed."

Hearten laughed with delight. The idea of turning those dreadful hounds back on the enemy so thoroughly delighted him, and he said, "I for one am for it."

"I would be more comfortable with the notion," said Tawny, *"if they are given specific directives on what they can attack."*

"Yes," said Wisdom's Child, "I have seen to that already. This will enable any other refugees to get into safe land. Then we can send our two – and four-foot guards to bring them to Refuge."

"With the towns and villages safe, I am afraid that my people will want to move from Refuge to them," said Prince Aaron, "especially the Hazbastas."

"That is a good concern," said Hildy. "I do not believe that it would be a good idea for us to do that. We need to be together, for there is strength in numbers."

"Our removal of their wizards and the clean sweep of this much territory, plus the magic they sensed from the runners, will have them believing that a mage of considerable power has moved into these lands," said Wisdom's Child, "and I think that they will try and launch an attack on us. If they do that, we will not be able to protect those who are not within Refuge, for we will be at war."

"I will explain this to them," said Prince Aaron and Hildy together.

"You explain it, Prince Aaron," said Hildy, "and I will back you up."

"Hildy, what rank do you hold among your people," asked Prince Aaron.

Hildy sighed. "Much the same as Arms Master Hearten," she answered. "It was I who figured out how to kill the hounds, how to hold safe from them, and how not to panic. Because we live on the border of Asalawn, we have to deal with the worse our neighbors can give us, and all women have learned soldiery. The men and children know how not to panic no matter what and to take defensive measures. I am responsible for all of this."

"You have quite a bit of say then over your people," said Prince Aaron. "That will be helpful. If they, whose homes have been made safe from the kill hounds, choose to stay at Refuge, then the others, who are not of such great numbers, will also see the sense of it. Thank you for your support, Hildy."

"We have decided to join the land we have settled in, Prince Aaron. We will not go back to our decision without giving it a try and a try of more than a few months. The adjustment may take two or more generations. Our males are not happy with the idea of being equals," answered Hildy.

"How do the women feel about it?" asked Aloo, who was at the meeting.

"Some are for it. Others are not, and others are unsure," answered Hildy.

Captain Alessia gave her a sympathetic smile. "Change is hard, and everyone is having trouble with it. Especially not falling back into the self-centeredness that made us blind to what was going on around us, leaving us easy pickings so to speak for our enemies."

"Yes, we too fell into that trap in our different communities, and I with my work felt too important to be bothered with civil things," said Hildy with a sigh. "We are paying a high toll for our self-centeredness."

Prince Aaron sighed and gave Hildy a comradely hug. "We have all realized or are realizing this lesson, but now we need to focus on surviving. What else, Eldest?" he asked Wisdom's Child.

"First we need to get aerial spying done. We need to see if they have reserves they can send out from behind us. What harbors do they hold that are close to us? I am wondering, why did they send kill hounds, instead of soldiers into Hildy's land? When the time comes to send land spies in, I hope that Elder Tawny will have trained the two-foots to work with our four-foot teams. We will be able to drop them in at night via avian bag if I can find suitable crystals to lighten the bags so that nothing weighs more than what will just stabilize the bags for flying."

"And because they are lined with magic-resistant linings, the magic will not be detectable," said Captain Alessia.

"Yes, but I need to make sure there is not the smell of magic on the travelers. I think they will fly in magic-resistant suits and take them off when they land," said Wisdom's Child.

"We know what we will be doing today. Our focus is on the hunted," said Elder. "Let us get our day started. We have at least two hundred people to gather in today."

"And today will see the way clear for our children to reach Refuge," said Aloo happily.

◊ ◊ ◊

"Triss," said Prass as they loped along at a mile-eating pace, "Scaaz says that he has been teaching his family how to mind shield."

"Good," said Triss, "Prince Aaron sent word back to Refuge that all should have this training. We can't have the children of The Family showing us up now, can we? I believe that was the tone of the missive."

Prass gave a feline grin. "That should motivate some of the baulkers."

"I know it has really only been days, but I wish they would embrace change faster," was Triss' comment.

"Once we get everyone in and settled, Wisdom's Child wants to explore the lower caves," said Prass, changing the topic to a happier one. "I am going to be sure to be one of the guards."

"Sounds like a great plan to me," said Triss. "Count me in. Is Alassfan signaling that we are near?"

"Yes, let's slow to a walk and cool down a bit," said Prass.

"Works for me," said Triss, who slowed and then walked.

They met their refugees in about twenty minutes.

"Ho, Scaaz," said Prass, "it is good to see you."

"And I you," said Scaaz, "but I thought it would take you much longer to reach us. I know from my lessons that two-foots are not as fast as four-foots." Then seeing Triss looking at him with an amused grin flushed around his beak, he said in a flustered voice, "No offense intended!"

"None taken," said Triss. "Four-foots are faster than two-foots. I am a cross-country runner, so I have more endurance and speed, for a two-foot that is, for long distances."

"I remember you," said WyAla's oldest daughter. "You won the cross-country race last year in such a good time that people tried to say you cheated. But the judges would have none of that. They had watched you the whole circuit."

"Yeah," said her brother, "the other runners didn't start coming in until fifteen to twenty minutes later."

Triss laughed and answered, "I love to run. When I am stationed somewhere, I get up before duty time and run for ten miles or more if I have the light for it. I try to take different routes so I cover different types of ground."

Zelvet, a young canine, looked at her and asked, "You run just because you love to run?" She had such a funny look on her face that Triss burst out laughing.

"I know from what Lady Aloo has said that you had a joyless life under the Evil Mage. So the idea of doing something that you love to do must seem very odd to you," Triss said kindly.

"Oh," said all three of The Family, standing there, taking in this concept.

"This means we will be able to do things, as long as they do not break the rules, for the joy of doing them like you do running!" exclaimed Zelvet. She got so excited she practically did flips.

"Do you have a secret thing you love to do but have always had to hide it?" asked Prass in concern.

"Yes," said Zelvet, "I love to make poems and songs and to sing! And now when it is safe, I can!"

The two-foots looked on the young canine and could not help but share her and the others joy at realizing this.

"My guide says that this is a safe spot for you to rest and eat and that we have moved further from the enemy. Our warriors, both of this land and The Family, have been very successful in their strategies against them. Our leaders believe that tomorrow will see the end of them in the territory that we retake for ourselves," said Scaaz. "And I will take up my duty as your guide now, well, after I have caught my lunch!"

"You only have to go down the trail a ways to find your lunch, Scaaz," said Prass. "We couldn't imagine a harder or longer day for you than walking all this way, so we hunted for you. Ericks and Geoff are guarding it."

"Oh, thank you!" said a happy and hungry avian hurrying off.

"Scaaz has been so helpful and such good company," said WyAla. "But he was right his tail feathers were the biggest problem. He had to lean very far forward, and still they dragged. When we came to muddy spots, we made him stop, and the children held them up until we reached dry land again."

Everyone chuckled at this picture, and then Triss said, "Let me introduce the rest of our party now that Geoff and Ericks have arrived. They are some of the youths from Refuge who have shown some skill with the blade and hammer. The feline person with us is Prass, and the canine is Zelvet."

"I am WyAla, and this is my husband Masson. I am a healer and an herb woman, and Masson is a shaper of wood," WyAla said.

"What is the difference between a carpenter and a shaper of wood?" asked Prass.

"A shaper of wood releases from within the wood its beauty in shapes and forms not always for practical use but always for the delight of the eye," said Triss to her. "When they do create, the practical is always a work of art and something only the richest in the land can afford."

"Oh," said Prass, "this is something new to us also. Life is going to be so much more interesting now that we are free."

"How long have you been free?" asked Masson.

"Not long," said Prass. "Our elder, Wisdom's Child, was put in command of us decades ago by her father, the Evil Mage, told to train us for war, and that we were to be able to survive outside of his lands without magic. He tortured her ruthlessly as he drew from her the promise that she would see to our survival to the very best of her ability. But in truth, once we were trained as warriors, she knew he would fear us and kill us. So the only way we would be able to survive would be with his death. That is why he had to torture the promise out of her. He did not know what he was asking, but she did. And then one day, she became happy. At first, the mage couldn't find the happiness, which was never allowed in his land. He searched and searched until finally he created a very complicated spell and discovered that the happiness came from her, his child. He could not believe it, and he flew into a rage, torturing her mercilessly and demanding to know whom she loved. But she would not tell him, and he wouldn't have believed her even if she had told him. For years before, she had sworn her hatred for him. He had her thrown into a dungeon, and two weeks later, practically skipping with glee, he entered his throne room and called for her. He tortured her out of habit and asked whom she loved, but she, weak and bedraggled, would not tell. She told him she didn't know his name, and he said she didn't need to know his name. And putting the spell on her, he told her the minute she pointed at whom she loved, she would destroy that person utterly. She tried hard not to point, as sweat rolled from her brow. But slowly, her arm lifted, and she pointed straight at her father. He had time for a single shriek, and then his spell took him, and he died. She finished healing herself, gathered power to herself, and sent her voice throughout the keep and land, having everyone running for the aviary and the kennels. She helped us gather our children in bags and pouches she had made especially for our escape with all of our loved ones. When we got through the opening of the pass, she stayed behind and gathered more and more power until you could hardly see her. When the sounds coming from the keep reached a certain pitch, she threw up a shield to protect us. Still the blast was so powerful that we were tossed about like autumn leaves, and she was so injured that she couldn't regain consciousness.

"And that is why we were in your lands when the invasion started, well, six of us were, along with Wisdom's Child. I was one of the original guards and helped her rescue Prince Aaron and Healer Mavis from her burning cottage when the enemy left. They were so hurt that it was good that Master Mavis's healing worked. For Wisdom's Child is a master healer as well as our eldest war elder. Has everyone finished eating? Good, let us be on our way," said Prass, changing the subject.

"Wisdom's Child is the only two-foot member of The Family," said Triss, "and her name evolved from The Child, to Old Child, until now Wisdom's Child."

"What does she think of these names?" asked Zelvet.

"Now that is a good question," said Triss. "I don't think anyone thought to ask her about that."

"How old is she, and why is child always in her name?" asked WyAla.

"Because she is enchanted to never age or die and looks to be nine years old by two-foot age," said Prass. "Even we of The Family, who were always around her, have fallen into the trap of seeing her as a child. It is very frustrating, but she is generally kind about it or doesn't correct you at all."

"It will be nice to have more healers at Refuge," said Geoff. "With Healer Wisdom's Child working as a war elder, we are down to one, and The Family is arriving with many pregnant females. Elder Yass has told Master Mavis that they have trouble with births also."

WyAla looked surprised at his concern.

"My sister died from childbirth, her and the baby. We do not take child birth lightly in our household," Ericks answered for his brother.

"That would sober anyone," said Masson quietly. Then changing the subject asked, "How far do we have to go?"

"We were within ten miles from you," said Geoff, indicating himself, Ericks, and Zelvet, "last night and started for you this morning. Triss and Prass caught up with us about an hour ago and kindly slowed the pace. About thirty to thirty-five miles as we on feet go I would guess."

"That would be about right," said Triss, who had grinned at the kindly-slowed-the-pace remark. "So at a pace children can go, it will be three days before we reach Refuge, but your cave has already been reserved for you. Also, Father Flin was very excited about hearing of your survival, WyAla."

WyAla smiled with happiness that at this dreadful time, an old friend was to be found alive. "He took me out of the streets, fed, clothed, taught me, and found me a profession away from the Regent!"

"He has been doing such deeds for decades, and many have cause for gratitude," said Masson, putting an arm around his wife.

"You know, Triss, and, Prass," said Geoff, "we will make better time if we carry the next littlest ones. The parents are carrying the smallest, and we are a lot bigger than they are. Also, we are supposed to gather children and flee should the enemy come upon us."

"That is sensible," said Prass. "Scaaz is signaling that some are drawing near. Triss, take the lead, everyone else in the middle, Zelvet to the left side, and I will take the rear. That is the way they approach from."

Triss stepped up the pace, but the Wanz seemed to know of them and followed. "One holds a globe in his hand," Scaaz mind spoke Prass.

"We must put on more speed for they will never cease and only go faster. One holds a magic-tracking globe," said Prass. They went faster, but still not fast enough, and the enemy caught them in a clearing. They put the children in the center and fought with grim determination. Triss and Prass, knowing how to take the enemy down, were happy that there were only four coming at them. The first soldier to go was the lead soldier, with Prass coming at him from the side and knocking him down as Triss cut his legs off at the knees and cut off his head. They had finished killing their last enemy when turning, they saw Zelvet jump to block a sword thrust to the chest of Masson, taking the wound herself and falling to the ground. The two killed the soldier in moments and went on to those who were after WyAla in particular, also Geoff and Ericks. The children had made themselves as small and close to the ground as possible as they had been instructed and stayed put so their parents would know where they were. Triss and Prass took care of one soldier and Geoff and Ericks the last.

"WyAla ran to Zelvet and knelt beside her, offering comfort, as she looked at a wound that could only bring death. Her eyes welled with tears at the hopes and joys of this person being cut off so soon. Prass came quickly to her side and went to Zelvet's head. "Oh, precious one, how can this be? How cruel is war that you, our first poet, our first singer of songs, should die before we hear even one?"

"I hurt, oh how I hurt, and all my songs dammed up inside me about to burst will never be sung." Taking shaking breaths of pain, she asked, "Why, why when finally I realized my freedom?" Then she closed her eyes and died.

"We must run. More come this way, but from farther away. More of our soldiers are coming, those of The Family, for they are the fastest. We are being directed to where they can entrap the enemy and the avians can join in battle. What they can do to devastate the enemy in an open battlefield is much," said Prass, unshed tears in her voice. And as she ran, she thought, *"Here is one more freedom. Our grief will not be turned to dark power for the Evil Mage to use."*

Even when darkness fell in the understory of the forest, Triss, Prass, and the rest pressed on. Once free of the forest and in clearer running ground, they stopped and slept without a fire and replenished themselves with travel food and water. They arose before dawn, ate hastily, and started again. Triss, a good leader of two-foots, kept the pace to a fast walk for the oldest children as the youngest four were carried.

When morning was well established, Scaaz mind spoke to Prass, *"They are ten miles behind you, and there are starting to be a large number of them. Here is something interesting. A being is carried on some kind of chair by some of the largest Wanz I have seen. I have reported it, and Anvar is looking to see if it is a magic wielder."*

"Find us paths that the chair cannot follow," said Prass. "Triss, we may have a magic worker following us. They have over twenty Wanz, but there is one being in a sedan chair carried by four of the largest Wanz Scaaz has ever seen."

"Yes, I have seen such in the capital and on the main roads. Interestingly enough, those large carriers do not seem to be warriors, but servants only," replied Triss. "I take you instructed Scaaz to direct our path to their difficulty?"

"Oh yes," said Prass, and they continued on in silence, everyone concentrating on not lagging behind, while Triss concentrated on not pushing beyond what they could do.

"Geoff," Triss called to the lad in front, "let us take a rest."

"Yes, ma'am," he said in relief.

"Prass, let's go back a ways and see if what I was thinking is a possibility," said Triss.

"What is in your mind?" asked Prass.

"There are a lot of loose boulders and some small and medium slide areas," said Triss, "not enough to stop them, but enough to slow them down. They have the scent of magic. You and I can stay back and activate them while the others go ahead since you go faster than I and the avians faster than you. If they get here in time, we can pick off the mountainside those who are forced to climb and not use the trail. We should see if we can get a good boulder on that sedan chair, and if not, run like the wind."

"I like it!" said Prass. "Right now my heart burns in me for the death of Zelvet and all I want is their destruction!"

"Pretty much my sentiment," said Triss to her companion.

"I will give instruction to the others, while you pick out the most likely looking boulders to create the mayhem you were speaking of," said Prass and turning went hurriedly to get their party moving once more.

Reaching them, it was clear that the children had been crying. "What goes on here?" asked Prass.

"The children sorrow over Zelvet," said their father with rather watery eyes himself.

"I know how they feel, but we must honor her sacrifice and win the race against the enemy. In order to do that, you need to go on with Geoff and Ericks, who Scaaz will guide from above, while Triss and I drop big rocks on their heads and cause them all kinds of trouble. Scaaz's people will attack them from the sky, and during that time, you need to set a good distance-eating pace to get as far toward safety as possible. We probably won't get them all, and we won't know if we do or not until the other avians tell Scaaz. Once we have done the damage we can do, Triss and I will catch up with you," Prass explained. They nodded and started on their way.

Prass returned and found Triss a considerable way back from where they left the others. "I saw the boulders that you had marked, and that was a good thought, for we will be hurrying from one to the other."

"I have numbered how I want them to go down the mountain," said Triss with a smile that boded her enemies no good. "Now for patience. patience is not my strong suit, but one I learned under the harsh tutelage of a soldier's life."

They waited in silence for half an hour before the first soldiers started to climb the slope. It was as Scaaz had told them. The number of Wanz had grown from ten to more than forty. When the Wanz reached a point in their climb where Triss could only see one, they went to boulder one. Then the two, using their weight, shifted the boulder forward until its own weight started it down the hill. At the first sign of its downward movement, they ran carefully, making sure they used cover to the next boulder. Boulder one had the satisfying effect of wiping out the front group of the Wanz. But the group behind pushed them out of the way and rushed onward where they too met with disaster. It seemed as though the mountain was enchanted against them, for they never once got a glimpse of their assailants. This time, a small landslide was triggered that sent about ten of the enemy rolling down the mountain.

"Freeze, Triss," said Prass in a whisper, "magic is being used to try and find us." They stayed frozen in place for fifteen minutes, and then Prass said in a barely audible whisper, "Anvar gives us the all clear but says that we probably should withdraw and catch up with the others as quickly as stealth allows. She does say that this was a good idea for two reasons. One getting rid of over half of the pursuers, and two, it showed her quite clearly that it was indeed a magic wielder in the sedan chair."

Triss nodded and signaled for them to leave. They were painstakingly careful not to be discovered on their return. Only when they were sure they would not be seen did they put on speed, glad to run just for the sheer release of the tension.

It took them about an hour to catch up, and they motioned for them to keep going while Triss told them, "They have a magic wielder with them. We dropped half or so off the mountain before it tried to find us. It did not, but Anvar suggested doing more was a bad idea. So once she gave the all clear, we left," Triss finished, not even out of breath.

"We need to take up running," said Ericks, eyeing Triss enviously. His brother nodded in agreement.

They traveled the whole afternoon before they heard again from Scaaz about their enemy. *"The Eldest elder has taken an active part in this situation. She had us do so much without magic that I forgot she is a mage! She has netted the magic wielder, and the avians have attacked and killed all the rest of those who pursue you. She, Wisdom's Child I mean, will be joining you soon."*

Prass relayed this information to the others, and they stopped and rested, easing aching muscles. "Okay," said Triss after a minute, "every two foot at least and maybe you too, Prass, start stretching. Remember, the Eldest, Wisdom's Child, is a master healer. And you, WyAla, would get the worst of it being a healer yourself. Let's stretch and get the kinks out."

"I am stretching," said Prass. "I am stretching! How could I have forgotten? You do not know how embarrassing she can make it for you if you forget!"

A laugh was heard behind them. "I am glad that you remembered. You put in a remarkable amount of miles. I am grieved at the loss of Zelvet. I had hoped that finally I would get to hear the music in her soul, and when she had just realized her freedom, but better than freedom unrealized."

One of the children began to weep, and Wisdom's Child, opening her arms to her, received the grieving child. "She saved my daddy," said the little girl.

Hugging her, Wisdom's Child wept with her and smoothing her hair back said, "Zelvet was very brave. She was a warrior, and this was her first battle. Sometimes, warriors do not live through their first battle."

"When she was trying to gather breathe, I had mind-speech with her, and she gave me her songs," said Prass, tears rolling from her eyes as she lay down, and for the first time grieved as she should.

Wisdom gathered the child to her and went to Prass, sitting by the huge feline, comforting her and weeping with her. "Thank you, Prass, for saving some of the beauty that was Zelvet for us and for her parents. I have hidden in my bag a crystal that has some of her poems. When she could not keep them inside, I would have her think them at it. This was when she was a child. When she became an adult, she had better discipline and life was so busy that she no longer needed it and told me so. She was afraid the Mage would find it, so I hid it in the avians bags."

"She said she was giving me her heart to treasure it and use it," said Prass. "I wonder what she meant by that."

"It sounds like she gave more than just what she has created," said Wisdom's Child. "But you are the one, dear, who will have to decide what to do with it. I would talk with the two-foot bards. I think they will be honored to make known the works of Zelvet from childhood to adult."

"That is a comfort, Eldest," said Prass with a sigh and closed her eyes in quiet weeping.

"I will fix dinner this night," said Wisdom's Child in her healer's voice. "This has been too trying a day for all of you. And you, WyAla, are showing power, and so are your children."

"What?" said WyAla, jumping up with a shocked look as she rushed to Wisdom's Child where she worked by the fire.

"Yes, one of our avians, Anvar, can see magic. Except for Masson, all of you are showing it," answered the Eldest absentmindedly as she concentrated on dinner.

WyAla just went and sat by her husband. "But how can this be?" she asked.

"I am not sure, but I will look into it," said Wisdom's Child. "But not soon. We are very busy."

"While I am cooking, why don't you set up camp and bring in wood for the morning? You will not need such a fast pace to get to Refuge from here," said Wisdom's Child with a master's tone to her voice.

"Are you sure she is really old?" came a little whisper from next to Prass.

"She is older than the oldest person you ever met," said Prass. "Remember, magic was used to make it so she would never grow old. If she grew to a certain age, she would be able to come into her full power, and then her father would have been afraid of her. So he made sure she could not get older than she is now. But Master Healer Mavis says that any human being who has lived for decades is an adult no matter what she looks like, and she is Master Healer Mavis's healer."

"Really?" asked WyAla. She looked at Wisdom's Child and asked incredulously, "You bossed Master Mavis around?"

"Yes. She almost died from the wounds she received, and as I was healing from the magic blast, my power was low. Also, she seemed afraid to use hers, and that worried me, so I had to do the healing the old non-magical way. The medicine she and Prince Aaron had to take was pretty awful, but she mostly was a good patient," said Wisdom's Child with a smile at the shocked look on the woman's face.

"Yes, anything that would worry or frighten Master Mavis is something to worry or fear about," agreed WyAla after several minutes.

◊ ◊ ◊

When the family woke in the morning, it was to find a nourishing porridge cooking. With Triss at the cook pot, they looked around for the Eldest, and Triss seeing this said, "She is gone. She left last night after everyone had settled down. Now that her magic is coming back in full force, she finds she needs to use it constantly. So she flew back to be with the rest of the war council and decide on the mopping up and see if she could learn anything from the mage they netted yesterday."

"She can fly?" asked an astounded Geoff.

"Yes," said Prass, "that is how she supervised the mock battles we would engage in and how she operated the fake armies we fought against."

"What about the seeker/suckers?" asked Masson.

"She has removed them all and turned them to her purpose which is of course our purpose. The crystals and stones that caused the traps to function are what she used in the net she put over the mage she caught yesterday," said Prass.

"Just how much power do you think she has and how much would she have had, had she grown to her adult age?" WyAla pondered.

"That kind of boggles the mind," said Prass, "and I have the Evil Mage to go by."

"We have legends, but none of the wizards had the power she seems to display nor the ease of use," said Ericks.

"Well, except those in the tales of the Evil Mages and the twelve who battled him. It is believed that no one of such power as they has ever been born since that time," said Masson.

"It is believed that the Evil Mage of long ago was her father," said Triss.

"What!" exclaimed everyone.

"He stopped not only her aging but also his," said Prass. "If you can do that, the years hold no importance to you."

"When the spell was broken, he turned to dust," said Prass.

"Oh, well, that is a bit of good news then," said Masson in a greatly relieved voice. "I may still have bad dreams with the knowledge that such a creature was my neighbor all those years, but good news nonetheless." He had such a funny look on his face that all the grown-ups laughed.

"Well, we had better get our day started. We can walk, but it is still a ways to go," said Triss.

CHAPTER 17

Strategies of the RESCUER

"*Elder,*" MIND CALLED Wisdom's Child, "*how goes it with our prisoner?*"

"You were right to put up the shield. Even though he is losing power, he keeps sending out tendrils of magic, seeking to learn what he can," answered the great feline.

"How is the net doing for containing his magic?" she asked.

"It seems like it is getting full," said Elder.

"I will cleanse it, and then find a place to store it," said Wisdom's Child.

"You can cleanse magic?" asked Elder.

"Yes, I read how to in my journal. It was connected to my father, so I did not remember how to do it. I learned how to so I could feel clean after he healed me," said Wisdom's Child.

"I can understand the desire to feel clean after such a creature touched you, especially to your bones," said Elder with a shudder.

"I have arrived, and my, my, but he has been putting out quite a bit of power. Will you make sure that I am not bothered? I am not needed with the cleanup of our enemies with the exception of this one," commanded Wisdom's Child.

"It will be as you command, Eldest," said Elder respectfully and left, letting those who needed to know that their mage was back and at work.

Wisdom studied the way the captive mage was working his magic, finding it interesting and very revealing. Then settling on the floor, she began to strip the magic from the web, cleanse, and store it in an unassuming boulder that's inside was almost completely crystal. She sat there patiently monitoring the prisoner and his power level, as well as cleansing the magic and storing it. Finally, when he stopped spending his magic and all the sucker was pulling from him was his life's energy, she removed the net from him and had guards blindfold him and take him to a cave prepared for questioning.

Once that was done, she joined Prince Aaron and Eldest of the Hazbastas to decide on what questions they wished to ask. "I think we should not do this with mind-touch," said Wisdom's Child. "If they are capable of mind sendings, they are capable of mind traps. We can, however, monitor him for lies and partial truths."

"I would like him to be asked questions by a voice with an accent he would not recognize," said Prince Aaron.

"I also," said the Eldest of the Hazbastas. "I believe Kriss should be the one to ask them. He has a less deep voice than Elder, and his would come from an acceptable height, whereas Alaw's would be from too much height."

"That is an excellent notion," said Prince Aaron and Wisdom's Child at the same time.

"Kriss," called Wisdom's Child on the elder's net, *"we would like you to ask the questions, so as not to give too much information away. Let me remember our discussion for you."*

"That is a very good idea," said Kriss. *"I will be there right away."*

The floor of the cavern the prisoner was in was covered with a thick layer of straw, as was the hall before it, for silence sake. He sat as Wisdom's Child had commanded, tied to a chair and blindfolded. Hearing the rustling of feet on the straw, he began sniffing the air to try and discover something about his captors. "So you come with dogs fearing me so much, do you?" And he laughed with bravado. "And so you should. I am one of the strongest of the human mages in this land, and when my power regenerates, I will kill you all."

"You will not be allowed to ever have your power again," said Kriss. "It will be stripped from you."

The man looked frightened for a moment but decided to continue on the path of threats he had begun on.

"Enough," said Kriss. "We wish information and not a bunch of idiot talk." Seeing that the man was going to be stubborn until he did indeed have his power stripped, Kriss mind spoke to Wisdom's Child. *"I am sorry, dear, but you are going to have to strip him, as the mage did to those whose power he wanted."*

"I read of it in my journal, and how to do it, but it seemed so violent and cruel. Let us step out into the hallway and tell Aaron and Eldest what you want me to do," replied Wisdom's Child. And indicating to the other two, they left the room and went down the hall.

When they were sure that they would not be heard, Kriss began, "I have asked Wisdom's Child to remove the magic from this man ruthlessly as the Evil Mage would do. Having no hope of his power returning is the only way that we will break him so that he will cooperate. I am sure Wisdom's Child has figured out how to block his magic to keep it from returning, but as long as he doesn't feel the pain of the loss, he will not believe it will never return."

"I agree," said Prince Aaron.

The Hazbastas Eldest nodded her head in agreement, and seeing the distressed look on Wisdom's Child's face, she looked sternly at both men and said, "This will be done only with us three present and none, Kriss, none will know that she has done this. Many of your elders do not fully trust Wisdom's Child, including Lady Aloo, who has watched the person she has become from the beginning. Her commanding the clearing out of the enemy so effectively, even though she is the only one among us trained to take up such command, is also causing problems."

"Oh," said Kriss, "I had not realized that there was a problem among The Family. The youth seem to interact with you well, and you don't hesitate to have mind-speech on the elder or war net, but," he said thoughtfully, "you never have private mind-speech with certain individuals. I am sorry for not being better aware, Wisdom's Child. We cannot allow such prejudices to continue. We need to constantly treat you as our senior leader and also with friendship. You are correct, Eldest of the Hazbastas. This needs to be kept private among the three of us."

"I agree," said Prince Aaron. "Many at Refuge who participated in the fighting and realized the orders were from their healer had a terrible time with it. But your people said that you had no choice but to be a commander, for that is what your father demanded of you and that you had trained the elders to command also. But someone had to coordinate everything and see the big picture. It was a tremendous help when they could see it in that light."

"Still there is a deep sense of not right within me," said Wisdom's Child. "I will do this my way. In a way, I hope I will convince him of the loss of his power. I will need a sucker net, and it will need to be placed in front of him. We will stand behind him, and his head will be held in position so he can only look forward. He will feel his magic control center and all the lines of power leave his body. He will see them pool in front of him and know what they are. Then he will watch as they are consumed. I hope you don't mind if I leave after I do this. I think it is going to make me sick to my stomach."

"I will leave with you, and we can get some fresh air together," said the Hazbastas Eldest.

They reentered the room when everything was according to Wisdom's Child's instructions, and she removed the block. The mage feeling power coming back almost crowed in triumph. "Ha! It won't be long until I kill you all." And Kriss nodded to Wisdom's Child. She reached into the man's body where the magic was gathering. Touching it, she lifted the control area from his brain. He screamed in fear and then in disbelief as she lifted all the pathways where magic would normally have flown in his body. Out they came, pooling on the table before him, glittering with power, and then fading, growing smaller, and turning into nothing as the sucker pulled the magic into itself. He screamed in rage. His power gone, never to be his again. His eyes and inner senses told him so. He went into a panic, screaming and moaning. Hysterical over the loss, he was so upset that he became physically ill and passed out.

Wisdom's Child left hurriedly, and the Hazbastas Eldest followed her out. They just made it outside before Wisdom's Child vomited. She crouched beside a boulder and shook crying so hard the sobs racked her body. Eldest sat beside her and held her, rocking her gently, soothing her hair back, and having her wash her mouth out from her water bottle.

When Wisdom's Child had calmed down, the Eldest said, "Child, I know that you are more ancient than I. But I also have taken to heart, and especially now, that indeed with the loss of any memory you have associated with the Evil Mage, you are starting anew and so do not know how to buffer you heart against having to do such things. But I doubt if I would have responded any differently than you did. Your solution was the right one. There was no need to apply the cruelty of the Evil Mage, and to do so may have caused you to lose a battle you have spent a lifetime fighting. A battle that you wouldn't remember because it is associated with the Evil Mage, but you would have strong feelings about it.

"As a healer, Wisdom's Child dear," said the Eldest, "I am sorry for holding out on you and Master Mavis. I believe you should take a sleeping draught right after you have eaten, and then go to bed. You should eat as soon as we get back."

A weary Wisdom's Child leaned back against the comforting presence of the woman and nodded her head.

◊ ◊ ◊

Setting the chair and man upright, Prince Aaron stepped back to join Kriss. "Well, do you care to answer our questions?" asked Kriss.

"Why should I? I have nothing to lose," said the man bitterly

"We can return you to your master," said Kriss.

The man blanched. "They would feed me to the larva, for I would be of no use to them, except as their food."

"Then tell us what we want to know or we will make sure your masters receive you alive and well," said Kriss. "I don't imagine that they will be pleased that you botched your mission. Do they have other things worse than the larva that they can do to you?"

The man looked paler still.

"Let us start with your mission. What was it?"

"It was to find out who was stopping the magic flow from the luck tokens," said the man. "I was to find out what was happening in this area, for the Lazzindaphs had not reported in as they were commanded to."

"Then they detected new power in this area and sent me to capture this new source of power," said the man. "They did not believe that this person had a significant amount of power because the magics they detected were small."

"They were a bit overconfident," said Kriss dryly.

"Yes," said the man bitterly. "A mage who can fly, create magic equally as good as theirs for sucking power from a person, and strip a person of their ability to do magic is more powerful than the head mage would want to face alone."

"Now that you have gone missing, what do you think will they believe?" asked Kriss.

"That there is either more than one mage or they have underestimated the power of the mage that they sent me to hunt down, or that I met with an accident," answered the man. "They would only believe the last if my magic returned to feed the head mage."

"Which it won't," said Kriss.

"How many Wanz do they have?" asked Kriss.

"They have twenty thousand in the city. They have four thousand in this area, and they have thirty thousand throughout the rest of Asalawn. They are trying to keep the people of Lacy Downs sealed in their town and mines. We can't do any magic there. When we do, it is used against us," the man told them.

Kriss and Prince Aaron looked at each other with lifted brows and grins. Good news at last!

"Are there any people in the capital who have been able to hold out since this invasion started?" asked Kriss.

"Yes, a smithy is holding out, but he can't escape down the sewers for the larva has been loosed and their slime will eat you. And if it doesn't eat you, once it gets into your blood, you are poisoned and will die a terrible death. They sacrifice different Wanz to be their herders so they are not damaged by the high tide," said the man snidely. "The Wanz are so stupid they do not know how to be afraid for their lives. If they are told it is good for the hive, they do it."

"Has a hive with a queen been established here?" asked Kriss.

"No. That's somewhere else on an island," said the man. "The queen grants authority to a head mage, and then he can act in her place. They will do anything he wants."

"Is your head mage expecting any more ships in, and is he under the command of another?" asked Kriss.

"I do not know. They do not tell us much, especially we humans," answered the man. "The head mage is not human. I don't know what he is. To know is to be seen no longer, and that curbed my curiosity completely. He has those who worship him as though he is a god. I act that way, otherwise I might get to know what he is," the man said dryly. Then suddenly, he drooped.

Prince Aaron going over to the man saw that he was out and could not be woken. Shaking his head at Kriss, they left. When they got to the front of the tunnel, they came upon Eldest holding Wisdom's Child, who slept, her faced streaked with tears and such a sad look on it that both men felt stabs to their hearts.

The Eldest looked at them and said sternly, "Never ask her to do cruel violence, especially that of the Evil Mage. Her response was totally emotional, but it was as though to do that would have caused her to lose something precious of herself. Her solution was just as effective and not so physically cruel, even though it was harsh on the man."

"She never did such acts at the keep. Her father did them through her, but he could not force her to do them. He tortured her for days to get her to do them, and she refused. She would not have remembered that, and I should have," said Kriss, sorrowed at the hurt he had caused.

"And I having been around her all this time. I should have realized that she is not capable of such without great hurt to herself," said Prince Aaron. "So involved in what I wanted right now, I was not willing to look for a different way. I am glad she is wise and could find another way, but it still hurt her heart."

"We are all guilty of that one," said the Eldest sadly.

"Here, let me carry her," said Prince Aaron, and he picked her up from the Eldest's lap.

With his lifting her from Eldest's lap, she woke and said, "Let me walk, and let our walk take some time so that Eldest and I know what he said."

"All right, but first we need to get someone to clean him up," said Kriss, wrinkling his nose.

Wisdom's Child looked into his room and magically cleaned the whole thing, including him, but left the prisoner tied to the chair.

"I have cleaned him," said Wisdom's Child. "The fewer people he has interaction with, the better. But we need to make him a more effective prison than his chair."

"True," said Prince Aaron, "and one where he can take care of personal needs. He was quite obliging when we suggested we could return him to his master. There seems to be a head mage, who isn't human, but he doesn't know what he is and worked hard at not finding out. It seems when you do, you are never seen again. They have fifty thousand Wanz soldiers, and other Wanz they use as servants and to herd the larvae that are in the sewer tunnels to keep those who have successfully escaped trapped in the smithy by the docks. The slime of the larva will eat you as well as the larva, and if it gets in your blood, you die a very horrible death. They are holding the people of Lacy Downs at siege but cannot do magic against them because it backfires on them. His mission was to find out who was tampering with the luck tokens and fix the problem, to find out why the Lazzindaph had not reported in. I am assuming that is the name of the lizard men. Then when they detected your power on the runners, they sent him to first capture you. They assumed that you did not have much power because it was small magic according to them. Then he passed out."

"Maybe we can pull a raid for those in the smithy," said Kriss. "We would need to be able to do something to protect us against the slime and the larva."

"What about the roof?" asked Prince Aaron.

"At night, with the avian's bags, we could pull a raid. We would need to bring supplies and see how many people we could get out in one night. We may have to wait to get the rest and ourselves out," said Wisdom's Child. "I can bring a healing tent and do what I can for them. We will need a lot of water. I imagine that they are pretty dehydrated by now."

"The public waterworks are not something that can be tampered without the aid of an engineer, and my uncle would not let any in the city," said Prince Aaron.

"You can make a magic block on anything," said Wisdom's Child, not liking to burst his bubble of hope.

"Another question to ask our prisoner," said Kriss. "Also, why haven't they been able to capture the escapees through the roof?"

"A good question," said the Eldest. "In the histories, we were taught that all of the public works in the capital are guarded against the use of magic."

"They are?" asked Prince Aaron. "That was probably in the lessons after I turned nine."

"It would seem, Aaron, that some of the lessons will need to be attended by you," said Kriss. "Wisdom's Child, why were we not allowed to learn the history of this land?"

"The Evil Mage had the last say over which lands we could learn the histories of. I do not know why he did not let us learn about this land. Maybe Elder will know that. My records show the poor dear was forced to be with the Evil Mage almost daily, at least until he turned into such an excellent war elder," she answered.

"Yes, but he didn't like doing without him the whole day, so he still spent a lot of time there," answered Kriss as they walked into a hidden barn where the war councils had set up their headquarters.

"Why do I feel as though you were talking about me," said Elder, looking at them as they came in.

"Because you have keen powers of observation," said Kriss. "We were wondering why the Evil Mage never let us study about Asalawn."

"Now that is a good question, and I don't know if I have the answer to it. But I will think on it some," replied Elder. "You are looking tired, Wisdom's Child," he added in concern.

"The Eldest of the Hazbastas, who is a healer, is going to fix me a draught after I have eaten to make sure I sleep all night with no interruptions," said Wisdom's Child. "And I am looking forward to getting a night's sleep without any patients of my own!" With that, she went to the cook fire and got something to eat, took the draught that Eldest had made, and went to bed.

"I do not believe that she has slept in two or three days," said Eldest. "We require much of her, and indeed, there was much only she could do."

"With the removal of their mage as a threat to us and with them not being able to get ahold of him, I believe they may send someone stronger and with a larger army," said Prince Aaron. "We need to get Refuge secured and regroup our troops. Having the hounds as border guards, along with the avians, to see what is going on is a boon. But we also need two – and four-foot guards out."

"Also, we need incursions to rescue those who are still managing to escape from the enemy," said Tawny.

"Your generosity to my people at the risk of your own wrings my heart with gratitude," said Prince Aaron gratefully.

"We can do nothing else, Prince Aaron," said Aloo. "We have been where your people are now and cannot continence it happening to others."

"This is an attitude that I believe Wisdom's Child helped develop within us," said Tawny to the shocked amazement of her fellow elders.

"Over and over again, she would not harm us the way her father would when he wished her to. She suffered tortures for days rather than do to us what was done to her, and I believe that is where we developed this attitude," she answered them with a smile.

"Oh," said Aloo who blushed around her bill, "and I have been treating her with mistrust, she whom I should have realized I could trust the most. I am ashamed of myself and more so since I realize that she recognized my mistrust. How I must have hurt her feelings and she in many ways but a child. I have been harsh in my judgment of her and unfair," she ended remorsefully.

"Many of us have," said all the elders, "and we all should be ashamed for the good she has done us in spite of the Evil Mage. One of my amazements is that he did not know her true power. What she has displayed takes considerable power and knowledge. The mages he brought to tutor her did not have power close to anything she has displayed here, and she never displayed anything that the most advanced of them ever managed to do."

"Maybe her journal will have the answers," said Elder. "We do not need her for the cleanup or for questioning the prisoner. But we do need her for council on the border situation to get Refuge ready for an assault, how to muster our troops, rescue those from the smithy, and so forth. I believe that our seconds can handle the cleanup under the guidance of Captain Alessia, and the rest of us need to be in council tomorrow as soon as we get to Refuge. Also, we will be able to get The Family securely in Refuge without any worry about the enemy now."

"Good," said Prince Aaron, "then we need a good night's sleep and an early start."

"This meeting is adjourned then," said Alaw, yawning.

In the morning, they had breakfast and told Wisdom's Child what the agenda for the day was. "Good. Getting out and getting some physical activity is just what I need. The hike back to Refuge will do that," was her answer.

With her being the shortest, they let her set the pace but soon had to tell her to slow down. "Wisdom's Child," said the Eldest of the Hazbastas, "my child, remember that I am old."

"Oh, I am sorry. I must have been walking to keep pace with my thoughts," said a contrite Wisdom's Child, dropping back to walk with the woman so she would keep the pace comfortable for her.

"What were you thinking about at such a furious pace?" asked the Eldest.

"I was thinking of Refuge," said Wisdom's Child. "I remember short people from somewhere, and the system seems to remind me of them. I want to explore the lower caverns that Master Seth spoke of to see if they will jog my memory. I seem to think that in some way, they may be related to the keep of the Evil Mage but can't get any grip on that because all my memory is gone. So I have been trying to get other bits of knowledge to come forth." Then she sighed. "And rather, unsuccessfully, I am afraid."

"You will give yourself a headache doing that," said Eldest. "You cannot get back what is destroyed. But your journal might have something in it. It could be that you have been keeping one for a very long time. Maybe one of The Family could help you get a fix on the when of the people you are trying to remember."

"What a good thought," said Wisdom's Child happily and went right to the elder mind net. *"Is there anything in your histories or traditions about the Evil*

Mage's keep about short people who were amazing miners? Something about Refuge reminds me of them, but I cannot get a memory fix on them."

"They died about fifty years before any of us were captured," said Aloo. "My grand dame was a historian for the keep and read that they died due to the experimentations of the Evil Mage. He decided that he did not need them to shape his keep any longer and tried to change them into another type of creature altogether."

"Thank you, Aloo," said Wisdom's Child on the net. *"That will give me a when in my journal. After our council I will go exploring the lower caverns."*

"We would rather you didn't do that by yourself," said Tawny.

"Why?" asked Wisdom's Child.

"I know that it is in your nature to do things on your own, but we cannot afford to have our one and only mage get hurt. Also, you need more practice interacting with others dear," said Tawny.

"All right, but I will only take those two-foots who can carry five days supplies on their backs. I will want a guard of at least two four-foots and at least two soldiers of the two-foots. We will need a rope that is knotted at equal intervals, stuff for a fire, paper and writing materials, medical supplies, and sleeping gear. I believe we will find water down there, but we will take water bottles. If we don't find water, we will cut it short and come back for more water and maybe a contraption to haul all the equipment. All the tunnels seem to be the same width," answered Wisdom's Child.

"It would seem that you didn't think you were going to get to go by yourself in the first place," said Prince Aaron with a grin.

"It was worth a try," said Wisdom's Child with a twinkle in her eyes.

"Ah, a wise child indeed," said Hearten, laughing. This got chuckles from everyone.

The war council, being considerably closer to Refuge than The Family, arrived first and after eating went straight to their meeting.

"We need to keep an understory guard as well as an aerial guard," said Aloo. "We can see through the eyes of the kill hounds, but it is disjointed due to the speed at which they travel. They do not seem to have a walk speed."

"No, they don't," said Wisdom's Child. "They pace, and even that is at a high speed."

"This is trivial I know," said Hildy with a sigh, "but my people wonder why they are not taking orders directly from me, instead of from Captain Alessia and her lieutenants?"

"You, Hildy, are of equal rank with Arms Master Hearten and are needed here at the council. Because we do not know how the Hazbastas warriors are trained to work individually and as a group.

"Captain Alessia who is battle experienced was chosen because of this as commanding second, especially after this last round of battles with mixed troops. She is second to Arms Master Hearten. Do you have the equivalent?" answered Prince Aaron.

"No," answered Hildy.

"Then she must double as your second also," said Prince Aaron.

"She is also acting as the head second for The Family," said Elder.

"Thank you. Would you mind waiting while I explain this and get the word to start passing?" asked Hildy. "It is actually our men who are the worst about this situation!"

"No, go ahead," said Prince Aaron to the nods of agreement from the rest of the council."

"And, Hildy," said Aloo, "we can send this word out on the mind net and get word to your soldiers in the field."

Hildy beamed. "Would you? That would be great!"

"Done," said Aloo.

"Wow," said Hildy and left.

"I think she acts second to their Eldest also," said Wisdom's Child. "Even the new Hazbastas were thrilled to see them both here. When it was explained why they needed to stay at Refuge, they accepted it. Some wonder if they couldn't get pack animals and get some of the tools and crafting items to bring back. All their pack animals were killed by the hounds. I will be happy when we have our community set up so the children have a set schedule for schooling and the crafters are busy. We need to assign the salvage groups starting farthest and moving nearer."

"That makes good sense to me," said the Eldest of the Hazbastas coming into the conference. "Hildy asked me to be part of the conference. Then more than one Hazbastas will know what is going on. Thank you for pausing to give her time to set things straight among our people. I keep laughing. She is continually amazed that it is the men who are so protective of how things should be done and who should do what. She says that she thinks they need to have classes on how things operate here."

"You are not surprised by this?" asked Prince Aaron.

"No," said Eldest, smiling, "they have always had a problem with pride: theirs, their wives, their families, and their people. I do not know how to get them to realize that they need to think before they take insult, that they need the facts, and not to rush into hasty judgments. This is what I believe led to the abuse that caused us to deny them any authority in our society."

Hildy came in then and smiling said, "There. That is settled. The men were shocked and pleased that I am considered equal to Arms Master Hearten. Do you really think that they are ready for equality, Eldest?"

"I do not know, dear," said Eldest. "But not all of the men were involved in this little tempest, were they?"

"No, only three really and the others said, 'That is what Albet said,' and he said that Captain Alessia is the one who has experience in directing troops against the Wanz,'" answered Hildy. "So he is ready for equality, and the others that listened to him are. These others proved themselves troublemakers before the whole group and foolish."

"That is the way of it," said Eldest. "Now Albet will be listened to more than the others, no matter how much they scream and fuss."

"I think, Eldest, that I will be happy with just directing troops," said Hildy.

"I am sorry, Hildy," said Arms Master Hearten, "but you need to understand those kind of things when directing troops. Sometimes it is better to let the situation work itself out, and sometimes it is necessary to interfere."

"Rats!" said Hildy, and the others laughed.

"If you need lessons on how to use embarrassment to get your troops or even an individual to shape up, just ask Wisdom's Child for advice," said Elder dryly. "I do not think that those memories are associated with the Evil Mage, are they?"

"Hmm," said Wisdom's Child thoughtfully, "now that you mention it, no, they are not, and I remember all of them," she ended with a mischievous smile.

"All right, fresh material," said Hearten, rubbing his hands together, and Hildy brightened up, causing Eldest to laugh.

"Good," said Prince Aaron, shaking his head and smiling, "now that we are all here, let us begin."

"I believe that the two-foots on the border guard duty will need to have the nets for capturing mages with them, but they must wear magic-resistant clothing. Also, any four-foots with them should have such adornment unless there is something else that will work," said Yass, trying to get comfortable as her time drew near.

"That is an excellent thought," said Wisdom's Child. "I wonder if there is something that would be handier and can also repel magic sent at any of our patrols and even the kill hounds. If the enemy cannot kill them, they can very well be helpless against them. Also, those in the sky will need such things, for sooner or later, they will be discovered. I will need to think on this. And now I feel more urgency to find the crystals and other stones I seek for my work."

"The Evil Mage had us wear special shields when we were on guard room duty," said Elder. "They used the magic-resistant fabric: gold, platinum, crystals, and gems."

"Not in my memory," said Wisdom's Child. "Do you know whether he created them or not?"

"I believe that he did," said Kriss. "He measured us himself and muttered the measurements to one of his hands to write down."

"Then I may not have the knowledge to make this in my library or my journal," said Wisdom's Child. "But that doesn't mean that I cannot figure out how to do so. It says in my journal that I figured out how to keep the Evil Mage's magic from escaping his lands."

"Well," said Alaw, "at least one mystery is solved. I wondered why the magic could not get to you. Although it was trying, it seemed that it could not pass a certain boundary. You do not know how happy I am that you figured a way to contain it."

"It may be a temporary fix," said Wisdom's Child. "I am pretty sure that I and no one else had any idea how much magic the Evil Mage had stockpiled. If it was more than I calculated, it could build upon itself or cause a weather phenomenon and escape. If that happens, the amount of magic in this land could increase alarmingly, and we will have a hard time getting the Wanz and their master to leave."

"They will want to increase the number of Wanz soldiers and maybe lesser wizards at their command," said Prince Aaron thoughtfully. "We need to have a watch set farther out to sea also."

"The avians we sent to investigate the shores closer to this end of Asalawn say that there seem to be Wanz compounds where small port cities used to reside and that they must have prisoners for they bring food to a building every day," said Aloo.

"We will need to eliminate these outposts. They don't need to be at our backs, and we can use them so that our winged scouts can have a place to launch from," said Alaw. "There are cliffs with lighthouses that will make good launching sites."

"Then those are the places for our next campaigns. I need to figure a way to use magic to keep our border guards safe, to use it to penetrate the confines of our enemy and free those who yet may live in the smith," said Wisdom's Child. "I do not believe you need me for the campaigns you will be mounting, unless our scouts discover something untoward. Call me if you do. I need to get my whole library together, do some research, and get my exploration team together." With that, she got up and left.

"What is their guard like at night?" wondered Elder, getting back to business. "If they do not keep a guard at night, we would be able to free them during dark."

"The avians were told to do both day and night watches once we realized that they had prisoners. They release larva at night with herders. They have trenches that they fill with water from the sea that the things will not pass. They bring them live things that are trapped to eat, but they don't seem satisfied and are forever sniffling at the building the prisoners are in," said Aloo.

"If we could put them in metal tubs and dump them into the sea while eliminating their shepherds, we would be able to get to the prisoners," said Arms Master Hearten.

"If we eliminate their herdsmen and lure them with dropped food to cliffs, the avians could use the strife rakes and rake them into the sea," said Elder, remembering one of the maneuvers Wisdom's Child had taught the avians.

"If they are not too heavy," said Aloo, "there also need to be a way to keep them from returning the way they had come."

"I wonder how they would do on sand?" pondered Hildy. "Slugs don't like coarse ground, and sometimes we use ground-up seashells to keep them from the gardens."

"Now that is a clever thought," said Yass.

"I will have the scouts examine the surface that they are on. It may be that they do not like a rough way," said Aloo. "This would make it easy to put a barrier behind them or even to just corral them so we could get the prisoners free."

"The herdsmen will most likely not be fighters. But we need to be alert in case they are," said Prince Aaron. "They seem to have different Wanz for different jobs, and they do not do anything else."

"We need to speak more with our prisoner, Kriss," said the Prince.

"I will do that after council and give you all the answers," replied Kriss. "Has Anvar noticed any magic users or any magic in use?"

"Yes, at each place, but she says that their power is not great, and they have to have an object to boost their message sending which they do twice a day at a set time," answered Aloo. "Also, the locks on the building the prisoners are in are magically controlled. This seems to be the wizard's main function."

"What is the building made of?" asked Arms Master Hearten.

"It is wood and stone. The stone is in the lower portion and the wood the upper. The roof is steeply pitched with wooden shingles," Aloo answered.

"I wonder if a fire started at the top would cause them to free the prisoners. In the confusion, we could net the wizards and attack the troops at the same time. Then we could attack while the larvae are not out," said Kriss.

"If they feel that there is more magic to be had, they will not want the feed for their larva to perish, and they would not want to use their soldiers for feed," said Kriss. "What could work to our advantage is a daytime attack with fire on more than one building, but the prisoners' building first so they focus on it, then an attack from all sides and above. We would be able to see well, even though the same can be said for the enemy."

"We will still need our mage to be available if we do not successfully net the enemies' wizards," said Eldest.

"True," said Prince Aaron, "and we will need spears and lances with long metal points to penetrate the larvae and kill them. We cannot count them out of this battle."

"We had better speak with Master Adela then and get her the stuff she needs. She can choose which ever smithy is close by as it will already set up. That will save time which I do not feel we have much of," said Aloo.

"That is the best plan. Then we could disassemble it and bring it here to Refuge," said Prince Aaron. "I think we should gather as much from all the smithies we can find and bring them here. We may need more metal work done than we know."

"True, and I am a little anxious about what Wisdom's Child said about her father's magic causing a weather phenomenon," said Hildy. "Every now and then, I get this feeling. And if I ignore it, there is trouble the minute she said that the feeling started."

"True, you do, and it is usually about the weather," confirmed Eldest.

"Then let us heed it and get more acquisitioners out and prepare our troops for the next task, while Wisdom's Child and her team explore the caverns below and she figures out everything we have requested of her," said Prince Aaron. "Let us adjourn for now to get what further information we need."

◊ ◊ ◊

Kriss entered the prisoner's cave, and the prisoner sneered, "I smell that you have your dogs with you."

"You have a fine sense of smell," said Kriss calmly. "I have more questions for you. How would your master get reinforcements if he should choose to stay longer?"

"He would send to the hive for more larvae in their final hard state, just ready to be soldiers or whatever they have been chosen to be," the prisoner answered.

"Do the Wanz ever do more than one task?" asked Kriss.

"No, they do not seem to have the capacity," he answered.

"So a herder of larva would be just that and nothing more?" asked Kriss.

"Yes, nothing more. They are useless beyond what they are bred to do. Only the personal servants like what I had can do more. The soldiers can only do those things that associate with soldiering: camping, cooking, fighting, following orders, keeping their equipment in good repair. They have some flexibility to the kinds of tasks they can do. They could be herdsmen also, but most of the herdsmen are bred and are somewhat immune to the slime."

"Has your master been able to tamper with the public waterworks?" asked Kriss.

"No," said the man with a grin. "I believe that every mage who tried was sick for weeks afterward, and it was deemed a worthless effort."

"Why is it that your master has not entered the smithy from the roof and captured the people within?" asked Kriss.

"There is a strange magic there, and none can come on the roof without receiving great hurt or even death," said the man.

"Thank you," said Kriss thoughtfully. "Do you know how many outposts your master has?"

"Eight along the coast, five west, none east, and three in the mountains," answered the man. "You have a way to tell whether or not I am lying, don't you?"

"Yes," said Kriss simply.

"You do not seem like ruthless people. Why did you remove my magic from me so cruelly?" asked the man.

"So you would have no hope in it returning," answered Kriss in sorrow.

"I have built myself, my identity, on my magic," said the man.

"That was a mistake," said Kriss. "You are your beliefs and your values. All those intangible things don't have a thing to do with your physical person. Your magic was of your physical person."

"You lie!" exclaimed the man.

"No," said Kriss, "I do not. If magic made the person, all people would be created with the ability to somehow gain the knowledge to do it, and this is not so. You are either born with the physical capacity to do it or not."

"No. They taught me how to do my magic. It only came when I learned certain things," said the man frantically.

"That is not true," said Kriss. "They put a magic block on you and removed it little by little so you would think that you owed them your magic when in fact it was yours all along."

"They lied to me!" the man screamed. "All my life, they lied to me! You are telling me that only because I was born with the ability was I able to do the magic. They knew this and deliberately blocked me so that I would be grateful to them! How I have always hated my masters, but loved the magic. It was mine!" he finished in horror and rage. Kriss quietly left the weeping man.

◊ ◊ ◊

Captain Alessia returned to Refuge with the mop-up crews and was amazed at the noise and the joy of families feeling safe. She reported to Arms Master Hearten, Prince Aaron, and Hildy, "Our two-footed troops did great, and we had no casualties. As I was acting second for all the troops, may I give this report to the whole war council?"

"Certainly," said Prince Aaron, "I will call it. Wisdom's Child will be absent. She is studying her journal to see what she can find out about our home."

"The poor dear, to have so much of your memory destroyed has to be very frustrating. It is a good thing that she discovered her journal," said Captain Alessia.

"Why don't you grab a bite to eat and meet us at the usual conference room," said Prince Aaron.

◊ ◊ ◊

Captain Alessia met with the council scarcely an hour later cleaned and fed. "The mop-up went well with no surprises and no injuries. The enemy, as we thought, was completely disorganized without a leader. They fought, but it was no contest. I have set up the border guard patrols with teams that consist of four two-foots, four four-foots, and two winged. Their areas intertwine so that they are able to go to each other's aid and are in easy striking distance for aid from the kill hounds as well."

"Well done!" said Prince Aaron with the other leaders nodding.

"We have found out how many outposts our enemy has. Eight are along the coast and four at our backs. They are our next targets. We are strongly considering a daytime attack where we set the roof of the prisoners building on fire. We believe that they will free the prisoners in order to save the food supply for the larva," said Lord Kriss. "This will also give us the advantage of drawing the wizards out and having the light of day to fight in an unfamiliar territory."

"Why do you need to draw the wizards out to free the prisoners?" asked Captain Alessia.

"The locks on the buildings that the prisoners are in are magically held," said Aloo.

"If you have net casters, they can take a net to the lock and neutralize it," said Captain Alessia. "Also, is there a guard that is problematic at night?"

"The larvae, their slime is a form of acid and will eat through shoes or any other soft thing from what our prisoner said," replied Prince Aaron. "They have trenches that they fill with sea water so that the things won't go beyond their compound and herdsmen who keep them going where they are supposed to go."

"How do they clean the stuff up in the morning?" asked Captain Alessia.

"They put the water that was in the ditch onto the ground and soak it. They do it again and again at least ten times," answered Aloo.

"So the slime is really nasty stuff," said Captain Alessia thoughtfully. "If we could eliminate the herdsmen when the larvae first come out . . . I am assuming that is when everyone else is in?"

"Yes," said Aloo. "No one goes out until the larvae go in."

"Wow. That says a lot that is scary about them," said Captain Alessia. "But as I was saying, if we could eliminate the herdsmen when they first bring them out and while the things are feeding find a way to corral them, we would be able to slip the prisoners away in the night."

"The seashells would work. We have found that they do not like coarse surfaces," said Hildy. "I wonder what would poison the things."

"They say they are always hungry. What if we made sure they always had something to eat while we were freeing the prisoners and a big pile when we left?" asked Kriss.

"We could try different poisons in the last food they would eat so that if they made noises, we would be gone," said Eldest.

"We?" said Hildy, looking at her eldest.

"Oh, not me, dear." Eldest laughed. "I could not keep up, and there will be at least four missions."

"Four!" exclaimed Alessia.

"Yes. That is why the planning has to be done so carefully. We are having large lances with metal tips made for the larva, if there is need, and large axes for the Lazzindaphs' tails," said Prince Aaron. "But I worry about the other outposts. Now that the time for me to be ruler of this land is here, traders might start appearing, and that could be a very bad thing for us and for them."

"I will send scouts out to see if any have come," said Aloo.

"I think that we should send four-foots with you so that they may scout where your scouts cannot see," said Yass. "We need to see if they have any more soldiers stashed around this land."

Everyone looked at her with inquiry. And she continued on, "That is the only way they could have so thoroughly invaded your land. Having the chrysalises stored, then having a mage just say the proper word, and like magic, soldiers appear ready to do the mage's bidding."

"We have effectively wiped out four thousand of his soldiers. If more magic is to land here from the Evil Mage's realm, he will want us out of here," said Kriss, taking up the thread of her thought.

"You are right," said Prince Aaron grimly, "and we do not know if he used all of his outlying supply or if he has reserves."

"It is fortunate that The Family is of large enough numbers that this is possible, as well as the attacks on the coastal outposts," said Tawny. "I will ready my spies, and they will travel with your scouts."

"That is settled then," said Prince Aaron.

"I heard no sound of smithing," said Alessia.

"With the lands surrounding us and farther clear of the Wanz and their masters, we sent Master Adela and those she chose to a smithy," said Elder.

"Ah," said Captain Alessia, yawning.

"Well enough, council," said Prince Aaron, "we will meet again tomorrow. We have things we wish to run by the Eldest."

"True," said Elder with a grin, "me asking the questions instead of her. What a treat!"

Everyone laughed. "You know the one thing she seemed to have set in her mind was to ask you most of her questions," said Aloo. "She said so when we were escaping to here."

"Yes, she did," said Prince Aaron and Hearten together.

"Oh bother," sighed Elder resignedly. Everyone laughed as they left the council room.

CHAPTER 18

The Magical Stairwell

"WE HAVE DECIDED on a plan of attack," said Prince Aaron, walking up to Wisdom's Child. "We will kill the herdsmen when they first get out and quickly pin the larvae into a small area. We will do this with food and coarsely broken shells. The net bearers will use the nets to neutralize the locks, and we will sneak the prisoners out. Then the next morning, we will be able to battle the Wanz and wizards without worry for the prisoners or the larva."

"Why will you not be worried about the larva?" asked Wisdom.

"We plan to poison them," said Prince Aaron.

"That is a good idea," said Wisdom. "From what the war elder net sent me from your council, they are terrible things. You know, Prince Aaron, if the soldiers were to lead the prisoners into the woods, we would be fighting them in the forest where we have been quite successful. And if, after the prisoners are free, you let the larva go on their circuit, it will be quite interesting to see how the Lazzindaphs and Wanz get outside."

Prince Aaron gave an astounded laugh. "We will need to meet with the council again, for fighting them in the forest is a good idea, and we can leave trails that lead to traps. Also, the lizard men do not have as effective use of their tails within the forest. But one other thing, Hildy who gets anxious urges usually about the weather, started having one the moment you mentioned the Evil Mage's magic causing a weather phenomenon. The Hazbastas Eldest says she is always right when she has one, so we have increased the number of acquisitioners who are out gathering supplies. The trick is to get them into Refuge without leaving a huge trail."

"With a record like that, hurry is a good idea," said Wisdom. "I read my journal and found that these caverns may have doors with stairs that lead to other levels and into rooms. If we are able to go to different levels, we could have several roads into our hiding place. Also, I wonder if the magic that protects the roof of the smithy is something that is a heritage magic that some masters receive at a certain level or if they have magical items that they can evoke. I need to talk to Master Adela.

"I suppose my job is to be on hand if any magical healing is needed?" asked Wisdom, going back to the subject of the rescues.

"Yes, although WyAla will be at one station, Mavis at another, and Vetor at yet another. We have placed them midway between the outposts so that help can be reached quickly.

"Vetor is a Hazbastas healer, and from what Master Mavis says after quizzing him, he is at a high journeyman or early master level," said Prince Aaron. Then grinning, he added, "When he was done with his interview with Master Mavis, WyAla met him with a soothing draught, a cool towel for his head, and had him lay down for a massage."

Wisdom laughed. "You should have seen the shocked look on her face when she found out that I was Master Mavis's healer and had bossed her around. She was so stunned she just sat down by the fire in shock and didn't reply to the rest of what I had said for several minutes."

"That tells me quite a bit about what Master Mavis expects from other healers, and that more than we know may have been under her tutelage," said Prince Aaron.

"It is a good thing she was my patient and got to see my work firsthand as well," said Wisdom. "It sounds as though she might have been frightening to know as a student."

"Well, healers deal with life and death," said Prince Aaron. "A mistake can kill someone who would not normally have died."

"That is true, and I learned that in the keep, I believe. But part of that memory is associated with the Evil Mage," said Wisdom. "I have an answer back from our Master Smith, and she says that yes there is smithing magic that can make that roof untouchable by anyone but a master smith with good intent."

"Then she will need to be the first one to step on it and open the way for the rest of us," said Prince Aaron.

"True," said Wisdom's Child, "and you will have to follow her in, then me. I hope you will be ready to go in not too many nights time. I feel as though they are running out of time."

"I will be ready," said Prince Aaron.

"*All will be as you command,*" responded the elders on the mind net who Wisdom's Child had listening in on her and Prince Aaron's conversation and who had given orders for the rescue of those in the smithy.

"In the meantime, I am going to check the walls and floors on this level and see what I find, while things are still slow for me. I would like it if we can get to the lower level. I do not want us to be trapped by our refuge."

Triss spotting Wisdom's Child went to see what she was doing.

"Hi, Triss, I believe I have found the stairs to the lower levels," said Wisdom's Child. "Let us go to the pit over by the infirmary. But first we need a few things: a lantern, broom, something to collect dust on, and then in."

Mavs offered, saying, "I can retrieve a lantern, and I will ask some two-foots to bring the other supplies."

"Thank you, Mavs," said Wisdom. And a short time later, taking the lantern from him, she bent over the pit. This did not afford her the sight she needed, so she laid on the edge of the pit and edged farther over it, holding the lantern so that she could see all its sides. Mavs, getting nervous, laid his forelegs across hers to ensure that she would not fall. Then after a quick look, she fished her papers out of her pocket and sitting cross-legged scanned through them quickly. "Aw," she said and jumped up. Scanning the floor, she said, "Lieutenant Triss, hand me the broom."

"Yes, ma'am," said Lieutenant Triss, handing her the broom and following with a piece of bark to collect the dust she swept up and a bucket to put it in.

Taking the broom, Wisdom's Child carefully paced a distance from the pit and started to sweep, careful not to raise a lot of dust. When she reached a nook in the wall, she laughed and said, "Here it is. Please stand back from the pit a good five feet all around." When everyone was at a safe distance away, she seemed to press on something. At first, nothing seemed to happen. Then everyone heard a kind of quiet groaning, and all of a sudden, whoosh. As if by magic, a spiral stairway appeared.

This caused great excitement. Everyone came running over, about to form a mob in their curiosity, until Hearten with the voice of one who expects to be obeyed shouted, "Halt! Master Wisdom's Child and Capitan Alessia need to make sure of the safety of the stairwell before anyone ventures near."

At his command, all of those rushing forward stopped and looked toward Wisdom's Child who was reading more from her journal. She did a couple more mysterious things in the nook and said, "That should have the stairwell locked into place. It was designed to get from one level to the next but also to be a trap for one's enemies. If the locking mechanism is not engaged, it will shut, crushing whoever is on it."

"Captain Alessia, Lieutenant Triss, Mavs, and, Lieutenant Stella, will you come here so that I can teach you the ways of this mechanism. If we use it for practice, it will also test the strength of the stairwell's structure. Then we can be fairly confident that it will be safe for us to use," said Wisdom's Child.

"Um, yes, ma'am," they said, hurrying over to her.

After she explained the mechanism to them and they had practiced it several times, it was deemed safe enough to venture down.

"Let me go first," said Mavs. "That way, if something goes wrong, I with my four feet will have a better chance at getting out. Four feet are faster than two, and you Master Wisdom, we dare not risk."

"That is an excellent idea," said Captain Alessia.

Down went Mavs without any problems, not even a creaking of the stairs. Deeming it safe, Wisdom's Child followed lantern and paper in hand. When she arrived at the end of the stairs, she met a blank wall and sat down to read further. "We need to go back up three steps," she told Mavs, which they did. Once there, they scanned the walls; and seeing the slightest of indentations, she pushed it. In just a few moments, the door at the bottom of the stairs opened.

Mavs was about to journey down when she said, "Wait! A trap also lies there." She very carefully went down one more step. Seeing two outthrust stones, one higher than the other, she pushed them simultaneously; and in just a short time, people heard something click into place. Reading a little more to make sure she did not forget anything, she and Mavs proceeded through the door.

They stopped short, and looking up, Wisdom's Child said, "There seems to be a privy close to this area blocking the trail further up.

Farmer Seth said to his second son, "Bret, get what is necessary and let's get that cleaned up. This is certainly going to make it easier to locate where the um, waste deposit sight is so we can close it off."

"Nice choice of words," said Lieutenant Stella at the top of the stairs. I think a bucket of water and some lye soap will also help the situation."

"True," said Mavis as she sent one of the youth off to get them and some scrub brushes also. "I wonder if there is a drain that the waste water can be flushed into."

Wisdom, hearing her, held her lantern up higher and soon located a small drainage ditch running along the trail that seemed to have a drain hole at the downhill end of it. "Yes, it does. The big debris will not fit, but the dirty water and the water used to rinse the soap should have no problems."

Wisdom and Mavs rejoined everyone at the head of the stairs to make room for the cleaning crew.

"What an amazing feat of engineering," said Prince Aaron with admiration in his voice.

"While cleanup is going on here, why don't we see what we can discover about the rest of the pits," said Captain Alessia.

"A good notion, that way, everyone can learn how to operate the mechanisms so we can all be safe," said Prince Aaron.

Wisdom's Child, bowing to the Prince, led the way to the next opening. Looking down at it as she had done before, she didn't seem to find what she was looking for, so back to her writings she went. After she had read for a short time, she hopped up and ran to a wall. Using a cloth, she wiped the surface. This not being satisfactory, she asked for some water and a scrub brush. When they arrived, she cleaned first gingerly, and then vigorously, getting quite excited by what she was finding.

"This pit is for the transportation of heavy loads," she told her fascinated viewers. "Once the debris down below has been attended to, we will find a room that has a mechanism powered by a small draft beast such as a donkey. Let us go on to the next one!"

"This pit was the one that could hold water. This pit is what is used for ballast to move the lifting mechanism up and down. Fortunately, we have already filled it with water, for that is what they used for the ballast according to my notes," Wisdom's Child explained. "Let us move on to the fourth pit. This is also one which lowers and lifts."

Wisdom made sure that Captain Alessia, Lieutenant Stella, Lieutenant Triss, Mavs, and Prass knew what to look for and what to do to open, lock the bobby traps, and close the pits. Then she said, "I am going to leave you to handle any further work with the pits. There is so much more I am curious about." And she went back to her writings.

After studying her scroll for a short while, she jumped up; and going to where the wall seemed to end, she carefully searched. After finding more depressions and juttings, she continued to search, causing great curiosity in those with her. Then finding what she seemed to be searching for, she set the mechanism in motion. The wall of the mountain opened. It seemed to push itself away from the mountain, and then turned to the outside. Then she went back to the other openers that she had found and engaged another door – this one hidden as part of the floor. After first ensuring that no one was standing very near, it opened, and more stairs appeared. But they oddly had a ramp that went down with the stairs. After securing the trap mechanisms, with Prince Aaron and Arms Master Hearten fast on her heels, she headed down the stairs. Master Mavis and many of the elders of The Family followed also. They entered the back of an area that looked like a hospital.

Master Healer Mavis looking around said, "This is a hospital, and now I understand the ramp. I think that it was used to lower the wounded down and cause as little hurt to them as possible."

"I agree," said Forester Fern. "Look. They even made groves so that the wheels of whatever kind of cot they used would not run off the track."

"I don't think that they used wheels," said Elder as his keen sense of hearing picked up a new sound, and water started flowing down the ramp.

"I wish that we had some engineers here," said Prince Aaron.

"I agree," said Hearten, "although they would probably be like children with new toys, and probably worse than Scribe Uther if they were here."

"If we find any, then we had better be sure to bring their caretakers with them. Look how many it takes to keep Scribe Uther out of trouble," said Healer Mavis.

They went through the door leading out of the hospital and found themselves in a large cavern. "Let us go along the wall, leaving a mark at where we started, and see how large this cavern is," said Prince Aaron.

"We really do not have enough lighting for that," said Aloo.

"I will go and get more lighting," said Prince Aaron, excited to be getting to do some exploring himself.

"Here comes Prince Aaron with the torches," said Wisdom," and I am wondering if anything like it was in the keep?"

Elder asked, "Do you remember much of the keep, or was it too strongly associated with the Evil Mage in your mind for you to remember it?"

"I don't remember the interior of it at all," said Wisdom. "So it must have been strongly associated with him."

"Hmm," said Tawny, "this is similar to the keep. No wonder I was beginning to feel a vague unease. Living down here will be a bit uncomfortable for us older ones, but the younger people who did not have mage duty should be all right."

When they returned to where they were, wonder was in their eyes as a strange moss on the walls glowed, lighting up the cavern walls wherever torch light had touched it. Prince Aaron suggested, "Let us post the torches and lamps at equal intervals and see what the results are. I think that once one area of moss gets all the light it can stand, it transfers it to another section of moss."

Alaw went to the center of the cavern and could not resist the temptation to flap his wings, causing a shout to come from his companions as they were engulfed in dust and debris.

"Alaw!" called Aloo with mind-speech, not daring to open her beak for fear of what might blow in. *"Enough! You are about to choke all of us to death! You will just have to be patient. When the cavern is cleaned, you can try your wings."*

Looking sheepishly at his companions, Alaw apologized, "I am sorry. It is just so exciting, and when I gave a high keening whistle upward, it was a long time until it echoed back toward me!"

"I know, dear," said Aloo, wincing slightly, "I heard. And so did our friends. The next time you are going to whistle, will you *please* give us warning?"

"Oh dear," said Alaw in consternation, "I seem to have lost a lot of self-discipline in the excitement. I think I now have a better understanding of the challenges of self-discipline that our children will be facing."

Forester Fern chuckled from behind him. "With so much happening in your lives right now, it must seem as though your life under the Evil Mage was long ago."

"That is true, but though we are confident of his demise, we cannot help but know that evil still walks in the world," said Aloo. "And this evil seems to be even worse than him, which of course is why he feared it."

"You know," said Elder as he walked with the Prince back up to their level, "I remember that the walls of the Evil Mage's keep and the ceiling glowed. I thought it was magic, but it could have been this moss instead."

Once back up the stairs, Wisdom's Child closed the door to the outside. One of the young avians had been sent off by Brak to see if he could see the opening and reported to him that it could not be seen. Nor did he notice any disturbance with its closing.

"Good," said Hearten. "If we can have ways in and out that are not noticeable, it will be to our benefit."

"Let the war council convene," said Wisdom sternly.

Looking startled, Prince Aaron and all agreed to this.

◊ ◊ ◊

"We have to get moving on the rescue of the prisoners at the outpost and the elimination of the enemy there. I also, thanks to Elder's good memory, believe that I know how to make magic-repelling harnesses for all of our people. But I need special crystals and gems to do this. Can we get into Lacy Downs somehow, Prince Aaron? And would they have what I need?"

"Yes, and yes," replied Prince Aaron. "If I and a few others are flown there in the avian bags, we could be dropped into the town at night. Then I can scare the mayor to death by waking him in the middle of the night. I have done that before, poor man. When I explain what we want and what the situation is, I believe we will get the help we need, and we will also be able to see how we can help them."

"Good," said Wisdom. "It will take several days for our people to get into position so that we strike all on the same night. I want to use horses, so if the lizard men do manage to send words back, it will look like something done with very little magic and much cunning."

"That would give us time to fly there and back I think," said Prince Aaron. "Or am I over reaching what the avians can do, Alaw?"

"We have people posted almost the whole way there as scout teams," said Aloo. "They could relay you there in three days via a flight bag."

"And back in three with one day to get what we need," said Wisdom. "That would put us here in time for the raids on the enemy posts if we scheduled them for ten or eleven days from now. Would that be enough time to get the horses into position at the farthest site?"

"Yes, if they leave in the morning," said Prince Aaron. "I will leave it to the arms masters to assign teams and will go on whatever one they put me on."

◊ ◊ ◊

Two days after they left, they arrived in Lacy Downs in the middle of the night so that the enemy would not spot their arrival. The mayor and a few of his councilors with a reasonable guard were there to meet them. Other than that, there was no one just as Prince Aaron had requested. Prince Aaron had had an avian messenger leave a message for the mayor, instead of scaring him.

"Greetings, Prince Aaron," said the mayor. "We are thrilled to know that you live."

"I am happy about that myself, and it was a close thing as I was left for dead. But Master Wisdom's Child," he said, indicating Wisdom, "and her people came to Master Healer Mavis's and my rescue, and she healed us of our hurts. Master Wisdom's Child is also a mage of high ranking." And pausing at the looks on their faces, he continued, "I know she looks to be nine, but she is really over one hundred years of age. Her father, the Evil Mage of legend, wanted a servant that, due to blood ties, he could always control but didn't want that servant to rival him in magic. So he stopped her aging at nine. She finds her looks, which belie her age and wisdom, a nuisance. Our mission here at Lacy Downs is to gather certain crystals and gems for her to use in her magic to help us defeat the enemy."

Seeing the mayor and councilors about to object, he said, "They have completely taken over our land. They have killed all the elderly, the infants, men, children – mostly boys and girls to a certain age – and taken the rest of the girls and women up to a certain age prisoner. They have killed the Regent and are planning on taking the people they do have out on slave ships. We are trying to prevent this. They are the authors of the magic attacks that have been killing those who are even slightly gifted in magic. Very few of the people away from Lacy Downs have escaped. They sent their kill hounds to decimate the

Hazbastas. You here at Lacy Downs are the only ones who have your population and families intact.

"Mage Wisdom, using her magic against them, has defeated their lizard men and human wizards. We have learned that their ruler here in Asalawn is not human, but the human wizard we got the information from didn't know what he was," continued Prince Aaron. "We have but a few days to meet with those who will assault those holding our coastal and some border land outpost, but we need the crystals to be successful as they have wizards at these stations."

The mayor and the councilors were pale with shock at the news of the devastation of the people of Asalawn and at the realization of the loss of those they loved. "I am sorry, Prince Aaron. I did not realize that anyone other than us was being attacked by these people. We thought it was by consent of the Regent, but you say that he is dead?"

"With his head on a pike," said Prince Aaron, some satisfaction creeping into his voice.

"Our food supplies are low, and we are rationing," said a councilor. "Is there any way that you can help us?"

Prince Aaron turned to Wisdom and asked, "As senior elder of your war council, can you give an answer to there need?"

"Yes," replied Wisdom, "we will be able to get food supplies to you, but you need to know that my people, with the exception of myself, are not human people. They are of the species avian, canine, and feline. If I have enough of your crystals and things go as planned with our reclaiming of the outposts, we will be able to fly, in the night, stores of food to you. You just need to make a shopping list while I get the crystals and gems I will need. Oh, and be sure to add anything medicinal."

"Thank you," said the councilors.

"If you will come with me," said one of them, a man with reddish hair in the lantern light, "I will lead you to where we store the crystals. I am the master miner, and none will nay say what I command."

"Thank you," said Prince Aaron and Wisdom together.

They gathered the gems first. The prince and the master miner were surprised that not all of the gems she chose were of the highest value. She just smiled and went about her business.

As they went to the vault with the valued crystals, they went through rooms with crystals deemed of less worth, and Wisdom's Child stopped them. "Wait, can we have more light please. Wonderful! Here are some of the simple crystals I need. They are good for storing power and to attach to crystals that can draw upon them to keep the spell in them active. Several bags of these please. Let us continue on," she said in a pleased voice.

They entered the vault, and the crystals glistened in the light of the lanterns. Wisdom, wanting a better idea of their color and depth, created mage light and had the lanterns put out. "Oh yes, here is what I am looking for," she said, and the master miner was surprised to see her go to the smaller crystals, instead of the large. Glancing up, she saw the look on his face and said, "The magic I need for the crystals must not be cumbersome. The larger crystals would be for greater works, such as providing light for a small town," she said, pointing at a good-sized clear crystal."

"Oh," said the miner and the Prince together, then looking at each other, smiled.

Wisdom picked out the crystals she wanted, keeping them separated. When she had enough, she looked at the master miner and said, "You have been very helpful. Would it be useful to you and the council, the guild, and healing hall if you had crystals that with a word would light a room no matter the size?"

"Yes," said the master miner, "it would be."

Selecting the proper crystals, she asked the miner the number they needed, especially the healing hall. And thinking of them seeing to their patients at night got some smaller ones for light that would not disturb other patients. Then they left the crystal storage area and went outside.

In a little while, there were over seventy crystals that all a person had to say was light, and there was light. As each councilor belonging to one of the guilds and the mayor gathered their crystals, there were grins of delight on their faces. The master healer was well pleased, but she had come with another purpose. "I have those ill with lung fever and no medicine. As you are a master healer and a mage, can you heal them?"

"Yes," said Wisdom, "please lead the way."

"I will stay with our crystals and get them ready to go," said Prince Aaron in mind-speech.

"Good," replied Wisdom, a little startled that the Prince had used mind-speech.

They entered the Healing Hall and went to a ward that was kept separate from the other. Wisdom took out a crystal and asked, "Who is the worst?"

"Over here," said Master Eunice, bringing her to a child.

Wisdom used her healer's eyes and magic eyes on the child, and, seeing no magic interference in the child, began healing her. Soon the child was breathing normally, and her fever was gone.

"I sense in you, Master Eunice, the ability to heal with magic. Why is it that you have not done so?" asked Wisdom's Child.

"I have had none who could teach me," was her answer.

"You have great self-discipline, Master Eunice," said Wisdom's Child thoughtfully. "Are you adverse to mind-speech or touch?"

"I am cautious about it as I do not know how it works, but I know that I can do it," answered the master.

"I have the ability, if you will trust me, to give you both knowledges: how to do healings using a healing crystal and how to defend yourself with shielding. I can teach everyone here at Lacy Downs how to do shielding so that the evil ones cannot use mind blast to overcome them. Are you willing to trust me?" asked Wisdom's Child.

"I will trust you, but until the people here know you better, I would that you did this in secret. I will just tell them I am a quick learner, which is true," said the master dryly.

"It will be as you wish," said Wisdom's Child, and she mind spoke to The Healer, giving her the knowledge. "And now I will work with you to be sure you practice the knowledge correctly," Wisdom's Child told her as she handed her a crystal.

Master Eunice smiled, and the two women went to work on the patients, drinking an energizing broth after every two patients. Soon there were no ill ones.

"Thank You, Master Wisdom's Child," said Master Eunice. "I will train those who have the gift, and I will be sure that everyone in Lacy Downs knows how to mind shield. Being able to do so, and have it stay up always, will make life more comfortable for those with the gift of mind-speech and those without it."

"We have found it so at Refuge," answered Wisdom's Child with a smile as she and Aaron entered the bags and called to the avians that they were ready. The crystals and gems had already been taken away.

They arrived back at Refuge ahead of schedule, and Prince Aaron found out much to his surprise that he wasn't on any of the teams.

"We need you here more," said Hearten. "You are the cornerstone of our nation, the one person everyone is willing to follow, and we need you to keep the peace and Refuge running smoothly."

"Well, I knew that something like this was coming, but I will not be left out of our larger engagements," said the Prince quite firmly.

CHAPTER 19

The Rescue Begins

"ARE YOU READY Smith Adela?" asked Wisdom's Child.

"Yes," said the woman nervously.

Wisdom's Child grinned and, putting her arm around the larger woman's waist, lifted them both in the air, and they were flying back to Refuge at a speed no avian could match. When they reached Refuge, they didn't so much as land as they still flew, but upright and only a few inches from the ground, and entered Prince Aaron's chambers.

"Prince Aaron," whispered Wisdom's Child.

"What?" said the prince, coming instantly awake.

"I have the avians stationed near the capital with bags to carry the refugees out, and I have Master Adela. Would you like to come?"

"Give me two minutes and I will be with you," answered the prince in a whisper, but with excitement in his voice.

He was as good as his word and was surprised when Wisdom's Child put her arm around him and lifted him from the ground. They quietly left Refuge. Once out, she gained altitude.

"Hold firmly, but fear not, Prince Aaron," said Master Adela. "Our mage goes fast, but she doesn't lose her grip on her passengers."

"Thanks for the warning," said the prince, making sure that his grip was firm.

Wisdom's Child rushed them toward the capital. Just outside, they stopped; and she, the smith, and the prince got into avian bags. Anvar had located the smithy, so their avians knew where to land them.

First the master smith was landed. When she gave the all clear and disappeared down the trapdoor, the prince landed, and Wisdom's Child followed after lowering bags full of bags and some containing foodstuffs.

Master Smith Adela looked around the smithy at all the people there. She could barely believe her eyes. There must have been over two hundred people lying quietly. She went over to the largest person there and was relieved to see he was alive. It was her good friend and senior master Jerome.

"Master Jerome," she said, quietly shaking his arm.

He roused and said, "What, has another died?"

"No, Jerome, it is I Adela," she said.

His eyes flew open, and he looked shocked.

"I have brought aid and escape for the people here," Adela said to him.

"How can this be?" he asked.

"We have allies," said Adela, "and they and we have become a people, but they are not people like we are. They are avian, canine, and feline, but people nonetheless, and so large that if you did not know that they were people, you would be terrified."

"Master Jerome," said Prince Aaron, squatting down beside the man, "let me introduce to you a woman who looks nine, but is over a hundred. She is also a war elder, master healer, and master mage.

"Master Jerome, Master Wisdom's Child," introduced the prince. "She got stuck with that name because not even she knows what her real name is, and we got tired of forgetting she isn't nine."

"Hello," said Master Wisdom's Child, already scanning him with healer's eyes, "here drink this. It will give you nourishment and energy for the task at hand. We need to put your worst within these bags so my avian friends can fly them to safety."

The master smith did as she said, and he grinned. "Definitely a master healer." But he seemed to perk up quickly once all of the broth was in him.

With the help of Adela, he rose and led Wisdom's Child to the children and their parents. Prince Aaron and Adela started loading them in bags as Wisdom's Child put a healing necklace on them.

"How are you getting them up those ladders so easily?" asked Jerome.

"Master Wisdom's Child has magically lightened the bags," answered Smith Adela.

"Won't the wizards here detect it?" he asked.

"Not likely. The bags are lined with magic-resistant fabric and so do not give off a magic signature," she replied.

"How are we going to get all these people out of here tonight?" asked Prince Aaron.

"I have cloaked this room and am going to load the bags myself," said Wisdom's Child. "I brought over three hundred bags, and since we will not have people in all of them, the master smith can chose what to put in them." And she got to work, first putting healing necklaces on everyone, and then loading them into sacks. Because Prince Aaron was there and reassured them, they trusted her to help them, and there wasn't any balking.

"I have over a hundred bags left, Master Jerome," said Wisdom's Child with a smile. "Point, and if it will fit in a bag, I will load it. It doesn't matter how heavy the item is. It will all weigh the same once it is in the bag."

He looked at her in amazement and started pointing. Very soon, his smithy was cleared of everything but the largest items. "Come. We must go," said Wisdom's Child. "Into your bag, Master Smith." He did as she told him. And Adela lifted him as though he weighed hardly a thing and quickly went up the ladder, handing him over to his winged saviors. Then she and Prince Aaron got into their sacks, and Wisdom's Child flew them after carefully putting the smithy back the way it was.

Wisdom magically accelerated the flying of her rescuers, and they arrived at Refuge in the morning. The healers were ready for them. The bags were lowered gently onto cots, and the survivors were carried inside with much care.

Mavis had the hospital in the lower level cleaned, so they took them there. The beds were all right for the children and smaller people, but they used the adjacent room for the larger ones.

When Wisdom's Child flew in with Prince Aaron and Adela, there were some very angry people waiting for her. Before they could say a word, the Prince took command of the situation.

"Do not dare lay at the feet of Master Wisdom's Child the sin of putting me in danger," he said in a stern and angry voice. "I am a grown-up, a man, a person who has survived much and risked much for your sakes. Why do you think I will stop and cower in a cave now? I am sick and tired of you trying to keep me safe, shutting me up as though I were a child who had to mind. These newly rescued ones are my people. Master Wisdom's Child needed them to trust her, and she in her wisdom knew that if I were there trusting her and knowing her as a friend, they would cooperate with what she needed to do.

"You do not realize the strength, the magical strength of our mage," said Prince Aaron. "We rescued two hundred people, emptied a smithy of all its small items, and never raised an alarm nor were we followed by any magic spy. Anvar watched closely.

"I will not be going on any of the new missions coming up, but this is one that only my presence would make work effectively," said the Prince kindly, but firmly.

"I could not see any of her magic working," said Anvar, who had come during the Prince's speech. "At the keep, she displayed no such powers. If she had, the mage would have killed her, draining her powers from her with slow, agonizing torture. She had to have had this level of power at the keep. How did she manage to hide it from the mage? I think I just saw it done. I don't know how she did it, but I just saw it done, and it covered the avians also."

"Oh," commented the people. Prince Aaron and Adela along with them.

CHAPTER 20

Clearing the Outposts by the Sea

TRISS AND ARIS waited patiently for dark and for the herdsmen to bring out the larvae. When they did, both assassins were amazed at how large the larvae were, and they and the other assassins waited until the larvae started feeding. Then killing the herdsmen, they added them to the pile of food. Others brought bags and bags of coarsely broken shells and surrounded the larvae with them, while others brought more food and kept feeding them.

Those who carried the nets went to the locks and voided the magic, causing them to unlock. They entered quietly using crystal lights that their mage had provided for them. They found their prisoners and setting them free of their bonds signed for silence and led them out of the building and into the forest. Putting them on horses, they quickly got them from the area.

Back at the outpost, the larvae were being feed the poisoned food, and the coarse shells were being set in a pattern that would lead to the doors of the wizards and the soldiers. Then these people too disappeared. This happened at every site, except where it was surrounded by a marsh and horses were not feasible. They brought the refugees to the cliff and put them in carry bags and had them taken to Refuge that way. The rescuers went barefoot to the beach in the number there were of adult prisoners and made it look like that was how they were escaping. They came to where a stream entered the sea and followed it, finding several good places to set traps and hiding places to trigger them from.

In the morning, the Lazzindaph wizards woke and found dead larvae on their doorsteps. They called for the soldiers to remove them, only to find the soldiers were blocked as they were. They then ordered them to go out their windows and then remove the larvae.

The soldiers did this by using the prods the herdsmen used and dragged the larvae from the wizard's door. "Come," said the senior wizard, "we must check on our prisoners."

When they got to their prison, the door was open, and the prisoners had fled. The head wizard started to shake with rage. He ordered his soldiers to find traces of them and to gather the supplies they would need to hunt them down.

Then he had to report to his master that in the night, the precious larvae had been slain, along with their herdsmen, and the prisoners freed.

When he had finished with that report, he looked very pale and very frightened. "Come," he snapped at his second, "we have to get the slaves back, and we have to find who stole them from us. If we don't, we might as well kill ourselves because our master is furious. This has happened at four other outposts."

He was practically running by the time he finished this, and leaping over the larva slime, he entered their quarters and put on his war harness, his second doing the same.

He ordered all of his soldiers out. They followed the tracks of their prisoners into the forest.

Waiting patiently for them were the Hazabastians, Asalawnians, and The Family, all grimly determined that these evil invaders would not survive.

Knowing that the Wanz use their sense of smell to also locate people, the two-foots had coated themselves in fragrances of the forest. Lieutenant Triss and Aris, along with Sergeant Corey, Traw, Lasva, and Dasto, waited for the wizards. All had on the magic-repelling harnesses, and Triss and Corey carried two of the tail-chopping axes.

The lizard wizards practically passed by their ambushers in safety for they were running on all fours to keep up with the Wanz soldiers. But before they were past, Corey and Triss sprang forward and cut off their tails, eliciting high shrilling whistles of pain from them; and moving up swiftly, Triss and Corey removed their heads. They sent word via mind net about the wizard running on all fours as they had not done so earlier.

The attack on the wizards signaled the rest of the war party to attack the Wanz, and they wiped them out to a warrior taking some hurt, but no deaths.

So well was the surprise planned that except for the marsh land outpost, the results were much the same, and the wizards did not get off any spells.

At the marsh lands outpost, Tawny mind called for Wisdom. *"I have a feeling that these mages might be of higher caliber than those at the outskirts. It is closer to the capital and seems to have a greater number of slaves."*

"I will respect your judgment, elder," said Wisdom as she crouched beside the great feline while they waited for the Wanz to join them in the gully.

"Does everyone in the gully have magic-repelling harnesses on?" she asked Tawny.

"Yes, also there are more soldiers there than at the other outposts. I am wondering what else this outpost is used for," said Tawny.

"Good question, we will know as soon as we get rid of our unwanted guests," said Wisdom.

Tawny looked at her with lifted brows. *"We cannot go back with an unanswered question like that. We could be leaving an amazing amount of trouble behind us if we do,"* she said.

"True," said Tawny. *"Finally, they are coming. They don't seem to move with the same urgency as the other wizards either."*

"I have just instructed Anvar to check our new refugees for magic signatures or any other magic whiffs she can find," said Wisdom.

"Sage Wisdom," Anvar called, *"they have markings that have a faint hint of magic. Share eyes with me and see."* Wisdom did, and lifting the markings from the slaves, she brought them to the canyon. And estimating how far the slaves could have gone, she put them a good distance up it.

"Thank you, Anvar," she said and turned her attention back to those coming up the canyon.

The tension grew as the allies waited for the enemy to be fully in the canyon so they could engage the traps. And finally, about a half an hour after they had begun, the enemy was where they wanted them, and the order came, *"Engage."* And the traps jumped to life. The wizards of the enemy easily freed themselves, but while busy freeing themselves, those carrying the magic sucking nets attacked. The nets were created to work swiftly, so the wizards were quickly overpowered by them while their soldiers were swiftly being killed. The soldiers who were not trapped put up a good fight, but with the leaders being the first targets of the allies, they did not survive the battle.

"Let us go and see what we find within their camp," said Wisdom. *"I do not like how well tended it was, and we should be prepared for there were guards within."*

"Let us send in those trained for such forays first then," said Tawny, mind calling those whose training best suited the task. They slipped away, not needing to go to her for instructions, having received it with mind-speech.

"*Troops, gather, we need to secure the post and make it ours,*" said Tawny. "*Leave the canyon, but not noticeably if possible. We do not know if they can spy here should they notice something is wrong. This area doesn't lend itself to going unseen well, but do the best you can, far enough apart so if one small group is targeted, the others can come to its aid but cannot be targeted at the same time.*"

"*Yes, ma'am,*" was the quiet reply, and they started flitting from place to place, leaving the canyon.

"*We have very well-trained people,*" Wisdom mind spoke to Tawny.

"*Yes, we threaten them with a talk from you if they choose to do foolish things or do not pay attention,*" said Tawny. "*When our human soldiers saw what kind of effect that had on the four-footed and winged ones, they decided they didn't want one either. Alessia and Hearten really want to talk with you about discipline enforcement,*" she finished with a feline grin.

Those trained as spies and assassins went swiftly into the compound that the Wanz and lizard men had created and did indeed find those left behind and two of them even higher-ranking wizards.

"*Elder Tawny,*" reported Kerr, "*there are two more wizards here of even higher rank than those in the gully. Also, they have a squadron of soldiers left guarding the place.*"

"*Thank you, Kerr,*" said Elder Tawny. "*Eldest Wisdom and I will be right there. Please hold your positions if that is a viable option.*"

"*Wisdom, they have two more wizards of even higher rank and a squadron of soldiers,*" mind spoke Tawny.

"*We need to go in unseen, locate the wizards, and net them before they are aware of our presence. These two may be more tightly connected to the leader of the invaders at the capital, and we need for as little information to reach it as possible,*" said Wisdom grimly.

"*I will get a mind picture of their location,*" said Tawny.

"*Kerr, send me a mind picture of their location,*" she requested.

"*Yes, ma'am,*" replied the giant canine.

"*Good, they are not together,*" said Tawny to both Wisdom and Kerr.

"*Yes, and one is human while the other a lizard man,*" said Wisdom. "*It would seem that the species do not mix well.*"

"*A fact to keep in mind for later use,*" said Tawny.

"*I have blocked the human wizard's ability to do magic, so let us capture him,*" said Wisdom. "*It is not so simple with the lizard man. We will need to use a net on it, and I do not know how much knowledge we would get from it or how its mind works. I don't think we can chance this creature at this time. It will have to be killed.*"

"Has everyone gotten into the compound?" she asked Tawny.

"*Yes,*" said Tawny, "*I have the netters in place and am having some use those magic attack devices to lure the mages out. I have our spies ready to capture the human mage and avians with a carry bag ready to receive him.*"

"*Well planned,*" said Elder Wisdom with a smile in her mind-voice. She and Tawny carefully moved to where they could see where help would be needed and to be sure the netting of the lizard man mage was successful. At Tawny's command, the magic attack devices were set against the Wanz soldiers, striking their leaders and creating confusion. The mages hearing the commotion ran to where they could see what was happening, each mage taking a different route as Tawny believed they would and each arriving where she hoped.

The lizard man mage sought for the source of the magic devices but couldn't seem to locate it, and just as he was about to send out a magic blast where he thought it might be, he felt something fall upon him, tighten, and all of his power swiftly drain from his body, and soldiers were there to see he was no more.

The human mage could not find the source of the magic either, and when he tried to summon his magic, he could not. He could feel it, but it wouldn't respond. He found the block but couldn't break through it, and that was all he remembered as Wisdom, using her healer's knowledge, put him to sleep. Those waiting for him tied him up, blindfolded him, and put him in the avian bag to be taken to the area where they held the other prisoner.

These Wanz soldiers, even without their leaders, seemed to know their duties and fought fiercely. Tawny joined the battle and fought alongside Sergeant Marista. Together, they made an unstoppable team; and though the battle was fierce, the allies won.

Wisdom set up her healing tent and had the wounded brought to her to be treated right away. Once she was done there, she joined Tawny in exploring the outpost. As they went down into the sub-areas of the manner house, they found lots of food and goods stored away. They also found another stairway and went even farther down. Exercising extreme caution, should there be any guards down there, on they went, finding no guards. But what they found astounded and frightened them. It was a huge room, and there were stacks on stacks, hundreds of feet across and as far as the eye could see, of Wanz in their chrysalis form.

"*They are all in stasis,*" said Wisdom with mind-speech to Tawny. "*I believe that the moment they come out of it, they will be soldiers, or what other thing they were created to be.*"

"*This needs the full council of elders, not just the war council,*" said Tawny. "*I am pretty sure I know what needs to be done with them, but I do not want to carry the responsibility of that decision by myself.*"

"*I do not want to either,*" said Wisdom quietly. "*Let a guard be put on this door and let it be secured very well. We need to use the elder net for this conference, but Prince Aaron and his elders must also be included in this decision.*"

"*I will so notify the net,*" said Tawny.

"*Elders, Elders, Elders,*" said Tawny using the formal three call to call to meeting all the elders, "*we have come upon that which must be spoken of by all of our elders, including Prince Aaron and his. Yass, will you please have him call a meeting and be our voice so they know of what we speak and who speaks?*"

"*Yes,*" said Yass, rising in search of him. "Prince Aaron, there is that which has been found that needs the council of the elders, ours and yours. Can you call council now? It is very important."

"Certainly, and we will meet you in the room we meet for in war council," said Prince Aaron, who went to gather the Masters he felt best suited for the job.

"Yass, if you would have the Eldest of the Hazbastas be included, along with the master smith and foresters, I would appreciate it," said Prince Aaron. "We are ready here to hear about what has been found."

"*We have found a subterranean room of immense size with rows on rows of Wanz in their chrysalis stage in stasis. They are stacked twenty chrysalises high, and there more than a hundred rows of them. The room is so large that they seem to go back as far as the eye can see,*" reported Tawny grimly.

"*This is indeed something the whole council needs to discuss,*" said Elder. "*It is no wonder they disregard the wasting of their soldiers.*"

"Eldest Wisdom," asked Carly on the mind net, "*is there any way you can tell if they can be changed from their set course?*"

"*I scanned a few, but I do not believe that they can be. It is coded into them completely,*" answered the Eldest, Wisdom's Child. "*They would have to be unmade and start over for that to happen.*"

"*I am sad to hear that,*" said Carly with a sigh.

"*Yes, because most of them are probably soldiers and we must defend our people and our land,*" said Prince Aaron, sad but grim. "*I do not see that we have any choice but to kill them where they lie. Can creatures be killed in stasis?*"

"*Not that I know of. I would have to bring them out of it,*" said Elder Wisdom. "*It seemed to me though that they would stay in the current stage for a few days before they came out complete.*"

"*What is the thought of the council on this?*" asked Elder.

"*I vote that we kill them,*" said Verasa an avian elder.

"*Are there any opposing thoughts?*" asked Elder.

"*No,*" came the voices of the many elders of the mind net and those of Prince Aaron's council.

"*It is concluded that they must be destroyed,*" said Elder.

"It will be as the council has ordered," said Tawny. *"Thank you for breaking and coming to council."*

"You are welcome," were the replies. *"Not a choice I would want to make alone,"* came others.

"Well," said Tawny looking at Wisdom, "how do we do that?"

"I think that we will burn them before they become aware," said Wisdom. "I will study them and see if this can be painless for them, but with so many, I believe that is the only solution. We will of course need to assure good ventilation."

"I will go down with you," said Tawny, and they journeyed down to the unformed Wanz. Wisdom sat for some time just looking off into space, and Tawny just sat there silently beside her. Then she blinked and said, "I have rendered them unconscious, have torches brought down, and I will move them to the farthest one and start them burning from there. For some reason, I feel it would not be a good idea for two – or four-foots to be in there when they start to burn."

Tawny did as Wisdom commanded, and in a very short time, they had a hundred torches all lit and moving down to the end of the lines of Wanz. Wisdom dropped them on top, and they didn't so much ignite as explode. Scattering flaming debris and creating more explosions farther up the line and over to other rows, it was moving so quickly that it was halfway to the shocked people before Wisdom had the wit to say, "Run!"

One of the soldiers went to close the door, but Wisdom stopped him, "No, the fire needs the air to burn. Leave the doors open. All is made of stone, and the fire will remain below."

"Yes, ma'am," the soldier gulped, still looking shocked.

"That was most unexpected," said Tawny, checking her fur for any hot cinders.

"Most unexpected indeed," said Wisdom. "I do not think it will take long for that room to be cleared of the Wanz."

"No, ma'am, not long at all," said another soldier.

"Let's just sit on these steps until we settle down, shall we," said Wisdom.

"A good plan," said Tawny, and everyone sat and got over the shock.

"We are needed back topside," said Tawny after everyone had visibly calmed down. "Let us go back there. We can check down here later." There were no stragglers, as everyone was happy to go find something to do.

CHAPTER 21

Getting a Feel for the Enemy

"**W**ISDOM," MIND CALLED Kriss, "*are you available to come for the interrogation of the prisoner?*"

"*Yes,*" she answered, "*I think that he is high ranking and trusted by his master. I am concerned that his disappearance will cause a quicker reaction than we want.*"

"*That is alarming,*" said Kriss grimly. "*We need to be one step ahead of it.*"

"*I will call the war net up,*" said Wisdom. "*War net elders,*" she called three times, and they answered with members of The Family being mouths and ears for the Prince and his war council. "*I believe that this mage is of higher rank than the other and trusted by his master, so his capture will cause a greater alarm and possibly a faster reaction than we want.*"

"We need to hurry our troops back then and fortify the outpost you and Tawny captured," said Prince Aaron, with Yass sending his words out on the war net. "I believe that it will be the first one they try to get back."

"*I have given this thought already, but I wish to question our prisoner first and see what he will tell us,*" said Wisdom's Child.

"In the meantime, we can have our defenses in good order and will move some of the kill hounds to your outpost, Tawny," said Elder. "I would suggest that you stay there and supervise the defenses."

"I agree," said Prince Aaron.

"I am willing and agree with your judgment," said Elder Tawny, still at the outpost. *"I have a good group here, and it will be interesting to see what kind of traps they can think of."*

◊ ◊ ◊

Prince Aaron, Wisdom's Child, Elder Kriss, and Eldest of the Hazbastas entered the cavern of the new prisoner.

Kriss as before did the talking.

"Mage of our enemy, what were your duties at the outpost?" he asked.

The mage, blindfolded, refused to answer, and Wisdom put a spell on him so he must speak.

"I am to awaken the Wanz when called to by my master, my god," said the man.

"Why do you think your master is a god?" asked Elder Kriss.

"He has given me such power. He has made me practically a god among humans, and they must do as I bid," he said arrogantly.

"He gave you nothing," said Kriss.

"He gave me my power!" insisted the mage.

"You already had the power. Your master just blocked it, unblocking it a little at a time for rewards of your effort. He gave you nothing. If you are not born with the ability to do magic, you cannot do magic," said Kriss in a bored, everybody-knows-that tone of voice.

"You lie!" shouted the man.

"No wonder your master wanted everyone dead. If you talked to anyone here and they told you what I did, you would not be his willing slave. You might want his power. You may even have enough knowledge to figure out how to get power from him and weaken him, or even kill him," said Kriss. "I wonder why the hunt for everyone was so thorough. I don't imagine he allows you to associate with the people of this land."

"No, so what, he gave me my magic," said the mage, less confident than before.

"You, of course, have never heard your master lie to anyone before, have you?" asked Kriss.

"Well, yes, but it was for their own good or for my master's purpose," said the mage.

"And so was his lie to you," said Kriss.

"I think we should leave now and let him worry about what you have said," said the Elder of the Hazbastas with mind-speech. The others nodded, and they left.

"Well planted were your seeds of doubt," said Prince Aaron quietly to Elder Kriss.

"Yes," said Wisdom. "I imagine that he also was to be in charge of that entire army, he or the Lazzindaph wizard."

"I scanned him more thoroughly while you were questioning him, and I could detect ties, magic ones, to his master," Wisdom's Child continued. "It may be that through those ties, his master could break the block that I have established. I propose using the ties as a trap to pull magic from his master. I believe that if it feels that it is threatened by the contact, it will sever the ties."

"I believe that is a very good idea," said all three at the same time. "How soon can you do this?"

"I have the crystals I will need with me, and I will have this done shortly," was her reply as she sat on a stone outside the cavern. They stood by quietly while she worked, and as she promised, in a short time, she had the stones and the spells ready. They went back to the cavern where the mage was held, and saying nothing to him, she put the spells on the ties, also blocking any mind-speech he might be capable of.

"Now we wait," said Wisdom. "I suspect that this one was to report in more frequently than the others. He is a more powerful weapon, and trust doesn't seem to be strong among our enemies."

"I will send a guard to sit with Wisdom's Child, and we can go about our duties," said Elder Kriss.

"A good plan," said Prince Aaron.

Wisdom's Child waited with her guard of two-foots and four-foots at the entrance of the cavern, making no sound and going unnoticed by the prisoner. In about two hours, one of the ties to the mage's master activated. It was very quickly severed from its master. It tried another and another with the same results until it just severed all the ties and did not try any longer.

The mage, feeling the ties being cut and finding himself totally bereft of contact with his master, went into hysterics. He screamed and turned and twisted in his chair, knocking it onto the floor and then flailing around on the floor in his panic.

Wisdom, having called the other questioners when he started panicking, ordered the guards to stop his flailing about by throwing some cold water into his face. That seemed to help him calm down, but he still sat there and wept.

"Well," said Kriss, "your master has deserted you. You are on your own, and you cannot access your magic."

"What do you want?" asked the unnerved man.

"We want information about your master. What likely his plans might be now that he has lost the four outposts by the sea. We have also removed and destroyed all the magic traps that have killed so many magic wielders in this land, along with all the troops that were anywhere near us. We have reclaimed a considerable amount of Asalawn back. We are aware that he is after magic and life power and his plan is to drain this land to death."

"He will come against you. He has troops stored up, tens of thousands of them, that will come to life with a simple spell," said the man.

"Were the ones at your outpost the only ones?" asked Kriss.

"No," said the man. "He has stores all over this land."

"Do you know where they are?" asked Kriss.

"What if I do?" asked the man, a sneer in his voice, as he thought of his master's power.

"Yours have been destroyed," said Lord Kriss quietly. "They burn explosively."

"You could not destroy them," said the mage emphatically. "They were in stasis."

"We took them out of stasis," said Kriss simply.

"You cannot have the power to override my master's magic," said the man, becoming alarmed.

"We had the power to trap him if he tried to contact you through any of the ties he had with you," said Kriss.

"No," said the man.

"And we have the power to remove your magic forever," said Kriss.

"No, you don't. Only my master can do such things," said the mage.

"Your master has run away. He did not even try to free the ties to you from the spell that was on them. He simply cut them and ran away," said Kriss with a sneer in his voice. "It would seem you overestimated his power."

"I have seen him do great things. I have seen him change into whatever shape he wants. He can look human or like a Lazzindaph or a Wanz. I have seen him take on the shape of a mighty lion or a kill hound. I have even seen him take on the shape of a dragon," answered the mage.

"Shape shifting, but what spells can he work?" asked Kriss broadly.

"He bespelled that stupid regent so he could do as he wished to the people of the court, and the fool always thought it was his idea," said the man.

"I don't imagine such a greedy and vain person with such paranoias as the regent was that hard to manipulate," said Kriss dryly. "I doubt it would have taken much in the way of spells at all. In fact, I think the regent had been groomed by your master from his youth to listen to his voice."

The man looked shocked. "How did you know? My master was sure that no one would know how long he had been planning for the downfall of this land."

"Oh, such a thorough invasion with troops popping up out of nowhere and a regent who feels safe with foreigners and not his own people, plus knowing that the magic traps had been planted two years before anyone with magic started getting ill, it was not hard to figure out. Your master must enjoy a long life," said Kriss.

"Yes, much longer than we humans," answered the man. "That is why he and his kind rule and we are subject to them. It is why they are greater than we are."

"Not really," said Kriss. "If that was the truth, that they are greater than we are, they would not have to stoop to such trickery as the magic traps and murdering the mages of power and the heads of the ruling houses. They wouldn't have to get people to be so focused on themselves and their families, work, and town that no one else matters as long as nothing bad happens to them. They wouldn't need Wanz slaves or human mage slaves such as you. If they were greater than us, they would simply be able to overpower us, and they are not able to do so unless they resort to trickery."

"But that is to keep from having so many deaths," said the mage.

"Obviously theirs, not ours," said Kriss dryly. "They have wholesale slaughtered the people of this land. How was that preventing so many deaths? The people of this country were never a threat to anyone. They were too interested in their work and their families."

The mage could not answer this. The lies of his masters seemed larger and larger, and he could not get the fear of losing his ability to do magic out of his mind.

"What are you going to do with me?" he asked.

"We don't know yet," answered Kriss honestly. "You are a mage of some power and not a friend of ours, so you represent a threat to the safety of our people." He and the rest got up and left then, and a worried man found himself free of his chair and unblindfolded with water and food available.

"I think we should allow him to talk to our first prisoner," said Prince Aaron. "He had no problem believing that his master lied about the magic, and he can testify that we can and will remove the magic if we deem it necessary."

"We got a lot of information about his master though. That shape shifting was very interesting information, and it turning into a dragon really caught my attention," said Wisdom's Child.

"Legend says that all the dragons were slain," said Prince Aaron, smiling.

"What if they weren't? What if they just went into hiding and chose a different path to defeat mankind? If they can change into human form, we may have more trouble on our hands than we know," said their mage and eldest elder.

The three with her looked stricken at this thought and more than a little worried. "This is something that we will need to bring up in full council," said

Eldest of the Hazbastas. "We must hope for it not to be true but plan as though it is."

"But first we need to get more troops to Tawny's location and see what else we can muster as a surprise," said Prince Aaron.

◊ ◊ ◊

"The enemy is more cautious in their approach," said Tawny to Captain Alessia with a feline grin.

"Yes," said Captain Alessia with a grin of her own, "I wasn't sure those jellyfish would be as much a problem for them as they are for us which is why we made sure that part of the beach was thick with them."

"They are about to hit that noxious seaweed," said Tawny. "This should be interesting."

"I hope it won't," said the captain. "That stuff burns great, and if they can get it all over them, a little surprise we have for them tonight will cut down the number of troops facing us a bit."

"Really?" asked Elder Tawny, looking curiously at Captain Alessia.

"Yes, I am hoping that the fully developed Wanz are as flammable as their unfinished brothers were," the good captain answered her. The captain was in luck the Wanz soldiers and chair bearers just plowed through the stuff.

Captain Alessia grinned and spoke to Elder Tawny, "The tide is coming in, and they will only have one place to make camp and that will be crowded with so many people. The area has been saturated with juice from the seaweed, barrels of it. The sand seems dry on top, but it is only dry for about an inch. The rest is seaweed juice. Their movement and the weight they put on the sand once they lay on their bedrolls will wick the oil up, making it easy to ignite. We will send out flaming arrows in the night and illuminate it for them."

"Good, the less magic used the better. The Eldest wants to keep the confidence of their master falsely high. She has had a grim thought on what it could be and hopes she is wrong as does the rest of the council," Tawny told her captain.

"What does she think it could be?" asked Alessia.

"Her darkest thought is a dragon," said Tawny.

"I thought they all died," said Alessia. "That is what legend says."

"But what if they didn't and they have chosen a different route to destroy mankind? This is what she asked the whole council, as you can guess none of us were happy to hear her speculations," answered Tawny dryly.

"I guess," said the captain. "I am not cheered to hear them myself, but such speculations need to be spoken so we do not find ourselves unprepared."

"So you are willing to give our Eldest's idea some serious thought?" asked Tawny curiously.

"Eldest Wisdom's Child has not been wrong about anything yet, and everything she has put into motion has worked beautifully. If she says this could be a possibility, then I am going to listen, no matter how far-fetched it might seem to me," said Captain Alessia in a firm voice.

"And that trust, without evidence, is the same that I have," said Tawny in amazement. "She found out that the master of the mage we captured has a longer life span than humans, and when he showed his prowess through shape shifting, one of the forms he choose was that of a dragon. None of the other forms live that long."

"Dragons can fly," said Captain Alessia. "That means that we could be under aerial attack ourselves or at least observation."

"Our mage thought of that and has a passive form of magic that monitors the sky above us. It will activate once it senses something of say an avian's size or larger coming our way, and she went with a small avian size," Tawny told her.

"Just how powerful is our mage anyway?" asked Alessia.

"We don't know," said Tawny with a grin. "She made sure we did not know nor did her father know how much power she is capable of. I do not know where she stored it in the Evil Mage's keep, but she hid it somehow. She must have been storing it for decades, if not centuries, to keep herself safe. Otherwise, she would not have had enough power to protect us as well as she did."

"Wow," said Alessia, "it kind of boggles the mind, and now she is back to full power and is even storing some with everything she has been doing?"

"Yes, and I, who have been around amazing amounts of power, find my mind boggled," said Tawny with a chuckle.

At dusk, the enemy followed its usual pattern and set up camp. By full dark, they were settled down, and most were sleeping. Those about were humans on guard duty and some of the wizards that had accompanied the soldiers. Captain Alessia gave them an hour more and then quietly gave the command to fire. Her archers lighting their arrows launched them so they hit the perimeter of the encampment, firing on the center and finally throughout.

At first, there was not much reaction. But suddenly, the perimeter caught, and the guards shouted in alarm, then the middle and finally everywhere else. The Wanz were in a panic as their bedrolls and tents burst into flames, lighting them on fire; and once burning, it did not seem as though they could be put out very easily. The mages did their best, but while they were doing this, they were subject to arrows from the enemy and were killed to a being.

The allies were glad of the victory, but shocked at the completeness of it. They expected to get a dozen, maybe two of the soldiers out of the way, but to see hundreds burn to death was something they were unprepared for.

The magic of the enemies' wizards would go back to their master, and this time he would know that his army was defeated, and when. Tawny had everyone inside, including those who would normally be on guard duty. Wisdom had thought that this might put the creature into a rage and hoped it wouldn't think to take its revenge out on its captives.

"I worry for the captives," said Wisdom, concern in her eyes as she sat at council. "While the creature's eyes are here, is there a way that we can plan their rescue?"

"I don't think it will take vengeance on the captives. I believe that it thinks we are a whole new power coming in to claim what it was securing for itself," said Elder.

"None of the people left had any magic, and it knows that magic has been used. None of the people who escaped were of enough military might to wipe out his troops or even had the skill, and none were as clever as we seem to be. Maybe it thinks one of its own kind is making a play for the power it has stolen?"

"Yes, it doesn't think much of human intelligence," said Prince Aaron. "I agree with Elder. It must believe that we are a different people altogether. Especially as we have a completely different uniform than the one of this land. Hildy's suggestion was a good one, and having Alessia change the color of her hair was also good."

CHAPTER 22

Inland Outposts and Traders

"*WAR COUNCIL,*" MIND called Tawny, "*the overhead alarms went off, and something flew over, but it beat a hasty retreat when Mage Wisdom's Child's traps started drawing its energy from it. I don't think it will be back, but I wouldn't bet on it, not if it can take other forms.*"

"That is why there are gate crystals and door crystals. They will activate and cause the entrapment of anyone who bears magic that tries to enter," said Wisdom's Child. "I expect him to use treachery now and probably human form. If it is fast, it might get out of the trap before we get it, and that will be the end of those tries. But do expect the attempt and maybe others. You don't know who or what it might enlist or use as a spy. There are lesser crystals that will glow pink when someone or something with a tie to him enters. I will be there after this meeting to give you classes on magic traps and devices."

"Prince Aaron, along with the concerns that Tawny has brought to us," said Aloo, coming upon him as he left practice, "our scouts have seen trader caravans coming to your border outposts."

"That is bad. We have not liberated those areas yet, and they may fall into the hands of the Wanz's master," said Prince Aaron. "They come because they know that my reign begins. We need to free those outposts and send the traders on their way, telling them to come back in a year when we will have either succeeded or they will be dealing with a different land."

"Let us call for a war council. We will have to move on this situation quickly," said Aloo. "Fortunately, all of the seeker/suckers in that area have been removed. Master Wisdom's Child ordered it to be done as these would be our next areas to clean up."

"She thinks ahead quite a bit, doesn't she?" asked Prince Aaron.

"It is habit of her to do so," answered Aloo.

"Habit?" asked Prince Aaron.

"It is also a habit of yours, Prince Aaron," said Aloo with a smile as they walked to the council together. Seeing his look of inquiry, she continued, "You both needed to do so to survive and to achieve what was demanded of you. Wisdom's Child's father demanded that she become the commander of an army able to think steps ahead of the enemy. You don't have that training. Your uncle tried to ensure that you would not know how to lead or govern your people, but I find that you are doing a fine job of it, and you are also trying to plan ahead."

"She knows more about war and strategy than even Hearten, doesn't she?" asked Prince Aaron.

"Yes," said Aloo. "We have been training for at least three generations to be warriors."

"And I seem to be having to learn as I go where the freeing of my land is concerned," said Prince Aaron. "Well, at least I have the good sense to let the Master War Elder lead. I am happy that she asks for and follows suggestions."

"Wisdom's Child does not believe in pride. She says the fall hurts too much, so it should be avoided," said Aloo, wincing in memory of such a fall.

"She is correct," said Prince Aaron, understanding in his voice as he remembered some of his own falls.

They arrived at the council and took their places. "The avian scouts have seen trader caravans coming to our border outposts," said Prince Aaron.

"Can they tell if any of the caravans have magic wielders with them?" asked Yass.

"Yes," said Aloo, "they do. Some of them of high caliber."

"That is bad," said Kriss. "The enemy cannot resist magic and will not allow those caravans to leave this country."

"We need to stop them before they reach the outpost and send them away," said Prince Aaron.

"It would be a simple thing to fly you and some guards to them in the night so that you might meet them," said Alaw.

"You would need to be dressed a little better," said Master Mavis.

"Not really when he explains that we are at war and what danger they are in because of the magic wielders within their groups," said Yass.

"I wonder, do they know what you look like?" asked Elder.

"Yes, they do," said Prince Aaron with a smile. "My portrait was done and sent to the other lands to keep up the pretense that I would be ruling my land. There are other princes that would have a better claim to the throne than my uncle, so he could not allow them to know that I was dead."

"Good," said Aloo.

"I will accompany the prince," said Wisdom's Child. "In fact, I will fly him from place to place along with some soldiers. Do we have any uniforms of this land in good condition?"

"No, and we do not want the new uniforms to be recognized," said Arms Master Hearten.

"The old ones will be best," said Aaron. "They will certainly say that we are at war."

"Also, we will bring kill hounds," said Wisdom's Child. "An avian will control them from up high."

"How many avians do you want?" asked Alaw.

"Twelve," said Wisdom's Child. "I will enhance everyone so that we can move swiftly. We need to get to the closest first."

"I want the rest of the war council to get a plan in action to conquer the mountain pass outpost and the rest of them. We will also need to see where there are postings of Wanz soldiers that seem strange. It might be that there is a wizard in residence to awaken more Wanz soldiers. I worry that there may be more hidden chrysalis sites," she added.

"As you command," said the council.

"I know I am being autocratic, but Master Fern says that the storm Hildy was nervous about is almost upon us and there is so much snow in it that it will bury buildings. This means that all of the family that is in the hidden barns need to come here to Refuge along with the cattle and food stuff for both people and cattle," said Wisdom's Child with a smile. "Now let's get busy."

◊ ◊ ◊

Wisdom's Child and Prince Aaron arrived at the closest caravan shortly after dusk, and they presented themselves to the guard who quickly ushered them into the Master Trader.

"King Aaron!" exclaimed the Master Trader before the guard even mentioned the prince's name. Rising, the man bowed. "To what do I owe the honor of this visit?"

"Alas," said Prince Aaron, "I come to give warning and direction rather than trade. Much as I wish it would be the other way around, my people have been storing trade stuff for some time in hopes that the trading would begin again once I reached the throne. Unfortunately, the Master Mage and his soldiers that the Regent brought in have invaded my land. They killed all the infants, elderly, men, and boys, keeping only women and girls of a certain age. We believe they chose them to be slaves so they could be hosts to the Wanz eggs which will then hatch and eat its host." Prince Aaron finished this quite grimly.

The trader looked shocked. "I have reclaimed much of my land and have found most of the people who managed to escape the slaughter. Also, we have rescued those along the coast who were being held in case there would be a need to feed the larvae once they were done with their host. We would not have you walk into a trap. I believe that they would lure you in land or just take your prisoners or kill you as they did us, especially as you have magic wielders and that is what they lust after. They killed almost all of the magic wielders of this land, with magic traps disguised as good luck tokens. They suck the magic and life out of the wielder. It is a slow and painful death, and the magic and life that has been stolen is sent to a container in the capital."

All of the people of the caravan were gathered around at this news, and there was shock on their faces. "How could they have so thoroughly invaded that an alarm wasn't sounded?" asked the trader.

"The Wanz who are the soldiers of the master mage, who isn't a Wanz, we do not know what he is," said Prince Aaron, "are people, not human, more like insects, and the larvae I spoke of go into a chrysalis phase designed to be warriors. When they are at the end of that stage, the mage puts them in stasis. They were hidden all about my land, thousands and thousands of them. And when he was ready to invade, he simply took them out of stasis, and they came out of their cocoon soldiers ready to fight. At the coast, we found an enormous cavern filled with these chrysalis. Our mage destroyed them."

"You say these seeker/suckers are disguised as luck tokens," questioned the Master Trader, "were they given to your people by gypsies?"

"Yes," said Prince Aaron.

"We have some, and our magic wielders have begun to feel ill," said the trader.

"Your route must have been known, or there was a code in the seeker/suckers that would activate when you came in this direction," said Wisdom's Child.

"Who is this child who speaks with such authority?" asked the Trader.

"This is Master Healer Wisdom's Child. She is cursed to always appear nine and to never die," said Prince Aaron.

"Who cursed her?" asked the Trader.

"Her father," said Prince Aaron.

"Her father?" wondered the Trader.

"He was an evil mage and did not want her to grow into her power and be a threat to him. He just wanted her to be his slave," answered Prince Aaron.

"Where is this evil mage?" asked the Trader nervously.

"He is dead," said the Prince.

"That is good to hear," said the Trader, deciding he did not wish to know more. And looking at Wisdom's Child, he asked, "Is there something you can do about these things and my magic wielders?"

"Yes, take me to the magic things first and I will turn them off and disable them," said Wisdom's Child. The trader took her to them, and she said, "If you would lift me up please so I can reach them."

A tall trader lifted her and she, using magic-resistant cloth, turned the thing off and removed it from the wagon. "Do you have more?" she asked.

"Yes, at the other wielder's wagon," said the tall Trader, taking her there. The same process was repeated, and then Wisdom's Child went into the magic wielder's wagon. "Hello," said Wisdom's Child, "I am a Master Healer and am cursed to always appear as a nine-year-old. Quite annoying, I can assure you. I was cursed by my father who only had me so I could be his slave. He is dead, and still I live on. Quite the curse, wouldn't you agree?"

The woman nodded weakly with a smile.

"What is your name?" asked Wisdom's Child. "I promise my healing will not touch your mind or your will. But I have been told that I need to practice my manners and quit being so abrupt."

"I am Healer Baleesta," she answered with another weak smile.

"I would like to repair the damage done by the seeker/sucker to you. It is a magic trap and was given to you as a good luck token by gypsies. Most of the magic wielders in this land died from these things. You are the first person I will get to work on who has been afflicted by one, so I will be very slow and thorough. Actually, I am always slow and thorough. May I start?"

The woman nodded yes, and Wisdom's Child began. The magic pathways of the woman were damaged, seeming to be slowly stripped from her. Wisdom's Child told her everything that she found and made sure the woman would not hurt from the healing. She also noted that there was damage to the organs, and using her healing crystal, she set about repairing what the magic trap had damaged. She worked on the woman for over two hours, making sure she missed nothing; and noting that the woman was pregnant, she checked the fetus and repaired any harm there also.

"What gender?" asked the woman.

"A girl," said Wisdom's Child with a smile.

"A magic wielder?" asked the woman.

"Yes," said Wisdom's Child.

The woman seemed to gain strength from such good news.

"I am done," said a weary Wisdom's Child. "How are you feeling?"

"So much better," said the woman. "Thank you so much for saving me and my daughter. I am so grateful to you. Is there anything I can do for you?"

"Not that I know of, except stay healthy, you know how we healers are," she answered.

"You had best go and replenish yourself. Theadius was ill when the seeker/sucker struck. Maybe you should have gone to him first," the woman said worriedly.

"I will do as you say," said Wisdom's Child, leaving the wagon. As she stepped on the ground, a woman screamed in her face, "Why did you do her first? My husband is sicker!"

"I was not aware of this, and the child the woman carries would have died had I not healed her first. Tell me, is your husband dead? Is he not better just for having the foul thing turned off? Or do you even know?" snapped Wisdom's Child in an irritated master healer's voice.

The woman stopped with her ranting, and Wisdom's Child walked around her to Prince Aaron who had a bowl of nourishing stew waiting for her. "I have never seen you chastise someone before," said the Prince bemusedly. "I must say, I did not see her in the wagon checking on her husband. Rather, she has been waiting the whole time just to scream at you."

"That is what I thought," said Wisdom's Child, eating the stew. "The trap sucks the magic pathways from their bodies inflicting excruciating pain."

"Then just having the thing off must be such a relief. I imagine he is asleep," said Prince Aaron.

Wisdom, using her magic, checked on the patient. "Yes, but he is very ill. I will need to awaken him before I work on him, although I am doing some work from here to make sure he lives. There is an insidious poison in his viens.

"Would you find a container? It doesn't have to be very large, but it needs to have a lid that can be sealed so I can store the stuff," Wisdom's Child asked the Master Trader.

The Master was upset to hear of the poison and went and did as Wisdom's Child asked. It took him only a few minutes to find the container, and when he handed it to her, she said, "Thank you, I will continue my work in the wagon. Would you make sure that woman stays away?"

"Yes, I will," said the Trader with a smile. And after Wisdom's Child was in the Wagon, he said, "I have never seen anyone shut Mastina's mouth so quickly before, and to me that was absolute proof that she is a Master Healer. They take no nonsense from anyone."

"Yes," said Prince Aaron, "some of the people who come from Wisdom's Child's land say that she can embarrass a person pretty thoroughly if they get out of line or do something stupid."

"Definitely a master healer then," said the Trader. "She does not come from your land?"

"No, her people are wandering people who needed a master healer for their master healer, so they were in our land when this horror started. They have been essential in the rescue and the clearing out of the enemy in a good three-fifths of my land. They wander because getting free from subjection of the evil ruler of their land caused it to be destroyed, and they aid us because they would not see us suffer from evil as they did," said Prince Aaron.

"You were graced greatly, King Aaron," said the Master Trader.

"I know this and thank the One God and His Son every day, usually more than once," said Prince Aaron, not correcting the trader.

By the time Wisdom was done healing the man and removing the poison from his body, the Master Trader had his caravan turned around and ready to move. He felt they were too close to the border and the Wanz could easily capture them, and as the King had told him that they could not see well at night, this seemed a good time to get some distance from them.

"I will keep this poison, Master Trader Hestel," said Wisdom's Child. "It is called cadishna. I will destroy it in a safe place so that none are harmed."

"Thank you," said Hestel. "That poison is forbidden in this caravan, and in many lands, it can get you killed if you are even suspected of having it. Is there any way you can see if there is any in my caravan?"

"Yes," said Wisdom's Child, "I will search." And standing motionless, she made a search. Looking at the Master Trader, she said, "Come with me." She led him to the fourth wagon in his caravan, which held Theadius. Master Hestel told Theadius that the poison that Wisdom's Child found within him was in his wagon, and the man paled.

Wisdom's Child led them to a cupboard that was closed tight for the journey, and the Master Trader opened it. It was obviously the cupboard of Theadius's wife, with all of her lotions and things inside. And unerringly, Wisdom's Child went to a container sitting in the back of the second shelf. The trader was holding her up to make sure she could see.

The woman screeched and tried to rip it from the hand of Wisdom's Child and was surprised to find that she was firmly held by King Aaron.

"You can tell this is poison by taking a bit of hair and dabbing it in the poison. It will lose all color and then turn the most verilant color of blue," said Wisdom's Child.

"Yes," said the Master Trader, "I know." And taking a knife from a sheath on his belt, he cut a piece of the woman's hair, opened the lid, and dipped the hair in; and it lost all its color and turned to an awful blue.

"Thank you, Master Wisdom's Child, and, King Aaron. You have saved us and kept murder from happening. We will return within a year and hope to find trade with you and your people."

"You are welcome, and now we must go to the other caravans who are on the other two approaches. You were the closest, so we hurried to you first," said Prince Aaron."

◊ ◊ ◊

"This caravan, Prince Aaron, is alive with magic, and much of it is not human," said Wisdom's Child. "Anvar, let me borrow her sight. It feels much like the magic of the head mage of our enemy. This could be a trap."

"In that case, let our netters get into position," said Prince Aaron, "and let's spring this trap."

They walked to the caravan and presented themselves to the guard who hurriedly led them to his master, and again, the Prince was recognized and referred to as King Aaron.

"To what do we owe this visit?" asked the Master Trader.

"My land is at war with invaders, and we want that traders be warned to turnabout and visit us again next year when we are sure that we have cleaned them all out," said Prince Aaron. "Your caravan seems to have magic wielders with it, and our enemy has a voracious appetite for such. Granted we could let you go through and use you as bait to draw them out, but that would not be very friendly, so I am telling you to turn back and visit again next year."

"We thank you for the warning!" exclaimed the trader. "Where did these invaders come from?"

"They were the Regent's protectors," said Prince Aaron dryly. "His head is now on a pike at the front gate of the capital. They have had years to infiltrate our land and set up their positions to slaughter our people."

"This is grim news indeed," said the Trader. "It is a wonder that you escaped!"

"We received help from people of another nation and so have reclaimed most of our land," said the Prince as he moved with Wisdom's Child to get the Master Trader and his fellow sorcerers in place.

"*They are trying to block mind-speech,*" said Wisdom's Child. "*We now have them in place, and I have created illusions of you and I. Step with me and we will be invisible to them. There is a hole in their net that they do not believe you can get through. Will it be all right if I give you magic sight for a little while so you can get free?*"

"*Yes,*" answered the Prince with mind-speech. "*This is amazing. Ah, I see the hole you are talking about, and now I am through. Can I keep the sight for a while?*"

"*If you like, it will not harm you. And it might be best if you had it, considering what we are coming up against,*" answered Wisdom's Child. "*I am allowing them to believe we are trapped, and now they have set many geasa on what they believe is us, and we are now out of their sight. Keep talking to the trader. The voice will come from your illusion.*"

"*They have cast their net, and our net casters have done the same and quite successfully!*" said Wisdom's Child with some excitement in her voice.

"*I will stop the sucking when their power is gone and they are physically weak,*" said Wisdom's Child.

"*A good idea,*" replied Aaron with mind-speech.

"*This is curious,*" said Wisdom's Child. "*The head mage seems to be fed power by another source. I have had a net put between the two, and it is absorbing the power. Lieutenant Triss will join me in finding this power source. In the meantime, Prince Aaron, you need to figure out how we can put an end to the abuse of these mages, but not strip them of their power. If the world found out that we could do that, we would have war at our door.*"

Wisdom's Child and Triss followed the magic stream to a wagon that looked more like a prison than a place to live. "The locks are magically held," said Wisdom's Child.

"I have an extra net," said Lieutenant Triss. "I brought it in case the power comes from someone not seen but who is the real power behind these mages."

"Good thinking," replied Wisdom's Child, and she watched while Lieutenant Triss disabled the lock and opened the door.

It was very dark inside, and Wisdom's Child brought out a crystal, said light to it, then handed it to Lieutenant Triss as they entered the wagon. Once in, they saw, chained to a wall on such a short chain that the creature could barely sit up without strangling itself, a lizard man of large proportions with its tail cut off and its feet and hands chained also. When they entered, it cringed from the light and seemed frightened out of its wits.

"Stop sending out your power," said Lieutenant Triss, and it instantly complied.

"What is your name?" asked Lieutenant Triss.

"I do not have a name. I am slave. Slaves do not have names, just functions. I do as my master commands or he will harm me greatly, or you will harm me for him," whined the lizard man, shaking like a leaf.

"Your master has tried to capture the ruler of this land with his magic and has been captured in turn," said Lieutenant Triss sternly. "He will be sentenced according to our ruler's decision. Tell me, does he delight in harming you?"

"Yes," said the slave.

"Is there a reason that he delights in it?" asked Wisdom's Child.

"Yes, old one," said the slave, "my people delight in harming yours, seeing your people as disgusting and worthless, only useful for filthy tasks and amusement."

"How did you become a slave?" asked Wisdom's Child.

"My people have always served the dragons. We have traveled with them from world to world as they gathered power to themselves and fed us some, but I spared my daughter the usual treatment at birth that makes our females slow and easy to rule and thus learned the true history of our people and that the females are truly our fiercest warriors, not us males. When this was discovered, I and my household fled. But because I had been trained by dragons and had given my loyalty to one, I was traceable, so I sent my daughters and sons away. The dragon lord I swore to was so wrathful it could not just kill or torture me. It wanted to humiliate me as completely as possible. So I am a slave to humans, and my magic is used by them. I have no way of accessing it, so I may not use it," ended the slave.

"These mages and other magic wielders of this caravan will be suffering a similar fate soon," said Wisdom's Child. "My question to you is, do you wish to remain their prisoner, for I am sure they agreed to never free you as part of the purchase price, or do you wish to be our prisoner?"

The slave looked at Wisdom's Child deeply in the eyes and said, "Your slave, old one, for I do not believe that the evil that rules the rest of the world does so in you."

"Evil is in everyone," answered Wisdom's Child kindly.

"This is true, but you fight it and do not follow where it would lead and have done so all your long life," answered the slave.

"You will have to give us your name then," said Lieutenant Triss with a smile. "You will be a prisoner, not a slave, and we have rules against abuse in our land."

"That is good to hear," said the slave. "My name is Fessthassa, and I am happy to be your prisoner."

Lieutenant Triss removed the collar around his neck and the shackles from his feet and hands. "We will steady you when you walk. We know that your people use your tails for balance, and to learn to balance without one will take a while, especially as you have been forced to lie still for so long."

"Thank you," said Fessthassa, his eyes blinking in surprise at their kindness. Wisdom's Child went out of the wagon first and held the door while Lieutenant Triss balanced Fessthassa down the narrow aisle in the wagon and then down the steps.

"There, that's the worst of it," said Lieutenant Triss as Fessthassa made it down the last step. "We will be walking on ground and not doing any more steps." Wisdom's Child moved to his other side, and they walked him to the outside of the wagon circle, the light crystal showing their way. Partway around, Lieutenant Triss signaled one of the guards to come and take Wisdom's Child's place as she was needed by Prince Aaron to deal with the caravan leader and the other mages.

"*I think, Prince Aaron, that you should pronounce their punishment upon them, and I should establish it from the shadows so that they do not realize who is doing the actual cursing, so to speak,*" said Wisdom's Child with mind-speech.

"*An excellent idea,*" said Prince Aaron, who stood facing the mages as they stood weakly before him. "I have no tolerance for what you just tried to do and will not abide people who do such things. I have thought about what should be done with you, and this is what I have decided. This is a large caravan, and these people need to make a living, not as your slaves, but as members of the caravan. I am aware of the usual split of prophet in a caravan and will have this be so from now on. You will not be able to avoid doing this. You will be cursed to always deal honestly with the people of your caravan, even if they are only temporarily part of your caravan. Your magic will be cursed to always be of good use and never put to such evil as you have done before. The price you will pay for trying to do harm, even if it is not by magic, will be very unpleasant." There appeared in Prince Aaron's hands necklaces for all the magic wielders of the caravan. He put the necklaces on the mages before he allowed the nets to be removed from them.

Stepping back, he said, "Also, you have cost me greatly in time, money, and magic, and so you will pay retribution. We have already selected one item from your caravan, and I will inspect and choose whatever I will, then you will turn around and leave never to come upon my lands again."

The Prince, standing by an amazing pile of stuff, looked at Wisdom's Child and said, "Well, one more to go. I wonder how the outpost cleanup is doing."

◊ ◊ ◊

Prince Aaron, Wisdom's Child, and their group walked into Refuge and were surprised to find that Arms Master Hildy had arrived before them. "How did you manage to clean up the outposts so quickly?" asked Prince Aaron.

"They had fewer soldiers and weaker wizards than we thought. As we had teams for every outpost, it only took us half an hour to do our job. We then explored around some, and at two of the outpost, we found cavern systems where they may have stashed some chrysalises. We were about to explore farther, but Master Fern gave the call-in as the storm will break in a matter of hours."

"Do we have everyone in?" asked Wisdom's Child.

"We wait only for those who have been supplying Lacy Downs," answered Kriss. "Having the Wanz soldiers move out really helped get the supplies in. How did things go at the caravans?"

"The first two make for good fire side stories, and the third was quite easy. They said that they had been approached by the gypsies but did not trust them, so their wielders were safe, but they would get word out about them. Wisdom also left cloth and instructions for turning the things off with them.

"Those crystals for lightening loads came in very handy, and we left no traces to our refuge from the roads. Many of the wagons were flown from the towns or the barns. Master Carter Hays has been having them disassembled here for our use."

"When everyone is in, let me know and I will close the door to this cavern. It has taken me awhile, but I have finally figured out where they hid that mechanism," answered Wisdom's Child. "First I want to take Fesssthassa to the infirmary and see what we can do for him." And she and Lieutenant Triss left, gently guiding him.

"Master Wisdom's Child, the last person has entered Refuge," said a slightly out of breath youth.

"Thank you, Francsen," said Wisdom's Child. "I will shut the door so we will be safe and snug."

Once the great door was closed, Wisdom's Child called a meeting of elders, masters, and the war council.

"We need to explore our new home while the weather gives us this time to draw our breath. We also need to decide how we are going to assault the capital, free the rest of the slaves, and reclaim what we can of the magic of this land.

"Dealing with their high mage will be for me to do, and I have already thought much about this. But the actual assault on the capital will have to be carried out by you. I will have to be able to completely concentrate on the enemy's high mage and any others he surrounds himself with. Please keep me up-to-date with your plans so that I can plan in a manner to do you no harm and maybe some good."

◊ ◊ ◊

Several days later, as they sat by a fire planning the attack on The Capital, Prince Aaron said musingly, "I wonder why she does it?"

"Why who does what?" asked Elder.

"Why Wisdom's Child works so hard for everyone. She is completely well now and in her full power. She has her library, and I know that she longs to be by herself. She could leave at any time. She doesn't need us. So why does she give so much of herself for us and especially for you of The Family?"

The originals of The Family looked at Prince Aaron as though he had grown another head.

The new members of the family looked at Prince Aaron, wondering what he was getting at.

"It can't be from the command of her father for that has been taken from her, so why does she stay?" asked Prince Aaron again to the shocked silence of The Family.

Aloo, Alaw, Yazz, Kriss, Tawny, and Elder looked at him worried and frightened; but before they could speak, Wisdom's Child herself appeared. And noting the looks on her friends' faces and the worried looks they gave her, she asked, "What?"

"Prince Aaron has asked us originals of The Family why, now that you are well, do you still stay with us?"

"Because I love you," she answered them. Then she smiled at them and added, "I hope you keep that in mind when I tell you that the storm, instead of giving us a rest, has increased our danger."

Everyone sat up in alarm, and Prince Aaron asked, "What do you mean?"

"The snow is loaded with magic, and much of it is unsigned. Therefore, it can be claimed by anyone," she answered.

They all sat there, taking in just what that meant, and imagined there enemy being strengthened.

Elder gulped. "Having had the experience of the evil mage that could leave Wisdom's Child battling for weeks, if not months, and turning our whole land into a terrible warzone."

"Yes," said Yazz, "all people will need to be within Refuge and as far underground as we can go."

"We will need to figure out how to get to Lacy Downs, even with this storm going on," said a grim Prince Aaron.

"I too can use this magic," said Wisdom's Child with a small smile, "and I wonder if the tunnel ways might not take us close to Lacy Downs, I can then use the magic to transport us the rest of the way."

"Oh," said Prince Aaron, blushing, "I keep forgetting to add magic into my logistics."

Everyone chuckled with sympathy.

"We must plan a caravan, bringing trade goods for those who will choose to stay in Lacy Downs, especially if this storm does not affect them. They will think they are immune to the danger," said Hearten.

"Well, this will start a new chapter for Refuge. We will be incorporating people who have not been through what we have been through. How will we handle this?" asked Master Char.

"That thinking must be for the morning," said Prince Aaron, stretching. "We will all think better for it, and we need to think for more than just a day."

"We will have time to think until we get there and while we are there," said Master Fern with a smile. "We need to see what kind of people we will be dealing with. Miners, like foresters, are a breed of their own."

"On that note, let us get ready for the night," said Wisdom's Child. "We are all still on the same bedtime, you know."

"So our next adventure will be a caravan and an opportunity to explore the tunnels on our way to Lacy Downs," said Prince Aaron to Wisdom's Child with a grin.

Wisdom's Child smiled back. "Yes, even at the speed we will need to travel, we will still need to explore, and I believe you should take up your authority and demand to go exploring. Otherwise, your job is going to drive you crazy, and your people and mine have already had that."